Will of the Heart

Darry Fraser

Copyright © 2012 Darry Fraser

ISBN: 978-0-9875148-1-3

ACKNOWLEDGMENTS

Thanks to Annie Seaton for all – there's always Limoncello!

Susi Parslow, as always for her eagle eye and her red pen

Simone Yvette, a big happy-dancing thank you for
the most marvellous title…it suits perfectly.

Friends in Alice
Nicky and Geoff Cooper who lent their names to two characters

Thomas McKay Kulgera, NT and Kangaroo Island, SA
for some pointers on NT stations, and the purchase and sales of
land and stock

The wonderful red dirt of Country

Note:
Will of the Heart started out in my early published years as half its
current size. It differs in content and style to my later works

1

The family's solicitor didn't have the guts to meet her stare, but if he had, he'd have been vapour. Nothing but a wisp of smoke on her horizon.

Justin West paced the anteroom of his office, ducking and weaving around her. 'What do you want?' he muttered. His glance darted back to his office door.

Toni MacDonnell stood stock still. *What the hell?* 'I want my brothers to hear this *thing* you reckon is for my ears only.' Nothing about this meeting, or anything else about her dad's will had her optimism rising.

She caught a look from Stacey, the receptionist, and the barely perceptible lift of her shoulders. Then the young woman donned a headset before concentrating on the computer screen.

The solicitor stopped a moment to pick lint from his trousers, then brushed down his shirt. Patted his pockets. He paced some more, flicked a glance at her. 'It's not as if this hasn't been waiting for you for a while.' He pointed at her. 'You could've come back from Adelaide earlier. Instead, you were off chasing your tail. All this would've been done and dusted, by now.'

That rankled. 'That's my private business. I'm here now.' Mouth set, she jammed hands into her pockets. Prickles, tiny stabbing needles scampered down her spine. Always this sense of foreboding when she visited his office.

His behaviour was downright odd these days, and he even looked a bit strange as well. Oh, he used to be okay—sandy coloured hair, brown eyes, decent build, dressed metro-meets-country. But over the years, he'd gone a bit peculiar. Lately, his lean, running-to-gaunt face glistened, and his clean-shaven cheeks, usually the colour of skinned potatoes, were ruddy. He seemed too stressed out, jumpy, just like he was today. He plain gave her the creeps.

Justin rolled up his shirtsleeves, tugged at his collar. Any wonder. Perhaps because his office was stifling—the temperature was forecast to be thirty-seven degrees Celsius today with sixty per cent humidity. The poor old 'swampy' air cooler wasn't keeping up with even the pre-summer temperature in central Australia. Had Justin outlaid for a reverse cycle that took humidity out of the air, rather than dumping it back in, he might be feeling better.

Surely to God, Justin wasn't that badly off financially.

He blotted his forehead with the palm of his hand. 'I've advised before. We don't have to have the boys here. This is the last codicil. And it's technically not even a codicil, it's just your father wanted it read formally, and it only relates to you. Or mostly. Your brothers are aware of everything else in the will.' Sniffing, he pointed a finger, again. 'You knew this would happening.' He rubbed his neck then stabbed a thumb over his shoulder towards his closed office door. 'You've just called me out mid appointment for no good reason, Toni.'

'Don't tick me off,' she said. 'I didn't call you out. You ran out here as if something was on your tail. I've been back for weeks now and you haven't answered any of my calls. What's all that about?'

He shook his head. 'In ten minutes. That's your appointment, whether the boys are here or not.'

She bent and picked up a manila folder by her bag, hugged it. 'We'll wait for Paul and Evan. And then we'll be done and not

3

have to come back.'

Justin straightened up. 'I have to get back in there—' he thumbed again towards his office, 'and finish up. If the boys haven't arrived by then, we'll press on, or it doesn't get done.' He stared at the folder at her chest then caught the frown on her face.

Toni held up a hand. 'And I say we wait for them, so it doesn't have to be repeated.' Turning her back, she found a chair in the waiting room, dusted off the seat of her jeans and sat. The precious wildlife park file was still clutched in her hands.

Justin swung towards his receptionist. 'Stacey, no more interruptions until I'm finished in here. No matter who it is.' He lasered a glare at Toni, opened the door to his office only a crack and sidled inside. The door shut behind him with a firm click.

Stacey gave Toni a small smile and rolled her eyes a little. 'Sorry about that. I shouldn't say, but he hit an alert which means I'm supposed to call him out here as if there's an emergency. Sometimes clients get a bit antsy with him,' she said, and ruffled her short platinum blonde hair with both hands.

'Not surprised they get antsy with him. Is there someone awkward in there?'

'No. Well, I shouldn't say that either, but I'm just about over it. He's a perfectly safe client, don't worry. It's probably that Justin is a bit out of sorts right now.'

Toni dropped the folder to the next chair and smoothed her hands over both sides of her head. Wisps of hair had escaped the single plait down her back, the humidity today turning the escapees to frizz. Stark contrast to Stacey's cool spiky cut. 'Hope I didn't upset the apple cart even further, then,' she said.

Stacey shrugged, smiled. 'Should be fine.'

Toni reached into her bag for a glucose hit, the last of her jellybeans. All this angst chewed up her reserves and she didn't want to have a hypo on today of all days. If only jellybeans fixed blood pressure as well. Thankfully, she didn't have that problem. But she was pretty sure it still pounded sky-high whenever she was around Justin West.

Back in the dim past, long ago, Justin had asked her out a couple of times. They'd got along well enough; they'd laughed and joked, ate heartily, shared a bottle of wine on those occasions. That was as far as it went. No spark for Toni, no zazz in it. Best to stay only friends. Best to stay only *friendly*. She knew the difference, and discouraged more dates, had been busy with other plans on all occasions he asked her out. Not that it stopped him. And that last time, not so long ago, when she did actually say, 'no thank you, Justin, it's not for me', he'd looked at her vacantly for a bit, and nodded. Cocked his head to the side as if he was trying to figure her out.

'We're not all bastards, you know,' he'd finally said, referring, she believed, to her ex. Her narcissistic, cheating, lying, drunken, druggo bastard ex.

She promised herself she wouldn't think of Sonny Murphy again. His behaviour towards her when he found out about the chemo's effect had been the last devastating straw. She shuffled her feet. Every time that last dose of chemo sprang to mind, the last lot of rotten cells being purged oh-so-long-ago, she felt the loss, grief. The grieving had seemed like an old companion but was now a companion she was a bit over. Way over. Eventually, she'd accepted the reality of her situation.

Pushing the thought away, she shuffled some more. Still, once Dad got sick, Justin kept his distance from her anyway. Except the last time. She'd returned from her usual round of check-ups, and from mopping up the latest disaster her ex had left her in Adelaide, and things had changed. Justin was being overly pleasant, and that was irritating. It was unlike him to be soft around the edges. He was usually straight down the line. Confident to the point of arrogance at times, as if he knew better than everyone else. Or maybe just better than her.

She pulled her phone out of her bag and checked the time. Eight minutes until her scheduled appointment. Forced to wait, and patience never a strong point, her thoughts drifted to home, MacDonnell's Run, the family station north west of Alice. A small parcel surrounded by much larger stations, the result of a sell off many years prior. It was home, nonetheless.

She wondered for the millionth time since her father died how she was ever going to live without it. MacDonnell's Run. The hills, craggy red quartzite outcrops of home, the solitude, her dogs and the big sprawling old homestead that she'd soon have to farewell. She had the house in Alice Springs, but it wasn't the same as Home.

And now it would never be hers to call home again. Her dad had sold it out from under his kids. That alone was enough to make her spitting mad, but whatever was in this last codicil for her—

Her phone chirped. An SMS had arrived. Before she could check, gruff masculine voices from within Justin's office reached her. She shoved the phone back into her tote, heard a thud, maybe a fist on the desk and then some snarled words.

Stacey's glance met hers and they both shrugged. Stacey returned to stare at the computer screen, absently ruffling her hair once more. Maybe she was hot and sticky, and messing it up cooled her down. She'd made it look windblown.

The voices lowered to rumbles but only moments later rose again, angry and urgent.

Toni grabbed up the file from the next chair, just in case it might have got away from her. Again, she glanced at Stacey who shifted in her seat but continued to concentrate on her screen and keyboard. Guess she'd have to be the picture of discretion sitting out here listening to Justin with his clients all day. At least he hadn't shot out in a hurry again.

Toni settled in for a longer wait, straightened out her legs, and noticed she'd missed more red dust on her jeans. A vigorous swipe over both shins fixed that.

She held her file away and checked her front. The seatbelt had branded a rusty-dusty swathe of central Australian dirt across her pale gray tee, missing one boob and sliding under the other. God, she looked like she was warrior breasted.

Crap. No wonder Justin had stared.

Not wanting to attract any more of his attention to her frontage, she patted herself down. Covering her chest with the file again, she held on tight.

The main door behind her thrust open. Toni swung around. Her brothers. The boys. Anytime, anywhere they 'arrived', the space seemed to contract around them, always looked smaller, felt smaller, as if barely able to contain them.

The two tall, lean, denim clad and dirty men wandered in. Taking up the anteroom as if it were their own, they filled it with quintessential Aussie—casual, fun-loving, confident.

The day's heat came with them, a hot shimmer that captured the dry earth scent of home. They tinged the office air with a drop of diesel fuel, overplayed by the faint aroma of a burger—most likely with bacon and beetroot—and of hardworking man-deodorant falling just shy of its job. Fine threads of red dust puffed off their boots as they trod towards Stacey's desk. Comfortable gait, easy smiles.

Evan snatched off his Akubra. He mussed his sun-bleached hat-hair and it fell into some arty do. Almost. Then he leaned across the desk. 'G'day, Stace.'

Stacey burned a neat red. 'Hi, Evan.'

At least someone in the family was having fun. 'Yeah, hi, Evan,' Toni said, drawing his attention.

Turning, he flashed a smile at her. Broad shoulders were relaxed, and his hazel eyes crinkled under a layer of road dust. 'Hey, sis.' Evan, with hair the colour of pale toffee and his freckled, boyish good looks, had a wicked sense of humour. He was usually a 'love 'em and leave 'em, and let's be friends' type of guy.

Stacey found something interesting in her desk drawer.

Paul, Toni's older brother took a seat alongside her. He lifted his chin towards Justin's door. 'Here we go again, Tones.' He flicked off his hat, dusty and bent out of shape, and tucked it under his chair. Slumped in the seat, he stretched out long muscular legs and steepled his fingers.

Toni's looks and personality fell squarely between her two vastly different brothers. Where Evan was fair, and fun, taking after their mother and her Nordic side, she was on the darker side, auburn tinged hair more the colour of treacle toffee, and nowhere near the dark molasses shade of Paul's wavy hair. She was a little bit freckly but not overly much. Her moods were more like Paul's, deeper than Evan's. On few occasions did her lighter side shine through.

Paul was brooding, with an underlying volatility, sometimes— she believed—like the wild Celts way back on their father's side. He attracted women like magnets, and most times he was oblivious. She couldn't keep count of how many had come to her hoping for the magic key to unlock him. Only one of them, a long time ago, had got to his heart, but burned him first. *And it only took one to burn you forever.* She pushed that thought away.

Stacey bobbed up from the drawer. 'Justin has someone with him at the moment. He shouldn't be too long.' She aimed her advice squarely at Evan.

All three MacDonnell's nodded, and said 'thanks' in unison. Evan took a seat alongside Toni and the boys settled.

Justin's feeble air-conditioner couldn't absorb the heat they'd brought in with them. A trickle of sweat slipped down under Toni's warrior-breasted front.

Evan flapped his hat in front of him. 'Jeez. Open a window, Stace,' he said, and before she moved, he got up to do it himself.

'Justin thinks the cooler won't work if—'

'If you've got an old swampie, an open window is good.' Evan reefed up the window behind her and almost immediately the clammy air slipped out. 'Just order a decent aircon. It's not like he can't afford it.' He took his seat again and aimed a wide grin at

Stacey. She grinned back and ducked her head.

'Everything all right, Tones?' Paul nudged her shoulder. 'You feeling okay?'

She nudged back. 'Justin seems a bit touchy, again.'

The boys glanced at her. The boys. Dad had always called them that, not that they were boys now. Both in their early thirties and hardened by life on the land in the Centre. A hot, unforgiving ancient land whose secrets few realised. Indigenous people on the land in their communities spoke of stories, sang their stories or painted their stories of harsh gods who once ruled. Man, who often put a foot wrong, ended up learning tough lessons—or not.

Her brothers were cattle station workers. Cattle station owners until recently. They mustered on horseback when they had to, in helicopters when they could afford to. Part of the crew, they'd camp out with their teams. They understood the bookwork and the budgets, their stock and bloodlines, and kept up to date with current concepts of hardier more adaptable land and stock practices.

The boys could build a new shed, or an additional room, or plumb a new bathroom. They'd mix the cement, pour the concrete, erect the frame and roof and walls and suddenly there was a new dwelling. Neither being electricians, they didn't run to the wiring at all. Safety and legal reasons prevented any half-cut attempts at repairs in that regard. Tradesmen from Alice would visit to wire. But the boys could do anything else. They'd get into the machinery sheds and work magic on any vehicle, pull it down to bits of bolts and nuts and flanges and pins and rebuild it, giving it new life. She would tinker there with them, but her heart wasn't in the sheds. It was in the great parched expanse of the paddocks at home.

Her chest swelled. Pride, a huge wave of it, pushed emotion to the surface. It happened whenever she thought of her brothers. She loved them fiercely. Nobody else would size up to them, she was sure. If there was, they'd have to measure up big time. Her dad had always laughed at that and said there'd be someone, somewhere to take care of her. She'd always answered that she'd take care of herself, thanks very much.

'There'll be someone else, someone better than Sonny,' he'd declared.

Sonny Murphy. An anxious murmur riffled through her and her feet shuffled again. Better off believing there'd be no one else, especially after what he'd said to her. Maybe a lot of men felt the same way.

Stacey cleared her throat as raised voices again came from within Justin's office. Sounded like Justin was coming off second best. She stared in dismay at the closed door.

And then it flung open. A man, a powerhouse sort of man filled the doorway. He aimed a shot over his shoulder. 'Your services are terminated. Don't bother to send another bill, we won't be paying it.'

Toni stared and a fierce scorch rushed heat to her face. He was tall. Solid. Inky black hair, dark eyebrows—an intriguing scar dashed through the left one—strong jaw and chin. Nose a little bent as if it had been broken. His mouth was set in a grim line and a distracted, frustrated haunt shadowed his eyes. Blue or grey, which were they? Maybe warm, maybe not.

Edgy and intense, he had just propelled himself out of Justin West's office.

Her heart thumped. But he wasn't good-looking. No way. *No way*. Just had something about him … Some guys have that thing that smacks you between the eyes, sets your heart rate galloping, and zinging and zanging goes on all over the place. He was that kinda guy. Not good looking at all. *No, no, definitely not.* Just the sort of guy that set your hormones bouncing into overdrive, and your thoughts mooshing around in your brain. That sort of guy.

Inclining his head, he took a deep breath. 'Great bloke, this solicitor of yours.' He halted a half metre from Toni's chair, his gaze clamped mercilessly on hers. Then the steely snap of his eyes cleared and his features softened.

She nodded, she thought. Hugged her precious folder with all her plans in it, safe against her chest. Her red dirt smudged, warrior-breasted chest.

He acknowledged her brothers with a nod. As he bent to retrieve a briefcase by Stacey's desk, the worn denim of his jeans strained over a well moulded butt. He turned and walked out of the office without a backward glance.

Toni let out the breath she was holding.

Stacey shifted behind her desk. Ruffled her hair some more. Patted it back into place.

Paul leaned in against Toni's shoulder. 'Maybe he's why Justin's been tetchy. Who's he? Never seen him before.'

'I don't know.' She pushed out of her chair and oh, you know, just sidled to the window. He'd be outside any minute and a second look at him would ensure she'd recognise him again. Therefore, of course, she'd be able to steer clear in future. *Of course.*

Jeez, how often did that happen—a thunderbolt from the gods? Certainly, not in a long while. She wouldn't act on it, not like in the old days. The past made anything else for the future impossible.

Evan sat forward. 'Maybe we should sort Justin out like he did.'

Toni glanced over her shoulder. 'There's not a lot we can do about Justin, he's still handling the estate. Hopefully after this afternoon, it'll all be over and we won't have to come near him again.'

Down below in the car park, the black-haired man came into view. Any distraction was welcome today. She watched the ramrod straight back, the broad shoulders and the snug fitted jeans. The confident stride, the powerful arms. One hand gripped the large briefcase, the other pulled testily at the mobile phone in his shirt pocket. *Look away now, Toni-girl. That's trouble in truckloads.*

Nerves a-jangling in her stomach made her hands prickly and hot. That's what thunderbolts do. You get all prickly and hot.

Damn it. No. No. No. Don't get things all muddled up.

Evan distracted her. 'Movement from the Hide.'

Justin West emerged from his inner sanctum. His hands wrung over and over. 'Welcome, welcome.' Then he waved them inside. 'Come in. Sit. Sit.'

Paul studied his fingers as he took a seat on the lounge inside Justin's office. Evan leaned on the wall by the window. Toni sat in the swivel chair opposite Justin, laid her file on the desk.

'You okay after all that bellowing, Justin?' Paul asked.

'Bit of a tricky customer that fella.' Justin glanced at Toni. 'He, um, is actually required to be here at this meeting. Actually,' he repeated. 'I'm under instructions to ...'

The prickly sensation surged. Toni's eyes narrowed. 'To what?'

'Well, to introduce him when he returns and I'm not at liberty to say any more until he's back in here.'

Toni sat forward. 'What do you mean?'

Evan settled himself alongside his brother. 'You think he'll want to come back in here after the strong-arm armed you handled him?'

Justin cut him a glare. 'Very funny. Actually, this reading really relates only to Toni. You boys don't have to be here.' Met with stony silence, and the deepening frown from Toni, he stuttered on. 'But as you are all here, you may as well hear it together—'

'Actually,' Evan completed for him.

'That's the general idea,' Paul stated flatly.

Toni shifted in her seat. 'This is private, Justin. What the hell has that man got to do with this?'

The door opened quietly, and that man let himself back in. She glanced at him. And only a glance because another eyeful would set her heart rate off again. *Too late.*

He nodded again at her brothers, and they each extended a hand.

'G'day, mate. Evan MacDonnell.'

'Paul MacDonnell.'

'Callum Parker.'

Toni offered a quick grip of his hand. 'Toni MacDonnell.' It sounded like she croaked her own name. Then he slipped into a chair on her right.

Evan, his eyes wide and a grin on his face, inclined his head in her direction. Toni squinted at him, mouthed what was clearly not a sisterly endearment. She spun around and glared back at Justin.

Parker, all polite and congenial, said, 'Please continue, Justin.'

'All right.' The solicitor shook the sheaf of papers in his hands, spread them then regrouped and stacked them. 'Let's get down to it.'

Toni started. 'Wait a minute.'

'Yeah, wait. What's this all about?' Paul eyed Callum Parker and back to Justin.

'If you'll just let me continue.' A crimson bloom spread on Justin's face. He pulled at the collar of his shirt. 'Let me read this.'

Toni opened a hand in Callum Parker's direction. 'No. No. No. What does Mr. Parker have to do with us?'

Justin still tugged at his collar while he scowled at her. 'If I could get on reading this thing of your father's, you'll learn soon enough. It's part of the instructions.' He sucked in his cheeks.

Toni sat rigid at the slapping down. Heat rushed through her. She stared at her father's neatly cramped signature on the single piece of typed paper lying on Justin's desk. Her throat constricted as she shot a look at her older brother.

Paul sat back, shaking his head at Toni, hands clasped over his stomach. 'We're all ears, Justin,' he placated.

The solicitor read from the paper on his desk. '*My darling Toni, this will no doubt come to you as a great shock, but it is for your own good...*'

The blood drained from Toni's face. *For your own good.* Never did those words *ever* mean anything something enjoyable.

Her brothers sat forward in their chairs, shoulders hunched, heads hung, listening.

'*...and is the last thing I can do for you as I face my death. It* *has been known to me for some time that I have this inoperable, bastard of a cancer and because of that, I placed MacDonnell's Run on the market, as you all know by now. At the time of writing, it has a buyer, a small group. The group is fully aware of my impending death and of all the conditions I have put in place.*

'By the time you read this, it will be clear that the sums left to you and your brothers are the total of what was left after the sale of the station. Not a lot. Paul and Evan will find their way even after the last few lingering debts have been paid off. However, for you, Toni, it will not be enough, not after everything you've lost.'

Toni wanted to swallow, but her throat had closed.

'The station debts are many and expensive. So, in return for a lower sale price, I included a clause or two that the buyers accepted. Subsequently, the new owners have agreed to take over all but the most personal of the debts.'

She didn't even blink for fear she'd miss something.

'One of those clauses in the contract of sale was that you, Toni, were to be offered full time employment by the new owners for a period of twelve months upon take-over date, which, because of the impending inevitable, is to be sixty days after my death, a date in the not-too-distant future from this time of writing.'

Toni squeezed her eyes shut a moment.

Evan and Paul both reached her side at the same time, the rough grasps of their hands on hers steadying. She exhaled in one or two puffs, gripping their callused fingers.

'The debts will be paid off, and you will all have a small inheritance at the end of the twelve months. You, Toni, will be gainfully employed until then. It will help. The new owners have agreed to this condition.

'Knowing you as I do, Toni-girl, if you decide not to work with these people, your—and your brothers'—meagre inheritance, or rather what's left of even that, will be held over for a period of five years in a trust fund. Justin West has prepared that detail in case you decide not to take up the employment.'

Another involuntary puff of breath escaped Toni.

'It is the only way an old man like me can now provide for you. Please do this last thing for me and know that I've done this because I love you.

'And I will always love you. Your father, Philip MacDonnell.'

Toni snatched her hands free of her brothers' grips.

Evan snorted loudly into a large handkerchief and Paul strode to the window, hands jammed into his pockets.

Justin pushed the paper closer to her, tapped her father's signature to bring her attention to it.

Smartly brushing away loose wisps of her hair, she stared at Callum Parker, shock holding off the tears behind her eyes.

His gaze in return softened. He went to the office door and held it open. 'Justin, we'll leave for a few minutes.'

Justin got to his feet. 'Actually, yes. We'll go, ten minutes or so.' All his idea.

Toni shrugged off Justin's pat on her shoulder as he went by. She turned back in the seat, leaned forward and grabbed the letter from the desk.

The door closed quietly. A moment passed.

She shot out of her chair. 'How could he?' she exploded and shook the letter at her brothers. 'Especially after selling up without first telling us it was on the bloody market. This is medieval.'

'You know the old man, Toni. He never wanted you to go without. And he felt bad about your health problems before, then the whole thing with Sonny.'

Toni's eyes swam as she looked at her brother. 'Paul, I've built my business up again. I'm on my feet. What was he thinking—that I can't look after myself, or that I'm a total loss, or what?' Anger and frustration squeezed her vocal cords. She would follow this up with Mr. Mackie, the accountant, check the validity of it.

Paul levelled a gaze at her. 'Don't be ridiculous.'

'What's so bad?' Evan stuffed his handkerchief into a pocket. 'So, he wanted you to take an extra job, earn some extra cash. He wanted you to be safe, after everything.'

'Working with the new people on the station? With someone else sleeping in my room?' She waved her hands in the air. 'And what of my shop?'

Paul sighed and rubbed his ear, blinking to clear his eyes. 'Old fashioned bastard. Still, after all that bizzo with Sonny Murphy—'

'Don't.' Toni stopped her brother with a curt wave of her hand. Words hurtled out of her. 'And what sort of job? Why hold you boys to ransom if I don't take it?'

Evan looked at his hands. 'I reckon he knew you'd refuse otherwise.'

Her glare swung between them. 'You both seem to have a pretty good grasp of it.'

They shrugged at the same time, didn't meet her gaze.

Toni's shoulders slumped. Her father had known her well. 'You're right. He knew. Had you two known the place was up for sale before me, as well?' They both shook their heads but didn't look at her. She ran her fingertips over the sheet of paper in her hand. 'Oh, Dad, you didn't trust me to look after myself.' Closing her eyes, she hoped to stave off the wave of disappointment and grief. 'You never did.'

'Be fair, Tones,' Paul objected. 'You were his little girl, after all. It broke his heart, what happened to you. And he never liked that prick, Sonny, and look what he did.'

Toni turned her face away, willed the burning in her cheeks to dissipate. Shied away from her brother's well-meaning support.

Paul went on. 'And he didn't like the idea of your shop after that, and you know it.'

She flicked a hand at the paperwork. 'That doesn't make this right.'

Paul moved away from the window. His eyes were red-rimmed, bloodshot. Tentatively, he gripped her shoulders in a quick one-armed hug. 'Twelve months is not so bad. It's not long,' he said and dropped his arm.

Another moment passed in silence. 'No. It could be worse. I could make you both wait the five years for all that money.'

Evan barked a laugh. 'All what money? Nah. We'd talk you into taking the job, anyhow. As it is, I reckon it'll take a year before we see any of the estate. You know what these things can be like, hidden traps and taxes and payments and all the rest.'

Toni sighed. 'I know. I know, but—'

Paul held up his hand forestalling her. 'Don't worry about us. Just do it for a year, you need the money. You can't blame him for wanting to look after you. Was his job, after all.' He bumped her shoulder. 'The time will fly. And it might be interesting.'

Toni swiped at the stupid, angry tears threatening to land on her cheeks. 'At least the shop pays for itself, now. I'll could still run it, maybe if Mary-Anne goes full time.'

'See? You've got a plan already,' Evan said.

'But now there's suddenly a lot more to think about,' she said, fidgeting, her boots scuffing the carpet.

'It'll work out.' Paul looked at his younger brother and back to her again. 'Just take it easy.'

A light knock and the door opened. Justin West slid back in. 'I'm sorry that clause came as another shock to you, Toni. But ethics and all that. I was under instructions, you know, not to say before.' He took his seat. 'Are you ready for some final details?'

'There's more?' Toni felt tension crease her forehead again.

'Just the Who, and the When and the Wherefore.' Justin concentrated on the papers in front of him.

Callum Parker slipped back into the office and took up his seat.

Oh. She'd momentarily forgot about him. The man who'd caught her eye when she thought the world was just about right-side up again. Her pulse thumping in her ears, she said, 'Go ahead.' She stalked back to her seat, her father's letter still clutched in her hand. Air whooshed out of her as she plopped into the chair.

'If I may?' Justin outstretched his hand for the crumpled sheet of paper. 'The Who is a consortium. Three major partners. Big money, in property. A family business.' Justin's gaze slid to the man sitting quietly in the far corner as his hands smoothed out the paper. 'A brother and sister and the sister's husband. They're the directors, and they have access to many resources if necessary. More money, that means.' He glanced up momentarily and Toni gave him her best evil eye. 'The, ah, brother will be living and working on the station.' He paused and swallowed. 'In your house, actually.' He looked directly at Toni, a flush suffusing his cheeks. 'Don't worry, I don't like it either.'

What the hell did he not have to like? But she knew what was coming next. She just knew it. Could not believe what she was about to hear. Silence suspended in the room. A shiver crept up one side of Toni's body, tightening her scalp and prickling the back of her neck. Slowly, she turned her chair. Couldn't move her neck, couldn't blink, or swallow. She locked eyes with Callum Parker.

'You,' she accused him.

He lifted a shoulder. 'Me,' he agreed quietly, the dull shine of his eyes impenetrable.

'When will you be moving out there?' She forced herself to stare into those calm grey eyes—or were they blue?

Justin said, 'The request is for tomorrow.'

Toni's mouth dropped open. Air rushed in and lodged in her throat as she swivelled back to face the solicitor.

Justin coughed, tapped his thighs with the palms of his hands. 'It's only a request. Technically, they don't own a thing until settlement, but there's nothing to stop the deal going through, so take it as gospel that the station is sold, unfortunately, for all of us.' Justin hung his head a moment. 'Until the first of November, twenty-three days from tomorrow, they pay rent to you if their request is granted.' He hurried on, not looking at Toni. 'The Wherefore. You will be required as live-in bookkeeper, personal assistant and liaison officer, you name it, you're the one. I have here a list of duties required.' A forefinger rested on a few stapled sheets.

Toni reached over the desk and snatched the document from under his finger. Frowning, she glanced over the very professional job specification. She couldn't believe it, couldn't take it in.

'There is one very good bonus in all of this,' the solicitor began.

Toni looked at him in disbelief. 'Bonus?'

'Go on, Justin,' Paul invited. 'We're listening.'

Callum Parker leaned forward.

Toni's heart thudded. She closed her mouth, clamping her lips shut.

'The salary. They're offering sixty thousand a year. That's around eleven hundred, just off the top of my head, per week. Before tax, of course. And superannuation on top.'

Evan whistled through his teeth. 'Wow, sis. Go for it.'

Paul nodded his approval at Callum Parker. 'Why not? It's in your best interests, adds extra to your kitty.'

'No way,' she cried. 'I'm not accepting it.' This, after the sale of MacDonnell's Run, the station. Her home. This, her father's backhanded leg-up, so to speak. Humiliation flooded in. Her dying father's help after the fiasco with Sonny Murphy. *Embarrassing.* She felt hot with a slow burning, simmering heat that had nowhere to go.

'The hell you won't take it.' Paul eyed her. 'You need it.'

'Now, Tones—' Evan began.

'Everybody, everybody.' Justin held up his hands for silence. 'The money, less tax, has already been paid into Toni's bank account. Don't ask me why that's happened—it's unorthodox, but one of the principals insisted—'

'My bank account?'

'I had your details for the disbursement of the station's funds, remember, so when the money came into my trust account, I deposited it into yours.' Justin pushed a paper across the desk. 'Now Toni, I have to have your signature on this document, and this one for the bank, and this other one and then you restart your lives.' He pushed more papers towards her. 'Bear in mind, this is not technically a codicil, but it does form a part of the original conditions of settlement.'

Toni turned again to stare at Callum Parker, who merely inclined his head. 'This is ridiculous,' she said. 'This is all crazy, and wrong and—'

'Yes. Yes.' Justin tapped the sheet of paper, offering her his pen. 'Sign here, alongside this signature.'

'One of the principals insisted?' Her stare bounced to the tall man then to Justin, who kept waving the pen at Toni.

'He could speak up, but obviously, he doesn't wish to.'

Callum Parker briefly looked to the ceiling.

'I bet you think it's all very convenient and neatly tied up,' Toni grated at Parker. She swung back to Justin. 'Is there nothing I can do about it? This is like some stupid Gothic movie. No one gets trapped by these things this day and age.'

'Actually, it happens quite a bit. Usually not a trap, because it's never a problem if there's big money involved at the end,' Justin said. He leaned back in his chair, a smirk beginning.

Toni narrowed a glare at him.

Paul spoke up. 'Dad put this in place, Toni, no one else.' To the lawyer, he said, 'You recommend anything, Justin? Is there anything we can do if Toni—?'

Justin shook his head. 'You don't have the money for a court case,' he said baldly. 'It'd make things long and drawn out in Probate. It's clear and concise in the contract that both parties signed.'

Toni held out her hands, palms up. 'But Dad did it without my consent.'

'He didn't need your consent to put it in the contract.' Justin laced his hands on the desk. 'If you don't agree to the condition, your inheritance is held up for five years. That's the part that if you fight it, all the money will go in legals. Trust me on that.' He stared at the papers under his hands, shuffled one to the bottom, rearranged the rest.

Callum Parker cut in. 'Your dad just made it a condition of the sale that you would be offered full time work, and you have been. The rest is up to you.'

Toni's fight leached. He was quite right. She snatched the pen, then hesitated.

'Sign it, sis,' Paul encouraged, and glanced at Parker.

'Yeah, go ahead, Tones. It'll be right.' Evan lifted his chin in the paperwork's direction.

It was a long few moments before Toni finally hammered her signature on the paper. Justin took it out from under her clenched fist as quickly as he could.

'Of all the damned ridiculous—' Toni threw the pen to the desk and spun around to face the man in the corner. 'Who do you think you are?'

Callum Parker met her glare. His eyes gave nothing away as he studied her.

Her mind was blank but her gut trembled. *Fight or flight.*

Then he reached over and took the signed paper from under Justin's hands. He held it up to her. 'Your new boss.'

2

Callum Parker stood as Toni shot past him out into the reception area. She flicked a glance in his direction. It seemed polite. Not the force-ten glare it could have been, like the glare he'd been the recipient of earlier.

Evan nodded at him as he followed his silent sister out the main door. Paul MacDonnell remained, waited until Justin stopped hovering and retreated into the Hide.

'Mind if we have a chat a bit later?' Paul asked Callum.

''Course not. Over a beer sometime, maybe?'

'I meant today, if you've got the time.'

Callum nodded. 'Sure. I've got an hour or so, after that I have a couple of phone hook-ups I need to get to.'

'Won't take an hour.' Paul looked outside to see Evan and Toni walking to her car, her arms waving. 'I reckon my sister will go to her shop, but Evan will join us.'

'Great.' Callum hadn't brought anything back with him into Justin's office, so he waved Paul ahead of him as they left the building. 'Thanks, Stace,' he said, turning back to the receptionist. 'Sorry about the yelling.'

She smiled. 'Used to it,' she answered then took an incoming phone call.

Outside, Paul was waiting in the car park. He leaned up against an older model white Land Cruiser coated in fine red dust. MacDonnell's Run was emblazoned along the side doors in bold black print, though the sign itself had webby cracks, and bits of the old stick-on vinyl were flaking. The panels had dents and scratches, mostly well-worn in.

Callum dug in his pocket for his keys, aimed the remote at his own Toyota nearby and unlocked it. 'I'm at the Mercure,' he called across to Paul. 'Meet in the bar poolside, if you like. We can grab a coffee.'

'Will do.' Paul headed towards his sister's vehicle where Evan waited with her.

Callum climbed into the four-wheel drive, turned the ignition. Flicked on the air-con and waited a few beats until cooler air hit him. He'd parked under shade, but the build-up of heat inside the car was like a furnace. Be easy sixty degrees Celsius. He tapped the steering wheel, sure his fingers would sear to it. He never thought he'd be the guy wearing driving gloves, but the bloody thing was too hot to grip.

He poked about in the glove box, pulled out a leather pair from his golfing days and tugged them on. Even they were hot, but at least he'd be able to drive away without the skin on his hands melting onto the wheel.

Some things you never forgot about the Centre, but others, like the temperature inside a vehicle in summer could take you by surprise.

He remembered the old Vauxhall his dad drove when he came into town from their station. A Vauxhall of all things. They'd had four-wheel drives—Callum reckoned they might have been the old land rovers back then—but then when his dad had the accident, they were left with nothing but the old Vauxhall. His mum had to drive when they finally came to town to live. For that car, his mum had knitted some sort of steering wheel cover for driving in the heat. It'd had many covers over its life, that car. The heat perished just about all of them to dust.

He smiled at the memory. Wondered why he even had that memory. Wondered why the hell he was thinking about his childhood at all right now. Once the bull had fallen on his dad, his childhood, life for the surviving family, was anything but happy.

The trips south, the Adelaide hospital barely able to cope with the sort of injuries Dad had sustained. The long drawn out recuperation. His mother's helplessness. The frustration he felt as a young teenager powerless to do much but watch his dad wither, survive, adjust to life in a chair then a bed then die.

At least the family had friends around them before they had to give up their life on the station. Phillip MacDonnell, father to the three Callum had just met in Justin's office, had been one of those friends.

He reversed out of the parking bay. Driving away, he saw Evan and Paul with their sister heading towards their vehicles.

The boys wouldn't be long behind him.

3

The central Australian sun beat down on Toni's head, and the baking heat of the carpark tarmac underfoot shimmied up her legs.

Evan snatched off his hat and waved it over his face, jammed it back on his head again. 'It's too stinking hot to be standing out here arguing about it.'

'I'm not arguing,' Toni fired back, and leaned against her car. That was too hot as well and she popped off it. 'I just don't think we had enough time to look at everything properly before Dad's contract was signed, sealed and delivered.' She rubbed her forehead then folded her arms, scuffing the gravel at her feet.

Paul held up a hand. 'Listen, guys. Dad looked after all of that. It wasn't like he couldn't at the time. And don't forget, we weren't made partners or anything. We had no say in it. There was no succession planning.' He pulled keys from his pocket, unlocked his vehicle by remote. 'I didn't have a clue anything might have been on the nose, Toni. And you were in Adelaide clearing up that—'

'I know where I was,' she snapped, then regretted it. 'Sorry. I'm not saying it's anyone's fault.' Her phone pinged in her bag. An SMS. She'd look at it later.

'You are,' Evan disagreed. 'You're saying we didn't look hard enough while you were away—'

'I am not.'

Paul held up both hands. 'Hey, stop.'

Toni ignored that. 'I'm saying Dad chose not to bring us into his decision-making at all and now the whole thing looks like it's been right royally stuffed up.'

Evan's brows met. 'It's not stuffed up.' He shook his head. 'You just don't like it. No one's forcing you to take the job, Toni.'

She threw her hands in the air. 'It's not about the job.'

'You're pissed off because you have to work for the new guys,' Evan pressed.

'I don't have to work for the new guys. Stop making like this is about me.' Toni wiped her forehead again, a swipe of new perspiration quickly dried. 'This is about Dad selling the place up to clear his debts. What if we find that those debts were so much bigger than we were led to believe?'

Paul squinted at her. 'What are you talking about?' He pushed his hat higher on his head, the black hair shoved back with it.

'She doesn't know what she's talking about. You just got a feeling in your water, haven't you, Tones?' Evan said, into the hot air over his head.

'Don't be a dick.'

Paul blew out a loud breath. 'Any reason, Toni?'

Toni shook her head, tried to calm down. 'First, how could the debts possibly have been so big Dad practically had to give the place away?'

Paul chewed a lip. 'Don't know.' He looked at Evan.

'Second, how can any of us trust Justin West to do the right thing?' Something niggled her so badly about it all but she just couldn't explain herself.

Paul's voice was low and modulated, as if speaking any louder would upset the apple cart. 'Can't see how he could get away with anything. Mackie Accountants have been all over the books and the contract. They handled the sale in conjunction with Reddell's Station Agency. The settlement statement says it all.' His hands were shoved into his jeans pockets, and he didn't look at either of his siblings.

Evan looked around, agitated. 'Dad was up to his eyeballs. Why else sell for such a low price? All we'll get is the price of whatever stock is left.'

Toni stared at him, wide-eyed. 'And so, you reckon the bottom line is right, do you? How can that be?''

Evan's mouth downturned. Tawny bristles on his chin glinted gold in the late afternoon sunlight. 'Well, yeah, I thought there'd be a bit more in it for us after the wash up.'

'Didn't you check the figures?'

'Didn't you? Don't yell at me. That's what Dad paid all those other bastards for.'

Paul held out his hands again, his dark eyes red rimmed. 'Okay, enough.' He nudged his hat back off his forehead, wiped the sweat with his forearm. 'There's a copy of the settlement statement at Toni's house. We'll have another look.'

Evan scratched the back of his neck. 'We've already looked.'

'We'll look again. At everything.'

Toni waved a hand. 'It won't be just in the settlement. It'll be in the whole bunch of figures he had to show the buyers beforehand.'

'A station sale isn't like other sales, Toni,' Paul said.

'I know that but we should check all the outgoings for the last couple of years. At least do that.'

Her younger brother shook his head. 'Justin said we couldn't afford to fight it.'

'Evan, we won't be fighting if there's something illegal,' she said. 'It'll stand for itself.'

'If what's illegal?' he asked.

She pinched her lips before continuing, then wiped them over. 'What if Dad was … What's that word when you're sick and not thinking right?'

'Compromised,' Paul supplied. 'Taken advantage of.'

'Yeah. What if he signed off on bad advice?' she said, appealing to both her brothers. 'What if he paid for stuff that he didn't need? Or thought he was getting good returns from. Or something.' She knew she was picking at straws. Angry now and fit to burst, there had to be another reason for their lack of funds.

The baking heat of the day hummed in the silence between them.

Again, Evan shook his head. 'He had all the advice from—'

'But he was sick.'

Paul shrugged. 'We were here, though, the whole time.'

'But not advised or consulted.' Toni scuffed a foot. 'You didn't get involved.'

Evan exploded, his hazel eyes under twisted brows. 'There you go again—blaming us while you were away dealing with that arsehole.'

Paul intervened. 'Toni, to put it the right way around, Dad didn't involve us. Any of us.'

Toni rounded on him. 'But you get it, don't you, that it doesn't add up, that there's hardly any money?'

Evan folded his arms. 'Why'd you wait this long to speak up? You just want to put a fire up someone's arse because your eyes were off the game and—'

'That's not it,' Toni said between clenched teeth. 'If there's anything illegal—'

'All right.' Paul glared at them. 'We'll look harder at the books. We'll go see Mackies and ask questions. More questions. We'll go over things with Mo at Reddell's.' He flexed his hands. 'Let's just stop the screaming match.'

Evan pulled out his phone and squinted at the screen. He nodded at his brother. 'We gotta go.' He climbed into the passenger side of Paul's vehicle.

Paul bumped Toni's shoulder with his. 'We'll have another look at it, Tones, I promise. Don't worry.'

She sniffed. 'If there's any shonky business going on, if there's the slightest problem, we'll use the money in that account they set up to pay for the legal stuff.'

Paul squeezed her shoulder. 'We'll be right,' he said. 'See you.' Her big brother climbed into the driver's seat, gunned the motor and drove off.

Toni turned, aimed the keyless remote at her car and the locks clicked up. Pulling open the driver's door, she slid inside and shoved the key into the ignition. As the engine turned over, she reached across and flicked on the aircon. A blast of hot air fanned her face and neck and she lifted her collar to catch it. It'd take a minute or two to begin to cool down.

What a mess. What a morning. What a—

Her SMS alert pinged again. She rummaged around in her bag, found the phone and tapped the button on the screen. *Loser* appeared as the contact name. Three messages waiting. Staring at the screen, her heart sagged, but the pulse pounded through her veins. Sweat popped out despite the temperature dropping inside the car. Her hand shook.

Still this bloody reaction every time. Get a grip. It's just texts. You haven't even looked at them yet.

But any contact at all from Sonny Murphy would not be good news.

4

Good that Paul had stopped him and called for a chat. Callum wanted the brothers on side. He was fairly sure they already were, but hearing it for himself, from them, would be best. Changing the structure of the station, from cattle only, to more diverse options, would take strong management, strong policy and good marketing. Certainly, both MacDonnell brothers had those skills and more.

Their sister, however, might prove challenging. Hopefully, she'd be as co-operative and engaged as her brothers with the changes that would come for the Run.

Philip MacDonnell hadn't helped the situation. He'd insisted the new group not flag the last condition regarding his daughter before she'd heard it in last reading. As far as Callum was concerned, it was Philip's only mistake in the whole sale process.

He let out a long breath. Still, so far, so good. He knew Philip loved his kids. From his hospital bed, he gave Callum a fair idea about what to expect from each of them, especially his daughter, Toni.

It was a couple of months before he passed away. In the hospital ward, the old man had gripped a photo of her.

'Headstrong, stubborn. She can get all hot and bothered at times. When you meet her, you'll reckon she can take care of herself. But I know that when I go, she'll have nothing. As a kid, she had a rough trot, and again lately. Rough. That's why—' He'd stopped to draw in what easy breath he could. His hand with the photo in it floated down to rest on his chest.

There hadn't been much left of the man Callum remembered from his childhood. The broad shoulders had shrunk, the body had wasted away, and the big happy face had shrivelled as the cancer chewed its way through his body. His frame was skeletal, his skin appeared translucent on his wasted arms, and hands. Before the illness, Callum had been able to see Philip's likeness in both his boys, more so in Paul.

He'd placed his hand over the old man's. 'Philip.' He glanced outside the palliative care ward caught the eye of one of the nursing sisters who hovered nearby.

Philip MacDonnell waved her away. 'Cal, I wanted you to see her picture. She's beautiful, just like her mother, and Nettie was a beauty. Irresistible. Toni's full name is the same—Antoinette. She looks so much like her mother. Died too young, my Nettie. Couldn't have that for Toni. When she was diagnosed …' He moved his restless hands out from under Callum's, fluttered paper-thin skin-and-bones over his feeding tube. It was clearly hard for Philip to talk about it, especially in his last few weeks. 'Antoinette MacDonnell. But Toni hates using her full name, Antoinette.'

When she was diagnosed? Who, his wife? His daughter? Surely not.

Callum remembered he'd stared down at the sunny-faced woman who smiled at him from a photo print. She was certainly beautiful, no denying that. Against the backdrop of a Central Australian red desert dune, her hair, the colour of peat-smoked whisky, and her skin lightly tanned, honeyed from life in the Outback, stood out as a breath of fresh air for him.

A smattering of freckles to add youth to the unspoiled beauty which radiated from her face. Eyes which were dark toffee delights, like thick, burnt caramel. Her mouth …

No one else had attracted a second look from him in the seven years since Sylvie had been in his life. Oh, sure, the one-night stands had come thick and fast after Sylvie had found the greener pastures she was chasing, but he'd tired of that life quickly.

No one had caught his eye since, or his interest, and the couple of women who persisted in trying to nibble away his reserve, soon gave up. They hadn't opted to stay around any length of time. So, he stopped looking. Stopped expecting the right one would be around the next corner, and just got on with it.

And now, Toni's photo in his hand, he felt she might be the very thing he'd been looking for. He'd stared at her image, knew he was caught, hook, line and sinker. In the picture, she was—no question about it—the most gorgeous creature he had laid eyes on in years.

In the flesh, at today's meeting, she struck him exactly the same way. She was older than in the photo, of course. He couldn't ignore the rush of blood and the thud of his heart as he spotted her in Justin's reception area, clutching a manila folder, staring at him. As he gripped her hand, the shake in his own had surprised him.

But he had a job to do. Couldn't be distracted. The last conversation he'd had with Philip MacDonnell meandered back into his thoughts.

'She's the reason for that clause in the sale.' Philip's voice had faded to a rasp as he sank against the pillows. Just the effort of breathing exhausted him. 'And she's not to know until after—' A pointed arthritic finger remained in the air between them.

'I know.' Callum had taken the old man's hand in his again and squeezed it gently. 'It's all taken care of. Don't worry.'

Philip nodded once, his hand resting in the younger man's. 'You're like your dad, Cal. Pity we lost touch. I wished I'd have known him better when he lived around here.'

'You did all right when he needed you,' Callum had said and looked down at Toni's picture again, his mind not on his father.

'You keep that photo, Cal. I don't need it. I'm glad you'll look out for her. But she won't thank you, or me, for that matter.' Philip

MacDonnell closed his eyes, breath caught in his throat.

Now, the clause in the contract of sale was going to break her heart. It seemed it was the price to pay for her father's long-ago kind act towards Callum's father.

He shook it off. Maudlin feelings of his own dad's early death and the late memories of Philip MacDonnell's passing were catching up. He'd be glad when this part was over and done with and they could all move forward.

He turned right at the Todd River, drove along until he took a left on to Stott. The Mercure came up on his left and he pulled into the driveway, headed for the parking bay outside his room.

Inside, glad he'd left on the air-con, he tossed his keys onto the bench and poured a long drink of cold water. He chugged it down and checked his laptop. Among others, four emails from Marnie, his sister. He'd have to catch up with developments after he'd seen the boys. It was one of the phone hook-ups he'd mentioned to Paul earlier.

He left his room locked, headed towards the bar by the pool. By the time he got there, Evan and Paul were already taking up space inside at a low table. There was a third chair vacant.

Paul ordered a long black for himself in a mug, an iced coffee for Evan and—?

'Long black for me.' Callum sat, rested his forearms on the table.

Paul was ready. 'We didn't know what Dad had in mind for Toni.' He leaned forward, his elbows on his knees. 'I reckon she's in shock.'

'It's fine,' Callum said. 'No matter how she heard the news, it would be hard to take.'

Evan pulled a hand through his hair but said nothing.

Paul tapped his fingertips together. 'We don't have any problem with your mob being the new bosses. Nothing like that.' He checked his brother and continued. 'We're happy to work with you, happy to maintain any connection to the old place. We appreciate you wanted to keep us on.' A muscle in Paul's jaw worked, his chin flexed. 'We all do, me and Evan, and Toni.'

'Good to hear,' Callum said. 'You both have your own jobs, that hasn't changed. You know we want you to stay on. In fact, the deal included you.' The coffees arrived, and a rich, heady espresso aroma wafted over the table. 'Without you, all three of you,' he emphasized, 'it would be tough going for us.' Callum sat back. He sensed the brothers were about to launch a case for their sister.

Evan's casual slouch didn't disguise the discomfort and concern in his eyes. And Callum felt Paul's unease. Maybe the brothers were going to ask something else of their new employers.

Paul came to the edge of his seat, the steaming mug of coffee in his hand. 'She's going to find it hard to adjust.'

Callum inclined his head. 'Okay.'

Paul put his mug on the table, his jaw set, stare intense. 'She doesn't want to be looked after.'

'Doesn't look like she needs to be,' Callum said.

Evan looked at his brother, took a swig of iced coffee. A little white moustache of froth appeared at his lips before he wiped it away. 'Yeah, well.'

'You're right there,' Paul said to Callum, and looked to be considering his next words. 'She and Dad each had a different way of looking at the same things. They were pretty much two peas in a pod, but they'd come unstuck, time to time.' He scratched his head. 'Too much alike, I reckon. But Dad had calmed down a helluva lot in the last years. Not sure about my sister.'

Callum waited. All right, so Toni had something of a temper. He figured as much from the meeting earlier, when she'd barely reined it in. Maybe she was like her dad, maybe not. What he remembered of Philip was a man who measured his reactions.

Evan sat forward. 'Then she, um. There was a problem with her… and then a bloke who—'

Callum didn't want to hear about any other bloke. 'Not my business,' he stated, and held up a hand to stop Evan going any further.

Evan gave a snort. 'Right, but it means all blokes are bastards.'

'Ah.' Callum picked up on cue. 'Could be hard going, then?'

'Just sayin'.' Evan continued. 'Us two aren't exempt, either. But we had a chat in the car on the way here. We can make it so that things work out smoothly enough.' He glanced at Paul who kept his eyes on the coffee mug.

Callum frowned. 'Something I need to know? Because if there's going to be real trouble over all this, I'd want to fix whatever it is before it gets broken.'

Paul shook his head. 'We have a few things to look at, extra business we hadn't anticipated. That's not your concern, so, that aside …' He looked across at Evan. 'Keep going, bro.'

Callum reckoned he was being sized up by the younger brother, who always seemed a little detached, unlike Paul. Usually he had a youthful glee about him, though it wasn't evident right now.

Evan flexed his shoulders, took another long swallow of iced coffee. He smacked his lips over the froth on his mouth and kept up a forthright stare. 'We want you to know that, yep, Toni is gonna be hard work,' he said. 'She's gonna be hard-headed, she'll want her own way. She's not afraid of a fight. Guess growing up with us she had to defend herself.' He shrugged at Callum, and his dark ginger eyebrows creased. 'She came unstuck, though, with—'

Paul interjected. 'So, she's tough. Won't take any fooling around. But she's had a rough trot. A real rough trot and we *will* look out for her.'

Callum leaned back in his chair. *Just what Phillip said. Great. Now these two are gonna read me the riot act.* And that would be okay. He was a professional. As he'd said all along, he had a job to do, and no amount of staunch opposition would stop him from doing that job. He took a couple of swallows of his coffee. He needed the caffeine to keep up with this conversation.

Evan kept going. 'So, let her have things straight up. Tell her like it is. No namby-pamby.' He finished his iced coffee and put the glass down on the table.

Paul sputtered a laugh. 'Namby-pamby. Where'd you get that from?' His cheek twitched as Evan shrugged. He turned back to Callum. 'Yeah, just keep things straight up. That way, things will go to plan,' he said. 'We don't want anything going wrong.'

'Right,' Callum said. 'Fair enough.' Still waiting, he stayed tense, puzzled.

'But if the shit hits the fan with her and she gets all bolshy,' Paul began, retrieving his coffee and downing it.

Evan cut in, po-faced. 'We'll look after you, too. We just wanted you to know that.' He stared at Callum a moment then burst out laughing. 'We got your back, mate.'

Paul's face split in a wide, relaxed grin.

Callum, relieved, barked a laugh. 'You both have my grateful thanks.'

Paul, eyes wide, and still laughing, looked over at his brother. 'He's a poor bastard, bro. He thinks we're kidding.'

5

Justin West sat at his desk and peered out the window. No one could see him. No one was around. He watched as the MacDonnell family argued in the carpark and then took off, Paul and Evan in one vehicle and Toni in another.

He'd already seen Callum Parker reverse and drive away.

Who the hell did he think he was? Oh yes, bought the station, did he, he and his team. Well, that didn't give him the right to make demands or anything, or to tell Justin his job. Mr Fucking High and Bloody Mighty. More money than manners. As usual.

'Good riddance. Good riddance,' he said, aloud.

Crissake, stop talking your thoughts, stop repeating yourself.

His hands stilled over a white sheet of paper folded down the length of it on top of the desk. His palms were hot, as if the lies he'd written burned him, stirred under his skin. He snatched his hands up. Stupid thought.

Drawn to the paper again, he opened it, read the typed legal-speak silently, his lips moving.

I, Philip MacDonnell, in this last codicil to my will hereby bequeath one quarter ownership of MacDonnell's Run to Justin Dwayne West of ...

What possessed him to begin such a fraud? And such an amateurish attempt, at that. No wonder he never completed it. But it had sat there, tempting him from under the other papers Toni had to sign. He could easily have slid it under her nose. She was too agitated to—

He'd very nearly done it. But too crazy, even for him. Wasn't it? He wouldn't be doing it only for himself. He just wanted to show the family he was part of them. And he was, even if the truth hadn't come to light yet. Soon it would. Real soon.

He shook his head. Drops of sweat popped off his face and, worried they'd land with a soft splat on his desk, he withdrew a clean, pressed handkerchief from his trouser pocket. Mopped his forehead, mopped the rest of his face. Mopped the desk.

Air-con on the blink. Though he knew it wasn't only that.

In his madness, he'd nearly presented Callum Parker with a forgery. He'd nearly done it, shaking with rage and frothing at the mouth like a rabid fool.

Oh, it had Philip MacDonnell's signature on it, all right. Just not a signature meant for such a document. Such a clumsy document. A clumsy, clumsy attempt. He was a forger, a fraud. A man should burn the evidence of his forgery. Burn.

Mo Reddell at the stock agency knew he was mad. Though he wouldn't find anything to blame Justin for.

Eric Roycroft had something in place so that if— No. No. Roycroft would keep his mouth shut, too. It wasn't time. Besides, Eric didn't know that Justin had something over him. Insurance, you could say. He hadn't done anything stupid. Not yet. He'd stay in control, get past this. Get past this extreme emotional state. This ridiculous state.

Head in his hands. *Maybe get some help. God knows I need it. It's a madness. It must be a madness.* He pressed a fist against his pounding heart, and the heat in his chest felt like it blasted from a boiler. He mopped some more. *Relax. Breathe.*

His eyed another envelope on his desk. It needed to return to safe keeping. The results in there from the lab would do him far more good than a botched attempt at fraudulently claiming an inheritance. He was sure of that.

He'd do it the right way, with evidence. With DNA evidence. *Calm.*

He had evidence, which he knew would be conclusive. So, what had he been thinking with that forgery? Trying to measure his breathing, his heart rate slowed. Checking the forged document on the desk, he stared at the signature and felt a sadness creep over him. At the time, it looked as if he nearly had a perfect plan.

The paperwork was all wrong—slight problem—but the signature was Philip's. Then Justin closed his eyes, groped for the paper on the desk and tore the thing in half.

Reaching behind, he flicked the switch on his shredder, pushed the two halves of the forged codicil through the cutting teeth. *Make confetti. Make lots of confetti.* He switched off the machine, grabbed the wastepaper basket underneath and swirled his hand through the tiny scraps of paper, mixing everything up together. If anyone snooped around in his shredder bin they'd have a hard time—

Fool! No one would do that. Fool! You're making it worse because of your bloody ridiculous paranoia. Tonight, he would take the whole lot home and burn it. That's what he would do. Burn it tonight. Burn the lot. Burn all the confetti.

For now, he had to be normal. Ready for work. He picked up the signed documents Toni and the others had left and walked to the door that opened to Stacey in the front office. He took a deep breath and pulled it open.

She looked up from her computer. 'You all right, Justin?'

He nodded, blew out the breath. 'Lodge these, would you, Stacey? All the usual processes.' He flipped the documents on to her desk.

She looked at documents, picked them up then looked at him. 'Okay. Will do.'

'And, um.' He looked around the empty reception room. 'Uh, when's the next appointment?'

Her gaze was steady. 'Tomorrow at two pm. Your bank manager. His office.'

6

Toni stared out the window and into the mall, busy now with late morning shoppers, and hardy, hot-weather tourists.

In the solitude of her travel shop office in the main street, she hoped some peace and quiet would allow her to sift through her feelings about Sonny Murphy's three texts.

Her heartbeat had slowed only a little, her fight-or-flight response was still zinging. Justin West's revelation, Callum Parker, her father's affairs... Sonny Bloody Murphy. Wild thoughts darted in and out of her mind, each one hard to grab and sort from the others.

Too hard. She pushed her thoughts away from Sonny Murphy's messages. She needed to concentrate on the fall-out from the meeting earlier in Justin's office. The texts would have to wait.

The shop was closed for the day. She remembered that Mary-Anne, her soon-to-be-elevated-to-manager staff member always closed the shop early on Mondays to pick up her kids from school, their father on late shift at the space base.

So, it didn't matter she was still in her station clothes, no one was here, no one would be dropping in. She'd change when she got back to her town house in Cromwell Drive.

It took a couple of deep breaths, and some glowering before she could make sense of her father's condition in the contract. To talk herself around to some form of accepting the inevitable, without feeling like her chest would burst.

'Ridiculous,' she said to the empty office. 'Why did Dad think we couldn't handle the Station? We would've coped. Somehow.'

It was the only lie she told herself over and over. She knew, her brothers knew it as well, that the debt had been insurmountable. A sale had been the only way out of their father's predicament. And really, the only way the debts could be paid by any sensible purchaser would be to demand the sale price of the station be reduced.

So many debts. Why had Reddell's allowed it to escalate? Millions of dollars had seemed to leach out of the property, leaving her and her brothers barely thousands between them until the last of the stock could be sold.

What the hell had Dad paid for over the last couple of years?

Her stomach tightened, and an ache deep down behind it caught her breath. Then disbelief, and impotent rage scorched through her as she relived the shock of her dad's last letter. At least at that moment, it had hammered the other issue of Sonny Murphy almost into the background.

But it wouldn't be hammered into oblivion, dammit. It loomed large. Both issues made her head hurt and her face pinch. Angry, scalding tears welled and fell. She swallowed down the choking lump in her throat. Hadn't felt like this since Sonny Murphy's last betrayal. *Frustration. No control.* At least here in her office she could let go if she was going to. A show of grief in private wouldn't encroach on her brothers' own grief.

Still she held off. Had to think clearly, had to get on with life, had to get on with things, despite the added blow of her dad's last condition. She knew she could.

But the other thing with Sonny. She still had a shared mortgage with him. It had kept her broke and always on her toes, jittery and tense, hoping she'd manage to pay her share of it each month. Hoping she wouldn't have to find his share as well. All the coloured balls were in the air and she felt like a juggler, clumsy at best.

So the only thing that had kept her going forward was the plans for the wildlife sanctuary. That was worth something, surely. In the years since the last of her treatments as a teenager, and since having seen the last of Sonny, she'd thrown herself into the project, pored over reams of business plans and marketing devices, waiting for the opportune moment to approach the banks for development.

It was the only thing that kept her sane.

Then the news of the sale of the station. Her dad's death. She hadn't even had time to run the idea of the wildlife park past her ailing dad. And she'd have needed lots of time to convince him of its merit. There wasn't enough time to do too much at all, as it turned out.

Maybe the new owners would lease back a small portion of the station to her, if she asked nicely. Glancing at her notes, she shook her head. It was too early. She didn't have the fight in her right now to face up to big business and multi-million dollar wheeler-dealers.

Don't dwell on it. No time to dwell on it, on any of this, much less on something you can't do anything about.

She jotted down a few extra points, marking her thoughts on paper in case the force of raw emotion wiped them from her memory. At times like this, the keyboard just wouldn't do it for her. Her head was bent over the lined pad as she scratched away, the pen clenched more tightly in her fingers.

But the tears refused to be ignored. Before she could swallow them down, they spilled over. She gave in, the weight in her chest too much. She plonked her head in her hands and sobbed. Between sniffs, she heard footsteps falter close by.

'What's the matter, kiddo—lost your all-day sucker?'

Toni looked up at Ben Whyte, a mate for years. She let out a little broken laugh. 'Bit emotional.' She swiped a tissue and pressed it over her eyes. 'Silly to be bawling this late in the day about it all. Should be out of my system by now.' She sat up. 'I'm the sucker. Wait 'til you hear this.' She slid her mobile phone off the desk and slipped it back into her tote-bag. If there were any more texts, she didn't want Ben catching who they'd come from. Ben hated Sonny Murphy's guts. Every time there was a mention of his name, he broke into a rant equal to that of a guilty politician at question time.

He perched on her desk, all six foot of lanky city boy, dressed to kill in outback Alice Springs. 'You tell me yours and I'll tell you mine.' Ben had city style about him, always looked like a fashion mag model. Smooth good looks, dark blonde hair, brown eyes. A sense of humour that had you chuckling long after he'd gone. His partner of ten years, Josh, was just as great a friend to Toni as Ben was.

Toni relayed the details of the codicil. '…And that's about it. I don't know what to make of it all, but the Parker guy seemed right at home.'

Ben lifted a shoulder. 'So, it's all tied up and sold, lock, stock and barrel. And he's got money by the sound of things, and lots of it. Such a problem. Is he single?'

Toni snapped a glare at him. 'How the hell would I know that?

Not the least bit interested, anyway.' She threw herself back in the chair. 'I'm the one stuck with that awful bloody condition. I feel like a pawn in someone else's chess game.'

'Come on,' Ben drawled. 'It's me you're talking to. What's the real problem?'

Exasperated, Toni flicked the paperwork on her desk. 'All of it, especially Justin West's part—'

'That crook. When will you sack that guy? You know I can't stand the sight of him. Besides, now your dad has gone and you don't have to keep him on, I'll let you in on something. I'll tell you my—' Ben stopped when he saw her stricken face. 'Sorry. Mouth is running away with me.'

She put her head in her hands.

Ben tapped her shoulder. 'You've got company,' he said close to her ear. 'He's a chunk of hunk, that one, isn't he? I'll be off. See you later.'

She looked up as Ben said, 'G'day, Callum,' and excused himself.

*

Callum Parker watched Toni glance up from her desk. She wasn't happy, that much was clear. Despite her frown and reddened eyes, his breath stopped in his throat as he gazed at her.

'Sorry, we're not open.' She pointed to the *Closed* sign on the door.

Not the opening line he'd hoped for. He thumbed over his shoulder at Ben's retreating form. 'You mean just to me?'

'Not just to you. We close Monday afternoons every week. Ben is a friend of mine, comes and goes as he pleases. Can't seem to stop him.'

Callum took a glance at Ben's departure. 'What if I'm here to buy a flight ticket?'

'But you're not.'

'No.' He leaned a hip on the desk opposite hers and folded his arms. 'I thought I'd see if you're feeling any better about things. Maybe we could have a longer chat without all the hype.'

Warm, dark eyes glared at him—or, he supposed, they might usually have been warm because now they were red and teary. Her brows twisted.

Jesus, Philip. Now I've got your daughter's tears on my head. Not good.

Her mouth he'd earlier noted as generous and sensuous, was set, drawn tightly. Her chin puckered as she struggled with her mood.

'Right,' he said. 'Not a good time.' He pushed off the desk. 'Apologies. I'll leave you in peace for a while.'

She blinked. 'No. Wait,' she said. The glare she gave him was a force ten. 'I'll only be doing it for my brothers.'

'I'd prefer you'd do it for you, as well. You're not being held to ransom over this.'

She stood up. 'My brothers are.' Her eyes flashed. 'Twelve months. That's all I'll do.'

Had her father said headstrong, stubborn? That wasn't the half of it. He tried again. 'That's all your father requested of us. To be honest, we believe it'll take at least that long to get everything sorted. You're the obvious one to help us with that particular part of the job.'

She held his gaze for long seconds, then turned away. 'I don't like how it's happened.'

'That's clear,' he said, trying to step carefully through the conversation. 'I fully understand you thought there wasn't a lot else you could do.'

Her shoulders rolled forward as if some extra weight bore down on her. 'The condition was put there without my knowledge.

Behind my back.'

'It was part of your father's conditions for us. We agreed to make you an offer and that's what we did.' He knew he was repeating himself, but he wasn't the enemy here.

She looked over her shoulder at him, then back to stare out the window.

'We wanted to show good faith.' He shoved hands in pockets. 'That's why we opened a bank account and deposited the year's net pay,' he added.

She nodded, and once again only partly turned toward him.

'Do you think you could manage lunch, now? Maybe it's a good time to go over the job specifications. Get it out of the way.'

'I'm busy with other stuff right now. Thanks all the same.' Toni dusted off her jeans, seemed to make a big deal of it, patted down the front of her pants, and slapped at the sash of dirt on her shirt.

At least her tone had softened, and the line sounded genuine enough. Headstrong and stubborn. She had no clue of the effect she had on him. How her proud, sad face made his heart beat a little faster. How those angry, furtive glances at him sent a coil of heat unfurling deep in his gut. One day he'd tell her of the conversation he'd had with her father. But not today. Today was not the right day.

She returned to her desk and stood behind the chair. Her hands clutched the back of it, and those dark caramel eyes glinted.

Something arced in him, sharp and unrelenting. Something he'd missed all this time, for years now, it seemed. Something he'd barely realized until that glint spoke to him in waves. He shook at what he hadn't known was there. A deep connection that crept up on him and clouted him behind the ears. What if she rejected him and his offer outright? *What are you thinking, idiot?* He faltered, unused to a waver in confidence. But that only deepened his resolve. He had to test it.

'Fine,' he said, keeping his tone agreeable. 'Then how about we make it an hour and a half's time? The Stockman's at one thirty.' Waiting for a response, he watched frustration, and what he suspected was indecision move over her face in chin puckers and brow lines bent out of shape. When no answer was forthcoming, he said, 'One thirty, it is then. Sharp.' He turned and let himself out.

She'd either be there, or she wouldn't.

7

Toni bristled. Her eyes felt like they were steaming.

His cool grey eyes widened in an apologetic smile. '…there wasn't a lot else you could do.'

Her heart lurched. She blew her nose. Watching her hand shake as she discarded the tissue, she knew she needed to eat to raise her blood sugar. Extreme emotion depleted her stocks, but if she was careful with her diet, she was fine. She'd grab a new packet of jellybeans on her way home.

She blew out a long breath. Callum Bloody Parker. Her new boss. His whole stance oozed chilled-out. The broad shoulders were loose, hands pushed deep in his pockets. His face, angular and confident was softened by the dim light of her office. His generous mouth curved in a warm grin. That dark, dark head of hair…

She sniffed back the last of her tears. Squared up. Well, he'd have some questions to answer. And some conditions to meet of her own. All right, buster, one thirty, sharp.

She locked the shop and drove by the pharmacy for some lollies, then headed on to her house to change. She wasn't going to dress in the smart, corporate gear she usually wore when she was in her office. It required clean jeans, and boots and a sassy top. That would be the dress for lunch at the Stockman's.

Then again, would it do to antagonise the new boss? No. It would not.

She'd better get that through her head, quick smart. If she didn't toe the line, her brothers would suffer the consequences. She didn't want that. So, shrug off the resentment towards Callum Parker, towards this whole thing and get on with it.

Not easy to do when it felt impossible. Impossible, that is, to shift her attitude. But if she couldn't do it, it might cost all of them five years.

Once at home, the aircon flicked on and the cool air driving down the temperature, she headed for her bedroom. As she tossed her bag onto the bed, she heard the SMS alert ping again.

Heat rushed to her face, her pulse thudding. That would make four messages from Sonny Murphy, for sure as anything, it would be him. This was his usual tactic when he wanted something. He'd just keep plaguing her with messages until she answered.

Despite being urged to block his number or change her own phone number—why do that and have him hunt her down some other way—she allowed the contact so she could keep tabs on what he was up to. To a certain point, of course. She knew he lied through his teeth to her, but she was still locked into a mortgage with him and he had to be jollied along to pay his portion of it. He had refused to sell the place. If she blocked him, or refused contact, chances were he'd leave her well and truly in the lurch and disappear off the radar, never fulfilling his responsibilities.

And she certainly couldn't afford to go bankrupt—

A fifth message alert.

Groaning, she flicked the screen. Sure enough, five messages but only three from Sonny. The two others were from her contact at the bank.

Oh no.

That meant she'd better look at the *Loser's* messages. Her stomach dropped, her gut hurt in the clench, hands shook as she thumbed open Sonny's texts.

I know you won't answer a phone call. Ring me

The second one was pitiful, but typical. In the beginning, she'd rushed to answer texts like these, fearing he was sinking into this depression thing he cited. But now she knew it was a ploy. He didn't have depression. He had manipulation strategy.

Ring me. I don't know what to do about this and it's making me sad

She could just hear the mocking laughter.

The third one. A cryptic threat, again typical of his style. *Don't ignore me Toni*

Sniffing, she reached across to the dresser, plucked a tissue from the box and blew her nose loudly. *Bugger you, Sonny Murphy.*

The texts gave no clue to whatever he was up to. They were the same kind Sonny sent all the time, normally in the wee small hours of the morning, freaking her out about his state of mind, but generally just designed to keep her tethered.

Keep his control of her. Send her mad. Narcissistic bastard.

Over the last few months, she hadn't wanted to turn off her phone at night as her brothers and her friend Nicky had suggested, because her dad was so sick. The hospital might've called at any time.

The text messages from the bank urged her to call as soon as possible. What had happened now? It must be about Sonny because her end of the deal was all up to speed.

Worried, anxious, she thought back to the last time she'd checked the joint account for the mortgage deduction. Only a few days or so past, and the money for the month's repayment had been there, intact; he hadn't 'loaned' from it as he'd often done in the past.

The deduction had been due yesterday. With her dad's letter, the reading of it in Justin's office and ... and everything, it'd slipped her mind. She hadn't checked. She should check the balance every day. Every waking hour.

Oh no. Oh no, don't tell me it's happened again. He's 'borrowed' and we haven't been able to cover the repayment.

Staring at Craig Sherwell's contact number at the bank, she pressed the call-back. With the niceties out of the way, her usually pleasant and helpful bankie sounded a little short with her.

Her heart sank. 'What's happened, Craig?'

The voice was distant. 'Toni, we can't fool around with this anymore. We're going to demand repayment of the loan in full and we'll have to come after you solely if it can't be paid jointly. Can you find funds to cover the arrears?'

'Arrears? Didn't the last payment go through? I haven't checked the account today but there was plenty of money in it.'

The moment's silence gave her all the answer she needed. She bet Sonny had done it again at the last minute: skived off with the funds. The last time it had happened was months and months ago. She'd had to borrow from Paul to make it right, but Sonny had sworn that it was a last time one-off. Again. And he still hadn't paid her back.

After that, she'd asked the bank to alert her immediately if the same thing happened.

Why the hell she trusted that Sonny would do things the right way was beyond her. That was the bloody problem—she always believed what he said. Still she believed, to this day.

Except this day was the last. Absolutely. She'd do what she'd decided to do a while back—create a sole account in her name and as soon as his funds landed in the joint account, she'd transfer them to the new one, and have the mortgage deducted from there. It would be totally under her control at that point.

Craig's voice sounded tetchy again. 'You wrote me a letter regarding the account.'

'A letter? No, I didn't.'

'I've got a letter here and it's got both your signatures on it.'

Stunned, breath stopped in her throat. 'What's it say?' she

croaked.

A rustle of paper, and a throat clearing grumble delivered the news. 'I'll remind you of what it says.' He sounded as if he didn't believe her. *"Dear Craig, yada yada... Toni and I will have to delay repayments indefinitely. We will voluntarily apply for bankruptcy—"*

'No!' she cried down the line. 'No. I didn't write that or sign it or anything. Craig, I'll get the money to you.'

'I need it transferred today.'

'Sure. Sure.' Toni thought hard again. Paul or Evan would have to see her clear again. *Shit shit shit.* Three and half thousand dollars. She'd be in debt to her brothers forever at this rate. Her heart missed a beat as a thought slithered by. Why was the bank in a dither over a payment missed by a day or so?

Craig cut in, his voice loud in her ear. 'So, have you got the funds?'

'I'll get them. There's no way I'd deliberately let a repayment slip, no way. Or apply for bankruptcy. That's just ludicrous.' But another moment's silence from him was killing her. 'What?'

'You haven't asked how much it is.'

A chill. Another oddly skewed moment. It occurred to her that she could hardly breathe. 'Three thousand, five hundred and something.' She paused. 'Isn't it?'

The voice hardened a little. 'Hmm. Really? You're telling me you're only behind by yesterday's repayment?'

A pulse gonged in her head and she groped for the bed to save herself from falling to the floor. 'Isn't it?' she asked again, breath blurting out.

'Surely you've checked your statement?'

Toni thought hard. She received statements on internet banking from the joint mortgage account. 'The repayments have all been deducted. I've seen that they've come out...' She hadn't seen any housing loan statements for a while.

Disbelief hit her. How had Sonny done it? How had he tricked her? Why had he done it?

Craig's voice was still hard. 'Well, you might've seen deductions come out of your account, but the funds are clearly being transferred elsewhere because the bank loan has not been serviced for nearly five months.'

Pain clanged between her ears. Thoughts crashed together, desperate thoughts. A quick, scrambled calculation put the arrears over seventeen and a half thousand dollars. 'But you were supposed to notify me if something went wrong.'

She heard another rustle of papers. 'There's a file note and a change of authority here. You've signed it to say we're to notify Sonny if there are any problems.'

The air went dead. She'd done no such thing. Would never have done that. 'He's forged my signature.'

'Uh huh.' The disinterested tinny voice broke the silence again. 'And we haven't been able to locate him.' She heard his sharp inhale of breath. 'You've had reasonable warnings about this.'

Her words spilled out. 'No, no, no, I haven't had any warnings, otherwise I'd have responded. Tell me what you need me to do, right now. Right now, Craig. What do I need to do?'

A sniff, a long inhale this time from Craig. 'You'll need to transfer all the arrears, of course, and the late fees.'

Toni squeezed her eyes shut.

'But if you pay twenty-one thousand, one hundred and sixty-two dollars today and send me the transfer receipt, I'll waive the late fees. That amount will put you a month ahead.' |Another silence, then, 'You'll need to send me the transfer note before close of business today. Otherwise we'll start foreclosure proceedings.'

'No,' she ordered abruptly. She fell back on the bed. *Shit. Shit. Shit.*

'I'll give you the direct loan account number. Do you have a pen, Toni?'

'Yes, I have a pen.' She sprang off the bed and ran into the kitchen, flipped over the grocery list and grabbed a biro. Craig reeled off the necessary account numbers and Toni promised him she'd transfer the money.

She hung up. Stared at the black screen of her phone, devoid of numbers or instructions or contact messages or life on the outside of this total mess.

That bastard. That thieving, lying, cheating bastard. Twenty-one grand. How the hell was she going to find that sort of money?

She flicked the phone again and scrolled to Sonny's last three messages. Something had happened—his plan had been foiled somehow, whatever bloody plan it was ... otherwise why would he text her?

She stabbed the call back button on his SMS and it went straight to message-bank. The prick probably had it shut off his phone on purpose, knowing he'd have reeled her in and she'd be trying to get hold of him. Two minutes she'd give it and she'd call back.

Pacing up and down the hallway, in and out of the kitchen, she tried the call-back again. Message-bank. No way would she leave a message. The moment he heard her voice grating at him, he'd know that she knew. And by showing any emotion whatsoever towards him, he'd shut down and she wouldn't get anything out of him.

Pacing, pacing. Stop. Stop the panic. If he calls back, you need to be calm.

She checked the time. Twelve thirty. There'd be time enough to transfer the money if she could convince Paul to advance another lot of funds to her.

Even if the bastard doesn't call back.

What a mess. The house in Adelaide would *have* to be put on the market and sold She'd have to put pressure on Sonny to agree to it. But the market being what it was, to get rid of it fast maybe they'd have to sell it for less than what they bought it for. They'd talked about that in the odd times when emotion didn't get in the way. When his lies didn't have time to surface. But really, how would she know if what he said was ever true?

And if they did sell the house, they'd barely clear the mortgage. Wouldn't matter. As long as it did clear the mortgage, she'd finally be free of it. And him.

But then, if it didn't clear the mortgage …

Her laptop. The bank statements. She banged the phone onto the kitchen bench, charged back to the office, the smallest bedroom in the unit, and booted up the computer.

Fumbling with the password, on the third go she made it past the bank's security. Clicking open the joint account, she could see clearly the orderly repayments coming out by the month. These were supposed to be credited to the housing loan account.

She clicked open and downloaded older statements—same deal. No discrepancies. How had he done it? How had he got away with it?

She tried to go back even further. Then remembered they'd opened it as a joint account and after their last split, it had remained the account for the mortgage only. So, he had access, jointly, as she did. He would simply have diverted the funds to another account that only he had access to. How else could he have done it? She stared at the last few months' transfers.

The coded reference message looked exactly the same as it ever had, but when she delved a bit deeper and checked the status of the transfer, there it was. Transferred to an account number she didn't recognise.

Had the bank notified her of the change? They probably had, but maybe in all the goings-on with her dad, she'd simply overlooked it. She traced back further still and there it was, beginning nearly six months ago. The transfer's destination account had changed. And she never thought… had no reason whatsoever to check. He knew she'd never think to check that far back.

The utter, utter bastard.

She collapsed against the back of the chair, her head spinning with the enormity of what faced her now.

But what could he want, trying to contact her? Was he going to gloat that she was liable for the debt? Was he about to take off and in a fit of—?

Good God, that's exactly what he would do ... Take off.

Her phone jangled. Where the hell—? She raced back to the kitchen and grabbed it up. *Loser* on the screen. Him.

Heart rate pounding. 'Where are you?' she yelled. So much for calm.

'Yeah, it's only me.' He always made the same greeting, long and drawn out. 'I'm guessing by the way you're screeching, the bank's been in contact.'

Heat slithered over here. 'Where are you? What have you done with seventeen grand?'

'Haven't done anything with it, but I'm about to.'

Toni listened hard, tried to still her hyper breathing. And there it was in the background. The overhead roar of an aircraft. 'You're at an airport.'

'Sydney. Boarding in ten, and off to foreign shores. I needed the money, Tones.'

Her teeth slammed together painfully. She hated him calling her by the pet name her family used. She heard her short bursts of breath echoed back to her.

'Sorry,' he said. 'Hard times.' The drawl was meant to demean.

'You're not sorry,' she blasted.

'Okay. I'm not sorry. Have it your own way.'

She was desperate for an answer, desperate that he stayed on the line, but the smart-arse drawl was his way of controlling the conversation. She rattled on. 'We have to sell the house. Have you signed papers so we can sell?'

'No.' He drew that out as well, as if he'd thought long and hard about it. 'You'll find a way to pay it off, and I might need a bit more money later. So, if you want it sold, you'll have to pay me out.'

'You've already stolen—'

'Now, now, now,' he drawled.

Another jet roared over the line. Over that noise she could hear the mirth. Could almost see him smirking, taking delight in the abuse he was aiming at her. Again.

She spluttered. 'How will I know you'll sign the papers to sell it to me? I can't sell it without your signature on the papers. How can I pay you out? How can I trust—?'

'You don't have to keep screaming.'

Toni wasn't screaming. She ignored him, waited.

'I can hear you just fine. Hold on,' he said, and a muffling of sound occurred, as if his hand covered the phone.

Then she heard, 'Sure, doll, I'll be there in just a tick.'

And he'd said it deliberately clearly. Clearly enough for her to hear. The blow landed in her gut and she staggered back, the chair behind her scraping across the floor as her weight pushed it. Frightened she'd fall, she grabbed the kitchen bench and clung to the corner to steady herself.

He was with someone. Of course, he was. He'd sworn all along there wasn't anyone else. That it was just him and his depression driving him to do all these awful things. The drinking while on his meds. The old 'poor me, it's not my fault, I'm not responsible for anything'. All the excuses she no longer believed, or even heard. He couldn't bloody lie straight in bed.

'You still there? I have to go,' he said, all drawly and condescending.

'No! Don't be such a—'

'I'm not a nasty person, Toni. I'll be back in touch when you've calmed down.'

'What?'

And the line went dead.

She stared at the phone. Glared at it. Squeezed it. Shook it. Growled aloud at it. Stomped her feet. Then promptly sat on the floor and the breath blew out of her. So angry tears wouldn't even squeeze out. Her gut had started to ache. She had to stop…

Twenty-one grand. Where the hell am I going to get—?

For a second, the storm clouds stopped swirling madly and a brilliant flash of light cracked through.

That new bank account of Parker and co's.

Scrambling to her feet, she took off for the office again, logged back into to the bank site. Her hand shook on the mouse as scrolled down. There it was. Antoinette MacDonnell, Parker Inc. Steadying her fingers, she double-clicked. The balance came up, fully cleared.

A shade over forty-six thousand, eight hundred dollars. Her net wage for the year from Callum Parker's company.

Swallowing, breathing deeply and resting her hands on the solid timber desk that had been her mother's, she ordered her thoughts. She sat for a full minute ordering calm, ordering a quiet mind. Her hands weren't having any calm. They shook uncontrollably.

That money. It was her only solution right now. It would alleviate the stress right now. Was there a downside? No. Oh sure, it meant for now she was letting Sonny Murphy off the hook, but it also meant she could breathe, that she could get the bank off her neck, that she had time to re-think the rest of it. Maybe she had enough money left to engage a lawyer—not Justin—and pressure Sonny into selling up.

Even if she didn't do that, or couldn't do that, the rest of the money would help her get by with the loan repayments until she could figure out something else.

Her hands hovered over the keys. She clicked the 'Make a Transfer' tab. Sat another moment while the pros and cons filtered through. It still all seemed good. Clear.

Concentrate. Concentrate.

She tapped the 'From' tab and selected the Parker Inc bank account. Then she pushed away from the desk and ran back to the kitchen to grab the piece of paper with the loan account details on it.

Back in front of the laptop, she keyed in the six-digit bank, state and branch number backtracking and correcting over her clumsy mistakes, then keyed in the account number itself.

Double checked everything, a shaking finger under each number ensuring it was correct. Next tab was the amount. She tapped in the figure Craig had cited.

21,162.00

She stared at it. Not a lot of money if you were talking cattle stations. She laughed aloud at that. But a lot for Sonny to have raked off the top and got away with.

Money she couldn't afford to lose. She'd have to find a way to fight him but she knew if she did, she'd lose the last of what she had. For the moment, though, she had breathing space.

Typing in the reference number, she followed up with Craig Sherwell's email address so he would receive the bank transfer receipt. Still her hands trembled. It was nearly the point of no return. And then a little voice said, 'easy come, easy go'. She saw herself angrily signing the paperwork accepting Callum Parker's offer of employment and the payment earlier in the day.

Deep breath in and she hit the 'Transfer now' tab. The funds disappeared from the new account, whisked away before her eyes. Saving her sanity.

Mum would have said she'd just had six month's growth frightened out of her.

Mum.

Logging off, Toni put her head on the desk and bawled.

8

How do you dress when you're feeling wrung out, trapped, betrayed?

Bloody hell. Get over yourself.

She tossed up sassy, or a cool summer dress, which fitted to show off curves she really didn't feel like showing off. Toni held the sassy outfit higher as she studied it. A real smack in the mouth if she wore that. Then she lifted the dress. Too girlie, too feminine. She didn't feel like that, either.

She picked a corporate suit off the hanger, held it in front of herself before the mirror. No and no. No power dressing either. It's not a contest. And we don't do immature shenanigans. Play it straight down the line.

Sassy, it is. A floaty sleeveless number in reds and greys and white, over a white fitted tank top. Still, it showed off a little boob and curve, but only a hint. She unclipped a black straight-leg pant from its hanger, a most suitable piece to accompany the top. A pair of black, funky wedges on her feet would finish the look. She held up the top and pants to the mirror.

Done. But bloodshot and squooshy eyes stared back from her reflection.

Oh well, they're starting to look all right again, thank goodness. Will just have to pretend no one notices.

A quick check of the time and she dashed to the bathroom, freed her hair from the plait and raked fingers through it. As she showered, the last of home dust twirled down the drain in a rush of sudsy water. Drying off, she knotted her wet hair high on her head, stabbed a couple of bun-maker combs into it, and that would hold until she was ready to let it down again.

Undies on, pulling pants on, shrugging into her tank top, she thought about the station, deliberately not dwelling on the ex, his problem and the bank. Her problem.

Taking a couple of deep breaths to centre herself, she ticked off last minute jobs to cover.

The remaining stock would have to be rounded up and sold off, for one thing. That was a given. She and the boys had met a truck just before dawn that day to take a load away, and trucks had been out at the station for weeks carting stock off.

The flimsy tunic floated on over the tank.

There was only one muster to go, the last one, maybe a couple of hundred steers left to track, and truck. It would have to be done on horseback. They couldn't afford the chopper again. Thankfully, it was only a small paddock. A couple of days' ride would cover it.

Shoot. Her hair was all weird. Dragging out the long-pronged wide combs, she shook it and twisted the still-wet mop back up again, securing it again.

She'd make time to be out there at the station with her brothers, the last time as owners of the place. Would have to be soon, she knew.

Had other purchases been made by the new owners? The machinery had been sold separately—the vehicles, the plant and equipment. She had no clue what was still out there for them to use during the change-over period. That all needed to be negotiated for smooth operations.

Still seemed to be an awful lot to get through. How would she manage all of it? Her heart rate surged again, just because it could. *Dammit. Concentrate. Stop the rattling.* Standing still a moment, she surveyed her own room

Household goods. Though the new company wouldn't get much of that. There was her mother's family's old furniture, lovingly restored when she was alive. It kept the main lounge-room set back in the early 20th century, all leather and timber and lush settees; the only nod to the harsh central Australian country were sturdy legs and feet on some of the pieces.

And Parker wasn't getting his hands on her beloved dogs, that's for sure. That was a given, of course, but still. She'd make a stand if she had to. Toni would not part with Chipper and Sudsy. She'd leave with the dogs before she was ever parted from them and bugger her brothers and the five years.

She couldn't imagine anyone asking that of her. Chipper and Sudsy. One kelpie and one kelpie-cross-coolie as cheeky and busy as a room full of kindergarten kids. Chipper was a rich red-brown and Sudsy had a merle coat which made her look as if she'd just come out of a frothy bath—until she'd rolled around in the dirt and whatever else she could find. Usually a dead something, or a soggy something.

Chipper was a smoocher and Toni loved his joyous leaps when she'd turn up for the day. Suds was the older of the two, bossy and confident.

They'd both sneak into the homestead at night and if Toni was feeling a bit town-ish, they'd stay in, and sleep at the foot of her bed in her old room at the homestead. That had been a big no-no when her mum and dad had been living out there.

More often than not, Toni and her brothers would drag out their thin swags, line them up along the length of the veranda, and the dogs would crawl up beside whichever sibling belonged to them. The only strict instructions were to each dog—no moving off the veranda or else they'd be tied up.

Her dad had finally given in. He had built in a section of the veranda with framework and fly-wire to guard against the incessant flies by day and mozzies, other bugs and creepy-crawlies by night. So many different dogs over the years, had come to live on that wide veranda, and suddenly she couldn't wait to see her beloved two.

Best to get this meeting over and done with and think about heading out to the homestead soon. With one last look in the mirror, determining the puffy eyes looked almost normal, she shut the house and drove to the centre of town.

Parking close to the Stockman's Restaurant, she crossed Todd Street and hesitated at the door. Stepping inside, adjusting to the dim light, she returned the warm greetings of other locals.

Ben came into focus. He waved and came over.

'Hello, Ben,' she said. 'I didn't expect to see you so soon.'

'I live here, too, you know.' Ben steered her through the lunch-time crush. 'Forgot, have you?'

'I mean, what are you doing here at the restaurant? I'm meeting someone.' She looked around but couldn't see Callum Parker.

He looked at her, surprised. 'You are? Didn't I say come to lunch? Could've sworn— Oh well. I wanted to tell you something this morning, but I didn't have time.' He leaned in to her. 'I resigned from Reddell's today. There's a lot to tell, but I'm sworn—'

'That's important news,' she cried, and stared at him. 'You should have said.'

'Well, yes, but that Mr. Hunky-Chunky-Money-Bags appeared before I got around to it. Since it's clearly not me you're meeting, I bet it's him.' He lifted his chin. 'He's over there.'

Toni refused to look behind her. 'I don't think he's hunky.'

'You so do. Oh, I forgot. You're off all men.' He stopped, squinted. 'Are you all right?' He dipped his head to look more closely at her eyes, then pulled back. 'Sure, you're fine. You're glaring at me and you've set your mouth in that straight line. That means you're not fine, and you're not telling. Fine.' He looked over her head. 'And correction, he's not over there any longer, he's right here.' He bent to her ear. 'You and I will have to catch up

another time.' Ben looked up at the towering man approaching.
'He's all big, solid muscle, baby, and I bet he has a big something
to match, too,' he whispered.

Callum Parker was now too close to do anything except offer
him a thin smile and hope Ben would just shut up.

'Hello, Toni. I see you made it.'

Accompanied by the frank appraisal in his eyes, Parker's even,
friendly tone cut short any snotty response she felt rising.
Something about stating the obvious. He seemed to study her for a
moment. So much for thinking she didn't look like she'd been
bawling for the last umpteen hours.

Then he turned to Ben. 'G'day, Ben. Good to see you again.'

Again? Toni looked at Ben, the unspoken question in her wide-
eyed stare.

Ben slid her a glance. 'Uh, we met at Reddell's a few days
back. More to tell, like I said.'

'And I see you two know each other.' Callum glanced at them.

Toni's stare turned into one of those *what-the* frowns at Ben.

Ben gripped the outstretched hand. 'I've been a loyal friend of
this one for about a hundred years, even though she can be quite
thick at times.' Smiling widely at Parker, he said, 'Good to see
you, too.'

Toni rolled her eyes. A besotted fan.

Callum inclined his head. 'Toni and I have some business to
discuss, but ah, maybe you could join us for a drink after lunch.'

Ben didn't hesitate. 'Thanks, not today. I'll leave you to it, I
know what it's like trying to get things moving along.'

'We'll see you some other time, then.'

'Look forward to it.' His eye was on Callum Parker but he
leaned over and pecked Toni on the cheek.

She tried to stall him, a hand on his arm. 'But your news, Ben.'

'Don't wail. It'll keep.' Ben melted into the crowd.

Callum steered her towards his table, a file tucked under his
arm. 'Loyal friend, is he?'

'He usually says "Loyal Friend of the Bewildered".'

Callum laughed a delighted, hearty chuckle. Toni managed a smile despite herself.

'So, a drink?' he asked. He directed her to the table for two by the window overlooking Todd Street, and pulled out a chair. He dropped the file to the floor under the table and sat in the chair opposite.

'A white wine would be good.'

He lifted a hand towards the bar, and waved, a reminder of his casual confidence. His gaze settled on her, his scrutiny open. 'Are you all right?' he asked.

She sniffed in a big breath. 'Aside from all today's revelations and goings-on, I'm fine.'

He waited a beat. 'Great.' He picked up the wine list and studied.

The waitress, Lizzie, swooped on their table like a spur-winged plover. After a smirky glance at Toni, her attention fixed on Callum, she asked if he was ready to order.

'Give me two minutes,' he said to her.

'I'll be back in two minutes then,' she said and set off for the bar again.

Did she just flutter her eyes at him? *God sakes, the Besotted were everywhere*. Toni snorted to herself. Well, she wasn't one of them, though she could admit Callum Parker was worthy of a second look, decked out as he was like bush royalty. Not that she liked the look. Much. While he studied the list, she evaluated his wardrobe.

RM Williams gear, head to toe, she reckoned. Expensive, but casual. Open neck pale blue shirt, sleeves rolled up to reveal smooth forearms, lightly tanned. Moleskins and, as she looked down, chestnut coloured RM boots, too. If she could get a closer look, she'd be able to tell if they were Classics or Signature. But she'd have to get on the floor to do that. *No way*.

'Dry and crisp or some sort of fruity sweet?' he asked, frowning a little as he read.

'Uh, dry, thanks.'

Signature boots, I bet. That meant hand-made to order. And she bet he was sporting a RM belt too. Add another hundred and forty bucks, easy. If the boots were Signatures, all up that amounted to nearly seventeen-hundred-dollars' worth of stuff he was sporting, not counting his socks and jocks. Not that she'd take a look there, either.

She loved RM stuff. Loved it, hankered after it. Had a much-loved hand-plaited belt that was the last gift her mother had given her, years and years ago now.

Mum.

Maybe she should have worn a more classic outfit. She'd dressed too casually, damn it. Absently, she straightened the hem of the top. Perhaps it was a bit frothy for a meeting. No time to get nervous about it now.

'Thought there might have been a bit more on this list.' He turned the page over and back again.

'Just a nice South Australian one will be fine,' she said, waved a hand, all conducive, all high society.

He glanced up at her, and down to the list again. Probably thought his lunch companion was a poor country hick. *Jeez.* That sort of thinking always sets me up wrong. What the hell do I care what he thinks? Her feet shuffled. What, again? Was shuffling of feet some sort of signal from her sub-conscience? Because she was not interested in Callum Parker. Or any man. At. All.

Finally, he waved for Lizzie. When she arrived—like the road-runner—Toni had never heard of the bottle of white he ordered. Lizzie dutifully recorded it, nodding and smiling. Congratulating him on his choice, she finished with the drink order chit-chat then turned to Toni. 'You should introduce me to your date, Toni.'

Toni felt her smile twist. 'Not my date. Lizzie. It's a business meeting. This is Callum Parker.'

Lizzie's sweet smile—so unlike her usual barracuda gape—was

plastered on her face, her over-made-up, botoxed-to-buggery face. The one with the false eyelashes and the tattooed eyebrows. Shaking his proffered hand, Lizzie said, 'Elizabeth Horden.'

Callum lifted a little from his seat and sat again. 'Nice to meet you.'

'Likewise.' Lizzie turned back to Toni and the stencilled, tar-painted eyebrows rose. 'Sorry, my mistake about the date thing. It's just you don't look dressed for a business meeting, that's all. Felt sure you were just having some fun,' she said and added, 'Finally. Antoinette.'

Toni kept the twisty smile. 'Oh,' she said, nodding, as if Lizzie's comment was a surprise. Everyone knew Toni never used her full name. She felt a blush scorch across her face and she was pretty sure smoke was about to come out her ears. The furnace inside would curl her hair.

It was a definite dig from the waitress. At high school, Lizzie was the one they called 'Lizzie Borden' because she always seemed so poisonous. She knew Lizzie's tactics of old. Usually, the woman didn't get under her skin these days, though not because she didn't keep trying.

Deep breath in.

Lizzie swished off with a smirk over her shoulder.

Callum Parker. 'She wouldn't know yet that you're my new employee,' he said, eyes creased in the smile he aimed at her. 'Mistook you for—'

'She knows who I am, all right,' Toni said. 'The news would already be all over town.' She looked over her shoulder at the retreating figure of the other woman whose butt cheeks lifted and wobble-dropped in her hip swing.

It looks like a bag full of knees. Floozy. Obnoxious tart.

That made her feel better. Toni turned back. Callum was the picture of propriety. His eyebrows creased over blue eyes, or grey? Bugger it, she couldn't decide which. His nose—obviously broken by someone who'd laid one on him—was crooked, his smiling mouth generous. His frank return study of her was unsettling. Definitely unsettling. And was that a goddamn twinkle in his eye? Or was it sympathy?

That stunned her.

He tapped his fingers lightly on the table. 'I'm sorry this whole business is difficult. I know how hard it is—'

'Please.' She held up a hand, politely, careful not to make it a command. 'You don't know anything about how hard this is. Any of it. But I appreciate your saying so.' Her heartbeat pounded, and the phone conversation with the Loser ambushed her again. She set her jaw. Would not teary-up again. *Would not.* 'We should go over the specifications.' She rearranged the serviette carefully across her lap.

'Wouldn't you rather wait for the wine?'

She lifted her shoulders. 'The sooner we're straightened out, the better. We can move forward. I really do want this to be as conciliatory as possible.'

'All right, if you like.' He waved a finger in her direction. 'Talking of straightening things out, I'm presuming you own more corporate style outfits.'

Shouldn't have worn the sassy. She didn't miss a beat. Was not going to be railroaded. 'I see you're in your best business suit, too.'

'I'm not having a go at you.' His gaze was direct. 'A month or so after settlement, there will be some very influential people visiting. Potential investors.'

She crossed her fingers. 'I missed reading about clothing in the job specification.' *Hardly read a word of the bloody thing.*

An eyebrow raised, he kept his eyes on hers. 'You will be meeting with some top echelon business people. You'll be the one, I hope, to do the promotions for the company, for the station. If we need to talk a clothing allowance—'

'I own a busy travel agency. I don't wear jeans there.'

'All right. Good.' He nodded. 'And speaking of the travel

agency, perhaps that's something else we need to talk about.'

She sat up straight. 'No, we don't. My shop has nothing to do with anything in Dad's will.'

'We need to talk about it,' he insisted. 'But perhaps another time.'

'Perhaps,' she conceded, warily. No one was going to sidle around her again.

Lizzie brought the wine to their table, set it down with a smile at Callum, who said that he'd pour, so she left.

Toni moved the cutlery and the basket of bread rolls for something to do. 'Can we order a meal now and get going on this? I have another couple of meetings of my own this afternoon.' *Liar, liar, liar*.

'Certainly.' He beckoned another waiter who hovered nearby. 'We'll both have the prime beef, thanks, Andy. Medium rare for me, too.'

Nope. Now was the time to stop this, to nip it in the bud, right here. He would not intimidate her, not at any time. Certainly not at the very beginning of this whole fiasco. Certainly would not take it upon himself to order her meal for her.

'I can order for myself, thanks all the same.' And she watched him look at Andy then spread his hands as if bewildered.

Andy bent closer to her. 'Toni, I've already got your usual order. I told him what you always have.' He showed her his order book. *Toni Mac 1 x p. beef mr*

Silence descended on the table.

After a moment, she nodded at the waiter, said, 'Thanks, Andy. Beef is fine. As usual.' And Andy headed for the kitchen.

Those cool eyes of Callum Parker's were fixed on her; she could feel it. He expected her to speak first, she knew it. Focusing on the elegant glass of wine, she reminded herself not to swill today. She wouldn't. Those bloody blue eyes, or grey or whatever-the-hell. Heat itched her in hands and her chin firmed up. 'Waiting for something?'

He nodded. 'For you to bite some more.'

Another moment of awkward silence hung between them. Every miniscule beat, every nanosecond of it, dragged.

He drew his legs back under his chair. 'How's Ben in the mix here?'

'We're friends, that's all.' She checked the restaurant for Ben but couldn't see him. 'Nothing to do with this situation. My friends are nothing to do with this other business.'

In that second's silence, Toni watched as high tensile steel replaced what had been friendly amusement in those blue-grey eyes. The gun metal sheen that flattened his stare was cold, and for the first time, she caught a glimpse of her real opponent. No escape. She'd locked herself in.

Callum Parker's low voice belied the frown. 'Finding time for personal relationships in the first few months will be tough with the schedule we have planned.' He waited a moment. 'I might have agreed to the condition of sale brought to us by a very sick man, but his daughter had better live up to expectations. Remember, you've been paid, in advance.'

Another heavy thud of heartbeat. Paid, and half spent. Toni went blank but the creep of heat inside flamed her face again.

Callum raised his brows. 'Your mouth is closed. That's a very good thing. Time to talk business.' He tapped the table. 'The job specifications,' he began. He reached to the floor and brought up the manila folder, slapping it onto the table. He pulled out a pair of wire rimmed glasses and put them on. 'Have you read it all?'

'Some,' she said. Like, the title, and the subtitle. She couldn't bring herself to look at the damned thing after the meeting earlier.

'Good. Let's go over it together.'

The hours. Seven in the morning until nine in the evening.

Piece of cake.

Every second Tuesday off.

No big deal.

A vehicle only on that Tuesday and only with permission from him if she were to take it the ninety-minute drive to Alice from the Station on personal business. Insurance issue.

No way! In that case, she would have her own vehicle out there with her. The station did not own that. She'd bought it herself despite her father's protests that the station could buy her a vehicle. And a good thing, too, as it now turned out. She'd go to Alice from out there whenever it suited her.

And no personal visitors permitted to stay over until things were up and running.

'You're kidding. That'll never work out here.'

He moved on. Entertaining. She would host his visitors and chauffeur them over the property when required.

Didn't seem so bad.

He hadn't mentioned shopping, thank goodness. Not for clothes, God knows you just need jeans and a shirt, and a sturdy pair of boots. There was mail-order for all that, anyway. Shopping for supplies, she meant. It always fell to—

'Now, supplies for the kitchen, staples for the pantry and so on,' he started.

'That's a cook's job. Lorraine's job.' Then she hesitated. Oh God, she hadn't thought properly about Lorraine, and Bob Bolton, her husband, or Two Bob as he was known. 'Do Lorraine and Two Bob still—'

He looked at her over his specs. 'Do you cook?'

'Lorraine is the cook,' she answered sharply, then realised that Lorraine and Two Bob might no longer be employed out there.

He stopped a moment, as if he would say something about that and then changed his mind. 'I'll take that as a no.'

'I will not be doing the cooking.'

'I'm talking more with Two Bob about a number of other issues,' he said, abruptly, and turned the page, peering at the next clause. 'You'll be trained on our computer system and programs.'

She focused on the tip of his nose. Her lips were tingling after half a glass of wine and now they felt like two tyres. She smacked them together forestalling any more tingles. They still felt like two tyres. She just plain shouldn't drink white wine, but it was too bloody hot to drink red. Maybe a gin and tonic. Or a vodka, lime and soda—

'Or do we have to start you from scratch?'

'From scratch?' Her head felt fuzzy.

'Computers.'

'Not from scratch. I already work with computers. I do all—'

His glance silenced her. He kept reading. 'You'll oversee the builders.'

'I have no experience in that.' She grabbed a bread roll from the basket in the middle of the table. Needed food.

There was much more. She was to do the book-keeping and send full accounting reports to Adelaide once a month. Personal assistant, answering to him, organising his office, his correspondence, appointments, travel …

This whole thing was just a bloody citified regimen for the next twelve months written by someone with no idea about living on a station. Just had to look at him to know that. Those clothes—no matter they were RM's, he'd never seen work in a paddock, that's for sure. *Great.* But now she was well and truly stuck with it. She had medical bills to pay, a mortgage to clear. And had to get the Loser narcissist off her back. She'd need money. She needed a plan. She needed this job, like it or not.

He moved on. 'Investor liaison. You'll need some training for that, too.'

Toni sat stony-faced.

In her silence, he said, 'We've yet to decide whether to re-stock the place immediately, or to revegetate. The boys will want a hand in all of that, I'm sure.'

'I've had experience with stock, too.'

He nodded but appeared to let that go as well. 'Now, to your wildlife park idea.' He took off his glasses and tossed them onto the table.

She flinched, dumbstruck. Who told him about the wildlife park? There was no way she'd hand the file over to him. It was hers. *No way.*

Callum Parker stared at her. 'Think of your brothers.'

'I am,' she answered coolly, despite her frantic mind. The file. Where was the bloody file? She remembered. She'd left it on Justin's desk earlier. It was safe.

He nodded. 'Then we shouldn't have any problems. You'd be fully aware that it would never compete so close to the Desert Park in town.'

Toni leaned forward and words rushed out. 'It's a different model. There's room for one that's out bush and offering accommodation and—'

He held up a hand. 'I'd like to see what you've got. We'll do our own feasibility study, of course, but no promises.'

She sat back, lowered the tone of her voice. 'It's my plan, so it's not up for grabs. You don't get it for free. I've worked too long and too hard on it.'

He lifted a shoulder again, focused on his wine, twirled the stem of the glass between his fingers. Then, 'When can you be out there?'

The empty, stern tone had disappeared. Toni couldn't think straight. 'Next week. Monday.'

He shook his head. 'Before then. I have to return to Adelaide later this week to tie up things in the office. How about Thursday? Does that give you enough time?'

'That's only three days away.'

'I could have said tomorrow. As requested.'

The wind fell out of Toni's sales. What would be the point of arguing about when? It would only stall the working relationship further. She was boxed in. The sale of the station was the reality. And being prickly and churlish was tiring. Tiring her. 'All right. All right, Thursday. I'll be out there Thursday.' If not before, she thought. She folded her napkin and stood up. 'Well. If that's it?'

He cut her a look. 'That's not it. Our meal's just arriving.' He indicated the waitress heading towards them. 'Please. Wait and eat with me.'

She sat again just in time. Lizzie sashayed over and gently slid his meal on the table. As her meal was plonked in front of her, a splash of sizzling sauce leapt onto Toni's top. A low hiss escaped her. She kept her eyes on her plate. If she cut Lizzie the look, the woman would turn to dust.

Lizzie told them, 'Enjoy,' and left.

Callum topped up Toni's glass. 'Eat up, drink the wine. You'll need to know a lot about wine for the clients.'

Toni drank but without her usual gusto. She didn't trust herself to drink much at all around this Callum Parker.

'I believe you still have personal possessions out there.' His knife glided through the beef and his fork stabbed a good-sized piece.

'Of course. It's my home.'

'And your room will always remain yours.' He ate, appreciating every mouthful.

'Thank you so much.'

Callum shifted in his chair. 'I know there are not many rooms in the main house. Any objection to my taking your father's room when I'm out there?'

She didn't miss the nod at compassion and it jagged her. How could she object? It was only a room, after all, and soon it would be empty of her dad's possessions anyway. It was the biggest room, and still had the full-size desk in it, as well as the big bed and the dresser her parents had always had. She'd have to move those things quickly. He wasn't getting his hands on those. Her sails deflated further.

She was about to answer when he said, quietly, 'Perhaps you'd like some more time over that one. Anyway, anything you deem your family's property—'

Only thousands of square hectares.

'—please pack away, except, of course your personal requirements.' He looked at her. 'I've no interest in pilfering your possessions if that's what you've been thinking.' He leaned over his meal again, savouring every bite.

Her conscience targeted by his soft voice, she said, 'I never thought of this as robbery.'

'That's encouraging.' He went back to his steak.

Moments ticked by.

Toni fidgeted. 'Look, I'll leave the packing up for a while and you can see the house as my mother had it set up. It's been like that a long time.'

His gaze flicked up to meet hers. 'Your dad told me of her illness.'

Toni stopped a second. *Mum's illness? Mine, too? Dad wouldn't have, would he? God, no! Get a grip.* A deep breath and the words came fast. 'It's very traditional and there's a lot of history there. We have to decide what to keep and what to donate to the museum in Alice but it might even be useful remaining where it is. It connects you to the providence of the place...' *I'm rattling, I'm rattling.* But maybe some things can stay as they are, for a while, at least.

His eyes lit up. 'It's up to you, of course, and I'd welcome it. I like family connections. It's important to have heritage present. Something to gift the grandkids.' His smile only lasted a moment.

She sat stock still. *Grandkids.* Had she even given a thought to him being married? Test the water. Hurry up. Get it out of the way and save yourself any wondering. She put a smile in her voice. 'Oh. You're a family man?' she asked and cut a slice of steak.

He shook his head, looked away. 'I have a niece and a nephew, twins.' A dimple deepened as he leaned forward over his plate. 'Twins go way back in my family, can trace them to the first Irish immigrant ancestors here in Australia, at the goldfields. They're in nearly every generation. But my sister can't have any more kids. Up to me to produce, apparently.' His mouth set for a moment, then he loaded his fork. 'So, you'll be out there Thursday?

She poked at her steak with the cutlery. 'Okay.'

'Good. The house itself isn't really our focus. What's yours will always belong to you.' He pointed at her plate. 'Eat.'

My station belongs to me. But she nodded agreeably enough, put the kid-thing out of her mind, and took to the prime beef once more.

Driving back to the house on Cromwell, a long road winding through the golf course estate, she glanced at the job specification file tossed onto the passenger seat.

Would have to sign off on that, too, in the near future, because she'd already used part of the funds.

Oh, so what? It was her money, now. Maybe she'd just quietly forget about signing off. There was no hurry right at this minute, so Callum Parker and Co could wait.

She parked outside the house and sat in the car a moment longer. Taking the keys from the ignition, she rested her head on the door frame, her eyes closed. Through the open window a hot breeze fanned her face.

Callum Parker. She liked him despite her best efforts. She couldn't help it. There was a flutter in her belly when she thought of him. It shouldn't be happening. Especially not when she'd heard, clear as a bell, that he intended to have kids.

And besides that, she didn't know if he was married or not, or even in a relationship. Wasn't like she'd flat out ask him. Too obvious. How embarrassing would that be? No. Best to forget about it.

She'd made sure any feeling she might have had for anybody after Sonny was well and truly stopped before it started. Not even buried, but completely wiped out. So. She would set about wiping out this stupid hormonal response to Callum Parker and stop it in its tracks. Didn't need it. Didn't want it.

She bowed her head and her chin tucked to her chest. There.

Done.

So not done.

How could it be so strong after just one day?

Come on, Toni. Wipe it out. This isn't for you. Besides, it'd be like a book title, 'Sleeping with the Boss'. *Forget it. We've been over this. Relationships are not for you anymore.*

Her heart felt like it banged around in her chest. Her spirits, already low and weighty, dropped even further. In the immediate, she put dreaming about Mr Bloody Parker out of the question. Inhaling to hold that thought, she shifted focus.

Breathe. One, two, three. Put it out of your mind.

Breathe. Turn your mind to home.

The station. Right. Home. Right.

She would go out to the station mid-morning tomorrow. Spend a couple days there, on her own with the dogs before her official start on Thursday. Before the other real work began. She'd have to face up sooner or later to the fact that her father was no longer there. Better to get it over with in private, before the new company people arrived. No one would bother her out there. She would have time to get her head straight over the latest Sonny Murphy debacle and work out a game plan.

A trickle of perspiration rolled down her cheek.

Geez. Get the hell out of here. It's bloody hot in the car, you fool.

Inside the house, she aimed the remote at the aircon and dumped the job file and her bag on the floor, kicking off her shoes, she grabbed her phone. First things first.

She called Mary-Anne to discuss the new, unavoidable developments and Mary-Anne's new position managing the travel agency. All that had to be in hand and rolling along smoothly. She was most certainly not going to discuss the travel agency with Callum Bloody Parker.

Mary-Anne met her in the shop late in the afternoon after the kids had been picked up from school. Her husband, Rod, was on early shifts this week at the base so he was home to mind the kids while they made new work arrangements.

They worked around the kids' school hours, around Rod's daytime shifts, devised new shop hours, talked about the need for holidays, which Toni said she'd make sure to look after. It all needed to work. It looked good. They shook hands in a very business-like manner, and both burst out laughing.

Excited to take on the extra responsibility, Mary-Anne rattled on. She'd love every bit of it, and how much the extra work and wages would mean to her.

Toni groaned inwardly. She'd be broke at this rate before she got to thirty. No way could the travel agency afford two full-time salaries. She'd have to fork out most of her own wage to pay Mary-Anne manager's rates. In fact, a better thought—she'd forego her wage. That way, perhaps a little more capital would build up in the business.

At least now there was the extra nest egg to back her up, compliments of Parker Inc. She would borrow from it if she had to. The mortgage payments had to come from somewhere until she could get the house in Adelaide sold.

She might be tied to the new company for longer than she cared to think.

Another groan. *Damn you to hell, Sonny Murphy.*

More first things— she would get the real estate office in Magill to send her up a Sales Agency Agreement. First opportunity she got, she'd have the bastard sign it. The last email Toni sent was to the estate agent requesting the Agreement.

Mary-Anne left with a hug.

As she turned to lock up the shop, her phone pinged. Her stomach clunked until she saw the screen. Paul had sent a message saying he and Evan would spend the night swagging it at the Hayes' place, east of town. So, she had her house to herself, tonight. Good. No one to see her tucking into the wine and the self-pity.

Now back at the house, with a cool sauv blanc decanted in the chiller, she decided that she could do without any more self-pity.

It was time to step up. Time to be in control of what she could control, and not worry about what she couldn't.

9

Driving home. How perfect it was, bumping over the home straight leading into MacDonnell's Run. Now that she'd made the turn from the main road onto the long station track, she had about half an hour to go.

She loved the roar and crunch of the big four-wheel drive's tyres racing over the dirt road. It blasted out behind in billowing, dense russet clouds.

To the north, low lying dusky pink hills crept up in the distance. Small clusters of casuarina, the desert oak that dotted the roadside amid the rocky outcrops, always gave her a sense of belonging. Over the years, they'd become as familiar as family.

How long would she feel like that? Forever, she hoped, no matter what happened.

Good thing she wouldn't be driving too long into the afternoon sun today. Already after midday, she'd make the homestead long before the sun's glare would slow her up.

This time on the drive, she seemed to see every old familiar thing anew. Stopping as she sometimes did, she got out to stretch her legs, and stood a little way from the heat of the vehicle. A grey shrike-thrush called, low and as melodious as a flute. Bright parrots of brilliant green flashed from young mulga trees and Gouldian finches rushed past, darting to and fro nearby. Kangaroos would be here, but it was too early in the day for them. She stayed awhile, sat in the dirt by an old corkwood tree that had a young 'un sprouting nearby. In this arid land, the flora and fauna and its low hum of life always bolstered her spirits. Always a solace, a comfort.

Which was why ages ago, before her dad passed away, she'd begun to draw plans for the Desert Freelands, her wildlife park concept. And her dream. How could she possibly leave it all behind? She couldn't. It was in her blood, in her mind and in her soul. The land demanded great love and great respect. She understood how indigenous people felt for it, had empathy with them. It was also her land by birth and she could not let it go. Why had her dad thought she could?

Heavy of heart again, the earlier solace a bit ragged around the edges, she stood up, slapped dust off her jeans and brushed bark off her shirt. She climbed into the car and started the engine. The motor gunned while the aircon cranked up again. She reefed out a bottle of water from her cooler-bag and chugged down half the contents.

Back on the track, she sped over the last fifty kilometres, slowing when the homestead came into view. Although there was a grassy plot in front of the verandah and the steps, the fine red dust of the track carried, as though stirred too vigorously. She didn't want to spend the rest of the evening sweeping it out of the house.

She pulled up, wound down her driver's side window, killed the motor.

The silence of home took her breath away. A lump lodged in her throat as she imagined for a split second that she could hear her Dad yelling 'G'day'. There would be no more yells of greeting from him.

Missing her mother's greeting had long ago taken its place in her life. She still remembered her bright smile and the happy wave of welcome whenever she came home. *Taken too early*.

The silence didn't last long. A flash of rust, of suds moving with the speed of light, excited barks and yips and frenzied round-and-rounds, two dogs madly galloped and danced over the verandah and down again around the car.

Chipper leapt at her window and Sudsy was yelling at her from the dirt. As soon as Toni stepped from the car, Sudsy hurled herself into her arms and squirmed and barked and breathed dog into her face. Toni couldn't help laughing aloud as Chipper tried to do the same. She had to run with them up and down the verandah steps until all three came to a stop. Chipper sat quickly, then Sudsy. Toni sat between them on the steps, an arm around each dog.

After a moment tears trickled over her cheeks unchecked, as her grief, her anguish, her frustration flowed naturally, taking its own time. She pulled a face to staunch the flow of tears. Sudsy helped and licked a few drops. Chipper sidled on to her lap. Toni poked about in her pocket and came up with a couple of dust-tinged tissues and eventually let out great wracking sobs.

The dogs stayed with her, and the musty smell of hot, dusty dog was a welcome scent long remembered from childhood.

Slowly, the sobs subsided and gave way to a few deep gulps of air. Suddenly aware of another presence, she looked around in the fading light, wiped her cheeks and eyes. Lorraine, the station cook, stood quietly in the yard watching her.

A tall woman, in her late fifties, or older—hard to tell—stood at the end of the veranda. Her dress, a loose shift in yellows and oranges, mid tans and white. A natural fabric, silk or cotton. Fabric painted by her cousins and set to screen printing to be sold. Proceeds would help fund health and education in outback communities. She always seemed to have cheerful clothes, and Toni envied her easy, confident grace. Her black hair was short and fluffy, and her ears dangled with hand painted beads. Lorraine came towards her. Her feet, clad in leather sandals, made no noise as she padded across the soft, powdery dust of the yard.

'G'day, Lorraine.' Toni sniffed. 'You goin' all right?'

'Yeah, Toni. You goin' all right?'

Toni stood up. 'I think so. Better out than in, don't you reckon?'

Lorraine touched Toni's forearm in a gesture of sympathy. It was all she would do to acknowledge Philip MacDonnell. Indigenous people didn't like to speak of those who'd passed on. 'Better out, I reckon. Will you be eating in the house or down with us tonight?'

'I'll eat here, thanks, Lorraine. Wouldn't be much company right now.'

'Okay. But you just yell if you need me or one of them boys,' she said, speaking of her sons. 'You got company.'

Toni looked at her. 'What company?' She sniffed again and swiped a tissue over her eyes.

Lorraine jerked her head and Toni followed its direction. Behind the machinery sheds, she saw a big four-wheel drive vehicle parked in the shade.

'Who?'

Lorraine's lips twitched. 'Talkin' to Two Bob, now, out in the paddock. Talkin' to you, later, I reckon. Tall, black hair, a handsome fella. And rich. Can tell by the weight he carries in his pants,' she said and walked away, chuckling her low, delighted chuckle. 'Family jewels and all.'

Toni stared at the car. Tall, black hair, handsome. Out with Two Bob in the paddock, is he? Getting his city clothes grubby, perhaps?

'Lorraine,' she shouted to the retreating woman. 'Where did he go?'

Lorraine, whose lean shoulders lifted slowly and dropped, didn't bother to turn around. 'Dunno, Toni. Maybe to look at them fences with Two Bob. Maybe you better wear your jim-jams tonight and lock up.' She gave another mischievous chuckle. 'No nudie runs to the bathroom for you.'

It was no use trying to get more out of Lorraine. She clearly thought it was all a fine little joke and was tickled with the mischief. Lorraine waved a hand over her shoulder and wandered back to her little cottage alongside the old cellar, the dogs charging around her.

In the good old days, Toni and her brothers had played hidey over there. In and out of the fusty hole in the ground that had housed freshly hung meat and the cook's home-made jams and chutneys. It'd been a great hideaway from Mum when she wielded the wooden spoon aimed at their backsides.

Toni grabbed her bags and headed inside. She threw her things into the front bedroom that had been hers since she was a baby and marched outside again, stepping off the verandah in a huff. The dogs came back to her.

She would ignore the fact that he was here. Ignore it. *Oh, get a grip. Don't be stupid.* He must have high-tailed it out to the station just after dawn to beat her here.

She wouldn't dwell on it. Wherever he'd gone now, he'd gone on foot and wouldn't be too far away. That is, of course, unless he'd wandered off somewhere and was delirious in the heat, slowly perishing out there in the western desert in his fancy RM's, his skin parched and peeling from his bones et cetera et cetera.

Standing in the middle of the yard, she tapped her booted foot, and turned from side to side hoping to catch sight of him. This was no good, no good at all. Where the hell was he? When she caught up with him, she'd tell him to get the hell—

'Hi.'

She spun around, and powdery red sand spun around with her. There he was, large as life. He stepped around the untidy stack of fencing wire and droppers between them and took her breath away. In an old, faded red, brushed cotton shirt over T-shirt and jeans, which fitted his long lean legs better than he knew, he looked at home, in his element and master of his universe. His boots were sturdy, dirty, and well-worn at the toes. Not RM's. Maybe Blundy's, or Rossi's. Her gaze roamed all the way back up to his old Akubra, sweat stained and battered; maybe something had chewed on it. He looked like he'd worked out bush all his life. And he was grubby. Outback dirt, dust and diesel grubby.

The dogs bolted at him, delighted.

'I didn't realise you'd be out here today,' he said. 'Welcome home.'

The smile made a dimple again. A dimple she had certainly noticed before. He bent and ruffled both dogs as they barked and yipped around him. Nonchalance carefully applied to his tone. She knew that. Full, generous lips curved in a smile designed to make her knees weak. She knew that. Sparkling eyes commanded all her attention. She knew that. And she couldn't take her eyes off him.

Did it show? Her breath puffed out in a frustrated huff. 'I didn't realise you'd be out here today. What are you doing here?'

'It's Tuesday, the day I requested to come.' He patted both the dogs one last time and straightened up. 'I've been checking out the home yards. I needed to catch up with Two Bob, meet Lorraine, and I was about to check out the—' He peered at her. 'Are you all right?'

Was she all right? *What did he mean by that?* Here he was, imposing on her life and her privacy, and he asked if she was all right.

'What are you doing here?' she repeated.

The smile slipped from his face. 'Truly, I just decided to come out. So, I came early this morning. I had to come out, at some point. And it is Tuesday, we pay rent from today.'

She hadn't remembered signing anything to that effect. Or had she? Toni wasn't having any of it, no matter who signed what, or not. 'This is not going to work. I wasn't expecting you to be out here today.'

He inhaled long and exhaled slowly. 'Yes, it is going to work. We will make it work. I wasn't to know you'd come early, either.'

If she'd been wearing a collar, she would have been hot under it.

He bent to the dogs again who still had dog-frenzy. He rough-housed them going down on one knee to play. 'I love your dogs.

I've had a couple of hours with them. I miss mine.'

She softened just a bit. 'You have dogs?'

He kept his eyes on Chipper and Sudsy playing around his feet. 'They're long gone now.'

'Oh.' What Toni couldn't see in his face she heard in his voice. 'Chip. Suds,' she commanded and the two dogs came to her, sat by her side. 'Listen, um ...' she began again, firming her resolve, she hoped.

'Callum,' he reminded her.

'I wanted to be here on my own for a couple of days.' That had come out all soft and—soft. Firming her resolve was on a trial and error basis, it seemed.

'You will, no problem. Two Bob is taking me to the eastern paddocks. We'll stay out there for a night or two and then I go back to Alice.'

Her eyes narrowed. 'Straight back to town?'

'Absolutely.'

She didn't trust his smile. And why was he going out overnight with Two Bob?

A vehicle careened around the sheds, and the flat-sounding horn blared across the silence. A dusty arm shot out of the window as if it were halting the cavalry behind. The car skidded a little and stopped, bouncing back into the cloud of rusty whirling dervishes it created.

Callum Parker pointed to the canvas roll-up in the back of the ute. 'You see that? It's my swag, and we're going. See?'

Two Bob hung out the window waving at her from the battered old land rover. 'Toni. Toni. Good to see you, Toni.'

'Hi, Two Bob.' She gripped his hand. His fingers squeezed hers for just a second or two as his big brown eyes showed a flicker of sadness. Then it was gone. There was a trace of wood smoke on him, and a faint whiff of the sandalwood soap Lorraine liked him to use in the shower. An unlit rolly hung from his mouth, waiting for a match. Greying whiskers on his chin were in tufts as if he hit-

and-missed with the razor a few days ago. He might have been fifty, he might have been seventy.

Two Bob pulled a hand through his curly brown-black hair, the ends of which were sun bleached. 'You tell my missus to cook you up good tucker for a coupla nights. Me and this one,' he said and lifted his chin in Callum Parker's direction, 'we're gonna go by that creek tonight, won't be back in time for tea.'

'All right,' she said and laughed a little.

'So. There you have it.' Callum tipped his hat and that dimple appeared again. 'I'll see you later.' He pulled open the side door and swung into the cabin.

Two Bob put his foot down and the vehicle roared off.

Toni shut her mouth before the dust choked her. She watched as the rickety old vehicle ploughed away, and stood in the middle of the yard until her heartbeat slowed.

Bloody man. Bloody, bloody man.

The dogs had wandered off. There had to be something else to do other than stand in the middle of the yard in the hot sun. Like sit in the shade somewhere until some other interesting thing happened. Maybe like dinner. The dogs had the right idea. Toni climbed the steps of the veranda again and went into the house from the main door.

No point thinking about the man with the black hair and the blue-grey eyes. And the dimple. So, what about the dimple. Nothing special.

Shoving that thought aside, she stood in the hallway. Home. She closed her eyes and breathed in the scents of a lifetime. Warmth of the timber, cool of the stone walls, lemony furniture polish, the sharp aromatic scent of ti-tree drifting through, wafting out from the drawer of the hallway dresser. She even imagined her mother's favourite scents of rose and lavender floated from odd nooks in the house.

Lorraine kept the place dusted and aired while the family had been in town, but Toni loved to open the place so the dry breeze could float through. It kept the place alive. In summer, as it nearly was, the heat rose to the ceiling. She walked from room to room and opened every door and window that had a flyscreen on it.

Down the end of the hallway, she threw open the door to her mother's lounge-room. Complete with restored furniture from her grandmother's day, it was a room of refuge and comfort, and somewhere that spoke of home as much as her beloved paddocks.

Many antimacassars, doilies, dressing table runners, tablecloths, serviettes, and milk jug covers had already been donated to the museum in town. She'd kept the old hand-stitched quilt, and crocheted knee rugs for the freezing winter nights, and packed them away in a heavy trunk laced with camphor. They were stashed in the Alice house. She couldn't bear to part with them.

Lorraine's home-made lemon scented polish fragranced the room, and the dark timbers of the settee and the low tables by each chair gleamed in the daylight. Leather seats were shiny, not a trace of the outside red dust on anything. Lead-light lamps dotted strategically, and she knew only the one tall lamp was electric. She looked up at the small chandelier hanging from the ceiling, the crystals twinkling in the mid-afternoon light. Another of her mother's additions.

She pushed up the front window and felt the warm air rush in.

The ceilings were high enough to keep the house cool, but fresh air—minus the flies and the bugs—was what Toni craved.

She left the lounge and crossed the hallway to her room. In contrast to her mother's taste, Toni had set up her room in minimal style. The first time she began to earn her own money, she'd saved up and bought a simple bedroom suite of distressed birch. A queen size bed, two bedside tables, a dresser with six drawers, in pairs side by side, complete with a mirror. The bed had its covers neatly made, the sheets, she knew, would be fresh. Inviting.

Good on you, Lorraine.

She opened her window, the air cooler this side of the house than the other side and backed up to sit on the bed. The view was of the long driveway into the property. The curve of the track was wide and it made a sweeping turn down a low hill until it dropped out of sight. You could always hear someone coming for much longer than you could see them.

Old Bill Dodson had built the original house out of the iron oxide tinged stone, rocks baked in the sun and stacked to fit one on top of the other, stuck together with red mortar. It had a bough shelter roof, but neither walls nor roof had proven very good when the rain came. He'd sold the property to Philip MacDonnell and with Two Bob her father built the present homestead. The old earth and stone hut had eventually fallen to rubble and was now almost non-existent.

She stood up, headed out of her room and across the hallway. Before grabbing her overnight bag, she opened what had been the boys' room, and her job would be done. Heaving wide the solid door, she marched directly across their large room to the French doors leading onto the veranda. Her mother had insisted the doors be for the boys so that their comings and goings late at night didn't disturb anyone else in the house.

No one mentioned that they needed to tread softly on the jarrah floored verandah, or that after the rain, the timber on the doors would swell with moisture and squeal as they opened. The boys never snuck anywhere.

The room was filled with all manner of paraphernalia, complete with king size single beds, a huge free standing old wardrobe that was mainly used for target practice rather than for hanging clothes, a desk and chair, an assortment of boots flung here and there, and bullets spread over every other cleared space.

Lorraine was known to make the beds occasionally and when she did, it was the only cleared space in the room. She would dump everything else on the floor.

Back across the hall and down from the lounge room, Toni tentatively opened the door to her parents' room. It was almost bare. Her father had moved a lot of stuff out when her mother died.

He'd lived frugally, sparsely since, after his Nettie had gone.

The big old timber desk was there, pushed against the side wall. The heavy dresser was worth keeping, though it was too dark and ornate for her tastes. It was empty except for two large framed pictures on it. One, a picture of the homestead as it had been when Philip bought it all those years ago. The other was her parents' wedding photo. It always took its place on the left-hand side of the big oak dresser.

She put her hand on it, wondering about the dreams and hopes that day had held for her parents. Squeezed her eyes shut and pinched her nose to stall the tears.

The bed was only a double. Neither of her parents had wanted a bigger bed. Her mother had said she always liked to be close to her husband and he had agreed. But it would have to go. It was old, the timber dried out in the harsh heat, the mattress was as old as Toni, older, she was sure.

There were two chairs on either side of the bed, as well as a nightstand on her father's side. A string hung from the ceiling for him to tug when he wanted electric light. If it wasn't broken, it didn't need fixing, he'd always say.

She crossed to the window and pushed it up. The view from here was across the home yards and the track leading off to the southern paddock. It was a two-day drive to get to the boundary and back. Not a large property by Territory standards, but it was hers. Or it had been.

Toni purposely kept her thoughts from straying. She concentrated, wanting to commit each rock to memory, before she lost it to the new owners.

She loved the homestead's design, as energy efficient as it could be without modern technology. Sixty-centimetre whitewashed brick walls, a wide verandah and doors to each room opening out on to it, much like the town house in Cromwell Drive. The kitchen floor was sandstone cut from a local quarry near Alice Springs and sealed for durability. The newly installed solar system heated water drawn from the house bore and a generator for electricity hummed for sixteen hours of the day before lights out.

Some of the 'modern' appliances dated back thirty years, like long distance telephone. Before there'd only been a radio telephone with calls limited to a particular timeslot and to twelve minutes each.

The phone was her dad's only nod to the modern world's communications. He hadn't wanted any internet or mobile phones on the property. despite his three kids insisting. In the end, it hadn't mattered.

Mainstream humdrum of modern society was far away from here and now. For once, she was grateful for it.

The cavernous station kitchen beckoned. A long timber benchtop spanned the width of the room. Underneath the old cupboards and drawers housed tableware, cooking utensils and pot and pans. On the other side, the window over the sink faced north. Unadorned, it held a hazy vista of mauve hills in the distance, and another paddock worthy of two to three day's drive. A wide, free standing bench, complete with utensils drawers and storage cupboards stood in the middle of the room.

Fresh vegetables were on the bench and in the old fridge Toni found beef steaks. Lorraine had clearly known she was coming today, but how? She shrugged. In earlier times, Lorraine's sixth sense was legendary. The half dozen bottles of white wine chilling down were welcome, too.

Heading outside to the car and lugging in her overnight bag, Toni decided to get herself unpacked before settling for the afternoon. Then she showered quickly, scrubbing her face free of make-up and the dust of travelling home. Donning an old pair of cut-off jeans and a large tee shirt, she wandered back to the kitchen.

A glass of sauv blanc poured, she diced vegetables for a stir-fry. She grabbed a couple of frozen bacon rashers and chopped them roughly. Everything went in together, and as she cooked the aroma wafting from the pan started a growl in her stomach.

To keep her sugar up, she popped a couple of jellybeans from the handy bottle on the bench. Scoffing them down, she reached for the few carrots and celery sticks that had not found their way into the pan. She hummed, munched some more.

It hit her with a thud how her new way her life would be. Emotions had still been still raw after the Loser's phone call before the meeting yesterday. She admitted—with today's clarity—that she hadn't properly dealt with Callum Parker and his approach.

Poor man had only wanted a business chat at lunch yesterday, a casual visit to property today, which was, after all, almost his. He wasn't to know how fragile things were. How volatile her emotions...

Poor man.

... How hard her temper was to contain. Thank God, he was out bush for the night; he might have ended up like the carrots and celery.

Poor man. Poo to that.

She wouldn't think about it.

As for Sonny Murphy, if he kept his distance, she could work around whatever crap he threw at her. One day it would end. The day they sold that house. The only two concrete things she had to do was to get him to sign a sales form, then get him to sign off once they got an offer. He was just as likely to say he'd do it, then not. A real piece of work, that Sonny Murphy.

Toni took her meal to the verandah. Chipper and Sudsy joined her, quietly hoping for something to fall their way. A setting sun, its vermilion glow blanketed the Run and her beloved desert. The night's stars flickered high in the western sky and more were beginning to appear as the light faded and twilight slipped into darkness.

Callum Parker's voice, 'welcome home,' edged once again into her thoughts. *A bloody earworm.*

She ate slowly, then took her dishes back inside. Fed the dogs on the verandah. Waited until they'd finished and then sent them off for business before she brought them in. They went to the foot of her bed and knew they were not to move from there until told.

Toni knew Two Bob would take Callum to Sleeper Creek to camp. Oh, so beautiful there… It was okay to dream if that's all you had. Imagined herself sitting with him under the night sky. It wasn't difficult to recall the timbre of his voice—*earworm*—or the smile on his face.

Had her dad deliberately put Callum Parker in her sight thinking she would need such a person? How like her dad to believe a woman needs a man. And a man needs a mate.

She wondered about that. Wondered about Callum Parker and a female mate. Where was she? He wasn't the type to be living his life alone, no way. He'd have a beautiful woman somewhere in Sydney, tall like he was, and graceful, probably rich and have a fancy, fashionable degree in a subject like… Toni didn't know what. Maybe he had a wife and they were just waiting for the two-point-four kids or whatever it was these days. Or two sets of twins.

Didn't matter. If she wanted to dream about him, she would. *It's okay to dream.*

She went to bed thinking of the broad shoulders, wondering if his chest was coarse with wiry man-hair. His hands, she'd noticed, were strong and lean and dry. How would they would feel wandering over her body, lazy and confident? She closed her eyes and, in the dark, pictured his face above hers, his whispers. Imagined the pressure of his body alongside hers, the lean, hard limbs and flat stomach, powerful arms and strong hands.

It's okay to dream.

If she repeated it often enough, she hoped the hurt and sadness would become part of her life and diminish quickly.

Exhausted by emotions in turmoil, she said goodnight to her mum, her dad, to the dogs. As she drifted towards sleep, she squeezed her eyes shut and forgave herself the hot-and-bothery tinglings Callum Parker invoked—she really shouldn't be thinking of the boss that way, anyway—turned on her side and slept.

Dreamed of a black knight ransacking and pillaging. She breathlessly chased him through dark tunnels and dank hallways, her skirts rucked high, her bosom bouncing and heaving, her belly still tingling.

It was a long night.

Hammering on the door, someone calling her name.

God, I'm exhausted. All that running around after dark knights.

Her eyes popped open. Watered as daylight streamed in the window across her face. The hammering on the door stopped. Toni swung her legs out of bed and sat, dazed for a moment. She fell back onto the bed again and groaned. She was tired as tired could be. She must've had a dream, there was no-one calling her name…

'Ton-ee, Ton-eeee.'

Ah! Recognising the voice, she called back, 'All right. Hang on,' and tugged on a light dressing-gown. Taking a couple of deep breaths to steady herself, she opened the bedroom door.

'Hi-i, it's me-e,' a diminutive woman before her sing-songed. 'Oh wow, you don't look too good. Your eyes are all red and puffy.'

Toni hugged her friend, Nicky Cooper. 'Are they still? Nice to see you, too. How'd you know I was here?'

'Hang on to that. Come on, into the kitchen. We'll talk there. I'm doing breakfast.'

Toni tightened the belt on the cotton wrap and tottered into the kitchen. Perched on a stool at the breakfast bar, the aroma of freshly brewed coffee seemed to permeate every pore of her body.

Nicky poured two cups and bent over them, inhaling deeply. 'I love your coffee.'

Wrapping her hands around one of the mugs, Toni sniffed appreciatively. 'And you do a good job making it. I'm glad you're here. I really needed to see you.'

''Course you did, is why I came.' Toni's dark-haired pixie-faced best friend gave her another quick hug. 'I couldn't get you on your mobile, out of range maybe, so I rang your brothers in town. They said you'd be here, wanted to be by yourself but too bad, you got me. I jumped in the truck and came over.' She shook her head. 'But when I got here, you were so fast asleep that I let the dogs outside. You didn't stir and that was about an hour ago.'

Toni hadn't heard a thing. 'Out like a light.' She rubbed her eyes, scraped fingers through her hair. 'I didn't hear a thing.'

Her friend thumbed in the direction of the yard and Toni looked out the window. Nicky's big old F100 sat over by the sheds. It usually sounded like a Boeing jet taking off, so she couldn't believe she'd slept through its arrival. 'There's the proof. My broom wouldn't have made it in time.' She grabbed an apron. In her black short sleeved tee, black skinny jeans and the apron tied around her middle she looked like a café waiter. 'Yeah, left at five this morning, it's only just gone eight. I couldn't let you sleep a moment more—thought you were dead.' She stopped suddenly. 'You know what I mean.'

'I certainly felt like it. It's a bit hard to get going.' She sipped her coffee, her head still fuzzy as thoughts bounced around in it.

It was hard not to think of what would come next. The mortgage repayments. The juggle about Sonny, and the thing with Callum Parker. At least the Sales Agency Agreement for the Magill house had been emailed to her. Printed out, and filled in as much as she could, it only waited for Sonny Murphy's signature on it. She'd stored it at the Alice house.

'Don't worry about it. I'm here for the day. Geoff Cooper doesn't need me in the yards.' Nicky always referred to her husband by his first name and surname, her quirky little affectionate thing for the man she married.

'Your husband's a saint,' Toni said.

'Yeah, he knows. So, you haven't eaten. I've found eggs, there's fresh tomatoes, orange juice. And I'll cook. Why don't you go have a shower?'

Toni's legs felt like weights as she dragged herself into the bathroom. The shower refreshed her, and though her eyes were puffy and red-rimmed she felt a lightening of the load, the exhaustion receding. Thoughts of Mr. Bloody Parker were easier to push away.

After pulling a brush through her wet hair, she applied a spray of toner and generous amount of moisturiser to her face. Brushed her teeth and dressed. Just in time to see a great pile of food on the table.

'Are you feeding some army?' she asked Nicky.

'Go on, eat. You know you need to. Besides, just look at you, skinny thing. Got to fatten you up.' Nicky took Toni's arm and turned her around. 'No meat on those hips of yours, legs straight like twigs. Good thing you got big boobs, we can tell you're a woman. You should be fatter though. It's a sin you should be so good looking and skinny. My mother will tell you that, and more.'

'You and your mother.' She paused for another mouthful. 'I don't feel good-looking. And I'm not skinny. I'm a healthy size.'

Toni found herself reaching for a fourth piece of toast even after polishing off the couple of eggs. At this rate, she might not remain a healthy size.

Nicky rattled on. 'Well, Geoff Cooper rang Paul to, you know, chat about guy stuff and Paul told him that Ben had reported, so to speak. You know, about the new guy and all that.'

Toni stared at her friend, shook her head. Bush telegraph still never ceased to amaze her. 'It goes around fast, doesn't it?'

'Ben reckons he has the hots for you.'

'Not for me. Ben's got the hots for the new guy, more like.'

'Yes, probably, but don't be daft, not Ben. This new guy, this Callum Parker has the hots for you.'

Toni blurted a laugh. 'I'm sure he would much prefer a blonde bombshell before anyone like me. Besides, he's not my type, and even if he was, you know I'm not going anywhere near any of them.'

'Yeah, right.'

Toni shrugged. 'Can't dwell on it. I've got a new job to get under control. I've got to sort out how I feel about what happened yesterday.' Deciding against talking to Nicky about the extra Sonny Murphy issue, she drained her coffee. 'That and the fact that Callum Parker has been out all night on the station with Two Bob.'

Nicky exploded with a million questions, waving her arms in the air demanding answers.

They left the house to take a walk around the gardens and the house sheds. Chipper and Sudsy came careening around the yards especially excited to see Toni awake and on two feet. They gave Nicky a respectful amount of attention as a visitor to the pack.

The girls wandered past Lorraine's little cottage and the old cellar nearby, dogs charging around them.

Life was good here and the hard work was mostly rewarding, although not so much financially anymore. Times were tough. As conversation once more turned to the station, Toni's spirits drooped. Nicky tried bullying her into a better mood but by the time they'd come back to the house and were once again in the kitchen, it still wasn't working.

'Nicky, this Callum Parker. He's going to take over. I've got to be out here—'

Her friend tut-tutted. 'Just tell him to naff off.'

'Yeah. Never mind that he's the bloody new boss around here and he owns the whole bloody place.' Toni blew her nose and took a couple of deep breaths. 'I wish he'd just bugger off. Just complicates things having him out here in our space.'

'Yep, it's no good at all. What's he want, anyway?' Nicky emptied the contents of the coffee pot, refilled it with fresh grounds. 'Bit greedy if you ask me,' she said po-faced. 'Fancy thinking he can throw all his money around, buy the station, employ you with a little blackmail from your dad and think he can come visit his own place. Of all the nerve. I hate that.' Placing the pot on the bench and filling the kettle, she threw her hands in the air. 'Who the hell is he, anyway? Some city slicker who wouldn't know his backside from his frontside.'

'Stop. I'll hurt myself laughing.'

Nicky gave her a stern look. 'You're thinking too much, too soon. You have the travel agency barely back on its feet, and you've got your brothers. Let the station go. Just see the job through.' She raised her hands to staunch the protest. 'No, no, I'm only saying give yourself some time. You've been through an awful lot these last couple of years, Toni. See what this fella has to say. Seems to me like you mention his name and go a bit shaky on it.' She poured steaming water into the plunger. 'Just an observation, mind you.

'He's got my home, that's why.'

'Sure, it is. Well, is he single?'

'Who knows? Who cares? What's that got to do with it? I couldn't give a toss.'

'Yeah, yeah. Sheesh, all that denial.' Nicky wagged a finger. 'But they're not all Sonny Murphies, you know.'

Toni flicked loose tendrils of hair off her face. 'Far as I'm concerned, they may as well be.'

'If he's single,' Nicky started, pointing. 'Marry him—but we do know how buying cattle stations can drain your resources,' she said and laughed, 'so only if he's got pots of money left after settlement on the place.' She poured two coffees, splashed milk into her own and pushed a cup of long black across the bench top.

Toni shivered, grimaced. Took a sip.

Nicky looked at her. 'Already thought of that, have you?'

Toni scoffed. 'Not even close. The guy wants kids.' Heat burned in her cheeks.

Nicky inclined her head. 'Wow. You cut to the chase quick. What's it been—a couple of days? You gonna get married and have kids already.'

'It came up in general conversation. There's no point me even thinking about a relationship—' she held up her hand to forestall

Nicky's protest, '—even if I was thinking about it, which I wasn't. Which I'm not.'

Nicky put her cup aside and rested her elbows on the bench. 'You put up with a lot of crap from Sonny Murphy, and still do, I know, and you worked hard through a lot of things that came out of that.' She squeezed Toni's hand. 'Just don't give up on all men.'

'I know now I put myself *into* a lot of crap—'

'But you came out,' Nicky insisted. 'With flying colours. You're just putting yourself down by staying in retreat.'

Toni stared at her coffee, wrapped her hands around the cup. She felt a foot shuffle coming on.

Nicky still pressed Toni's wrist. 'Sonny wins if you just give up. He wins, and so does his rotten, stinking, immature behaviour.'

The familiar lump that usually rose in her throat when she and Nicky spoke of these things was absent and had been for some time. It was a mark of how far she'd come out from under the stranglehold of a narcissist. She was certainly glad of that. But she knew her confidence had been rocked hard and she didn't know how to steady it, or how to fix it, if she ever could.

Nicky squeezed Toni's wrist again then withdrew her hand. 'I've been thinking a bit more. I think Sonny did what he did because, with you, he was punching above his weight. He knew, didn't he, that he could never give you what you wanted.'

'What he thought I wanted. So why be a complete cretin, and an arsehole? Why not just say he wanted out? Why do all that emotional damage?' Toni threw her hands up, frustrated with herself. 'Bugger it,' she snapped. 'I've always got the same idiot questions. Never any sensible answers.'

Nicky folded her arms on the bench. 'Because there aren't any sensible answers, only that he got his jollies off on it. No sense at all, except to him. Except to drag you down lower than him. Which he couldn't do, I might add,' she said, and took up her coffee. 'We know that.'

'We, the psychologists.'

'Yep—we had a little practice there for a while with him. And he is an arsehole. No mistake. But you're in a much better place now, and you've started your own life again.' Nicky tapped the table. 'So. Drink up, then I have to head home. I'll be back in town on the weekend if you want to catch up.'

Toni gave her a nod. 'Now that sounds good.

10

Nicky left after lunch to take the eighty-kilometre trip back to her own home.

The rest of the day sped by despite Toni's low mood. She'd spent most of the afternoon on the verandah reading, thinking, pacing up and down when she knew she should have been packing up some of the personal items in the house.

Later, she'd prowled around in her mother's formal lounge, checking for sneaky dust and straightening a book here and there. Should have known better with Lorraine on the job before her. Pushing open the door to her father's room once again, she took one look at the bare necessities and decided she couldn't get started in there either.

So, it was back to the verandah, trying not to nod off in the chair.

The dogs kept well underfoot. Lorraine had come through the house and checked the pantry, made a list. Toni poked her head in the laundry and, finding little to do, had come back to the kitchen.

'There's not much around here to keep me out of mischief these days, Lorraine,' Toni said, leaning on the kitchen bench.

'Just the calm before the storm, I reckon.' Lorraine wiped down an already spotless draining board. 'That new fella has big ideas. And Two Bob. Reckon they're a good pair.' She flicked a glance at Toni.

Toni's radar had picked up. 'What do you mean?' She straightened, felt her eyes narrow.

'Two Bob reckons he works like a real good ringer. Reckons he has country in him.'

'Reckons Callum Parker is an indigenous man?'

Lorraine snorted. 'Not skin.' She tapped two fingers over her heart. 'Country, in here. Reckons he worked country for a long time.'

Toni stared. 'Why's he and Two Bob talking? What's going on?'

'They been talking a long time before now.' Lorraine dropped her gaze and wiped some more over the clean benches.

Startled as she was by the revelation, Toni knew that whatever insight Lorraine had, it wouldn't be forthcoming. 'I see.' She tried something else. 'Have you talked to Callum Parker before today?'

Lorraine shook her head. 'Not me. That fella, I reckon he likes you for talking to.' Then she smiled, a big grin with large white teeth. 'Going off to bed, Toni. See you tomorrow.'

'See you tomorrow.'

Lorraine padded outside, her soft footfalls echoing along the veranda and down the steps into the darkened night.

The desert scent of dry earth dust wafted in on a sprite of warm breeze.

What on earth could she have meant? It was pointless pressing the issue; Toni knew Lorraine of old. If she didn't want to impart anything, it didn't get imparted. It would remain a mystery until Lorraine decided to give her some more clues.

Toni thought some more about what Lorraine had said. Maybe Callum Parker knew Two Bob from somewhere else. Or maybe met him when negotiations to sell up first started.

Toni had still been away at that time. Trying to recuperate after the last operation, the last of the chemo. Then trying to stem the financial life blood, leaking out in torrents, after Sonny Murphy's earlier clandestine efforts. Masses of credit card debt. Bills left unpaid in her apartment in leafy Magill, a suburb of Adelaide, even though he swore he'd paid them. The little 'holidays' he took here and there while she convalesced. Toni had been unaware of the 'guest' he always took with him.

For the millionth time, she raged, asked herself how she could not have known what was going on. But she hadn't. She believed every damned excuse. Her fists drummed the bench. *Stop it. It was well over*. No need to revisit it time and time again. Dealing with narcissism was among the hardest of emotional abuses, but damned if she was going to let it be her undoing.

Stop!

Nicky was right. She was in a much better place now. A better space.

Really? Thing was, she was left with a total lack of confidence. Total lack of trust in her worthiness. No amount of willing it so would return that. It had to be worked on, they said, worked at, rebuilt bit by bit, they said. *They* being the counsellors.

Toni shook her head. Enough of that. Now it was time for bed. She shot a look at the clock. Fifteen minutes to go before the generator closed down. Racing into the bathroom, she peeled off her clothes and under the hot showery needles of water, lathered up quickly, then rinsed off.

No more thinking about Callum Parker and rightly so. She had no space, or right, to entertain thoughts of having a man in her life. Especially him. *Sleeping with the Boss*. Even if she thought she could, it was not a good idea.

Dry, and padding naked to her bedroom, she threw on a long loose t-shirt. She climbed into bed and the generator shut off. Darkness fell lightly, and everything was quiet except for a faint distant hum. A vehicle somewhere miles off, maybe an aircraft high overhead. Sound travelled lightly over a still night.

Reaching over, she switched on her battery light. Chipper and Suds shuffled together at the foot of her bed. Toni settled against the pillows, and dragged a sheet over herself, pulled out a book from one of the bed-side drawers, glad to have a few minutes to read. Checking the little bedside clock, she realised it wasn't even nine in the evening. How wonderful. She'd get a good long night's sleep – hopefully a good, long, dreamless sleep if the full moon later didn't keep her awake half the night.

She heard the hum more clearly. A vehicle after all, coming up the driveway, still far away. Five minutes passed before its lights showed, and another ten minutes before it pulled into the house driveway.

On security alert, the dogs went crazy before they figured they knew the vehicle. Her eyeballs rattled at the din of two barking dogs inside her closed bedroom.

Two Bob's old machine clattered up the driveway and skewed to a halt at the front door. The horn honked. Then it veered off past the house and stopped a little way, most likely at Lorraine's. A car door opened and slammed shut moments later.

In the stillness, and without a generator shredding the silence of the outback night, she could hear a gnat breathe. Next thing, the vehicle revved and headed back towards the house.

A large, bright rising moon glowed. Callum Parker climbed wearily out of the passenger side. He headed for her verandah carrying a bag of sorts. Two Bob yelled goodnight and the vehicle roared off again.

What—?

Sleep fled as her heart thundered. She threw on a light bathrobe, pulled the belt tight and stalked down the dim hallway.

Toni ordered the dogs to sit and be quiet as she thrust her feet into boots she kept by the front door. She switched on the torch that hung on a hook overhead and pulled open the door. The dogs looked up at Callum Parker as if they'd just arrived in heaven.

He stood there, his shirt smudged with dirt and dried sweat, and with a wicked grin splitting his features. 'I'm back.' Dust creased in the lines of his face, darkening the dimple.

'Oh, it's you,' she said, tightening the silky wrap and folding her arms.

He stared at her for a moment, the dimple twitching, and carefully placed a leather satchel on the floor. He dusted off his jeans. 'Expecting someone else?'

'Not expecting anyone, especially not you two. You were camping out.'

'That was the plan. I've caught you unawares again.'

'I thought you weren't coming back here.'

'I'd seen enough of that side of the property. I decided to stay another night out here and see a bit of the other side of the place. So, we came back.' He towered over her in the doorway. 'I thought as it is only early evening,' he said, illuminating his watch and checking the time, 'I might share this with you.' He bent and pulled a bottle of Chardonnay from the satchel. 'By way of a peace offering.'

'Early evening is like seven, not nine-thirty.' Toni hadn't much time to think much less take her eyes off the dancing muscles in his chest. They tensed and waved under the soft cotton of his red dust and grime smudged T-shirt.

'It's not even nine-fifteen,' he emphasised softly. 'And I have just been driven three hours for the undeniable privilege.' He beamed his killer smile, dimple fully activated.

'You didn't get that at the eastern paddocks,' she accused him, pointing to the bottle, and shivering despite the night's warm air breezing past them in the doorway. Suddenly conscious of her nipples pushing against the soft fabric of her wrap, she folded her arms again.

'I confess. I stashed a few things at Two Bob's just in case.' His gaze moved down, the smile playing at the edge of his mouth. His eyes flickered swiftly over her bare legs. 'Nice look, those boots with that night thingy you're wearing.'

Toni stared at her grubby work boots. 'I'll just be a minute. Dogs, bed,' she ordered. She kicked off her boots, turned and followed Chipper and Sudsy into her bedroom.

'Take your time,' he called after her. 'I'll find my own way to the kitchen.'

Toni slammed the door to her room harder than she'd intended. Bloody imposition. She didn't tell him to naff off, though, did she? Or say *no, don't come inside*, did she? And she wouldn't throw him out, would she? Oh no, that would be rude and besides he has brought a delightful bottle of wine. And he does own the place. Yeah, there is that. She wouldn't dwell on that.

Toni hoisted off the dressing-gown and the t-shirt, stepped into clean knickers and a pair of jeans, and threw a loose shirt over her bare shoulders. Dragging the brush through her hair once more, she tried to be calm, and remembered to flick off her light. She slipped quietly back into the hallway, breathed deeply, and firmly told her stomach to calm its butterflies.

She ordered Chip and Suds to stay, but they weren't having that and so happily trotted after her.

'I can't see a thing.' Callum Parker had found his way to the kitchen, and from the direction of his voice she knew he was at the breakfast bench.

In the pitch black inside the house, she walked easily around the bench to the cooker and pressed a switch on the mantel over the old cooktop. A battery light came on.

He had found a safe seat and was resting his elbows on the bench.

'Why don't you take a shower? The water would still be hot,' she asked, her eyes adjusting to the soft light.

'Later,' he said. 'Glasses in there?'

From the old sideboard cabinet, Toni brought out two over-sized crystal goblets. She stared at his hands as he poured her wine. Heat flushed her features. She looked up.

'I honestly thought you'd still be up.' His clear gaze met hers.

Toni resisted the urge to button up her shirt further—like to her eyebrows. Instead she swung around and sat on a stool opposite him. In the soft light of the kitchen, those eyes of his were a slate grey, challenging and depthless.

'We don't keep city hours out here,' she stated.

Callum sat back. 'It was a long, hard couple of days and I just—changed my mind. I could go back to Alice tonight, I suppose.'

'It's hardly very far.' Her throat was dry and her heart had begun to pound again. 'You're just used to getting your own way.'

'Old habits die hard,' he agreed with a tilt of his head. Then raised his glass. 'Cheers.'

The wine tingled on her tongue. How long had it been since a man brought a bottle of heady wine to her in her own home? Stop those thoughts quick-smart, solo-girl.

He leaned towards her. 'I really didn't think you'd mind if I came out here earlier. You certainly came out earlier.'

Aroma of hard-working man reached her. 'This is my home,' she flared, and felt her cheeks roast beet red. 'Or do you mean I'm not supposed to be out here without your permission?'

He set his glass down, folded his arms on the benchtop. 'It's entirely understandable you're having difficulty with the transition. I get it.'

Patronising. A snappy retort bubbled to her lips and stopped there.

He leaned closer, took a deep breath. Toni shut her mouth and moved her seat away a little, her eyes on his chest as muscles rippled underneath the T-shirt. Why couldn't she just lift her eyes and concentrate on the paint work of the ceiling?

'I haven't seen a lot of the station, and I need to see more, and quickly. Get myself acquainted fast.' His gaze met hers again. 'And you were the one who mentioned seeing the house the way your mother set it up.'

'Yeah, but I didn't mean tonight.'

A glitter replaced the dancing twinkle in his eyes. His arms came off the table as he leaned back. 'You're making it sound as if I'm some sort of predator. I have to be out here, sometime. Might as well be tonight as any other.'

Toni stared at the neck of his t-shirt that didn't quite contain the springy black hair curling up from under the collar. His arms were well muscled, his hands callused and brown. Strong hands, male and demanding.

She would not lick her lips. 'We only have the generator on until eight pm or so, if that. Up at dawn, et cetera. I just wasn't expecting you.'

It was a good attempt at disguising ill manners.

He nodded and took another swallow of wine. 'Sorry.' He didn't sound apologetic. 'I've been out on the property, working. Treat me as if I've just wandered home after a days' hard yakka.'

She wished he'd wandered home to someone else. *Sure.*

'So,' he continued as if the matter was closed. 'Do we sit here and talk, or can we go somewhere more comfortable?' He twisted on the stool, expecting to leave the kitchen.

She pointed out the door. 'You need the shower.'

'All right.' He put his glass on the bench. 'Shower first, that's reasonable. I'm more than looking forward to it. But then we talk. Agreed?'

Toni eyed him. What did he want to talk about?

'Hey, the shower? Point me in the right direction.'

She and the dogs led him down the passage to the huge old station bathroom and supplied two great towels from the hallway linen cupboard. Well-practiced, she found the battery light and turned it on. Reaching under the basin, she plucked out a large fresh bar of soap.

He immediately stripped off his shirt and bent to take off his socks. Such a glorious sight, she backed up to the doorway. Both dogs sat beside her at the open door, and all three stared, open-mouthed. *Thank goodness only two of us have our tongues hanging out.* She was sure it was both dogs. She shut her mouth, just in case.

A mat of dark hair covered the muscles on his chest … they were rippling things, bunching and relaxing with every move. His forearms had tanned darker than the rest of him—what she could see, at least—but the skin she was looking at had a golden hue swathed in a light dusting of desert.

As the fly came undone and the pants were shoved down over his hips, a fluffy patch of dark man-hair appeared over the top of his undies. 'Don't suppose you'd go out to my car and grab my bag, would you? Need clean jocks and stuff,' he threw over his shoulder.

She turned her back before her legs wobbled. 'Don't use too much water.' Slammed the door to the bathroom as she left. The dogs moved smartly out of her way.

'Thanks,' he yelled, voice muffled by the rush of shower water.

Stuffing her feet into boots again, she grabbed a torch and stomped outside across the yard to his car. It took her an age to drag the huge duffel bag out of the vehicle. She couldn't get the back-hatch door open—she'd had to get into the car to hoist it over all manner of man-stuff thrown onto the seats. Then she half lugged, half dragged the damned thing inside, trailing dust and dirt with it.

Cursed as she dumped it at the bathroom door. Lorraine would curse her tomorrow for all the mess.

'Can you throw it in?' he called.

While she stood there, contemplating yelling, 'No,' he flung open the door.

She stared. His hair, black as the ace, shone with water dripping from his tousled head. The fragrant soap scent on his warm skin clocked her on her head. The towel drooped around his waist. Man-hair again in a few damp licks started under his navel. A zing zanged through her, all the way down-to-there.

'What kept you?' His cool, damp hand closed over hers as he took the bag. 'I'll be out in a minute.'

She snatched her hand from his and turned for the kitchen. *He's off limits, girl. Way. Off. Limits.*

11

Carrying her wine, Toni led him to the small formal lounge room and flicked on one battery lamp. Its soft spritely glow illuminated the room her mother had furnished a lifetime ago. The room that had been her refuge too, and one that Lorraine fondly kept so well.

The things in it were much as they had been when she died.

Old family photos, sepia, black and white, faded colour in various frames, some pieces of carnival glass, antique crystal cabinets. Gone was the delicate lace crocheted by maiden great-aunties, but still it was a room belonging to a by-gone era. It had been a tough life with very little comforts to compare with today. A female room, not overtly feminine, but welcoming with the warmth of family, hearth and home. Toni was very much at peace in it, her own private space, her own special cocoon within the enveloping security of home country. Her country.

So, what on earth was she doing showing Callum Parker a precious room such as this? She should have packed things away immediately she arrived and not wasted time in a girlish hormonal funk.

Slipping into a large club chair, she tucked her legs under her. Callum eased his long frame over the only piece of very masculine furniture in the room, a mahogany leather chesterfield opposite Toni's seat.

He'd dressed in clean jeans and boots, and another T-shirt,

rumpled from the duffel bag. He looked comfortable, at home. At that moment, he certainly looked for all the world as if he belonged here.

Gazing around him, he nodded. 'It is a beautiful room. Your mother must have cared a great deal for it.'

Wanting to gulp down her wine to put out the fire, she forced herself to sip. 'Mmh. What would you like to talk about?'

Callum studied her over the rim of his glass. 'Perhaps we could talk money. Yours. What you could earn from us, over and above what you already have in that bank account. Then there's the issue of your wildlife park idea. I still want to see that file.'

That bank account. The one with only half the money left in it. 'The wildlife file's not here.' He could talk money if he liked. She'd need to earn all she could, but he wasn't getting the wildlife park for nothing.

'Or we could talk about the fact that you might want to opt out before settlement on November first, despite the money already paid you.'

Again, she stared into those steely grey eyes. *Opting out was not likely any longer.* As she swallowed some more of her wine, her chest thumped. Was her heart always so boisterous? Her ears were ringing with it. Her throat was dry, her lips needed balm. Perhaps another sip would cool all the heat. Or perhaps it was the wine playing havoc, even just a few sips.

'I wouldn't do that,' she threw back at him. 'If I did, that would negate the—'

'I'm not going to fence with you,' he interrupted. 'I'm glad you've decided to work with us.' He placed his glass of wine on the table and settled back into the leather lounge, hands behind his head. 'You, not your father, signed the agreement after the codicil, and you pocketed a good deal of cash in advance.'

She said nothing. The agreement made her without defense, and spending half of a year's wage to save herself, meant that she was trapped, and of her own making. No use grizzling about it.

'Ball's in your court.' He frowned. 'You don't want to end up holding your brothers to ransom for their right and proper inheritance—'

'I don't want that.'

'Your so-called solicitor should have told you to read the fine print protecting us.'

A pounding bubble of anger slid under Toni's collar. She unfolded her legs and set her own glass down on the side table. 'You—ah, terminated his services, unquote.'

'Trust me, his ethics are more than a little skewed.' There was a low rumble in his voice. 'But that particular incident in his office was on my account, not on yours. He is still your solicitor. Not my business, but I'd say he's not a very good one.'

'It's all right, I can read the fine print myself.'

'You do that, but maybe get a second opinion.' His intense gaze settled on her a moment then he sat up straight. 'I want a friendly working relationship for the long term, not a short bout ending with a technical knockout.'

A technical knockout Toni didn't need. She needed the job more than ever, and the time to make her plans. She took a deep breath. 'I'm good to stay, I said so. Look, I was just about to go to bed when you arrived—'

'Won't keep you long, then, and I have my swag. I thought I might doss on the floor, or the verandah. Unless there's a room I could use for the night?' He swallowed the last of his wine and went to the kitchen.

'I haven't packed up my father's room, yet,' she said to his back.

'Didn't expect you would've yet,' he answered from the other room. Returning with the wine, he topped up her glass and placed the bottle, nearly empty, on the table nearby. 'But couldn't we talk more? Don't go just yet. Put our cards on the table. Shouldn't take long. Then it's out of the way.'

Too many questions tumbled around in her head. Where to

start—put her cards on the table? He wouldn't want that. Besides, where his company was concerned, she didn't have any cards to 'put'. That was the main difference between them. He had huge resources by the sounds of things, and she had very little. And it would likely slip quickly through her fingers. 'Clearly, to do what you've done, you have a lot of money, you and that company of yours.'

He turned and sat on the edge of the chesterfield closest to her chair, pulling off his boots. 'The company, certainly. Next?'

'What are you doing?'

He shot her a look. 'I'm taking off my boots. I shouldn't even be wearing them inside; I've forgotten these things. And I don't usually sleep with them on, even though they are my Sunday best.' He set them aside at his feet and patted them. 'I have two pairs, if you'd like to know. One for work, and one for socialising. These,' he said, pointing at his feet, 'are the socialising pair.'

She ignored that. 'Are you on the land somewhere?'

'Does that surprise you?'

'Yes.'

His sigh was brief. 'I'm not on any land of my own, right now, but I was, growing up. My parents had land around here, as a matter of fact. East a bit. Dad sold up after one of his prize bulls fell on him. Earned himself just enough from the insurance to keep him in medical expenses and, for the day, a modern wheelchair.' He flexed his toes, stretched his limbs. 'He taught me to hang in there and keep going.' He leaned into the arm of the lounge not far from her. 'That's what I do best—hang in there.' The soft lamplight mellowed the angled lines of his jaw. 'I wouldn't have been able to work with Two Bob over the last couple of days if I didn't know what I was doing. Might be a bit rusty,' he continued and stared at his hand in the low light. 'But I helped repair a couple of fences. Mustered a few stragglers. Checked a couple of bores. Fixed a gate near Sleeper Creek.'

Toni knew the gate. Her brothers had meant to fix it ages ago.

'So not just a city slicker,' she said, and raised her eyebrows.

He snorted. 'Suppose not. Freshened up a couple of calluses I didn't know I missed. And I think I passed Two Bob's scrutiny. I'm here to work, and that's what I'm doing. Our plans will be revealed as everything rolls through the correct channels for approval.' Then he stifled a yawn. 'Sorry. It's just hit me. Not used to it, must be soft after all.'

'There isn't a room available here for you, tonight,' she said, sitting up a little.

'So you said. Doesn't matter. I can sleep in here, or on the verandah, though I reckon the mozzies might carry me away.' He leaned forward again. 'Tomorrow I'd like you to show me around, not Two Bob, so it'd be a waste of time and money to go back to Alice tonight.'

The retort slipped out. 'Money's not all we think of around here.'

'Perhaps you should think of it a bit more.' Callum shrugged. 'And I don't believe in wasting time. There's not enough of it.'

She reached across to take her glass from the table, hoping a sip or two might settle nerves. He moved at the same time she did, offering her glass before she could reach it.

'Thank you.' Her fingers touched his briefly as she took the glass and set it down. She changed her mind about sipping and settling nerves. It wouldn't be a good idea. 'I should really head off.'

'Thought you might have welcomed some company.'

'Well, I—' She hesitated, mindful, for some reason, of her manners.

'Just company,' he said, cool grey eyes studying her.

At any other time, before the thing with Sonny, his invitation would have had her leaping across the coffee table and crawling on to his lap. Pushing her breast into his warm hand, his fingers teasing a nipple, his other hand gliding over a bare thigh until it found a warm, wet—

'Okay,' he continued, a cooler light now shining in his blue-grey eyes, 'Maybe not.'

The rumble of his voice throbbed through her, vibrated along her bones.

'Perhaps you're right, it's best to go to bed,' he said, and inclined his head. 'I'll make some space on the floor here.' He stood up, turned his back and began to clear furniture. Then looked at her still sitting. 'But if you're going to sit there ...' He kicked his discarded boots under the chesterfield.

'No, no. Good night. Don't forget to turn off the lamp.'

'Sure. I'll just head outside and grab my swag.'

Toni beat a hasty retreat. Inside her bedroom, she locked the door. Would that be locking her in or locking him out? Either or, the thought terrified her. Sort of.

She undressed and slipped into bed. The cheek of him. The cheek of her. She was glad she'd locked the door, for one reason or the other. It didn't matter which, as long as neither of them gave in.

In a huff, she flicked off her lamp and the room plunged into darkness. Then she heard a loud thump and a louder expletive. Callum must have bumped into something trying to find his way outside. She listened as he found the front door, stepped onto the verandah, and cursed some more as he stumbled in the dark. He exploded with another curse as he picked his way across the yard in the pitch dark to his vehicle.

Maybe that big old moon wasn't glowing in the night sky quite so brilliantly now. She muffled her laughter as it bubbled to the surface. A moment later, she saw a light bobbing its way back to the house. Heard his footsteps on the verandah as the light swung across her bedroom window.

'Goodnight, Toni,' he said as the curtains drifted idly in the torch light.

When sleep eventually came, it was disturbed and hot.

12

At Reddell's Stock Agency in Alice, Eric Roycroft pulled at his collar. Damned good thing no one wore a tie these days, too bloody hot. God almighty, wearing a tie in this heat would be ludicrous. Did anyone even still wear a tie?

Sitting at his desk, he checked his watch. Eight o'clock. Heaps of time. He looked over the top of the computer monitor to the main door of the office.

All good, no one else is about. I'm alone.

The computer booted up. He waited for the thing to finally go through its paces. Once the program loaded, he entered his username and password and waited for the hidden files to spring open.

The bookkeeper had done her job, the invoices and the payments made to him duly recorded. Gazing at the entries, he drilled down to invoices from AgAnswers. They were all there, amounts for consultancy adding up more than four hundred thousand dollars. All approved for payment by the old man Phillip MacDonnell's Power of Attorney. Justin West had done well.

If they sat tight, they'd split the proceeds. The sale of MacDonnell's Run had now gone through, and with unconditional settlement pending, he'd be sitting pretty. Nobody would look too much into things now. Signed, sealed and delivered.

MacDonnell's accountants, Mackie and Mackie had finished with the books and all had been cleared.

He switched his attention to another column of figures, clicked open the file he highlighted and checked invoices from BioSoil+. More funds adding up to hundreds of thousands of dollars. Another amount he'd have to split, unfortunately, if Justin West played the game, but it was worth it.

Easy pickings. Eric Roycroft sat back. He'd retire after this last lot; had flagged his retirement to the boss, Mo Reddell so it wouldn't come as any surprise. He'd take himself off somewhere. Maybe bunker down for a while to make sure his tracks were well covered. That idiot, Justin West, would have to be watched. Don't trust him. The bloke had something else up his sleeve, Eric was sure of it. He looked like he'd blow a gasket if he didn't rein in his temper. But Justin was also up to his neck in it, so he wouldn't risk blowing the whole show, would he? The guy would have to get himself on medication before too long. The sooner the better.

They were so close to getting away with this. So close.

He pushed his chair away, crossed his feet at the ankles, and laced his hands over a bulging belly. A little too much condition, but nothing a few long laps in the pool and a few sessions in the gym wouldn't knock off. Maybe have his hair buzz cut too, or maybe go totally bald, get a whole new look. He ran his hand through thin hair, not happy when a heap of strands came out, tangled in his fingers. He brushed them off to the floor. He'd already shaved off his moustache because his neighbour's kid said he looked like some old detective on the tele. Tom Sellick, for crissakes. Still, the moustache had to go. The skin under his nose felt soft and raw as he touched where it had been. Pale compared to the rest of his face and the boys at Reddell's had kidded him about it. *All part of it, boys. All part of moving on, with a load of moola.*

The front door banged open and Steve Russell strode in, a gangly thirty-something insurance rep for the company.

'Mornin', Eric,' he shouted and headed for his office.

'Mornin',' Roycroft shouted in return. He scooted his chair closer to the computer, clicked on 'close' and waited until the encrypted program shut off.

13

Callum Parker was the first thought in her head as she woke,
mainly because she'd done nothing but dream of him all night. She
lay in bed and strained to hear if he was up and about.

She waited barely a minute before she was sure he was not.
Swinging her legs out of bed, she sat up. Then reached for her
other robe, her ugly old thick terry-towelling one. The one far too
hot for this time of year. She pulled it tight around her and crept
towards the bathroom, dogs on her heels.

Peeking into the lounge room, she could see the foot of his swag
on the floor. Good. He was still asleep.

She shooed the dogs outside.

Why she was creeping around in her own house? It was hers
until settlement. She lengthened her stride and struck out for the
toilet, just as normal, and did what she had to do. Then still
muttering about men and inconvenience, she headed for the
bathroom and pushed the door open.

Steam misted over a tall, broad form at the basin.

'Oh.' Toni stood stock still.

'Good morning.' His face was lathered with shaving cream and
the razor moved swiftly over it. 'What a pleasant surprise. No, no,
don't go, I'm nearly finished.' He splashed the last of the soap
from his face and grinned at her.

She stared at his reflection. Nobody should look that good first thing in the morning. And he certainly did look good, all damp and everything, part wrapped in a towel. Again. The towel, loosely tucked around his waist, looked desperately precarious and she feared a sudden mishap if she kept staring at it. So, her gaze strayed back to his reflection in the mirror and the dark mat of hair on his chest. Its trail spiralled out of sight beneath the soft fabric that hid nothing of the very defined masculine bulges.

He reached for the other towel and swiped it vigorously over his face and neck. The one at his waist moved enough to give her a start.

No, no, no, no. This isn't fair.

She put a hand to her hair. Suddenly wondered why her mouth had gone dry.

'Don't mind me,' he said, not making any move to leave the bathroom. That dimple appeared again.

'I'll wait.' She headed out the door, which closed behind her with a thud.

Outside, she leaned on the wall and tapped her foot. He'd sneaked into the bathroom ahead of her and was making her wait in her own house. He could at least have the courtesy to hurry up.

She heard him brushing his teeth, then heard two short bursts from a spray can, probably deodorant, the clang of metal and glass as his toiletries, she presumed, were thrown into a bag and then the flick of a towel against the wall, for God's sake.

The door pulled open. 'All yours.'

He sauntered off in the direction of the lounge room. Toni watched the taut butt work with each stride. That towel had a life of its own. She dived into the bathroom just as he turned to go into the lounge-room.

Caught perving for sure. Not good, Toni. Get a grip.

Not long after, she emerged from the shower and marched to her room to dress. The rich aroma of freshly brewed coffee drifted through the house. Inviting. Comfortable. Homey.

She wished he'd just leave.

Oh sure. So why take more time than usual to up-fling her hair into a scrunchie? And apply light make-up—out here at home. Who wore make-up out here? Or pull on a stretch T-shirt and climb into some stretchy jeans instead of a flannie shirt and saggy– baggy denims, and oh-so-casually enter the kitchen.

Callum Parker was at the stove, poking at eggs that sizzled happily in a pan. He turned. 'Toast?' Jeans, butt-hugging. Singlet, pec-hugging. Open shirt over that. Socked feet. Killer grip on the egg slide.

Her mouth finally moved. 'Look, let's get this straight.'

'Good idea.' He looked over, those grey eyes crinkled at the corners. He lifted his eyebrows and smiled. 'Sunny-side up, all right?'

She rounded on him at the stove. 'Those are my eggs you're cooking on my stove.'

'One or two?'

She cut him a look.

Callum Parker put down the egg slide, turned off the gas, reached for a couple of plates. He leaned back against the bench and folded his arms.

'Organised to have a pleasant breakfast in the fresh air.' With a lift of his chin he indicated down the hallway out on the front verandah. A small table, complete with cloth and linen napkins, set for two.

'Where did that come from?' she asked, immediately distracted.

'Brought it with me. Now,' he said and turned back to the eggs. 'Sunny-side up?'

She helped with breakfast, held the plates while he loaded eggs and toast on to both, watched as he forked slices of fresh Roma tomatoes and large white mushrooms to accompany them.

A giddy rush of warmth sped through her, at odds with her feelings. How could that be? Uneasy, she wondered, when his gaze lingered on her face, whether her freckles were covered up. Was her hair looking right? And what—you just forgot a splash of perfume? What were you thinking?

Taking the plates, he headed for the outside table. 'I cooked. You can grab the coffee.'

She poured two mugs of long black. It wasn't all that surreal. *I mean, both feet just need to be planted firmly on the ground, not flailing about mid-air like some desert fairy.* The mugs landed on the table outside with a firm thud, small spillage ignored.

'So,' he was saying as he started on his eggs. 'I'd like to see the western paddocks. What do you think?'

Her breath caught. 'They're a good two and half hour's drive from here,' she protested. 'I didn't expect you'd want to go as far away as that.' She felt warm all over. Hot, really. Probably the early sunshine. Might well be another scorcher today, and top forty-five degrees.

He lightly tapped the table. 'We can stay out overnight, swag it under the stars, get another early start tomorrow. I have all the camping gear, we won't be caught short.' He pointed to her barely touched plate. 'Eat.' Then caught her glance, stopped chewing. 'What?'

Double meaning. *That overnight word had a double meaning.* 'No. Not overnight. I have too much to do for that.' Bloody hell, why didn't she refuse outright? What's the matter with her?

'Like what?'

He seemed intent on her every word. He held her stare until her stomach flip-flopped. She carved into some toast with her knife. 'Like—'

'Like a little bit of packing up. Nothing more than that until we start work in earnest.' He watched her chew for a bit. 'I'll wait for you to throw a few things together and then off we go.'

Toni shook her head and swallowed the lump of toast. This was inviting trouble. There'd be no come-back either—she'd have consented to be out there with him and if anything happened ... *Off we go*, she repeated numbly to herself. *I can't just off-we-go!* A flare lit up behind her eyes. 'I can't just off-we-go,' she railed.

'And I'm certainly not going overnight.' She tucked into the other slice of toast, carving up the egg as if it needed biological dissection.

He hesitated a moment. Held up a hand and then dragged it through his hair. 'Of course not. Not overnight. Sorry, didn't mean to—'

She nodded. Exhaled. But her heartbeat pummelled. 'It's all right.'

'No, it isn't. I didn't mean—I'm just in a hurry and there's so much to do, so I—' He rolled his shoulders. 'I know you and your brothers have the place under control but I have a job to do. I want to look over the place as soon as possible, that's all. I know I can't do it all in a couple of days.' A lock of hair fell across his forehead. 'And let's not forget the job you have to do.'

The job she had to do. Oh yes. 'All right. A day trip. Not sure how far we'll get starting this time of the day.'

'Better than nothing.' He held her glance for only a moment more.

They ate in silence, and she managed to finish hers ahead of him, but only just. He pushed his plate away, leaned back, and swallowed his coffee.

She watched as his hand brushed through that unruly black hair again, his head bowed, a bit shamefaced, perhaps. Well, good. 'Thanks for breakfast,' she offered, and hoped that would smooth things a little.

He stood up and reached across to take her empty plate. 'Glad you enjoyed it,' he said, terse.

It could have been a plate full of cardboard. She'd hardly concentrated on the contents while she sorted out what it all might have meant. A thought struck her. 'Do you always do this sort of thing when you've got a job to do?' She waved her hand over the table.

'I have to eat. Someone's got to cook,' he fired in return and the blue-grey eyes zapped her, electricity arcing off steel. 'I remember you saying very clearly that you don't.'

He strode past her down the hallway. Toni heard him dump the dishes on the kitchen sink and when he returned, his tone bit into her. 'Being cranky about the condition in the will isn't on us. Or me,' he said. 'Your father put the conditions of sale into place, knowing it would save you from the station's financial burden. And my company has given me certain directions. Okay?'

She had no response for him this time and looked away, tossing it all over. Shrugged inwardly. What was it she really objected to? Him? Oh, sure. Frustration? Lack of financial capacity? She couldn't change anything about the process; Justin had made it clear she couldn't fight it. The family had no money. Not her fault. At the same time, it was clear there was nothing more she could do about it. Not a damned thing.

That was it. *Lack of control.* No question. So let it go.

Perhaps her father was right after all. He'd made the sale of the place. He'd been sure of what he wanted for his kids. None of them had had a say in the running of the place. None of them were partners in the station. Her dad had never gone down that track. And none of them had a sale in the selling of the place.

Lack of control.

Perhaps it wasn't so bad not to have the worry of the place and its debts, either. Her dad had looked out for her and her brothers. Had made sure they'd be debt free. Poor as buggery, but debt free. Something to celebrate, wasn't it?

So, why be upset, really? And surely not with the people who bought the place. Wasn't their fault. And Callum Parker was her new boss. She had a job, at least. Nothing else to be said for it. A shift in momentum was required. She would make the effort. For now. And keep herself to herself. At all costs. A new life.

Toni looked up at him. 'You're right. You're absolutely right. I'll just be a minute.'

She waited long enough to see the look of surprise light up his face.

14

Callum had a white-knuckled grip on the steering wheel as the vehicle bounced over the corrugations in the dirt track.

He couldn't get Paul and Evan's warning out of his head about their firebrand sister. Yet Toni had rolled over about coming out to the western paddocks without so much as a hiccup. Barely a protest especially once he'd withdrawn the overnight thing.

That had just slipped out. Wasn't something he'd put a lot of thought into. Overnight seemed sensible, logical. But she sure hauled him up on it.

Then she just seemed to make a turn-about-face without so much as a how-yer-goin'. Maybe that meant she really didn't mind the day trip. That thought stayed with him a while. He'd be on his toes, though. There could be an ambush at any minute. A wild-eyed gorgeous woman might leap on him to—

Idiot.

He glanced across to be sure there weren't any teeth bared so far. Dared only a glance and the vehicle bucked. 'This is some of the most spectacular country I've ever seen,' he shouted over the roaring of the engine.

'It is,' she shouted in return. 'Been a long time since I've been out this way. It's drier than I thought. Glad of that extra drum of water we decided to grab, just in case.' She pointed out the window. 'See that mountain range? Beyond that is country signed back to indigenous people.'

'I know,' he yelled.

She looked startled by that, but only for a moment or two as the vehicle jumped under them. Then she directed him through the long wide valley, over the sandy desert track pot-holed with bulldust, the finest, powdery sand filling deep holes gouged by rain and heavy-duty vehicle tyres from days long gone. Days when the muster might have headed trucks over this way.

They'd been driving for almost ninety minutes since leaving the home paddocks.

'I've forgot how rickety it is on these tracks.' She laughed delightedly, gripping the handrail above the door frame.

'Rickety is not the half of it.' Callum glanced across at her again. All things were bouncing abundantly. He looked back to the track because low down, his gut tightened.

The constant thwack-thwack of wheels and the jangling of his bones took his mind off that. The deep corrugations and washed out tracks reminded him of days he'd since forgot. As a child, he used to be able to sleep when travelling over this sort of country.

'Wait,' she shouted. 'Do you see that hill over there, the one with the flat red wall on the left side of it?' She waved a finger to follow up.

'Yep.' He kept his hold on the jumping wheel.

'Let's head over there. Something to show you.'

'It's off the track.' He steered the vehicle into the spinifex.

'Only a kilometre or so, won't take long. We can get out and stretch our legs.'

'If I'm still in one piece when we arrive.' When he looked over, she laughed. He couldn't focus properly for all the bouncing around everything was doing. Car, boobs, balls ...

'Outback,' she yelled by way of explanation.

'What are you laughing at?' he shouted, then laughed himself, acutely aware of the bountiful boobs under her T-shirt. If he was sure he wouldn't drive up the nearest tree, he'd have stared at her chest all morning. His hands tingled as he wondered about the soft weight of her bobbing breasts nestled in his palms.

They both yelped as the vehicle bounced into a ditch and bounced out again, throwing them both around the inside of the car. Shit, need to concentrate on driving, not on bountiful boobs. 'You all right?' He struggled with the wayward steering wheel.

'I've got the oh-shit handle here, I'm fine,' she said, hanging on to the passenger grip above her door. 'I've forgot how much fun it is.'

'If you say so.' His throat rasped from yelling. 'But you're right, it's great.'

The last hundred metres or so, before Toni called a halt, took them back to a speed slower than walking pace. The vehicle tiptoed over the obstacles in its path, the clearance under the car allowing it greater agility.

'And the city slickers want to smooth out all our roads and take away the adventure. All in the name of progress, they reckon,' Toni yelled.

He raised his voice again over the bump and grind of the car as it made its way towards the hill. 'They'll never get their hands on this place if I can help it.'

The look she gave him appeared to mean that she didn't believe a word.

*

'Pull up here,' Toni said. She directed him to a reasonably stable area to park.

He switched off the ignition, slumped over the wheel. 'That was great.' He grinned broadly at her, took off his sunglasses and wiped sweat and dust from his eyes.

Her smile in return was thin. Too bad he was oblivious to it. She looked away, remembering why they were out here. It had ended so swiftly for her. Her father selling out the place to this man and his comrades. A year seemed like forever again.

Oh, don't continue to be a maudlin idiot, Toni.

'Well, what's to show me?' He slipped his shades on again, reached over the back seat and unclipped a heavy padded bag. He grabbed a well-equipped camera. As he unfolded out of the vehicle, he clapped on a hat and slung the camera strap over his shoulder.

'This way.' She climbed out and grabbed her hat. Hesitating, eyeing off the camera he held, it occurred to her it might have been a mistake to have brought him to this particular spot. He'd exploit it, she knew it. This was a precious piece of land. She shook off the wasted sentiment. It wasn't hers any longer. And even before her family had come to buy it, it belonged to a race of people who'd lived here for eons.

All she'd ever really had of it was in her heart and her soul. No one could take that away, at least.

They clambered over rocks barely covered in the dusty terrain until they reached the base of the hill she'd pointed out. It loomed large over them.

Callum stared up at it. 'Fantastic,' he whispered.

He stood beside her, his arm brushing her shoulder, but it wasn't familiarity. She knew it for what it was. Understood it because she often felt it, too—a sense of being very, very small, inconsequential in a place that generated such awe, a place to be revered. Human contact made the solitude diminish a little, and by being there, they shared the dense mass of time that had passed over millions of years.

Her arms goose-bumped despite the blazing heat. She started to climb up the rough path in front of them, picked her footing over loose pebbles, careful not to slip.

'Here,' she said. 'It's here at the base of this boulder.'

He followed her up, taking the path in a couple of long strides. 'Show me.'

Crouching at the base of the flat rock as it rose out of the hill, she pointed. 'You see?'

A heat, other than the dry desert air, thrummed over her as he leaned closer, his shoulder pressed to her back, casually, at home. His breath fanned her cheek and a sudden thrill rushed to her stomach.

He wasn't looking at the wall of rock, she was sure. It felt like his gaze was on her. Toni shuffled, pretending to get a closer look herself and he followed, which only annoyed her. 'Look.' She twisted to glare at him, and that only put her closer to his face. Her fingers tingled.

'I'm looking.' He focused on the rock behind her.

'There,' she said impatiently, twisting back to point. 'It's a petroglyph. The Old People chiselled them into the rock, long before the New People arrived.'

'What old people?' He squinted at the circles pitted deep in the red boulder.

'An ancient race of first people. No-one knows who made these pictures in the rocks. There are also some close by Alice Springs, at Ewaninga, and some at N'Dhala Gorge in the east. There's probably heaps of them, but they're the accessible ones.'

'I know both those areas.' He took a closer look. 'I knew these were here somewhere, but I never dreamed… Two Bob says—' He stopped. Then, 'There are more around here, aren't there?'

He pushed the sunnies to the top of his head. The camera came up to his eye, and he snapped off a dozen shots. When he looked back at her for confirmation, his grey eyes were intense, startling.

She faltered. 'Well, yes and no. We know there are some are old paintings, a kangaroo, a hand in silhouette. They're not as old as this. There's probably lots of sites we don't know about.' Damn. She'd led him to the very thing she probably should have kept him away from. 'What was that about Two Bob?'

He concentrated on the pictures in front of him. 'You don't know what you've got, just in this place, alone.'

'Oh yes, we do,' she said, decisively, making sure he understood that.

He snapped several more shots of the petroglyphs, moving the camera to catch different angles. 'Show me the others. This isn't so far out that we couldn't make it a day trip for tourists. Good selling point.' He turned and began the climb down the path. 'Come on, back to the vehicle.'

Toni struggled to keep abreast of him as he strode to the base of the hill and over the rough terrain. 'I had no idea you were interested in this sort of thing, for tourists.' She climbed in the car, buckled up and picked grass seeds out of her socks. 'The terrain isn't too good. It's fragile, would need studies by wildlife experts, botanists, geologists … Inclusion on Sacred Sites register, perhaps.'

He seemed to mull over that. 'Should already have been done.'

'You have to know that they're here, first.'

'Now, we do. 'He then turned the ignition and the big vehicle roared into life. 'Which way?' He turned the car back towards the track.

'Same direction,' she said, over the din of the wheels on the huge corrugations. They were finally back on the original two-wheel track.

Tourists. Selling point? Did this sudden interest in ancient art have something to do with the plans for redeveloping the area? She thought better of taking him to another prolific area with more petroglyphs and faded paintings. Instead, she would head him east, and pretend to search for something she would, suddenly, have great difficulty finding. Even if he did own the place, he still wasn't privy to her land's ancient secrets. Not yet, anyway. A man had to earn his way around here, that was one thing she'd learned the hard way.

'Of course,' she yelled over the racket made by the wheels on corrugated ruts, 'these sights are sacred and while they're on our property, they are protected, registered or not. Really, no-one knows they're here, not even indigenous people. If you want to develop, you have to declare the sites. It's a minefield of red tape.'

He glanced at her and shouted back, 'I know that. But Two Bob knows they're here for sure.' His face was inscrutable.

Yes, Two Bob would. He and her father had roamed every inch of this place in their day. Her glance narrowed on him. His jaw was set as he concentrated on the rough track, the fun and laughter seemed to have gone.

He drove cleverly. She watched as he dodged ditches, rode the camber of the track, swung around bulldust holes and tore over corrugations. The muscles worked in his arms and in his jaw. His features set in grim determination as he fought the bucking vehicle. As he concentrated, his wide mouth, usually generous and laughing, was a firm line. Good looking? There was something about him. *Something*.

Yeah, like Something pressing all your buttons. Those old buttons you thought were all rusty. Like Something about getting up close, needing the— Stop. So much for never going there again.

Vexed. That what she was. Vexed. A person did not want to go near a man again and yet here she was thinking only of getting up close and wondering what that would feel like. See? *See?* Hopeless.

Large, strong hands gripped the wheel. Corded muscles worked in his arms. Oh, no. Tingles again. And she was the one worried about him touching her. It was all she could do to keep from throwing herself bodily across the car. She laughed at the thought of it. At this speed, and the incessant bouncing of the vehicle, she'd end up flying out his window and landing in the spinifex fully five minutes gone before he even realised.

The vehicle plunged further along the difficult track, his resolve keeping it on whatever path he could make out.

'What are you laughing at? This is the roughest track I have ever driven on,' he yelled across to her. 'You want to take over?'

'I've been on worse heaps of times,' she yelled back, dismissively.

He threw her a look. 'So, where's this other place?'

'I'll have to get my bearings.'

When the vehicle ground to a halt, taking one or two last bounces before the wheels came to rest, he leaned over the steering wheel. 'Feel like I've worked out at the gym for an hour.'

She opened the door and slid out. 'Now let's see. Just which direction is it?' Hands on hips, hat jammed on, she swivelled slowly.

He climbed out of the car after her and stood near the bonnet. 'I'm not on a wild goose chase, am I?'

She looked over the vehicle at him. His denim shirt was open to the waist, the old faded singlet underneath smudged with red dirt.

He dusted himself off and straightened up. 'Have you suddenly lost your memory or have you decided that these other sites are too good to show the likes of me?' That same muscle rippled high under his singlet.

A laugh in her voice, she said, 'Of course not.' She stood taller. 'It has been a long time since I was out here, maybe three, maybe four years.'

'Country wouldn't have changed much in forty thousand years, much less just four. Haven't got time for games.' He stood, hands deep in his pockets and looked around.

'It's not games,' she retaliated and felt a band of steel snap across her chest. 'Maybe my poor old memory is just rusty. So, bugger it, let's say I plain don't remember. We can go back to the station now and you can go on to Alice.' She turned on her heels and stalked towards the passenger door. 'Maybe Two Bob can help you find more of these sites some other time.'

'I'm sure he can, but that will have to be after settlement.' He shortened the space between them in a couple of strides. 'We had a deal. You show me what I want to see.'

'A deal,' she scoffed. 'You didn't even know these were here. The deal did not involve exploiting precious sites, nor my generosity.'

'Generosity? Is that what you call it?' Striding alongside her, he said, 'You've implied that there are a number of these sites on this property and that they should be protected by law. It's your job to show me around. I'll get to Two Bob later. Let's make it a good start, so stop a moment.'

She stopped. His flinty stare pinned her attention as if his hands had pinned her arms. *Breathe, girl, breathe. Breathe, Toni.* She tried again, forced the steel band to loosen. 'I'll need some time to pinpoint the landmarks.' She fumbled in her pocket and withdrew a chapstick for her lips.

'Fine.' Impatient. Short.

'That was the deal. I'll show you around. But only that.' She unlidded the chapstick and stared at it, thinking hard.

'Only that?' He slipped his hand over hers, moved the moisturiser to her mouth. He made a long soft drag on her bottom lip. Locked his gaze on hers, then he dropped her hand.

Her heartbeat pounded hard behind her eyes. 'Only that.' She smacked her lips together, the balm smoothing over both.

He shook his head abruptly, sighed aloud. 'You drive a hard bargain,' he said. 'But a deal's a deal. Come on, let's keep going.'

Toni swiped over her lips again and pocketed the chapstick. She climbed into the vehicle, weary of the joust. It was the heat of the mid-morning sun that blazed down on her hatted head, wasn't it? Not the heat coming from Callum Parker. Tingles zinged and zanged over her again, light and feathery. Tingly all over, for goodness' sake, as if a fever gripped her. It wasn't a hypo, she'd had plenty to eat. She snatched off her hat—lot of good the hat did—and threw it into the back seat.

He gunned the motor. The big vehicle picked warily over the deteriorating track until there was just no more track to go on. He stopped and the engine idled.

He turned to her. 'Now where to?'

Toni looked out the window. A quandary. Why take him to the sites when he'd exploit them and ruin the area? Selling point, he'd said. Then again, could he and this new company save the sites for future generations?

'Hello?' he asked, waiting for an answer.

She couldn't look at him, but she couldn't lie to him either. 'Truthfully, right now nothing looks familiar to me. I seem to recall turning off the main track again, but just where is beyond me at the moment.' Lifting her shoulders a little, she studied her hands, knowing that the truth now sounded as lame as her evasions.

He hammered the steering wheel. 'I'm willing to protect it. But only if you help me.'

She sniffed and looked into the distance, forward and behind. 'We've come too far, I think. Perhaps the turn-off is back there about two hundred metres.' She tilted her head in the direction.

'Shit. Great.' He turned the vehicle around, and it bumped and thudded over sand and potholes. She pressed into the seat and gripped her seatbelt as they began to bounce over the terrain once again.

Damn. Now she was stuck out here, in the middle of the desert, miles from home, with him. A not-too-happy him. She'd be a captive audience as he'd talk about how he was going to make this station work again, how capable they all were, how clever are his new plans for the place, how good it all would be out here.

Didn't she want that? For it to be good again? Yes, but only if she owned it—

Oh Dad, why did you ever put me in this position?

Her face scrunched. Emotion bubbled, tightened her throat, threatened to dim her vision and spill on to her cheeks.

'If they're as great as you say,' he shouted over the din, 'it could be big for us. Really big.'

Toni fixed her gaze on the wide-open spaces outside. Couldn't stop the overflow of tears, dammit.

'Toni?' He leaned forward, hanging over the steering wheel, and tried to catch her eye.

Silently, fiercely, she berated the upwelling in her eyes that wouldn't stop. She knew he saw tears trickle down her face. Bet there was even dust rolling down with them. A big, fat blob of good old central Australian pulverized red dirt.

Callum looked at the track, and back to her again, swore softly. He snapped gear shift into neutral, kept his foot off the brake and the big four-wheel drive to bounced to a power-less halt.

'Hey, hey, hey,' he said, his voice full of concern. He reached across and gently thumbed the tear away, wiped it on his shirt, leaving a smudge of red. 'What's all this?'

Toni shook her head, squeezed her mouth shut and hoped another tear wouldn't roll. How awful—her face was screwed up, her mouth set in a horrible pucker. Her eyes swam with more tears that spilled despite her efforts.

Callum sat back for a second, grabbed his camera. 'Come on, out you get.' He jumped out of the vehicle and strode around to her side of the car. Pulling the door open, he beckoned. 'Let's go for a walk.'

The concern on his face would break her heart if she thought for one minute it was for real. But her anger had evaporated. Instead, her heart was a big mushy lump pumping squishily against her ribcage. She wanted to bawl.

Waving his hand aside, she climbed out of the car. 'Sorry,' she croaked, and reached over the back for her hat. The last thing she had wanted to do was burst into tears and full-on bawl anywhere near Callum Parker.

'Which way?' He scanned the countryside, one hand shading his eyes from the sun, the other clutching his camera.

She shoved her hat on her head and pointed. 'Over there.'

They trudged over the sand dotted with low spinifex and leafless mulga. Toni cleared her head and kept the vehicle in sight. Calculating how far they'd walked, she said, 'In a few metres, we should come to a creek bed.'

'No way.' Callum squinted ahead of him. 'There's no creek anywhere near here.'

He nearly bumped into her as she stopped suddenly. 'Yep,' she said sniffing, and pointed just past their feet. 'There it is. My sense of direction is not so bad after all.' A wobbly smile creased her face.

He stared below at a deep cutting in the ground, perhaps as much as four metres wide. 'Christ. I nearly didn't believe you. Would've fallen in.'

She nearly didn't believe she'd shown him. There were other places, but they would wait.

They picked their way down, crabbing sideways, careful not to slip. The rock face ran deep, but the waterway petered out, as if over time the rush of flood waters had broken down the soft sand and carried it away, leaving only the granite-hard material of the gallery itself.

'The air's cooler here.' Callum's voice was hushed as he stood in the creek bed. 'Uncanny.'

'There it is.' She pointed at a wall of rock behind his head. He looked around and examined the wall about ten metres long. There were the ancient carvings of one era and the faded paintings of a latter era standing silent testimony to the timelessness of the art.

He whistled low in appreciation. 'This is the best.' He glanced at her. 'I mean it, this is great.' He brought the camera up to his eye again and snapped away, walking the length of the wall.

She caught up with him. 'Do you notice you can't hear anything in here?' she whispered. 'It's like we've stepped into a void or something. Nothing. No flies, no wind, no call of birds.' There was nothing. Except breathing. Hers.

Except him.

In this silent place, she thought she could hear his heart beating. It was her own, of course, once again. *You stupid woman.* Another part of her wondered what he would feel like if she reached up and touched ...

Callum shifted his gaze from the ancient art and glanced down at her. Caught her hand, squeezed it gently then gazed back at the silent vista. 'It's humbling.' He held her hand.

You can't do this, Toni.

'I feel like I'm in some kind of holy place, again,' he continued, his voice hushed. Staring around him, her hand held lightly in his, the rough rasp of those freshened calluses was warm on her skin. Then he looked at her, his eyes dark, his gaze on hers, on her mouth, and his fingers curled around hers.

Toni loosened her hand from his grip and pressed her hat more firmly to her head. 'Noon day sun. Can send you bonkers.'

'What?'

'Let's get back to the car. I'm famished.' She clambered back up the wall of the creek bed. Her head felt funny.

He followed on her heels. 'What is it, what's the hurry? It was surreal back there.'

'That's a problem. It's too hot out, now. We need water. I'm hungry. Need to set up some shade to eat.' She tried marching away from him but he kept up.

He easily kept pace with her determined strides. 'It's not just the heat. I know that. Tell me. You can't stop any of this from moving forward.'

He was talking about the station changing hands, right? 'I know. I know that. That's not it,' she grated, whispering furiously as though in a crowded room and not in the wide-open expanse of the central Australian desert. She wanted to let out a yell. 'Damn.' She practically broke into a run for the car.

By the time she reached it, all that clomping and stomping at a jog's pace over uneven terrain made her steam up, but her sweat dried before it could cool her down. She was well used to it being so hot, it's just that he made her feel hotter.

'Then what is it?'

'I can't do anything personal. Hand holding, or anything,' she blurted. She ducked into the car to grab her water bottle. Twisting off the lid she let the contents slide down her throat. *Damn. Damn. Damn.*

Stopped dead at the car, he said, 'Well, good for you. No

misunderstandings there, then.'

Callum lifted out a fold-up table and dumped it in the shade of the vehicle. He grabbed two thick-set, complicated looking deck chairs, set them up, thumping them in the dust. Pulling two sturdy poles from the roof rack, he stove them into the ground, then pounded them in with the mallet he grabbed from under the driver's seat.

'At least we'll have some shade to contemplate lunch,' he said, and shot her a wry smile as he worked. He yanked a tarpaulin from the roof rack, dropped it to the ground and unfolded it. Attached it to the rack through the eyelets and then stretched it over to the poles.

At least some shade… She scrambled to help secure it. Toni hadn't exactly agreed to set up here. There were better spots, some waterholes to the west, and big stands of trees for cover from the sun… *Toni, just for once, don't offer an opinion.*

She pulled her bag from the car and grabbed a handful of jellybeans from her stash. She munched them down, all the while watching him settle in a chair under the shade he'd just made.

He pulled a beer from the esky and opened it with a crackle of aluminium. Froth erupted first, which he wiped off with a finger. 'Ahh, the serenity,' he said, without looking at her. Frosty bubbles glistened on what must have been an icy cold beer. He tilted it up swallowed a long draught.

She was always straight down the line—with everyone. So, it was better that she'd said it just now, clumsy as it might have been, blurted out and embarrassing, rather than later. The response would be the same as it always was. There was no need to face rejection again. Nobody would want a woman who had lost what she'd lost, who'd had her insides fried out. To tell a partner that she was unable to have children. Then get that bone-scarring blow when, later, he would tell her she wasn't what he wanted. Surprise, surprise.

And he seemed too good to be true. Which generally meant …

*

The swallow of beer was so cold it burned all the way down. Callum fought the urge to drain the can in one long draught but lost. When he finished, he looked at her standing there glaring back at him. Everything under the snug fitting t-shirt moved with every breath she took. He closed his eyes, groped in the esky for another beer.

Bloody driving me to drink.

And in that gully, in that silent, ancient corridor between the ages, if she hadn't pulled her hand away, they'd have gone there on the spot, he knew it, dust and dirt and ants and flies. Primal. Awe-filled.

He looked at her again. Those eyes, big and brown, full of mischief when they weren't clouded with whatever was bothering her. Her generous mouth would curve up seductively without her even knowing it. Beautiful.

Didn't want a personal relationship, huh? That's what she'd said, but it's not what it looked like, felt like. He'd wait. Hadn't meant to show his hand so early, so to speak, but there was something magic back there in that ancient space. He would have to wait a bit longer.

She still stared at him, then in huff sat on a jutting rock under the shade. Outlined by hugging jeans, her curves sent his pulse pounding through him. He breathed in deeply as she straightened, the push of breasts straining against the clinging top. Exhaling slowly, he closed his eyes, willed himself to get on with the job. The real job: the station, the paddocks.

He took a long slug of beer and when he looked again, she was dipping into her carry-bag. Her top gaped just enough to reveal a bra cupping a full breast.

He looked away and wondered how he'd handle the afternoon. Beer. Have another beer.

15

Toni glanced over at him. 'So, your sister and brother-in-law are your partners?'

He appeared relaxed enough, his long legs stretched out with ankles crossed, the second can of beer dangling from his hand. He looked for all the world as if he belonged here, out in the wilderness under a shady tree—well, tarp—king of his domain. And here she was, sitting, almost at his feet, on a bulbous rock, like some obedient subject of the realm. She shifted immediately to the other deck chair.

'Yep. We're our own bosses on this job,' he replied evenly. 'Other times we've taken on investors, but this time we decided to go it alone. We might need help later on, have to revisit when the time comes.'

She pushed her hat back. 'But you said you had your orders.'

'Figure of speech. I meant directions.'

'You are developers, then?' she ventured.

'We're not property developers. Well,' he said, and swallowed the rest of his beer. 'We are, I suppose, but not like you think. Not the marauding kind. The collaborative kind.'

'So, what are your plans for the place?'

He side-glanced her. 'Nothing concrete other than what I've already told you.'

She let out a breath. 'You haven't told me.'

'Think I did. About either re-stocking or revegetating. It's not a major concern right now, not an issue. We'll decide about that as soon as something comes to light.' He stood up, threw the empty can into the back of the open vehicle.

Toni looked over her shoulder at him. 'It's a concern to me.'

'Of course it is. But the place is sold to us.' Callum's blue-grey eyes were hidden behind his sunnies, but his tone was terse. 'Your father had no back-up capital to counter the mounting debt. So the instruction to Reddells was to sell. It's just a business deal.' He wiped a hand over his face, tiredly, then glanced at her again. 'And I am not the enemy.' He rolled his shoulders, stretched his arms high above his head, thrust the sunglasses onto his head.

The quiet, tetchy rebuke defeated her brewing argument. What would be the point?

Strong arms flexed. The muscles on his chest tensed and relaxed under his t-shirt. Thighs bunched in his jeans. And that face. Why was that face becoming only the most wonderful face she'd ever seen?

Something in the air changed. 'I didn't want any misunderstandings.' Her gaze locked with his.

He turned away. He nodded. 'I know.'

Perhaps the less said the better. She looked off to the west, the sun lowering as the afternoon marched on.

He turned back. 'Are those the only sites in this area?'

'As far as I know,' she said after a moment. There were other places, but not anywhere near as graphic as this last one.

'Yeah right.' He reached in and grabbed another beer. Then after a moment, he tucked it back into the cold esky. 'I might take a nap.' He collapsed his chair, which made a low stretcher of sorts. He lay on it, his feet hanging off the end.

She had a good book in her bag but when she settled back to read it, found she couldn't concentrate. Instead, she sat back and cast her eye over her beloved desert, silent and timeless.

Red earth, patchy scrub and bare limbs of dead trees, sparse, and dotted as far as the horizon. The curve of the earth was clear in the distance, and nothing looked any different in any direction. As far as she could see around her, everything looked the same. It would be scary to anyone not used to it.

Her gaze back on him, she watched as he straightened out, placed his hat over his face muttering something about being challenged.

It took a few minutes to realise that he'd fallen asleep, his chest rising and falling in easy rhythm. She closed her eyes, transported by the warmth of the day. The dry heat penetrated to her bones and the shield she's been so careful to maintain shook just a little.

When she opened her eyes, she glanced across at him again. Callum Parker had marched into her life, taken over her home and yet showed her patience and compassion. If only a little. Was she so starved of it—someone being nice to her, being normal towards her? Could only that little make so much difference? Had it softened her resolve to live a solitary life?

She burned at that. Surprised at the strength of her emotions. Of feelings she had worked hard to shunt, never to revisit again. When those blue-grey eyes had settled on her, the intense gaze was the most unnerving thing to happen to her in years.

The simple touch of his hand on hers. His fingers lacing hers in the hushed, timeless gallery had colour rush to her cheeks. Suddenly she wanted his body pressed solidly against hers, protective and—wanting her.

It was a delicious thought. Bad. And good. And ridiculous. Get over yourself. Surely the desert heat had scrambled her brains.

Sonny Murphy had been that kind of guy, too, before it all became fucked up. Don't entertain thoughts of a relationship with anyone else.

The thought was sobering. She knew too well if she allowed Callum to touch her again, she'd fall for him. Just like she'd always done before—and that always turned out wrong, wrong, wrong. Now, she couldn't go there. He wouldn't want her. He'd already said he wanted kids, and he was a city-slicker, probably too used to women much more sophisticated than she was.

But a bloke was a bloke. Maybe he'd never be serious about her anyhow, so what did it matter? What about if she just went in for a fling—

Are you crazy?

She didn't want just a fling. She didn't want just anything. Couldn't risk it, though. Just couldn't.

Toni sighed. Her resentment was misdirected, too, and she knew it. Callum Parker hadn't pressured anyone into selling MacDonnell's Run. The utter futility of fighting, first the process of business and second, the law, weighed on her. Hadn't Justin told her she couldn't afford to fight? And she didn't want to feel hostility and resentment.

Tears threatened again, and she blinked them away. Perhaps a sleep would do her the world of good, too. It'd keep her eyes off him for a short time.

She collapsed her deck chair, rolled onto it oblivious to the heat, but not oblivious to the strong, confident man who lay not too far away.

A feather-light finger touched her brow, and a low, rumbling voice whispered in her ear. 'Come on, Toni. Time to wake up.'

She shook her head, mumbled something over a thick tongue, not wanting to come out of the deep, afternoon nap. She felt decidedly heavy and unable to move for the weight of the day on her.

'Come on,' Callum encouraged. 'Time for a late lunch.'

Toni didn't want to wake up. She wanted to lie there in the shade sipping something icy cold and nibbling on something exotic and tasty—

She opened her eyes suddenly. 'Lunch?' She sat up groggily. Her eyesight was filmy… oh my God I'm going blind—

She focused and realised he'd hung a huge fly net over the shade sail. No blowies circled her like buzzing helicopters, nor the tiny flies, the bushies, flittered anywhere nearby. Some form of heaven.

'Very late lunch,' he qualified, squatting beside her. 'So, let's have ourselves a mid-afternoon nosh-up.' He handed her a wet and cool flannel.

Gratefully, she rubbed it over her face and neck. 'Nosh-up. Right.' She laughed politely. 'Crank the lid off a tin of braised steak, with a side of baked beans in tow. Beautiful.'

'Look at this,' he chided. 'Told you I was prepared.' He flung open the back doors of the vehicle. Under two heavy blankets was another esky and a stainless-steel trunk. He flipped the lid to reveal a box fully lined and padded. Each compartment held its contents securely.

When she stood up to take a peep, she stared wide-eyed.

He'd re-set the table with a white paper cloth that had been folded, and some napkins, gleaming cutlery, and champagne bowls.

'I found these over there a bit,' he pointed off to the east, 'though they're touch and go, sadly.' He gently withdrew a small bunch of desert roses from the esky.

Flowers? He'd found a patch somewhere, and that would have been a fluke. Shouldn't have picked them, though. Something else he had to learn.

She stared. 'They usually wilt so quickly.' God, that was lame. She brushed the cool mauve petals, limp now, and watched as the beads of moisture popped out on each one.

And he smiled his dimpled smile. A blush of pleasure warmed her cheeks. Oh yes, he was working on her.

'How has all this travelled so well over the tracks?'

'Built to task,' he said. He'd set up a wine chiller, complete with ice melting fast as she peered in to check, and a bottle of something sparkly.

He re-assembled the stretchers back into chairs. 'We need the food.' Reaching into the esky he retrieved a number of bowls with lids that he set out on the table.

'Amazing.' Her taste buds tingled along with everything else.

He poured two glasses of the sparkling wine. 'To our partnership,' he toasted and downed his.

Toni hesitated before merely tilting her glass. There wasn't much she could say to answer his toast, wasn't even sure what he meant. Our partnership? Words echoed in her foggy brain. Their partnership would be short-lived, a year at most, and purely business. The tell-tale flutter in her stomach was the final straw and brought her heavily down to earth.

He set up the rest of the table, laid out pâté and wafer-thin crackers. He'd brought smoked salmon, native cranberries, plump kalamata olives and feta cheese. Everything had been secured in vacuum sealed packs, nothing had gone to mush.

Oh, boy. Without the fly net, the bushies would be all over this. A moving mass of black dots impossible to swipe away as they crawled up your nose and in your—

Her eyes narrowed over the rim of the champagne flute. 'You'd have had to plan this days ago.'

A blue-grey gaze swept over her. 'I did. I do. I plan ahead.'

'How'd you manage it?'

He tapped the side of his nose. 'I have friends.'

His frank stare sent her blood racing. She knew it wasn't the champagne—she hadn't touched a drop. She glanced at the table again. *He's out to run that steamroller right over you.* No, no, he's out to impress, she contradicted herself, and a zap of delight brought a quick little laugh to her lips.

'Glad you approve. Shall we?' He raised his glass again and chinked it to hers.

And on that note, her inner guardian knocked her hard on the head. 'Yes, let's, then we need to pack up and get going.' She took a sip and set her glass down. Scraped a cracker with the pâté and popped it into her mouth as if she'd said nothing out of the ordinary. Which she hadn't.

It hadn't phased him. 'Sure. But there's still plenty of the day left. Least it's one-degree cooler.' He grinned across at her and loaded a cracker with some salmon. 'So, they tell me you'd been away a little while. And then Philip got crook.'

Toni tucked in her chin. 'Dad took a turn for the worse so I came back.'

'From?'

'Adelaide. I have a house there.' That certainly was the case. 'Have to sell it.'

'Where in Adelaide?'

She wanted to shut down this line of conversation. 'Magill.'

'Nice spot. Handy to the city.' He reached over for another morsel. 'Bet Philip was glad to have you back.'

'I was glad to be back.' She patted a forearm over her forehead. 'Cities are not for me, even a small one like Adelaide.' She helped herself to another bite. 'Don't get me wrong, it was great, I loved it. Mostly. The cafés and restaurants, the wine, the beaches, all of that. There are just too many people. And at the same time, it can be a lonely place.'

He glanced across. 'I have to go to Sydney every so often and I can't stand the place. I fit right in but I have to get out. I know what you mean.' He took off his hat, ruffled his hair and plonked the hat on again. 'I'm going to love being out here doing this, every night of the week.'

'You can't do this sort of thing every night.' Toni shifted in the seat. Oh, how she'd love to do this, every night. As long as there was a shower at the end of each day. And a comfortable bed. And a good fridge, with wine. She was over the city life, not over any of the comforts.

'I intend to do it as many nights as possible,' he said, stretching his legs. 'Especially out here. There are not many accessible places left in the world where you can be alone in thousands of square hectares. Then again, you could do it on a yacht in the Whitsundays, or overlooking the Blue Mountains perched high on a hilltop in a little wooden cabin.' He set his empty glass on the table.

Very comfortable in his little kingdom. 'You have a yacht, and a cabin in the Blue Mountains?' She sipped while her champagne was still cold, and marvelled that it was still cold.

He nodded, spearing a fleshy olive with his fork. 'The yacht's a bottomless money-pit, so it's hired out. Keeps itself. The cabin's just for family.'

Family. Perhaps it was his wife he took to these out of the way places. *Nah. He would've said. Wouldn't he? Maybe not. And I'm not gonna ask.* The thought stabbed at her. She steeled herself. His private life was not her business. 'So now, all you need is a station in the Centre and a pristine wilderness on Kangaroo Island and you have it all.'

He raised an eyebrow. 'We already have a station in the Centre. This one. And there's a couple of cousins on Kangaroo Island, one with a vineyard, the other with a seaside property. We just visit there.'

We? And that's serious money talking there. How could anybody have that amount of money? 'Just what is it you do?'

He sat back in his chair, reefed in the esky behind him for a cold can. 'In this case, I'm an investor. Generally speaking, I am a property consultant, glorified real estate agent. I work for a fee—a spotter's fee if you like—as well as a percentage of the sale from the vendor. Usual set up. My clients are those people who have more money than they know what to do with.'

'And you advise them on which ones are good or bad buys?'

He nodded as he tugged the ring-pull. 'I only have a few clients now, I'm trying get out of the business altogether. Time to do something else, like this. I'm lucky, my sister and her husband are the ones with the big money. I have a small stake, that's all, but it's enough for me to do what I want.' He looked at her over the can of beer.

Toni took another bite of smoked salmon. 'And was my place a good buy or a bad buy?'

'We wouldn't have come this far if it hadn't been worthwhile.'

His expression was closed. Perhaps the topic of conversation was touchy for some reason. Maybe out of bounds. So, her home had been sold to rich people who 'had more money than they knew what to do with'. Parker and Co. As long as he got a good bargain.

Anger trilled through her. *Tamp them down.* She gritted her teeth. 'You didn't really answer. Was it a good buy?'

He seemed to think about it. 'We were advised …'

'Go on.'

'The banks and Reddells suggested not.' He rubbed his ear. 'They said it was a bad risk. That's why your dad would never have raised the capital to get it out of trouble.'

Tiny bristles stabbed all the way up her spine. 'A bad risk.'

'It's business. For years now, banks have been tightening their lending agreements. It's difficult to convince the banks to stay with an obvious ... Well, it's not personal, nothing to reflect on you or your family. You're all capable, I know that. It's simply the way of business. And money.'

The heat built up from her toes up. 'And you and your colleagues have enough money to step right in when somebody else's chips are down.'

'It's business,' he insisted and took a long swallow of beer. 'Your dad had long discussions with us about a number of things. And the station was for sale at a very good price regardless of what the banks—'

Thrusting out of the chair, she grated at him. 'It's my home.' She stood over the table, her heart squeezing as she tried to withhold the pent-up anger.

'I know that,' he returned calmly. 'I'm sorry you're not happy with the way it worked out. And I repeat, I am not the enemy.'

Toni sat again and put her head in her hands. Then she straightened her clothes, brushed her top down as if it had gathered more dirt. *Make more of a fool of yourself, why don't you?*

He leaned back in the chair.

'I'll clear the dishes.' She stacked the empty plates in a pile in front of her. Packed their rubbish into a bag. Paper-towelled the used dishes and put them into their box to be washed up back home. Toni lidded the food bowls and stacked them back into the esky, put a stopper in the champagne bottle and stashed it there, too.

Standing, he rested the beer on the kickboard of the vehicle and began to pack down first his chair, then hers. 'Let's pack down the shade,' he said and began to lift the fly netting away from the tarp.

When she began to clean up around the campsite, removing all traces of their being there, she just happened to grab the same piece of equipment he bent for. Then handing him some of the gear to pack away, her fingers brushed his. To put something in her bag, she was just oh-so-close to him that she couldn't help but nudge his back, or his shoulder.

It was by accident, but almost as if something was guiding her to do it. Weird. She flamed red, confused at her ambivalent behaviour. Not in control of it. Her body wanted one thing and her mind told her it didn't.

The heat of the afternoon hadn't let up. By the time the car was loaded again, her armpits were damp and her back sticky. It wouldn't last long, but more than ever that shower at home was looking good.

Leaving nothing for the ants or the dingoes, she secured the back of the car for the bumpy trip back to the station and climbed in the passenger side.

*

Toni breathed a sigh of relief when she jumped out of his vehicle to open the last gate before home.

The lingering light following sunset diminished quickly. After the last few dozen kilometres, the promise of a hot shower and clean clothes beckoned like honey to a bee. Now on the home stretch, she closed the gate and re-tied the latch into place after the car had roared through. Climbing back in the car, she glanced at him, probably for the thousandth time since they'd left the camp at six that evening. He'd been polite, a little distant.

Back at the homestead, Toni felt as if she'd been away for ages, not just a full day. Was that a subconscious shift away from it, already? Not possible, surely.

In the headlights, suddenly the home yard was in need of a tidy up. Scrubby weeds had sprung up out of the red dirt, never a big concern before. Late dusk light gave the homestead a tired look, as if for the first time, it illuminated some neglect.

No. No, no.

And something else. With no stock in the yards, no cattle or horses, her home had no purpose. It was drab, unloved. It needed a reason to exist.

She stepped out of the vehicle and stood with hands on hips. She would have a much closer look through new eyes in the morning. She checked her thoughts. It wasn't her concern anymore, and her mood dropped a little lower.

It was then she noticed another vehicle parked at the house.

'Company,' Callum remarked as he climbed out of the car. Justin West marched out of the house onto the verandah.

Under the dangling globe on the veranda throwing a wobbly glow, Justin shot a glare at Callum Parker. He said, 'Toni. I came looking for you—are you all right?'

Toni swung around, hands still on her hips. 'Of course I'm all right. What's the matter? What are you doing here?'

'You were out all day,' he said, glancing from her to Callum Parker.

She straightened. 'And you were here to know that, were you?'

'You know I come out sometimes to check on things for—for Philip.' His shirt and trousers were rumpled, and his face unshaven.

Toni snorted, and let the obvious retort hang in the air.

Callum Parker did not. 'Philip's not around anymore to look out for. So, unless you're invited, don't come out here. This is not your property, nor is it any longer your business. In any way.'

Justin's glare was still on Callum. 'You haven't got settlement yet, and you weren't supposed to come out here until later.'

Callum sighed, and Toni felt the air rumble. 'You know, Justin, I'm tired of people forgetting that these days we own the place, or very nearly.' He opened the back of the vehicle. 'You know as well as I do, settlement's just about done and dusted. Just waiting for the date. You're the one not welcome.'

'I've got a better right to be here than you.' Justin took a step closer to the edge of the veranda. 'I can prove it.'

'News to me.' Callum turned his back and reached inside for Toni's bag. He dropped it on the veranda steps.

'Prove what?' Toni asked, checking from one man to the other.

Justin ignored her. He pointed at Callum. 'I don't want you out here with Toni. You had your instructions.'

'Instructions?' Toni glared first at Callum Parker then at Justin West.

Callum glanced at her. 'He's confusing conditions with instructions.' He headed for the house, grabbed her bag as he passed her, took the steps up to the veranda and called over his shoulder, 'I need to make a phone call. I'll be inside.' He shoved open the fly-screen door.

Toni followed him up the steps, stopped and looked back at the solicitor. 'What's going on, Justin?'

He muttered something she couldn't make out, paced up and down past her for a few moments, then marched inside behind Callum Parker.

'Justin, what is going on?' she asked again and trailed him inside. She stopped dead as Justin's hand came up in front of her face for silence. They were standing in the hall outside the lounge-room.

Callum leaned casually against the wall with his back to them as he spoke into the phone.

'Yes, all nice and neat. A real push-over. Don't worry about those details, she's got no say in it now. Just bypass her, all will be done by tomorrow, I believe. So, I'll call you...? All right, all right. I'll come tomorrow. I didn't want to, but...no. Okay.' He finished the call, turned, and saw Toni. Then, brows crooked, perplexed, he asked, 'What?'

Toni knew her face paled under the dust of the day's journey. *Just bypass her, she's got no say in it now.*

'Toni?' Callum took a step towards her.

'You keep away from her,' Justin grated.

Callum stared at the solicitor. 'What have you said, West?'

Justin sputtered. 'Me?' he finally got out. 'I want to know what happened out there. With you and Toni.'

'Hardly your business, mate,' Callum said.

Toni turned to the solicitor. 'Justin.'

Callum snorted. 'I couldn't go by myself out there, could I?'

Justin looked fit to bursting. Toni stood rooted to the spot.

Callum leaned back on the wall, crossed his arms. 'It seems your boyfriend here doesn't like the idea of our being alone in the desert.'

'I'm warning you, Parker.' Rage glittered in Justin's eyes.

'About what?'

'He's not my damned boyfriend,' Tony aimed at Callum. She might as well have stood on her head. Neither of them was listening to her. Too busy chest-butting.

Justin West's frame shook, his fists by his side. 'You know what he was up to out there, Toni?'

She snapped. 'I don't want to hear any more. I want you out of my home, both of you—and it is still my home, regardless of your ownership,' she hissed, looking at Callum.

Justin glared. 'I'm not going until I tell you why he wants the place.'

'Tell her, Justin.' Callum shook his head. 'Tell her what she already knows. Settlement is unconditional now. Go ahead, tell her.'

'I'll tell her, all right.' Justin turned to her. 'He wants the place for a cattle kingdom, we all know that on the face of it. And I bet he's told you he also happens to be very interested in that crazy wildlife park idea, hasn't he?'

She flinched. 'The wildlife park?' She hadn't given Callum any information about the wildlife park. She'd deliberately kept it out of his reach.

'That Freelands rubbish you wasted all that time and money on.' Justin stalked over to a tall-boy dresser further down the hall and snatched a folder from it. 'Yes, here it is, all the scratchings and scribblings. He won't need to ask for it now that he's got it for nothing, for a roll in the hay.' He scowled at her.

'That's enough, West.' Callum pushed off the wall, stood taller.

Toni couldn't care less about Justin's baseless accusation. She focused on the file. 'Where did you get that?' She pointed and glared at the solicitor.

Justin glanced at her, dismissive. 'You left it on my desk after the codicil was read.'

She remembered. 'Give it to me.'

'All yours, here it is. It gave me enough of a headache, God only knows. Bloody foolish waste of time. We all know that. Waste of time, and money. Money you had no right to spend,' Justin carried on.

Toni reddened as she held her hand out for the folder. All she could think of was how to get him out, shut him down before he embarrassed himself, and her, any further.

Instead of handing it to her, Justin dashed the file back on top of the tall-boy. 'No one in their right mind wants a wildlife park out here on prime cattle land, especially in competition with the Desert Park—more especially now that there's likely to be another one down King's Creek way. The cost would be phenomenal, even out of their range.' Justin tipped his head in Callum's direction. 'He wants the place to run as a cattle station all right, but a luxurious place, with tourist lodges and a restaurant, a one-stop shop and some token station hands.' He glared at her. 'He's got another agenda, too. But he won't get away with that. He might've got this place for a song, *a song*, but it's not over yet.' He sucked in a breath. 'And he's pressing all your buttons to ease him and his cronies into it.'

'Watch your mouth, mate.'

Pressing buttons.

Too conflicted, Toni waved her hand in front of her face. 'I don't need to hear any more,' she cried again.

'But I do, Justin,' Callum said, as if it were a pleasant conversation. 'Let's hear all about your part in this.' He leaned back on the hallway wall again, folding his arms.

The solicitor baulked. 'I'm not letting you get away with it.' Then he squinted. 'I know the truth about blokes like you. You prey on vulnerable women and you sweet talk them into doing what you want.'

Toni felt the heat surge through her. 'What a bloody ridiculous thing to say.'

Callum's hand snaked out, grabbed Justin by the shirt front, his voice so quiet Toni barely heard his words. 'Just remember, I do know how low you really are.'

'Get your hands off me. You can't touch me.' Justin looked over Callum's shoulder at Toni, making sure she could hear him. 'This is assault. You see? You see? Maybe you wanna ask him what he does for all his other lady friends, Toni.' He stretched up on to his tippy toes. 'He doesn't hide out in the desert dust, that's for sure. Let me go, Parker,' he said, and pushed hard.

Callum released him with a contemptuous shove of his own. He turned back to Toni and met her glare. 'Don't listen to any crap that comes out of him.'

She took a step back. She'd nearly been a fool again. So glad now to have fought off those stupid urges. Maybe Justin was just looking out for her. Maybe he was a better friend to the family than she believed.

Her heart pounded. And maybe she was right from the beginning. Callum Parker was just a con man. What had he said just now on the phone?

'I'm not a push-over,' she whispered, hoarsely.

Callum looked confused. 'I know that,' he said to her then glanced over his shoulder at Justin. 'You don't know what you're talking about, West.'

'Yeah? Then what was your phone call all about just then?' Justin stepped forward and glared at Callum. 'Who were you gonna bypass, hey? Who was the one who's got no say in it? Answer me that.'

'You sound like you've got a screw loose.' Callum's glance flicked over to Toni.

Justin puffed out a dismissive laugh. 'Well, who's got no say in it?' he demanded again.

Callum Parker's brow furrowed. 'A silly bloody bank clerk who's tried to mess up a deal with a finance company, that's who.'

'Yeah right.'

'And it's no goddamned business of yours.' Callum's voice rose.

'Justin, it's best that you go,' Toni said. She scuffed her boots on the floor, her breath little staccato puffs in her throat.

'If you think for one minute—' Justin began, his finger pointed at Callum Parker.

Callum advanced. 'Get out.'

Toni followed Justin outside and watched him retreat with a stormy glance back at her. He stomped onto the verandah, down the steps, into his vehicle and disappeared, great clouds of red dust following in his wake, billowing into the darkening night.

Toni turned and stepped back into the hallway, staring at Callum. Her heartbeat was wild. 'It's best that you go, too,' she said.

'You have to trust me on this, Toni.' He tucked his buttoned-up shirt into his jeans then patted himself down.

'That's a little premature, really.' She didn't make eye contact.

He pushed hands through his hair, pinched his nose, nodded. 'Maybe you're right.' He strode past her, seemed careful not to touch her. On the veranda, he turned back. 'That phone call was about a deal in Adelaide I have to attend now. Damage control.' He looked at his hands. 'I'll try and catch the red-eye tonight, if not, a flight first thing tomorrow. Either way, I'll be back in Alice on the weekend. Do me a favour? Don't listen to anything Justin West has to say from now on. Not a thing.' He waited a beat. 'He's not a friend of yours, Toni.'

Her chin came up but she remained silent, even when he turned and headed down the steps, across to his vehicle. She watched as he drove away into the night.

Justin better be driving like the wind because the devil was on his tail.

*

Callum had no interest overtaking the bastard on an outback track in the dead of night. Once he'd turned onto the main bitumen highway, he'd think about it. But cattle roamed this country devoid of fences. Justin West wasn't worth barrelling into a six hundred kilo Hereford and getting himself killed.

He sat well back behind the rolling dust clouds West left in his wake. Each time the air became a little thick with it, Callum slowed up. At one point, he wondered if Justin was deliberately slowing down. He sure as hell wasn't trusting him. Worse than a snake in the grass. A loose cannon. Definite screw loose.

His thoughts turned back to his night in the scrub with Two Bob. Was that the other thing West was banging on about, the deal with Two Bob?

Callum liked the man. Two Bob had a no-nonsense attitude. A successful meeting, sitting around the campfire, feet off the ground and watching the scorpions scamper around them. Just the two men talking over new plans, new arrangements.

Two Bob had taken his turn to speak. 'We came to live near the family when old man Bill Dodson had the place. There was more of us then, but my people moved off, towards town. Me and Lorraine stayed on. We liked the new missus. The kids. Our kids played with their kids.'

Callum nodded. Lots of indigenous kids had been on stations when he was a kid. It was only recently he realised they'd have been the traditional owners. 'Where are your kids, now?'

'Charlie's in Adelaide city, at uni. Animal doctor. Nyree, she's in Alice at the hospital, nurse's aide. Saving to go to uni.'

'They might want to come back here if we get this project up and running.'

'Maybe. Maybe Charlie if you get up the wildlife park. Maybe not Nyree.'

Callum had plucked a twig from the ground underfoot. 'You know that Philip wanted you to have your land, Two Bob.' Callum had already checked that Two Bob was all right speaking about Philip.

'Good fella, that one. We got our land back.'

Callum nodded. 'If you're happy we work together, we can bring some employment here, get some family members back.'

Two Bob reached over and pushed another long dry branch onto the fire. He'd watched as scorpions with their overhanging barbs had scurried about or burrowed into the soft dirt. 'Maybe. Country call 'em back, maybe.'

'Lorraine would be happy.'

Two Bob had laughed, his whole body moving. 'Lorraine would be happy. All that cookin'.' Then he'd set his mouth in a line, slapped his hands on his lean thighs. 'That Justin West. He's a crazy one.'

Callum had been surprised. How would Two Bob know about West? 'I agree. What's he done that you reckon he's crazy?'

In the roaring glow of the fire, Two Bob had lifted his shoulders. 'He was sniffing around old Philip when I heard him say something about being my brother. Some DNA thingamajig. I had to put me spit on a stick for him.'

Callum had frozen. Justin West investigating DNA? 'Is Justin your brother?'

The lift of shoulders again. 'Reckons my father is his father.'

Callum hadn't stared at Two Bob, but he'd wanted to. Stared at the fire instead. He asked, 'You think that's true?' Shit, if so, West could prove a bigger problem than they already suspected. Flames danced under his gaze as he waited for Two Bob's response.

'My old man was white. Bit of a terror. Could be he's that Justin West's old man, too. I dunno. But I don't reckon there's much family resemblance.' Two Bob grinned. He had browny-black skin and Justin West had pasty white skin. There were no other matching traits, no physical resemblance at all. None. It could be true, though. Same father, different mothers.

Jesus, but they didn't need that. No wonder West was touchy—if it was true. And if it was true, he could make a claim against MacDonnell's Run, especially if it came to light that Philip had deeded back a portion of the place to Two Bob.

And Justin West was well aware of it, sure as anything.

When Callum had looked across the fire, he knew that his friend knew it as well. Two Bob said, 'I know it could make trouble for the deal.'

Callum threw a handful of twigs onto the flames. 'Well, old mate, we better hope this DNA test comes to nothing.' They were both aware it would only prove blood relations, not whether one had indigenous forebears.

Two Bob had agreed with a dip of his chin. 'We better hope that DNA gone in the wind.' He lifted a handful of dirt and let it drift through his fingers. 'I've been out here all my life with my people. Justin West is not part of country, here.'

Now speeding down the station driveway and back on to the main road, Callum thumped the steering wheel.

Fucking hell—why hadn't the police caught up with Justin by

now? He hadn't been able to explain anything to Toni. He'd been warned that if he mentioned anything to anybody, he could compromise the case the prosecutor was building against the crooked solicitor. Callum could see the mistrust in her eyes when she looked at him and it clawed at him. That she looked at Justin West with equal mistrust was no comfort.

West had to go to prison for what he attempted to do to the MacDonnell family. Callum was powerless to protect Toni from the machinations of the law. He had to keep out of it.

Old Philip had discovered Justin's duplicity, but was too incapacitated to strike on his own. He'd called in the police, just at the same time Callum, his sister and her husband had registered an interest in the station. Philip welcomed their timely proposition. Callum's father, Alan, had been a mate from the old days in Alice.

Philip MacDonnell had saved Alan Parker's life out bush years ago after a bull fell on his leg. Callum had agreed to the clause in the sale of the station, employing Toni, in part to honour the old good turn.

Now, she didn't trust him. Ironic. Trust was 'a little premature', she'd said.

He glanced at the folder on the passenger seat beside him. So what if he'd pinched it. He'd taken the file, tucked it under his shirt and buttoned it up. Her wildlife park projections. He knew there was no way she'd let him see the work she'd done, but it was his only key to her. He had to get to Adelaide and his solicitor. Had to get the plans of the park scrutinised by professionals. Had to place a partnership contract as quickly as possible. Tomorrow. At the latest, the next day. It was in their plans to have a wildlife park, and if the model were Toni's, she wouldn't be able to resist if he came up with the right deal. If he made her his partner, a full share in his third of the company, she would have some ownership again. He knew it'd be something he could give back to her. A piece of her home. It was the key to her, he knew it.

Hands tightened on the steering wheel as he shook his head.

Why would he do that? Maybe he was soft in the head, had a few screws loose, himself.

She was nothing to him. Bullshit. He couldn't walk away and never think about her again. He couldn't work alongside her and not feel his blood heat up, his fingers itch to reach across and touch her. He couldn't let a day go by and not want to be by her side. But sometimes, the way she looked at him when she got mad …

He didn't need the whole place for himself. He'd talk to his sister and brother-in-law. Surely, they couldn't object. It would only be a part of his share, not a majority, by any stretch. If the park idea took off, they'd all benefit. Especially if Toni's plans were as good as any he could commission elsewhere.

He'd have kept his promise to Philip. The same promise made to Two Bob and Lorraine. To deed back land—which was rightfully theirs anyway. And to give Toni MacDonnell access to her own family home. He needed to. Because he was doing what he wanted—the right thing. It was one way he hoped he'd be able to have Toni in his life. At least to let her know how he felt, how he hoped they'd get to know each other, and work towards something more solid. Built on that trust she found to be premature.

Clouds of dust ahead thinned out again and he sped up a little.

All his money. All he had, had come from hard work. Hard back-breaking work. Either long hours at the desk, day and night or the physical toil on the building sites, or both. All of it culminated in this one project. This one deal that meant so much to so many people, to him in particular. Something to pay back the man who'd stuck by his dad when the chips were down. When the chips were cinders under his family's feet.

Now that the man was gone, it didn't lessen the need to fulfil the project he'd begun, and thankfully, his sister, Marnie and her husband, Bill were partnering him. Marnie's stake was as big as Callum's, and for the same reason. The Parker family owed the MacDonnell family.

With Callum's busted marriage behind him, the cost of long hours building his wealth—and half that gone in the divorce pay-out—he wasn't in the mood to let anything get in his way again.

Justin West could unravel everything Callum had striven for. The man was a weasel, and wasn't the only one in the mix, of that he was sure.

He thought more about what Two Bob had said about DNA. Thought about how the hell that could rise up and bite them all on the arse. Not possible. He thudded the steering wheel with the heel of his hand. If Justin West was to be caught, red-handed, no compromise, Callum couldn't say anything to Toni. Not a thing.

16

Evan rubbed a hand through his hat flattened hair and looked at Paul. 'What I don't understand is, why there's hardly anything left?' He tapped the bottom line of figures on the last page of the property settlement advice.

They'd made themselves at home in Toni's town house and had stashed a dozen beers in her fridge. A beer each in hand, two huge T-bones sizzling on the barbecue outside, a mound of spuds and onions nice and cooked—job done.

Paul rested his elbows on the kitchen bench, hands around his stubby of beer. 'Good question. Out of a ten-mil sale price, I'd have thought there'd be a little more left than a coupla hundred grand each.' His dark brows creased.

'A lot more. Twice as much again by my reckoning at least, after debts paid and fees and all that shit. There's a bloody lot of cash gone in paying bills before, though. The accountant's report shows all the expenditure, doesn't it?'

Paul took a long swig of ale. 'We all saw it. We all ok'd it. The old man must have spent more on sorting things than we thought. There'll be a bit more still to come from this last lot of cattle sold. That's all ours.'

Evan grabbed up his beer and took a swallow. 'Not like I'm blaming the old man. I just thought there was more to it than just this.' He flicked his hand over the stack of paperwork. It seemed like it went on and on.

'Had its fair share of debt, but still, something to mull over.'

Paul sniffed the air. 'Make mine medium.'

'Should be ready, then.' Evan wandered outside via the sliding screen door and shut it behind him. 'You know that Toni wants to meet with the accountants,' he said, through the door.

'Yep.' Paul said. 'Told me that when we left Justin West's office.'

'She was still mad as, then.'

'Don't blame her in a sense,' Paul said. 'More I look at it, something isn't right.' He walked to the screen door. 'Should've looked harder before now.'

Evan loaded the steaks onto a plate, grabbed the bowl of cooked potato and onion and brought them inside. 'Guess we left it up to Dad and Justin to sort.'

'I didn't see anything wrong with that at the time.' Paul followed him back to the kitchen bench. 'Not too late to ask questions, though.'

Evan slapped a steak onto a plate each, then piled on the barbecued vegetables. 'You don't think this new mob has something dodgy going on?'

Paul shook his head. 'Not them. But there's something I can't put my finger on. Maybe Toni's right. We should follow up with Mackie's, see if they can shed some light on it. Accountants can drill deeper into the figures, and they have most of the older paperwork.'

'Do we know what we're even looking for?' Evan sat on a stool at the bench, pushed Paul's plate across to him. He picked up the salt and pepper shakers and shook vigorously.

Paul pointed the neck of his beer at his brother. 'Yeah. A helluva lot of our money that seems to be missing.'

17

The dogs had bounded happily around Toni once Two Bob had brought them home in the back of his ute. They clambered up onto the verandah for dinner with her.

Dusky light spread a pink and gold haze over the kitchen bench. Throwing together another stir-fry dinner, she recalled the last few moments of conversation with Callum Parker and that idiot Justin West. She cringed, embarrassed for him. For both of them.

What the hell was Justin thinking? He almost seemed to be frothing at the mouth. Mortifying splutters of what Callum Parker might or might not have been doing… were they the words of a jealous lover?

Yuk. Toni pulled a face as she scraped freshly chopped vegies into the pan with a few diced bits of the beef Lorraine had defrosted. Hardly felt like eating, but she knew she had to.

And Callum Parker, so upbeat for most of the day, so friendly—and nice, then so terse and dismissive. Until the last moments when he told her he had to go to Adelaide to salvage some deal. His tone had softened considerably then. She hadn't even said goodbye. Neither had he.

Thank God, she still had her dignity. Hadn't fallen prey to any of it—not to Justin West's nutty accusations, nor Callum Parker's temptations.

Temptations. What a laugh. And heartily glad the wildlife park was still the ace up her sleeve, still the one thing she might be able to grow out of this mess with the sale of the property. The file was all she had now, and it was—

Where? Where was the file?

Frowning, she stared out the window into the darkening evening. Justin had it, had waved it at her. Then he'd dumped it on the tallboy in the hall. Rushing into the hall, she stared at the bare cupboard. Pulled open a drawer. Closed it. Tugged the heavy piece of furniture away from the wall to check if the file had slid to floor beneath it.

Not there.

She spun around. Nothing. She raced to the front door, flung it open, and charged out onto the veranda, checking the length of it. *Nothing.*

Memory of Justin storming out, but empty handed. And turning back to see Callum Parker getting ready to depart. Alone in the hallway, right by the tallboy. What had he been doing? Buttoning up his shirt.

Mind numb, she stood back in the hallway. Sure, sure, yes, she had a digital file, but hadn't scanned in all the jottings, all the notes she'd handwritten on the hard copy. All of the other ideas that had come after the original concept had gone to a draftsman.

Justin West had brought it with him to fling it at her. He wouldn't have taken it back with him. Made no sense.

So, if it wasn't here at the house, Callum Parker must have it. But why take it? She was professional enough to eventually talk to him about it. She just wasn't exactly ready right now. Is that why he took it—if he did? Like a thief in the night because she wasn't forthcoming? Was he a thief as well? Oh, ridiculous. She didn't want to think he was. Pressing her fingers to her forehead, she took a couple of deep breaths. Sure that the file wasn't in the house, she headed back to the kitchen, a throb of disappointment in her belly.

She just caught the food in the pan before it stuck, and shaking her head, realised how she'd become so caught up in web after web. Plating up, fork in hand and a glass of wine on the table, she ate without savouring her meal. Tried not to think of anything. Not the drive into the paddocks, not the argument, not the missing file. Not anything.

Weary, done with the day, she showered and climbed into bed. Through her open window, a waft of breeze barely moved the old lace curtains, and she turned on her side to catch it on her face. The last of the dusk light had faded after the generator shut off and she idly wondered if the new owners would install one of those fangly new solar powered ones. First, they'd have to install solar panels, or whatever. Big job. Big dollars job. She should investigate that. Might be something she could sink her teeth into…

Work. It's the only thing to do now, the only thing to concentrate on.

She'd square things away with Callum Parker once and for all. All of it. Clear up the wildlife park thing, go with the flow of the new business model at the station. Well, at least for a while because now, more than ever, she needed a job, and a secure one at that. Sonny Murphy and his thieving antics had made that a reality, if nothing else.

What had she been thinking—a few days' solace out here at home? Total destruction of her life was still going on around her and here she was, hiding out as if it wouldn't catch up with her. Turning on her back, she clasped hands behind her head on the pillow. *Total destruction. Hah!* A person needs to get back to Alice and do something, be proactive. Find solutions.

Yes, yes, yes. Know all that.

Her mind wandered. The bank was happy for the moment. And she'd foiled any more of Sonny's tampering with her funds. Could she charge the prick with theft? Probably not. It was a joint account. What about fraud? He had, after all forged her signature, the low, rat bastard.

Good luck with that.

Rolling onto her side again to gaze at the stars sprinkling the night sky, she thought about making a doctor's appointment.

Breath puffed out of her, then she inhaled deeply. Her heart beat jagged, but she knew having clear answers would be the only way she could go forward. First of all, she had to learn whether her health had been compromised. And not only by the chemo in the past, but by Sonny Murphy.

Then and only then would she face how to proceed, whatever the outcome.

Her chest swelled, and angry tears threatened. She beat them down. Tomorrow she'd begin the journey to find out what her future might look like. She'd make an appointment with her GP.

18

Toni found Nicky already waiting at the café with their coffees. Her friend's mop of curls and all-black attire was easy to spot in the busy eaterie.

Nicky shifted her handbag from the spare chair to the floor between her feet. 'Did you manage to get some time to yourself out there?'

Shaking her head, Toni sat opposite. 'Not much. I came back in on Wednesday afternoon.'

'Only after a couple of nights out there? I thought you might have taken a bit longer.' Nicky pushed a cup of espresso across to Toni. 'Did Mr Hunky-Pants stay again, too?'

Toni pulled a face. 'He got a phone call and had to come back to Alice. Said he had to get the late flight out.' She didn't mention the embarrassing visit by Justin West. 'I don't know if he's back in town or not.'

Nicky squinted at her. 'You okay?'

Toni shrugged. 'There's a lot to do now, things to plan.' She took a sip of coffee, savouring the burst of flavour. 'I can't afford to ditch the job,' she began and gazed into the little cup. 'I didn't tell you what Sonny did.'

Nicky groaned. 'What now?'

The story left Nicky open-mouthed, and then when she shut her mouth, speechless. The look on her face said it all.

Toni waved her concerns away. 'Too late for any of that. The sooner I'm done with the creep, the better. Only thing I can do is move forward, be positive.' Taking the coffee cup in both hands, she sipped again. 'Somehow get the Adelaide house sold and finish any association with him once and for all, before he destroys me financially.' She pushed back in her seat. 'Before I'm totally defeated.'

'You'll never be defeated in any way. And certainly not by that wanker.' Nicky's fingers drummed on the table. 'What else is the matter, Toni? I know you well enough. What is it?'

'That's all. Isn't that enough?'

Toni didn't want to mention the visit she'd just had to her GP. Nobody else's business, really, not even her best friend's. She ordered the fertility test, to be sure of that, for once. She hadn't revisited the notion of being able to conceive since she was told the first time that she probably had no viable eggs.

She was doing her best to be responsible with the chance of a new relationship. If that's what it was. It's what it felt like. But scared, and not ready, she was allowing herself time. She had told him that she didn't want anything personal. Nothing might come of how she felt, anyhow, so no use crossing bridges unnecessarily.

Doctor Pauline had been positive and agreeable, had written referral letters for a fertility clinic and specialist in Adelaide.

She also took the time to explain to Toni that she probably really didn't need a blood test after Sonny Murphy. After all, there weren't any symptoms of anything nasty, were there? Toni insisted, knowing it was the only way to tell the whole story. Results would be a little while coming in.

It was also a major tactic to put Sonny Murphy behind her, forever. No hangovers from the time with him, no ugly reminders. To find out about her health was at least a start in the right direction. She hung on to that thought.

Toni pressed her finger over the little round band-aid in the crook of her elbow. Hoping there was nothing to worry about, she put it out of her head. There was nothing she could do about the outcome, anyway. It was out of her hands.

Nicky narrowed her gaze. 'You'll tell me eventually, but I'll let you off the hook at the moment.'

'Gee, thanks.' Toni shifted in her seat. 'My most pressing concern is how much gear to take back out to the station.' A smooth and relevant change of subject. 'Most of my stuff is here in town now.'

'When are you expected out there again?'

'Officially not for three weeks, but on request, I should be out there already. There's nothing to do until the boss gets back. I've got no clue what he wants.' Toni leaned her arms on the table. 'I'll catch up with the boys and see if they know anything more.'

Two tall, lean, outback men caught Nicky's eye over Toni's shoulder. 'Speaking of the boys.'

Toni swivelled. Sure enough, Paul and Evan were striding towards their table.

'Sheesh, if I wasn't married,' Nicky murmured. 'But I wouldn't know which one to go for.'

'Yuk. Stop it. You've been saying that for years.'

Nicky tossed her a smirk. 'Thank goodness for Geoff Cooper is all I can say.'

'Me, too. Else you'd likely be either my sister-in-law, or not talking to me at all.'

As her brothers approached, Toni was aware of glances and stares at them from other women in the café. A low wolf whistle emitted from somewhere to her left. She snorted.

'Sis.' Paul ruffled Toni's hair. 'G'day, Nicky.'

Nicky grinned at both brothers. 'Just making an entrance or have you come to take her away to do some work?' She pointed at Toni.

Evan asked the occupants of a table nearby if he could grab the spare seat. After an affirmative nod, he pulled the vacant chair and sat down next to his sister. 'Yep, come to take her away. There's paperwork to trawl through.'

Toni sat back, craned her neck to look up at Paul. 'What's this all about?'

Paul bobbed down on his haunches. When he spoke, his voice was low. 'Seems there might be some holes in the expenses claimed by Reddells.'

Toni gaped. 'You found something?'

'We're not exactly sure what it is we're looking at, so we need you to check. Go over what we've found, before we take it further.' Evan spread his hands. 'You had your suspicions, so it could get interesting.'

'Oh boy,' Nicky said. 'Doesn't sound good. I'm going to go and leave you to it. I've got shopping to do before I head back out home.' She stood up.

'Sorry to mess with your coffee date,' Paul said.

'It's fine.' Nicky reached over to Toni and gave her a quick hug. 'I'll ring you. See you all later.' She grabbed her bag, waved and left the café.

Paul took Nicky's chair. 'We can have a coffee then get going. I think you're going to want to see this.'

Toni leaned over the table towards her brothers. 'So, you did find something? Then how come the sale went through without a hitch?'

Paul lifted his shoulders, mouth downturned. 'Don't know. You know all that stuff we left piled on your kitchen table? It's in there. We'll do some more sifting, but it looks like there's a couple of large invoices we don't know anything about. Some sort of consulting work done going back a year or two, up to the last few months.' A black look creased his features. 'And I mean large invoices.'

'Consulting work? What—'

'Heard of AgAnswers or Bio Soil Plus?' Evan asked her.

'No.' Toni wasn't sure she liked where this was going. It felt like everywhere she looked there was something fraudulent going on. She leaned back. 'Unless you two really want coffee here, let's just go back to the house. Too many ears in this place.'

'Sure. We can show you the invoices.'

'You told anyone else?'

Evan scraped his chair back and stood up, replaced it at the other table. 'Not until we're sure it is something funny and not just collective paranoia.'

Toni grabbed her bag and followed Paul. Evan followed her. As they left the café, the last things she heard were female voices greeting her brothers. She scoffed, and when her brothers grinned at her she waved them off and stepped outside onto the baked pavement of Todd Mall.

The aircon blasting away, overhead fans on in every room, the siblings sat at Toni's kitchen table.

Stacks of papers were on the floor, the one furthest from Toni's chair was for Legitimate invoices and payments. Another stack by Paul's chair was the Questionable stack. The clutch of papers Evan had under his elbows on the table was the Guilty stack.

'So, what do we do, now?' He rubbed the heels of his hands into his eyes then looked at her, blinking. His eyes were red-rimmed.

Paul had a glass of red in his hand and pointed it towards his brother. 'Not sure whether we see Mo Reddell first or go straight to the cops.'

Toni reached across and gripped an invoice between two fingers, reefing it out from under Evan's elbow. 'I don't think I've ever seen an invoice for a six-figure sum before.' Her stomach roiled.

'You've gone white, Tones. You okay?' Paul stood up, grabbed her jar of jellybeans from under the window at the sink. He shook a few into her outstretched hand.

'Too much to take in,' she said, her voice croaky. She munched on the lollies and hoped they would steady her ship for the moment. She stared down at the paperwork. This one invoice alone—if it was crook—would have far ranging ramifications, she was sure. 'Could Dad really have been swindled like this?'

Paul looked into his glass, his mouth twisted. 'Seems so.'

'But Justin was supposed to have—'

'Yeah. That's what it comes down to,' Evan said, squeezing his eyes shut and opening them again, as if clearing his sight. 'And Mackies, the accountants, as well. But they only work on what they're presented with.'

'Can't do anything about Mackies now until Monday. Not sure the cops can help us before then, either,' Paul said.

Evan tapped the invoice on top of the pile. 'Is this something Callum Parker and co needs to know about?'

Paul shook his head. 'Pre-dates the sale by a long way. No wonder Dad had to sell up fast.'

Toni checked the clock. 'Not too late to put a call into Mo Reddell. He might still be at the office.'

Paul sucked in a breath. 'He's out bush, on Tonkin's place, assessing an insurance job. Won't be back until late Sunday night.'

The three sat in silence for a moment. Evan pushed out of his chair. 'Sun's over the yard-arm somewhere in the world for me. I'm having a beer. Anyone else?'

'I'm fine with the red.' Paul lifted his glass a little.

Toni nodded. 'I'll have a red, too.' She poured for herself. A glass of wine might settle her nerves.

'And then later on, I'm gunna fire up the barbie.' Evan pulled open the fridge door and grabbed a bottle of Corona. He turned back with a grin. 'I asked Stacey to come over for tea.'

At least one of us is having fun, tonight, Toni thought.

19

Saturday mid-morning and Toni had been at her travel shop desk an hour. Nothing much had got done—there'd been a bit of quoting by email to do for her clients' travel arrangements. Mary-Anne had left a note saying she'd been struck down with the 'flu.

She'd been mulling over that when the side-door opened.

Callum Parker stepped inside. 'Hi.'

'Hi,' she replied. Her cheeks burned. So much for having practiced the what-I-say-when-I-see-him-next line for at least two hours. She put her head down to finish her mulling-over-note task, her heart thundering. At this rate, she'd have a heart attack before she was thirty.

'Lorraine said that you'd come back to town.' He stood silent for a moment. 'Thought I'd find you here. You weren't at the house.' He gently tugged the biro from her hand and set it down. 'There are a few things I want to clear up. Would you come for lunch again?'

Toni stared at the pen, caught the scent of his freshly laundered clothes. 'I'm really busy here, what with everything,' she deferred, still without looking at him. 'Mary-Anne's called in sick.' She pushed the note.

The heat around her was stifling. Perhaps the air-conditioning had broken down and she hadn't noticed until now. If he came any closer, she'd internally combust.

'Toni.' He inhaled slowly. 'We need to talk about certain ... About your working with me. I'll like to lay some cards on the table. I need to explain a few things.'

Toni pushed her chair back, looked squarely at him. 'You don't have to explain anything. It's all in the job description. Don't worry, I get it. I'll do what's required.' She stood up. 'I have to. I'll do the best I can. But you know I'm not happy about any of it. So, don't try and railroad me, or keep me in the dark. Or steal from me.'

'Steal?' A glint flickered in his grey eyes.

Toni sat down again with a thump. 'I want my file back.'

'Ah. The file.' His gaze held hers. 'A bit harsh. I didn't steal it. I borrowed it.'

'I want it back,' she said, and was heartened by her steady voice.

'All right.' He leaned close, hands thrust in his pockets. 'But hear me out?'

Pride was a huge lump stuck in her throat, so she tried swallowing. No good. She was thinking hard. Her stare dropped to the desk, to the sheets of paper stacked neatly in front of her. Smoke would soon start to curl from her ears.

'If you want to, you can still choose not to work with us. Then the wheels have to turn in another direction and the money already paid to you does have to be returned.' He sat on the edge of her desk. 'Your father—' He stopped. 'Since you don't want to have lunch, perhaps we can go over the details here. That is if you don't mind. And,' he added, 'if you are still prepared to work with us. With me, in particular.'

Her head came up. 'There's not much to talk about, is there? Nothing I can do. Paul and Evan have worked hard, they deserve to have what Dad wanted for them.'

'And you don't?'

Toni felt tears smarting her eyes. 'Dad only ever wanted me to be married off and taken care of by a husband and have a hundred babies.' She fiddled with the papers. 'He seemed to think that was all there was to it.'

'There's nothing wrong with your dad wanting that for you.' When she shot a look at him, he said, shrugging, 'Except for the bit about a hundred babies.'

She raised her hand to the insistent throb at her temple. 'He never liked the idea of my shop, or that I could run it myself.' She reached for a tissue. Blew her nose.

'Are you all right?'

'Yes.' Toni tossed the tissue into the bin and fell back in her seat. Her head was a little woozy. 'You may as well know that my brothers and I have found a few big discrepancies in some of the paperwork prior to the sale of the station. It's more than a little distracting.'

He nodded. 'I already know about it.'

Exasperated, she frowned. 'How? How do you already know?'

He cleared his throat. 'Paul told me. There was a message on my phone when I landed this morning.'

'Great.' Toni glanced around, not impressed.

Maybe her brothers had thought it was a good idea to tell him. Transparency, and all that. Wasn't that the new catchcry? Transparency for what, though? It had nothing to do with Parker Inc., as far as she could tell.

He lifted a shoulder. 'I'm happy to be aware of it. I'll have our solicitors on it to check. But I can one hundred per cent assure you that if there is a problem, it hasn't come from us.'

She nodded. She knew Parker Inc. was not involved. 'It's a lot to take in, right now, that's all. After everything else.'

'Perhaps you need a few more days off before you go out to the station again. Maybe some R&R.'

Toni knew he was keen to start the ball rolling for his own company. 'I'll be fine. I just need to get this place sorted.' She waved her hand across her messy desk and looked at him. 'And I want to know more about what's going on for the station. I know it's technically not my business any longer, but if I'm to keep working out there ...' When she was met with silence, she continued. 'And I want my file. It's my property, my project and it's private.'

Callum inclined his head. 'You want to get it off the ground? Could you access the finance you need for it?' He waited a beat. 'Leave the file with me. I've had a look at it and on first glance it seems—'

'With respect,' and she waited a beat, 'It doesn't have anything to do with you.'

'What if it's a worthy plan and can benefit the station? What if it has possibilities that we can run with? On the face of it, it does have merit.' He looked apologetic. 'I know I pinched it from the homestead, but not to steal it from you. To get it looked at by my people. I reckon if it's got a chance, it's better off with us than with you, on your own.'

She held his gaze. Conflicting emotions battered her and she felt the wind go out of her sails. 'Oh, go ahead. I can't raise any finance on my own, especially not now. We both know that. I can't fight you.'

'We don't want that, Toni. I don't want it. You would be paid for it. No need to fight—'

'Justin West was of the same opinion.'

He stood up, first thrusting a hand through his hair, then jamming both hands in his pockets again. 'Why even mention that idiot's name? Do yourself a favour. Get rid of Justin West once and for all. His performance out at the station earlier should give you a clue where his head is. He's no good, and believe me, your brothers are well aware of that.' He let a moment or two pass. 'I do want you working out there, with me. I really do. There's nothing I'd—'

She interrupted. 'Already decided. But only for my brothers' sake, like I said. Nothing else.' She wasn't doing it for Callum Parker. Or herself. Just her brothers. 'And I want to be able to run this agency just as successfully as I have been.'

Lifting a hand in the air, he gave a short shake of his head as if she'd missed something. 'I'll give you all the help you need.'

Toni needed all the help she could get. Taking it when it was offered was only smart.

'Do you think you'll need extra staff?' he asked.

Another moment fled before her decision was made. 'Possibly,' she said, and looked around her office in exasperation. 'I don't know.' She looked back at him. 'But I do know I don't want all my hard work here to go down the drain.'

'It won't go down the drain just because you're working with me for a year. I'll see to it myself. Let me promise you, it won't fail here just because you're working for me.' He stopped, dropped his tone. 'So, a deal? No arguments?'

Her head felt light, and her eyes had begun to fuzzy up. She blinked rapidly to clear them. She really must have something to eat soon. She waited a beat or two, knowing she had no other sensible option. 'All right. It's a deal. But I can't guarantee there'll be no arguments.'

He mulled that over. 'I can live with that.' Then, 'So, if I'm not to have your company over lunch, I'll see you tonight.'

'What's going on tonight?'

'Barbecue at your place, so the boys tell me.'

20

They were in the office of the house on Cromwell Drive discussing the station, before their guests were due to arrive for the barbecue. Toni slumped in her chair, fiddled with the hem of her top, a sleeveless, cerulean blue tunic overflowing pants.

'C'mon, Toni,' Evan chided. 'Be reasonable. It's just a bloody barbecue. What is it with you, anyway? Me and Paul working for Parker Inc out there is a bonus. He's going to fix up the house and sheds. You have to admit, the place is pretty run down, has been for years, and now we get the chance to do something about it.'

'It'll be all right, Tones,' Paul said. 'I reckon I'm going to enjoy working with him. He's okay. Thought you'd have figured that out, too, by now.'

Toni stared at Paul.

'Nice fella,' Evan piped up.

Toni squinted at her brothers. 'Are you two having a dig at me? When did you both meet him, apart from in Justin's office?'

Paul stood up straight and stretched, yawned. 'We've had coffee, and Ben rounded us up before Parker went out to the station for those couple of nights.'

Ben, my Loyal Friend. What is he up to? But she wasn't going to dwell on him now.

Evan waited a moment. 'Anyway, let's forget it. He's here tonight for dinner with a few others, and we're all gonna enjoy it.'

So, her brothers knew Callum Parker had stayed overnight at the station. 'He went out to Sleeper Creek with Two Bob.'

'Sure he did. And?' Evan looked at her wide-eyed.

'And nothing.' Great. The teasing had started. It'd be merciless, too, as usual. They'd give her a real sledging.

Her stomach rumbled, a reminder that she hadn't had food since the hastily eaten fruit this morning in her office. Her stomach might have felt like food, but she certainly didn't.

She followed the boys onto the verandah where the barbecue grill was heating up. It wasn't long after that she heard the first car pull up. Ben charged into the back yard with his partner, Josh, lugging an esky behind him.

'G'day, all,' he said and blew Toni a kiss. He shoved a bottle of red at her, while Josh loaded a few beers into the ice box outside, a large tin drum cut in half length-ways and filled with ice. 'Callum and his guests are just behind me, but I need a bottle opener for that,' he said, pointing at the bottle as he sailed past her to the kitchen. 'Reckon they're the other investors.'

Toni took a quick breath. Investors? Oh, my God. The bosses. She wasn't ready for this. She glanced down at herself. This blue thing—is it right?

Of course, it is.

But for all her bravado, she needed to make a good impression. Wanted to. She couldn't get back to her room quickly enough. Scrambling back into the house, she banged the bottle of red onto the bench, ran upstairs and pushed her bedroom door shut.

I'm not ready.

Toni peered into the mirror above her dressing table. Her face was perfectly made up. Her hair, falling free of pins and bands was thick and shiny and wavy and the blue outfit flattered her, even if she did think so herself. A second or two later she heard Callum's laugh from the back yard.

Toni checked her reflection once more and then satisfied but shaky, headed for the kitchen. She would carry salads outside to steady herself.

Where was her glass of wine? Where were her jellybeans?

Trying to juggle four bowls of salad, she picked up three successfully then attempted the fourth. Exasperated, she thumped all three back down on the bench and tried again. She had three balanced, just couldn't organise the fourth.

'I'll help.'

She whirled around. He was leaning on the door jamb, all six foot plus of him, solid, touchable, smiling at her.

'Oh, hi,' she said. 'Um.' Juggling two bowls of tossed on one arm and a bowl of potato salad in the other, mesmerised by those blue-grey eyes, she didn't move. 'Thanks.'

Her arms wavered under the weight of the salads.

'We'll fix this,' he said, the dimple deepening as he aimed a smile at her. 'You take two, I'll take two.' He removed both the salads. Then he stared for a moment. 'All right?'

She nodded and stared back before dropping her gaze to the bowls she was supposed to have.

'You know,' he continued, and looked about for a cleared space to put down the salads but didn't. 'Maybe you and I need to have a proper chat about another subject.'

'Another proper chat?' She grabbed her potato salad and the other one, whatever it was. He was looking at her steadily. Her heartbeat sped up, her pulse bumping ribs and things.

'That's what lunch would have been about today. Not so much about the station, truth to tell.' He licked his lips. 'About you and me.' His Adam's apple bobbed. The smile was still in place, but he looked a bit tentative, unsure of himself, maybe.

It didn't matter what she'd thought earlier, she wanted him. Against her better judgement. Despite any test results. She wanted him pressed against her thighs, the hard ridge of him pushed snug and urgent against her belly. She wanted to make love to him, now, up on the table in the kitchen, with her pants down around her ankles and her legs—

No, no, no. Jeez, get a grip.

'So, I'd really like to talk later.' He dipped his head, and despite four bowls of salad between them, kissed her firmly on the mouth.

He broke away, lifted his eyebrows. 'Bit personal, I know. Couldn't help it. Unprofessional, of course.' He smiled as if that didn't matter a damn. 'See you outside.' And with his two bowls of salad, left the kitchen.

She nodded as he left, not caring, not thinking of work, either. Her lips tingled. Her chin was scratchy where the stubble of his beard had rubbed. She looked down at her two bowls of salad.

'Man, what happened to you?' Ben caught her at the door. 'Gawd. Your lippy's all over the place, kiddo.' His eyes narrowed. 'And I bet Callum's got cherry red all over him too, hasn't he?'

Toni shoved the salads at him and ran for her bedroom again. She glared at her reflection over the bedside dresser. 'You're letting him distract you, and it will be so wrong,' she hissed aloud, wiping away the smudged lipstick with a tissue.

For God's sake, she going to have to put a stop to this. And what the hell possessed him to—? Straighten up, idiot. It doesn't have to go any further, not if you don't want it to. Shut it down. *What am I, all of a sudden—weak?*

This was just plain wussy. This was so not her. She would to stick with her decision. See it through no matter what happens next. She wasn't a child. Whatever he meant by kissing her couldn't be denied, but she had to manage it. Had to be responsible. Shut it down.

With a steadying few deep breaths, she re-applied lip-liner and lipstick as carefully as her shaking hands would allow.

Back down to the kitchen, she picked up a basket of bread rolls to take outside. She shouldn't have rushed. Her head throbbed. Should have eaten earlier. Should have drunk a gallon of water. Should have jumped off a bridge into a lot of deep water.

Well, she just wouldn't have any more alcohol. But food was the last thing she felt like.

The boys' laughter, and that of their guests reached her. The tinkle of glasses indicated a toast to something or other. Taking another deep breath, she headed for the door just as Ben popped back inside.

'Lippy's in better shape,' he whispered, shaking a finger.

'There's a reason why I ignore you, Ben Whyte,' Toni whispered back.

'You can't ignore your Loyal Friend.'

Outside, Callum Parker was talking to and laughing with the most beautiful woman Toni had ever seen. She stared, disbelieving at first, then dismayed, at the lovely woman who so obviously adored him, and who stood within the circle of his protective arm around her waist.

So, tell me again what did that kiss just mean? Clearly not what you'd begun to think, you great 'push-over'.

There he was, openly enjoying the woman's company, and in Toni's own home. She leaned on the door-jamb. How could she possibly fall for that? Did he think she was so stupid? Her lip curled.

'What's the matter?' Ben asked, following her gaze.

Not taking her eyes from Callum as he barked a belly laugh at something the woman said, she thrust the basket of bread rolls at Ben. Toni turned blindly in the doorway. *I am totally over-reacting. Totally. Of course, there'd be a woman in his life. I must have just misunderstood him, that kiss and everything.* She wobbled slowly back into the kitchen and Ben followed her.

'What is it? You look like you've seen ghost. Are you all right?'

She nodded. 'I'm fine. I'll just be a minute.' She leaned on the kitchen bench. Her head felt funny again, woozy, and her stomach was roiling.

Geez. Good thing she hadn't attacked him with those legs and arms and things a while back in the kitchen.

Ben waved the bread basket. 'Well, hurry up. You've got important guests. Come and meet Bill and—'

'I'll be a minute,' she repeated.

He peered at her. 'You need food, don't you? That's what—'

Callum poked his head into the kitchen. 'Still in here? Come on, I'd like you to meet some people,' he said. He took a couple of strides inside and grabbed one of her hands.

Attached by her hand, her treacherous, traitorous, mutinous hand, he led her outside.

'Toni.' Ben was calling from the kitchen doorway. 'Where are your jellybeans?'

How could she even be allowing this? Don't make a scene …

Politely, firmly, she pulled out of Callum's grip. He didn't seem to notice as he went to the woman's side. He placed an arm casually around her waist again.

Am I really this thick? What the hell is this?

He was talking but she hadn't heard a word. How was she to keep her poise, to prevent her voice from breaking if she had to speak? She felt sick. Vomity sick.

'Marnie, this is Toni MacDonnell, the ever-suffering sister of these two other MacDonnells,' Callum was saying, pointing to Toni's brothers.

The woman smiled warmly at Toni and held out her hand. 'Nice to meet you, Toni. Callum is full of praise for you,' she said, openly, sincerely. Studying her.

'Really?' She absently took the woman's firm handshake. Her mouth was dry, her voice trapped in a narrow airway that was slowly squeezing closed. What sort of horrible trick was this? Her eyes felt as if they were a little bit owly.

'Well, yes,' Marnie said, glancing at Callum. 'You run a small business, a large station, have single-handedly planned a major attraction for tourism in your area and have come up against him,' she said, indicating Callum beside her. 'I'm impressed. He's finding it all quite a challenge.' She poked him in the ribs.

Everyone around her laughed. Everything was so funny. Toni didn't get the joke. She just wanted to crawl back into her room. The fog was getting thicker. She barely heard a word said to her. Just an echo of that word from, oh, not-so-long ago.

Push-over.

'Would you excuse me?' she rasped. Her tongue had dried in her mouth. 'I'll be back in a minute.' She weaved a path to the verandah, stumbling as her feet missed the tiny step.

Callum caught up, gripped her arm to steady her then let her go. 'Are you all right?'

'I need to finish some paperwork in the office,' she said, her voice thin as she stepped inside and marched through the kitchen.

He kept up. 'Paperwork, now?'

She wobbled down the hallway, gathering more wobbly momentum as her temper grew. He was still right beside her. 'It isn't enough that you tried to seduce me,' she threw over her shoulder. 'You called me a push-over back at the station. Then what you said to me in the office today was, well— But the sleaze in the kitchen, just before you point out that woman... Something I should be aware of, is there? Let's keep things very professional, will we? Oh sure, we certainly need to have a proper chat, all right.'

Callum halted there and then. 'Backtrack a bit. Sleaze? I'm not following. And did you just say "seduce"? I've been breaking my neck to let you know I'm interested in you, the person, not just you, the employee.' He turned to look out the door and then back at her again. 'And I never called you a push-over—you're anything but.' He shook his head, bewildered. 'And what woman?' Then his eyes widened and he pointed outside, a thumb over his shoulder 'That woman? Remind me to tell you that you're not only stubborn, you're obviously deaf as well—which on its own is no big deal.' He shook his head again. 'I'd bloody laugh it if wouldn't be so goddamned rude. Perhaps when you finish your paperwork in the office you might take a moment to recall my introduction of that woman.' He strode outside without a backward glance.

Toni tottered into the study and shuffled some old papers stacked on the desk. She would do some work. He wasn't going to push her around.

The wooziness floated over her again. She should've had lunch, was feeling decidedly ordinary. What she wouldn't give for a Mars Bar right now.

Rubbing at the pressure in her temples, she glanced out the window, even as she told herself she didn't want to, even though she had to squint to sharpen her focus. From where she sat, she had a direct view into the back garden where everyone else chatted and laughed and was having loads of lovely fun.

She couldn't resist sneaking a look, staring at the new people at the barbecue. She watched Marnie as she talked with the others. She was exquisite. Tall, shapely, her figure full, her outfit screaming money and class. Her perfectly made up face was faultless. Just the sort of person she knew would suit Callum.

He moved up beside her. Bent and said something. The woman, disbelief on her features, answered him. A lock of his hair fell across dark eyes. She imagined it would hide the stark glint of steel.

Toni cringed. Oh, God. *I bet he's just said something to her about me. They'll probably go home laughing their heads off at me.*

Screwing up her face to staunch the flow of tears of frustration, she shook her head. What hope did she have after all? Just plain silly to think that all his fine words actually meant anything. Even if she did believe him, what could he possibly want from her when he had this woman at his fingertips? Her poise and elegance made Toni feel like she was some outback extra. Why would he be interested in a dopey hick from the bush?

And why make such a big deal, Toni? He wants kids. You heard him. That means you're out. She fumbled about for a chair behind her and sat with a thud.

And what did he mean—his introduction of that woman?

Ben skidded into the study. 'What are you doing?' His blond spiky hair was oh-so-metro tonight. 'Callum Parker's just cut a swathe through the night air this thick,' he said, demonstrating with his arms flung apart.

'I didn't realise he had a bloody girlfriend,' Toni grated him at him. 'Why didn't you say so, Loyal Friend? I've just made a fool of myself and—'

Ben tut-tutted. 'I already know you're a fool. Spare me the details.' He poked a long, elegant forefinger at her. 'Do you think I'd let anyone do that to you, again? No. I. Wouldn't. She's his sister, you great dill. Marnie and her husband, Bill—that bloke talking to Paul over there in case you hadn't noticed—are the other major partners in his company, the partners in his corporation. They're the bosses. Are you bonkers? They're the ones with buckets of cash.' He threw his hands in the air again. 'You're employed by her and him, and him.' Ben stabbed the air with his finger as he pointed to each of the partners.

Breath whooshed out of her. 'Oh, no,' she cried and clutched Ben's sleeve. 'His sister, and her husband? I don't believe it.' Pushing up out of her chair, she leaned unsteadily against the desk, blotting her forehead with the back of her hand.

'Now, now. You're panicking me. You've had a big couple of days from what I hear. Let's just take it easy and calm down. Gather yourself together, kiddo. What's all this about?'

'I'm so stupid, Ben.' Thoughts crowded her foggy brain. Her tongue felt thick, and emotion had started to ache in her throat. 'All this is making me sound so stupid.'

'I already know that. Callum's just figuring it out,' he said, no sympathy, but not unkindly. 'Come on, out we go.' He took her by the elbow. 'We'll get you something to eat. That's it, isn't it? You haven't had food. Come on, you can't hide in here now. Where are your jellybeans?'

'I can't do it.'

'You don't have a say in it, Missy Mac. I'm making you do it. Now, come on. You need to eat.' Ben propelled her back out on to the verandah. 'You're not going to botch up this deal by being completely off your head on a hypo.'

Toni met Callum's eyes instantly but it lasted only a moment before he turned away, a short shake of his head. She reached for a glass of water as Ben darted off to get her some food.

*

Marnie was right just now. He should be very careful about what he was doing.

So, he was careful, and he knew exactly what he was doing. Pursuing something he wanted.

She patted her brother's arm. 'I wouldn't be too worried about what she said. The way those big brown eyes of hers are following you I'd say she feels every bit for you as you do for her.'

Callum glanced across at Toni standing by the table on the verandah. His heartbeat escalated. He knew what he wanted, that was for sure.

Marnie smiled at him. 'Don't let a little feminine insecurity stop you, little brother. But like I said, be careful.' She hesitated. 'If there's anything I can do to help you out of your own pickle, let me know. I'll leave you to it, for now.' She drifted over to her husband and the others.

*

Toni didn't waste the opportunity. As Callum stood alone fixing himself a drink at the makeshift bar, she walked over to him as steadily as she could.

Her step never faltered, but it was still a bit wobbly. She'd eaten. Hadn't she? Couldn't remember. Maybe she'd caught Mary-Anne's 'flu, and it wasn't a hypo after all. When he stiffened slightly as she came close, and a tell-tale muscle flickered along his jaw, she had to take a deep breath. He lifted his eyes, the piercing glower alight in the grey shadows.

'Well?' he asked, flatly.

'There's no need to sulk,' she said, then at the astounded look on his face, she stumbled her apology quickly. 'I'm sorry. I didn't know Marnie was your sister. I misunderstood. I wasn't paying attention.' Her words jumbled over others as they came out of her dry mouth. She wasn't used to apologising to anybody.

Determined to stand and take whatever was coming, she met his gaze as straight up as she could. A moment's awkward silence and Toni knew she'd have to speak up again. She swallowed, trying to staunch the sourness in her queasy stomach. She lifted her chin, but the effect of a couple of glasses of wine earlier, gulped in a hurry and on an empty stomach, began to take its toll. 'If you're not going to say anything,' she said, 'then please shove a chair under me before I sink ungraciously to the ground.' And she grabbed hold of his arm to steady herself. She felt her colour drain. 'I think I'm going to fall over.'

'What is it?' He hastily cast about with his other hand to grab a nearby chair and pushed it under her.

'I need ...' Toni felt her centre drop away as blood rushed to her stomach. She was about to pass out. She gripped the arm of the chair and fell into the seat, head between her knees.

'What?'

'Food. I need food.'

Ben marched up with a platter of fruit, cheese and biscuits and shoved it under her nose. 'Here. Get munching.'

Beads of perspiration felt like they'd popped on her forehead and were running in rivulets. She swiped the back of her hand over her face. Damp. The rest of her felt clammy and shaky. Straightening slowly, Toni took some fruit, figs and apricots and chewed them down. Ben dropped the plate onto the table beside her.

Callum had stood back, watching Toni. 'What is it?'

'She has low blood sugar,' Ben said, shortly.

'I can speak for myself.'

Ben ignored her. 'Yeah, and that was all lispy.' He looked at Callum. 'This is a hypo, mild, but we don't want any other sort.' Topping up Callum's red wine from the bottle he had in his other hand, he eyed Toni. 'Over to you.' He walked away, a curt nod to Callum, the bottle of red waving at his partner, Josh.

Silence.

'Wait right there,' Callum said to her. He returned with a glass of water, a small plate of sliced beef and sausage from the barbecue, and a bunch of paper towel. He watched as she ate, as her colour slowly returned.

'Thanks, that's better,' she said. 'Fool that I am drinking on an empty stomach.' She patted the paper towel over her forehead. 'Sorry. That came over me too quickly.'

'You never said you have hypos. You okay now?'

'It's diet controlled, but sometimes I forget about it.'

Evan came over to check out his sister. 'You all right, Tones?'

She nodded. 'Don't think I've eaten since breakfast. Stupid me. I'll be fine in a few minutes. Wait for this to kick in.' She held up the plate of meats.

Evan looked at Callum. 'Get you anything?'

'I'll grab something in ten. I'll wait here till she's on her feet. It's fine.'

Her brother wandered back to where he'd come from. Toni saw him say something to Paul who nodded and glanced across. Then the grin split his features.

Bloody brothers.

Callum sat on his haunches by her chair. 'I sure as hell don't want to start where we left off.'

'No.'

He put a hand on hers. 'If it wasn't your party I'd suggest going for a supper at the Stockman's and then maybe a night of debauchery at my hotel.'

'Now, that's unprofessional.' She plucked another bite of sausage and wolfed it down.

'Yeah, but hopeful.' He did a Groucho Marx waggle with his eyebrows

She smiled despite herself. 'Technically, it's not my party, the boys asked you over. I should get myself together and talk to your sister and her husband.'

He squeezed her hand. 'Marnie and Bill are on the red-eye tonight and I have to take them out to the airport, so they won't be staying long anyway. After that, well, you can't tell me we haven't got something to talk about.'

After a moment, she agreed. 'We do.' The sooner it was out in the open, the better, but not here. Not tonight.

Once Toni assured him she'd lost the wobbles, he went and got himself a chair. She shared her cheeses with him as he sipped from the glass of red.

'About before, in your office,' he started.

She caught her breath. 'Can we leave it until another time? I'm really not on top of things and I want to be.'

'But we will talk about it. No arguments.'

Toni thought about the test results still to come. Thought about how she'd tackle having to tell someone something so private, without making it sound as if she had presumptions. She'd think of a script to recite, think of some way to avoid telling the truth unnecessarily, and then shun any further attempts at intimacy. 'We'll talk about it. But not later tonight. Maybe in a few days' time.' She frowned. 'And I can't guarantee no arguments.'

He nodded. 'Fine. Ready to join the party?' He stood and held out his hand.

She took it to be polite, then let it drop to brush herself down of the imaginary crumbs on her outfit.

Eleven pm and Toni's brothers were driving their own girlfriends' home. Chances are they wouldn't return tonight. Callum said goodnight to her, took Marnie and Bill out to the airport, leaving with a glance in Toni's direction.

He'd told her earlier that he'd revised the plan about her being out at the station immediately. He said he had more business with Two Bob and it would be a waste of her time to rush out there. Maybe she could be ready by the following weekend.

Calculating the days, and maybe the news she hoped to have by then, the packing and all the other things to put in place, she agreed. She would have enough time to do what she needed to do. She'd need some quiet time to get around the next direction her life might take.

Would take. She'd make it happen. Take a stand and just plain go forward.

Toni made little head way cleaning up then, but after an hour decided to leave the rest of it – it would wait until tomorrow. She switched off the outside lights and went to the bathroom, staring at her reflection as she removed her make-up.

What did he see? The same person she saw? The well-educated, self-made business person or the see-sawing emotional wreck in charge of her father's affairs?

She jumped at the sound of an approaching car, and the pit of her stomach curled in anticipation—or was it apprehension?

She really was trying to talk herself out of falling in love with him.

The car sped by. It wasn't him. She knew he wouldn't come back tonight. He hadn't been invited, she'd made that clear. Tension jagged her. Disappointment that it wouldn't be him put a spotlight on her feelings. She had it bad.

At least the night had been salvaged by laughter, friendly banter and spirited conversation between all the guests—Evan and Stacey, Paul and his new friend, Bec, Marnie and Bill, Ben and Josh—and Callum. Thankfully no one had mentioned the settlement, or the new plans or the dodgy invoices or anything that might have upset the night.

Weary, Toni reckoned her over-thinking and lack of food had simply knocked her out. She undressed, showered, and sat up on her bed, hugging her knees to her chest under the light quilt cover. At least in her private thoughts she could think all she liked about Callum Parker, about the man, not the boss. And she could think what she wanted, despite her campaign not to have a relationship with him. Or with anyone else.

Her heart thudded as if in protest, but she knew it to be true. She'd fallen for him the moment she'd seen him. And not even a week had passed.

At least it hadn't imbedded itself so deeply she couldn't cut it off, couldn't undo it.

Sure.

All this time she'd been thinking how tough she was after Sonny Murphy. How clever she was to avoid an attraction to someone else, to run a million miles from anything resembling an attraction. To save herself more angst.

Yep, to hide away and wallow in self-pity.

Whoa. That thought stuck. What the hell was she doing? All her tricks to remain immune to attraction—and this one had hit her for a six. And it wasn't letting up.

Callum felt something for her, too. She'd seen glimpses of it. Certainly in the creek bed with the spirits of ancient humanity crowding into the silent space. And then in the kitchen, a flutter of—what was it, hope, perhaps? The flutter tickled deep inside.

Only one way to proceed. Just be straight up, as usual, and lay her cards on the table. She would lay it all out for him if he wanted to be closer to her. Then she'd watch him run that million miles. At least then she'd be done with it.

Self-sabotage.

Oh, yes, because she'd seen it before—a man who looked at her as if she was half a woman. Not that Sonny Murphy was a real man. Not that his opinion was anything to be regarded.

Who was she kidding? It had cut her like a knife.

Sonny Murphy was toxic. She had to be shot of him for once and for all. The only way to do it would be to face what she'd been lumbered with all those years before. Illness wasn't her fault. It wasn't like she'd planned for it. It was her responsibility to deal with it. To own it, and not be pushed and badgered and bullied into believing she wasn't good enough.

Get on with it. Grow up. Make a stand. Face it.

Flopping back on the pillows, she groaned. She'd just have to spit it out. There was no right way to tell Callum she couldn't have kids.

21

Thankfully her puffy eyes had gone down by the time she'd climbed into her car to head north, then west for the long drive home to MacDonnell's Run. At least she could see clearly, and if she kept her sunnies on, her eyes wouldn't smart in the harsh light of mid-morning.

An hour or so later, the air was still when she got out of the car at her favourite spot. Things looked different, but the same. Same trees stood, same birds skittered past. But life would be different.

Not even thirty years old, yet. A couple of months to go. And couldn't have children.

Shove those thoughts aside. She was on to it. She was onto gleaning every last drop of modern knowledge and technology available to check her chances. That visit to Doctor Pauline had set it all in motion, including the determination to be rid of Sonny Murphy's noxious hold on her.

Someone would love her, regardless of either test's outcome. Had to believe that.

If only she wouldn't feel shunned when he turned away. As they all did. As they all had.

The heat hummed around her and the shade of the casuarina did nothing to stop the sweat popping, or the old anger to cool.

The memory of hospital visits long ago, surfaced as if it were only last month. Of lines of saline. Of needles. Of burning in her gut and windpipe. The nausea. The treatment had fried her insides—kept her alive, and fighting the good fight, but left her a shell. Young, frightened, but alive.

All her adult life she'd beaten down the anger, and the fear. Had finally thought she'd accepted her fate. Her brothers had been bystanders, as supporting as brothers, young, too, at the time, can be, but neither had known what to do about it. Her dad was heartbroken, especially as her mother had died of insidious ovarian cancer years earlier. Her mother's illness had been advanced by the time of diagnosis.

Then when she told Sonny Murphy she couldn't have kids, he'd used it to give himself a way out, taken it as a chance to turn on her.

Nicky Cooper had tried to set her straight. 'He's an opportunistic bastard, my darling friend. He couldn't care less about you not being able to have kids—he found his excuse to run, so he puts it back on you, blames you. Let's him off the hook.'

Bewildered, Toni had shaken her head. 'Why doesn't he just say so? Why put me through all this—the lies, the cheating…?'

'So that you can be the bad guy and tell him to piss off.'

'He says he doesn't want that.'

'Look at what he does, not what he says,' Nicky had pressed. 'He's saying what he thinks you want to hear.'

'All I want to hear is the truth,' Toni thundered for the twentieth time. 'He just has to say he wants out.'

'He's a coward all round. An emotional coward, too,' Nicky had muttered. 'And besides, he couldn't stand up straight if you nailed him to a tree. Which I'd enjoy doing.'

The analogy was on the mark. Sonny Murphy was a liar, and one who had a smile on his face while he delivered them, knowing you would take it. He'd duck and weave. Layer the lies so you wouldn't think to look further than the words. Then when you woke up to it, you'd smash your palms on your forehead, knowing you'd been a gullible fool again.

How many times had she let it happen before she finally said, 'no more'? It didn't matter. She had finally drawn a line, and now the mopping-up was in full swing. She would get better at beating down these demons. She had her whole life to rebuild now.

A deep inhale of hot Centralian air—careful not to suck in the flies that whispered around her nose—she climbed back into her four-wheel drive.

She had to be ready. Had to get her head in the right space to go forward. Accepting this next phase of her life would be the best thing she could do for herself, and from now on, she was going to grasp it with both hands and move forward.

No looking back. You are who you are. And you're good. You're okay.

Gunning the motor, she took one last breath of the doldrums and blew them out.

Home called, like it always did—a siren's song in the age-old land.

22

They sat in the kitchen of the MacDonnell Run station house, coffee brewing for a late morning smoko. The gurgle of the machine got louder as the water drew up through the grounds, and the sumptuous aroma of espresso wafted around them.

Tapping her fingers on the table, Toni stared at the cupboards in front of her. She eyed the plans for the new sheds, new cattle yards and a bigger bore for the house. All pinned on the old timber of the cupboard doors.

'What is it?' Callum leaned across to catch her eye.

She pulled back. 'Thinking about what you said at the barbecue, that you wanted us to clear up a few things. So, good a time as any. Fire away. Clear the air.' She hoped a small smile would look like she was inviting transparency and—whatever.

His gaze nailed her. 'I didn't mean it like that. I meant that I wanted to be honest about how I feel. So that we can go in one direction or another. Without any misunderstandings.'

Shit. She had her spiel all figured out and it didn't involve words like 'feel'. Shit.

She'd just have to tell him. Make it like general conversation. Like, oh yeah, and a medical issue when I was in my late teens and the treatment for it probably left my innards all fried off. Babies not likely, so stop using words like 'feel'.

Well, tell him. Tell him just that. Why not? Just say it. That'll fix everything.

Her voice was stuck again. Emotional coward. Nicky's words echoed in her head.

Callum rested his forearms on the table. 'I might be putting myself on the line here.' He sucked in a breath. 'There's more to it for me than just working together. I think you know that, and despite saying that you don't want something personal between us, I think there could be.'

Oh, God. Feel. Us.

Still waiting for a response, he lifted a shoulder. 'All right, if you're going to give me a negative, get on with it. I'd prefer an honest fuck-off or something.' He raised his eyebrows and the dimple appeared when he pulled a face.

She gave a glimmer of a smile, not an encouraging one. 'Not going to tell the boss to fuck off.'

Shifting in the seat and slapping his hands on his knees, he said, 'At the risk of really buggering things up,' and laughed at himself, 'I think you do feel something for me.'

There was that word again. She didn't want to 'feel' anything. Not yet. Not until it was all sorted. This was so not going to plan. She'd practiced over and over telling him that he needed to run for the hills, choose someone else.

Come on, Toni. Okay, let's start with Plan A.

He let out a breath before she said anything. 'Simple yes or no. Then we get on with it. Whatever it is.'

'You want to know if we'll sleep together.' Did she just blurt that?

A moment laid silent. A sort of dead space in the air.

Callum stared. 'That would be a part of my evil plan,' he said. 'Among other things.'

She tapped the table a few times. 'That's what you mean, though, isn't it?'

Nonplussed, he cast about for more words. 'Not only that. To get to know one another not just as employer-employee. And sleep together, yes. Eventually, or sooner. If it works out. If you want to.

Fingers crossed.'

He looked open enough but a bit bewildered gauging by the expression on his face, by the tentative smile. As if he didn't understand why she didn't get it.

He shrugged. 'I was hoping for something a little less, um, straight to the point. You know, like a hug maybe. For instance. At least.'

Straight to the point.

Rubbing his neck, he continued, 'You know, the idea where I say to you, "let's go for dinner" and you say to me, "okay, let's". And then we go, and we eat, and things. Maybe catch a movie in Alice. Or we could talk about ourselves, tell a few stories and—'

She interrupted. 'And sleep together. If we're to even think about going any further, we need to have health checks.' There. She'd said it. That was Plan A. Duly blurted. Her face flamed.

'I totally agree.' Hands held palm up, he said, 'That's easy.'

'I mean a blood test.'

He blinked at that. 'All right.' A slight frown appeared.

'And prove you've had it done, show the results.' No way was she believing someone on face value again. The flame in her face bloomed, moved down to heat her neck.

He gazed at her a moment. 'As soon as I can have it done. Why wouldn't I show you the results?' Folding his arms on the table, he leaned forward. 'You, too, right?'

'Of course. Me, too.'

He smiled, dimple-deep. 'Good. Great. That's out of the way. In the meantime, we talk some more. Eat that dinner, see that movie. Okay?'

'Maybe.'

'Get to be friends.'

'Friends. As in friendly.'

That slight wrinkle of the brow again and then a nod, and a shrug. 'Friends. Friendly. And then some, that's the idea. Besides, there's a helluva lot more here we need to be working on, so friendly would be good.'

Great. So, that part of Plan A was covered. Good. Left more time to plot an exit strategy.

Straight to the point, he said. Damn right. But it didn't feel right. Any normal person would be put off by it, wouldn't they? And why was he still staring at her like that, like all understanding and good with it? He should be a bit pissed off or something; asking him to take tests that questioned his-whatever-the-hell.

Toni stood up to pour the coffee. At the window over the kitchen bench, she watched a huge cloud of red dust drifting along the driveway. It was still far from the house, too far away to see the stones and the twigs spitting high into the clogged air.

Stunted patches of casuarina lining the track shimmered in the heat. The dust billowed over them like great rusty coloured cumulus clouds, the rounded towers of which could only mean one thing.

'Trucks are coming,' she said, over her shoulder. Her glance collided with his.

He nodded, held out his hand for the proffered mug of coffee, his eyes, the dark blue-grey, unreadable. 'Good. New stock, new blood, new business.'

She turned from the window, rested her backside against the bench. 'The old yards here won't hold stock for long.'

Callum stood up and walked across to the window, peering out in the direction of the track, and the clouds that rose in puffing blooms above it. 'These ones we'll truck right down to the yards Two Bob and his boys have fixed up. None of this lot will stay here.' He set his mug on the bench, hung both hands on the window frame above his head, and kept staring down the track.

'Two Bob and his boys fixed up the yards?'

He swung back to face her. 'Two Bob is now the proud owner of a third of the property.'

Stunned into silence, she only gazed back. A moment later, 'What?'

Callum cupped a hand over his mouth and wiped espresso crèma from his lips. 'See? Lots to discuss. More revelations for you. Part of the deal we struck with your dad was that Two Bob would be returned a piece of his land.'

'Dad struck a deal?' She shut her mouth to stop gaping.

He nodded.

Toni tilted her head. 'I understand the decision to buy a lease on a failing property. One with potential. But to give away a third of it?'

Callum shrugged. Pointed to the topographical ag maps pinned to the cupboards. 'It works for us. With the deal, Two Bob works his share of the place, buys and sells what he needs, manages it for his family, and works alongside the public company. Us.' He traced a finger along the boundary of the paddocks towards Sleeper Creek. 'When the infrastructure goes up, at least the first stage, we have the rightful owners, a working indigenous family here, and with their own stories to tell.' He turned to look at her again. 'It's good. Strong.'

Toni felt the rising steam in her gut. 'You could've said.'

'Wasn't my story to tell before now.'

Toni vaguely recalled something Lorraine had said, something she hadn't elaborated on. She stared at the maps.

There it was. A clear delineation of the land. The enormous paddocks that Sleeper Creek ran through, dry mostly, but with bores dotted along. She checked over the other plans, the architecture's drawings and began to see the picture more clearly.

No wonder Parker Inc was happy to sign off on the deal. And Two Bob? He must have felt pretty damn good about it, too.

'What things will change?' she asked and heard the demand in her tone.

'Not a lot from our perspective. Two Bob is working on a long-term plan. We'll liaise with him, you and me. Lorraine doesn't want much in her life to change. Her kids might return.' He turned his gaze back to the maps. 'Two Bob'll manage his own team.'

Callum looked relaxed, a hand shoved in a pocket, his other forearm resting on the wall as he studied the maps.

Toni let her eyes wander over the broad back, the denim-blue shirt, the moleskins pants, rusty-coloured dirt smudged over the tight butt, his feet clad only in socks, for being inside.

Stop staring at him. Only make matters worse for yourself. Her head hurt at the temples again. Too much damn thinking.

He was tapping the plans featuring an area near the house. 'And here, this will be where we'll build the new homestead. Then we'll double the size of the catchment area of the existing roof here.' He waved a hand above his head. 'Of course, I'd like this old place to stay as it is, maybe tidy it up, new roofing iron, another water tank. I reckon we can manage that.' Callum glanced over his shoulder at her. 'It's only a minor part in the big picture now, but if we drop another bore here,' he turned back to the map and traced a finger to the east, 'it should be easy to keep viable.'

Viable. As in her house. Well, hopefully that's what he meant.

A rumble in the distance distracted her a moment and when she checked, she could see one big double thundering along the track, the spewing clouds at the rear hiding anything behind it.

There'd be at least three trucks each pulling three bogies, she knew. So two others weren't even in view yet. Looking at the pace this first one travelled, it was only about five minutes out.

Callum was beside her peering out the window, his head over her shoulder.

Man-smells reached her. Maybe it was the hard-working deodorant after last night's shower. Possibly, but not likely, the after-shave or even the shaving crème he used. Surely not the shampoo … a sweaty hat and a day's perspiration would knock out any scent there. Something else? Not a scent, though, no. A sensation, a feeling. Like an ease in him that slid along her jittery nerves and made her feel as if things would be all right. As if any fears she had would be downsized to nothing, taken care of. As if he could be trusted—

Trusted? For God's sake.

If she even moved an inch she would be tucked under his arm and sidled up against that hard body. She inhaled. Surely, he'd feel her thudding heart pounding into the small space between them.

'Two Bob will have seen the trucks coming. I better get out there and be useful.' He smiled down at her. 'See you later for lunch.'

Had his lips brushed the top of her head as he left? Oh, shit. Swear to God, that was no good. No good at all.

She watched him stride off the veranda and jig down the steps and onto the powdery red dirt. He marched across the yard to meet Two Bob's old vehicle chugging around from the sheds. Her heart—like some sticky-beak neighbour not minding its own business—did a double flip.

Friends. They had to be just friends. Nothing more.

*

By dusk, the truckies had off-loaded near enough to a thousand head of young Hereford steers, all of which had been set down in Two Bob's yards another half-hour's drive west. There was more stock to come over the next weeks, and the station men, black and white alike in the paddock, though tired, were upbeat to be once again working on their beloved station.

Now, the truckies sat on their swags on the veranda of Toni's old homestead, beers in hand, eskies close by. Lorraine's platters of barbecued sausages for starters were handed around.

Steaks and potatoes sizzled on the nearby open flame grills, and Lorraine bent over makeshift tables scattered with bread and condiments. She grinned up at Toni when bloke after bloke dodged the large bowl of salad in favour of bread, steak and spuds.

Paul and Evan had come out a day or so back. They dragged out more chairs as the station workers staggered wearily up the steps for a feed and a drink before heading off for an early night.

Before dawn would light the sky, work would begin again.

The temporary builder's huts would be erected tomorrow. The

ATCO dongas—prefab huts—that already dotted the paddock behind the house would remain in situ, and an ablution block would be erected close by. Another huge generator was coming out from Alice tomorrow. A truck carrying a new diesel tank to be put in place, and filled with fuel to power it, would follow.

Nothing was going to slow the pace as Callum got his new plans underway.

Later, preparing for her own bed, Toni heard the soft rattles and the loud snores of the men asleep on the veranda. Sprawled atop their swags, they were mercifully protected from the mozzies by her dad's fly-wire screens.

Lorraine called a 'goodnight' into the hot and still air and slipped off to her house, her little torch bobbing as she went. Two Bob was on the veranda, snoring with the others, and Toni's dogs Chipper and Sudsy lay alongside him.

Paul and Evan shared their old bedroom, the fly-wire screen doors open, the room an extension of the veranda. Someone slept in a swag by the doorway.

The familiar sounds of their sleeping, the soft rumbling, rhythmic breathing had her catch her own breath. The silence of the night outside, and all these familiar sounds inside, stopped her up short.

This was home. And it would work again like the home she always knew. Except for a few small differences, that is.

She padded past her father's old room, the door pulled to but not quite closed. Callum moved about in there but hadn't noticed her going past.

The bathroom would be empty. The generator closed down just as she opened the door, so she headed for the battery light and switched it on.

After snibbing the door locked, she shucked her day clothes, turned on the faucets and climbed under the hot water. A quick wash of hair, and a quick but thorough sluice of all the important bits and she was done.

In the low glow of the lamplight, her reflection gazed back from the mirror. Damp strands of hair clung to her neck. Other than beads of perspiration forming on her upper lip, the result of a steamy bathroom, she looked calm. Serene, even.

So why the hell did she feel weird, as if all this was happening to someone else?

Shaking her head, she rubbed the towel through her hair, gathering as much as she could to squeeze excess water from it. She patted her face dry, wiped her front down of more perspiration and shrugged into clean undies, a long tank top and boxer shorts.

Brushed her teeth, and then she was ready for bed. A four thirty morning start didn't thrill anybody, but the heat of the day surged from the moment the sun soared over the horizon. That meant the cooler hours before dawn weren't to be wasted.

Toni padded back to her bedroom. Her mind was on nothing but collapsing on top of the sheets, so she jumped when Callum spoke to her from the shadows of the hallway.

'Heading for the shower myself. All clear?' he asked, his voice low.

Toni tried a bright smile, knowing he couldn't see it, but he'd hear it in her tone. 'All clear. All yours. Monster day today, but a good job. See you in the morning.' Moving towards her room in the dark, she hadn't realized he'd stepped in her path. She smacked into his bare chest. 'God, sorry.'

He steadied her with both hands on her shoulders. 'Me, too. Can't really see you. I'm not mortally wounded, though. How about I get cleaned up and we have a night-cap?'

'I need some sleep—'

'I'll be five minutes. And one quick drink.'

His hands were still lightly on her shoulders, and the scents of him at this time of the day were not reminiscent of anything remotely deodorised, after-shaved or shampooed.

'Okay,' she whispered. 'Five minutes, the old lounge room.

White wine? Beer?'

'Great. Beer for me.'

He angled past her and she heard him fumbling about in the bathroom before the battery lamp glowed again.

Finding everything she needed in the pitch dark, she got to her mother's old lounge room and switched on the battery light. Setting her wine, his beer and paper napkins to soak up the condensation on the coffee table, she lifted the windows as quietly as she could and felt the warm air glide over her skin.

The rumbling snores, assorted cadences, snortles, coughs and gurgles reached her ears. She smiled to herself. Eight men on the veranda, all sound asleep. That was the sound of home she remembered from a not-so-distant past.

Chips and Suds would be out there in their element. She heard them offer a little whimper of greeting each to her, but she shushed them and it stopped. They were fine.

Settling in a club chair, she heard the bathroom door open and close.

Callum Parker poked his head in the doorway. 'I'll be another minute,' he said.

'Sure,' she answered and looked away before any more drops of water ran over his bare chest and disappeared into the bath towel he'd wrapped loosely around his hips.

Hope he pulls on some pants.

She heard a couple of thumps and a whispered curse. Another lamp light glowed, illuminating a path to his room. A few fumbles, some heavy footfalls and he was back in the lounge, wearing a pair of loose shorts and a singlet, exposing smooth arms and the sprinkle of chest hair. His feet were bare.

He slumped onto the chesterfield and draped long legs over the arm. Reached across and grabbed up his beer. Lifting it in salute towards her, he took a swallow. 'Long day.'

'Strange day.'

He peered at her. 'You okay?'

'Yep.' She sniffed. 'Things are moving too quickly.'

'It seems that way, I know. Stock, machinery, builders. I've only got another day or so this time before I have to be back in Alice again.' He shifted to get comfortable. 'I'd rather be out here, with your brothers and Two Bob.' Chugging down another mouthful of beer, he sighed in appreciation. 'With you, too.'

Toni felt a twinge in her stomach. Friendship. She leaned forward and grabbed her wine from the table, took a long sip. 'More work in Alice?'

'No.' He looked across. 'I got me a doctor's appointment to make.'

She stood up quickly, wine slopped over her hand. 'Okay, look, I don't need reminding. I know I'm setting boundaries, I get it. So, let's not make a big deal—'

'I mean it. I'm there. No big deal.' Callum reached over and tapped his fingers on the back of her hand.

His touch was light, tentative again. Toni stood by the settee anchored to the spot, wine dripping from the hand around her wine glass.

He swung his legs off the arm of the couch. 'Sit with me.'

'There's no point to this if things don't work out.'

'Just sit with me.' He took her glass, wiped it off and set it in the table. Toni sat. The silence extended. Then he took her hand. His was warm, dry, and large around her fingers. Loose. He reached over and took up his beer again. 'Kind of nice, just sitting here like this.' He squeezed her fingers a moment. 'We're just winding down after a big day. We're just being friends.'

She waited a beat in the soft lamp light. The air around her was as silent as a desert night before a storm. 'Friends don't hold hands.'

He squeezed her fingers lightly again. 'Sure they do.'

Moving her hand out of his would be rude. Leaving it there would give him the wrong impression. So, she squeezed his hand a little in return and slipped it out of his, taking up her glass again.

23

Callum Parker sat in the GP's room and insisted. 'Doc, the type-specific test, thanks. I know I don't have any symptoms and I also know that doesn't mean anything.'

'Look, Callum, this is just a nuisance thing, no biggie. Lots of people have it, some don't even know they have. Why do you want a blood test? You use condoms. You just said you haven't got any symptoms.'

'Tim, I know as well as you do that sometimes there are no symptoms.'

'Won't tell us anything.'

'Shitting me, right? It'll tell me if I have antibodies, therefore the virus. I've had a blood test before, I was clear then. But that was years ago, and a few partners since.'

Doctor Tim inhaled, hunched over the keyboard and two-finger typed as he spoke. 'When was the last test?'

'Can't remember for sure. Couple of years back, give or take. I've got my paperwork somewhere.'

The doctor grunted. 'Won't mean a thing now. Sexual liaisons in the last three to six months?'

'Yep.'

'Condoms?'

'Always.'

Tim pushed away from the desk. 'I still don't think there's a need to do—'

'Doc, I need to show her I've done the test. C'mon.'

'All right, all right. Roll up your sleeve.' Tim poked around in the shelves behind him and withdrew a small sealed plastic bag. He peeled it apart and popped the syringe. Swabbed. 'Results will be three months from now, at least.' The needle jabbed in, blood sucked out. 'There. Done.' Tim swabbed again. 'Need a band-aid, mate? I've only got these kiddie ones.' He held up a little packet. 'Have one anyway. All the big guys do. This Tinkerbell one is popular.' Tim fit the plaster. 'Good to go,' the doc said, admiring his handiwork.

Callum paid the bill, headed out of the clinic.

As soon as he got back to the hotel, he hit the keyboard for research. For the first time in a long time he thought of the years with Sylvie, his now ex-wife, and after, and all the time since he had never worried about contracting any sexually transmitted anything. Because condoms were king, weren't they?

No, they weren't, the website told him. And he let that sink in as he read some more.

*

Toni peered at the document he put on the table, his fingers tapping it.

They sat in the station kitchen, the kitchen to which her childhood belonged. The place where she'd sat on her mother's knee and shucked peas with Lorraine. Where she'd listened to her dad tell tales of getting city slickers eating bush oysters, of branding, or going on massive droves, or death by steer or bull.

The kitchen where her brothers had pulled her hair, or she'd swatted them instead of flies, or swatted the long slinky centipedes that scampered over the cool slate floor.

Where innocence and the promise of a happy life lived.

She stared at the paper that told her he'd undertaken a blood test. She looked away. It used to be a safe place, here, in this kitchen. A refuge. But this minute she felt trapped in it, trapped by her life and the things she couldn't control.

Her own paper was still folded in her hands. It felt hot, but that was impossible. She was hot on the outside. Cold on the inside. Just plain uncomfortable. Sad. Strong. Weak. Resigned. Resolved.

Solo. But I'm okay. I'm going forward.

Callum waited. Glanced at her hands.

*

It struck Callum hard.

Not for himself. He'd had time to assume that things might not be right for her, especially after remembering that her father, and then her brothers had said she'd been doing it tough. It struck him hard that she seemed so traumatised by it, whatever 'it' was. He wasn't going gently-does-it, though. 'We have to wait for the results but at least it's done. Yours done, too?'

Emotion played over Toni's features, though she tried to cover up the struggle. The tell-tale deep breath, her gaze steadfast on the sheet of paper still folded in front of her. But it didn't prepare him for what she said.

'We can never have the kind of relationship you think you want. There'll only be a work relationship. Employer-employee.' She didn't even glance up.

He held his nose with a rough pinch between fingers. 'Not good enough, Toni. You'll have to explain.'

'Do I?'

He flattened his paper in front of her, his palm slapped on it. 'This.'

She slapped her paper down on the table. 'Honest, yes. Congratulations. I did mine, too.'

'Right. It means we have to wait, it doesn't mean you knock us out of the game.'

Still she sat without looking at him. 'I don't want to take anything further. There really is no point.'

'I didn't wrangle this test out of the doc because I thought it would be fun.' He tapped the receipt. 'There are two of us in this mix.'

'No, there's not,' she said. 'There's nothing but a squillion hectares in this mix. Nothing else.'

He pushed back in his chair, scraping the floorboards. 'Syphilis?'

'What?'

'Warts?'

'*What*? Don't.'

'Tell.'

Shifting her shoulders back and forth, she laced her hands. 'It's not that, though having tests are fair enough—' She stopped. Finally, she looked at him. 'It's something else.'

Her beautiful face was drawn, and tiny lines had trekked over the smooth planes of her cheeks. She looked like she'd lost a little weight. The sharper angles of her face made her appear tired. Tendrils of hair, otherwise pulled back into that thick plait, wisped around her face. Her dark honey coloured eyes were big, their gaze now on him.

He wanted to take her hand but didn't. 'Not life threatening?' Shit. What had Phillip said—diagnosis? He couldn't think. God forbid...

A hesitant shake of her head.

He breathed out a quiet sigh. 'So, tell me what could be so bad, Toni.'

She shook her head. 'I want to be honest, and it's nothing that would impact on your health.'

He tried again. 'Whatever it is, it can be worked through.' For some reason, he was thrown back to another time and another discussion with his sister.

Toni looked up momentarily, then fiddled with her paper.

'You don't want to tell me, now, okay.' He tapped the sheet under his hand again. 'But this paper here, this blood test, says that I trust us enough to check that we'll either be okay, or we'll manage things and be okay. I want it to be right.'

Again, the flutter of a look. Again, the fiddling with her paperwork. She looked briefly at him, then back to the paper. 'This is the order for my blood test,' she said finally. She unfolded the pages and waved the first one at him. Then, 'This one,' she shook out the other page, 'is a little older.'

It was tinged with yellow and had been folded many times. 'Yes?'

'It says, basically—' She lifted a shoulder '—that because of chemo to treat a disease just before I was twenty, everything got poisoned off, and just to be sure, fried as well. It's most likely I will never have children.'

Silence beat a thunder boom in his head. He hadn't expected that. He stared at her. Cleared his throat, frowning. Nodded, thought hard about his next words. He had none that would do justice, but he tried. 'That's a real—' He was about to say, 'piss-off', but any words would be wrong, inadequate. He remembered clearly how Marnie said she had felt after learning she couldn't have any more kids.

Toni met his glance briefly, but remained silent, still toying with the edges of her paperwork.

He let the moment stay calm. 'Dealt a shitty card there.' He sat up straight. 'But you could check again. That looks to be a fairly old paper. And there are other ways to get—'

'I know that.' Her gaze flicked up at him, then away again. More paper fiddling, her fingers flicked a corner back and forth.

He nodded, rolled his shoulders, felt out of his depth, like with Marnie, all those years ago. 'Take more tests. There are new technologies. They're making advances every day—' *Shut the fuck up, Parker. Your mouth is running off.*

'You sound like a bloody medical fact sheet. I'm aware of those things. There's no reason for more tests.'

'You can never say never,' he insisted, hearing his own auto response. *Shut. Up.*

'I'm not saying never,' she snapped, and those fierce, sad brown eyes darkened.

'Nothing's a hundred per cent.' *Just. Shut. The. Fuck. Up.*

'Don't patronise.'

He waited some more but emotion drained from her face. It was blank of any expression. She'd shut down. He tried again. 'I appreciate your telling me.' *Jesus, got any other lame statements, Parker?* 'Don't knock it on the head yet, think about it some more,' he said. 'I'm sorry about my reaction. I didn't realise— It was just a shock. For me. I wasn't expecting that.'

Her stare was clear, her voice soft, and the low breath she let out was sad. 'No need for me to think about it some more, at all. It just had to be on the table.'

*

There. Done.

She schooled her features not to look defiant, or defeated, or— or bloody anything. Let him think what he liked. She didn't give a damn.

'It doesn't faze me,' he said, still shaking his head.

That floored her. It wouldn't be true, of course. 'It should—you said you wanted kids,' she exploded, and shoved away from the table to stand in front of the sink. 'I'm not going to waste more time on it anymore. You want kids, that's understood. So, we can't start anything here. I'm not going to be any more than friendly.'

'I know it's hard to—' He stood behind her but not too close. 'You could give me some time, at least.'

'Take all the time you like.' Her hands squeezed the rail of the sink and she glared out into the home paddock. 'It won't change things.'

The dogs were lying flat out in the shade of the machinery shed. No breeze moved the flies along, so their ears flapped a bit. A little dust from two dogs' tail-flapping sprang up. Wide blue skies beat down with the heat of the day. Everything was the same as it had always been. Except it wasn't.

'And I'd rather this went no further,' she said. 'You needed to know that my reasons for not encouraging anything, or— responding to anything, are legitimate.' She looked over her shoulder. 'And I don't want it all over local news.'

'I would never talk about personal business.'

She looked away. *Yeah, well, I've heard that before.*

That was the one other risk she'd have to take right now: that he wouldn't say a word. Why would he? *You're being paranoid.* Surely, she wouldn't strike another person like Sonny Murphy again?

The silence from behind was killing her. She'd just wait it out. He'd see the sense of it. He'd walk away. He'd have to. He wanted kids.

A few moments passed before he finally did say something.

He cleared his throat. 'I've got a truck coming out with some furniture for my room. Some office stuff as well. And the technicians coming to set up the satellite and the internet and the rest will be out later today, too.' He paused, came to stand beside her at the sink. 'Until the boys get here, can you lend me a hand to shift some of your dad's old stuff out to the shed?'

Level ground. Even footing. She could talk about work stuff because that's all there was. 'No problem. Room will need a good clean once all that stuff's gone.'

'Great.'

He left her in the kitchen. She heard him walk down the hallway, open the door to what had been her parents' bedroom. Heard something being dragged across the floor. She suspected he'd pulled the dresser out from the wall.

She turned her back on the sight outside, gazed at the empty kitchen. The years of her childhood, her adolescence and her young adulthood all crowded out of it now.

Pull up your big girl's pants, Toni. Move on with the rest of it. He was polite to her, not oh-so-polite, just normal polite, as if she hadn't just told him to bugger off and not bother her again.

Callum just carried on as normal. When she got to her father's room, he had the dresser out from the wall as she'd assumed and was removing the drawers to make it easier to move through the house. When the room was cleared, they rolled up the carpet square and pulled and pushed it down the hall and out on to the veranda, where she helped him hoist it over the rail.

Disappointed in the state of it, Toni pulled a face. 'Not sure this can be redeemed.' She thumped it with her hand. Red dust flew off in all directions. Parts of it looked like something had nibbled the edges, a patch here and there was threadbare, the colour overall had faded. She could still make out the old stoic roses, but they'd seen their day.

'Maybe not. Might mean a new carpet square coming up. It's not sentimental, or anything, is it?' He gazed at her openly.

She shook her head. 'No.' *Normal conversation.*

The telephone and communications tech boys arrived soon after, which meant they had to abandon her father's old room. She had little to do until they'd finished surveying and had decided on a course of action.

When they did, it meant almost a complete gutting of the old office room. It was a task she gladly undertook. Her mind was taken off the conversation of the morning, her energy taken up moving and cleaning. There was something very esoteric in that.

Only once did Callum smile at her, eyes crinkling. He reached across to give her shoulder a quick squeeze.

Regret burrowed deep within her. But she returned a nonchalant smile and bent to flick on the old vacuum cleaner.

24

Eric Roycroft wasn't overly happy. Justin West had appeared out of the blue, standing at his desk looking crappy and stinking of stale BO.

'What's going on?' Eric flapped his collar and looked up at the aircon in his office. *Not doing its job.*

'I got this in the mail.' West was slapping an unopened envelope in the palm of his hand. A sheen of sweat glistened on his cheeks and a droplet clung to an earlobe.

Warm day out, Eric figured. No wonder his old aircon was struggling. 'And?'

'It's the results I've been waiting for. So, I'll need my share of the funds.'

Eric popped off his chair and sprang over to the door and shut it. He spun back to Justin. 'It's a little too early, mate. Dust hasn't settled, yet.' He sank down in his seat again. 'What's the hurry?'

'I heard the new people out at MacDonnell's are organizing for a deed transfer on part of the property out there.'

Eric stared at him. 'So? I thought your office was handling it.'

West shifted his feet, pulled out a chair opposite. He leaned over the desk, the envelope shaking in his hand. 'Not me. They've got their own citified team. Rug's coming out from under my feet.' He tapped the desk with a forefinger. 'So, I need the funds. I need to be able to back this up.' The envelope waggled.

Eric eyed the envelope than glanced back at West. 'You haven't even opened that.'

'Don't have to. I know what's in it.'

'Mate. The funds are tied up for a bit longer—'

'Then loan me.'

Eric laughed. 'I haven't got that sort of money.'

'You have, I know it.'

West looks a tad agitated. Not a good thing. Eric stood up and reached for the aircon remote, ratcheting the cooling up a couple of degrees. 'I don't, mate. Swear to God.'

'Where is it, then?'

Eric inhaled. 'In a safe place, where it's always been, until we get a bit of space.' He glared. 'It's still there, if that's what the look on your face is all about.'

Justin West rubbed a hand over his face and wiped it on his trousers. The sneer wasn't quite wiped all the way off. 'I need it,' he said.

The guy was a liability but he had to be held off a little while longer. Only two weeks to go before Eric could get out of town, retired, off to Queensland and beyond. Just two weeks and then the mad jerk could have his funds and Eric would cut all ties with him. Each one's silence was the others' security for the embezzlement. All he had to do was keep Justin West calm. 'I don't have access to it all straight away. How much do you need?'

'All of it.'

One point five mil. But only half was West's. 'What is this? You can't have it all, no matter what, mate. Not in the deal.'

'I'll pay you back.'

Eric hooked a leg over the arm of his chair. 'Not how it works, Justin. What the hell's got into you?'

'This,' he hissed and waved the envelope again.

'And what the fuck is that?' Eric snapped back.

'The DNA report. It proves my father is Two Bob Bolton's father, too. Meaning if he's got land deeded back, it's family land. Half mine.'

25

Tuesday again, and back in Alice for the new routine of picking up stores and supplies for the station.

Toni had checked with Callum. She'd be spending an hour or two at her travel shop, as well, catching up with Mary-Anne and relieving her for a lunch break.

It grated on her to have to ask permission to do anything, but it was best under the circumstances. Not only did she need a good working relationship, she needed the job in order to keep up the repayments on the Adelaide mortgage. So, toeing the line was the only way to go.

The other thing she needed to do was engage a real estate sales agent, track down Sonny Murphy and have him sign papers to get the property sold.

Anything else, including the awkward conversation last week with Callum Parker was put on the backburner.

She and her brothers had come into town in Paul's car. Callum said he'd be following in his own vehicle, for business with Reddells. Their paths wouldn't cross.

She sat at her old desk at the shop, now in a sleeveless top, a loose skirt and a pair of low heeled, strappy sandals. Much better for the short time in the office than her jeans and boots in which she had travelled. That apparel now sat neatly by her tote-bag underfoot, the jeans ditched hastily in the back room.

Callum. For two days at least, before now, every time they were in the same room together, she'd jump on the inside. It was almost as if by not revisiting that conversation, its presence had heightened. But he was a pleasant and attentive colleague, nothing more. It calmed her and saddened her at the same time. She wanted her body and brain to turn off so she could take a break from the torment. It was plain miserable. Her chest ached with a pain she couldn't describe. And it was her own fault. She knew that. But at least it was out in the open. All she had to do now, was deal with how it felt.

She squeezed her eyes shut. He'd soon spend his time jetting around the place between his investments or whatever-the-hell and she'd be here working for him. Alone and that would suit her.

Yet, when the office door opened, she held her breath and looked up expectantly, hope lifting her mood. Until she saw that it was Justin West who stood there, looking at her.

The atmosphere dropped. 'What can I do for you?' she asked, coolly.

He waved a hand in the air at nothing in particular. 'I came to apologise. For the other week, out at the station. I was definitely not at my best. That Parker gets on my goat.' A crinkled envelope was in his hands.

Justin eyes were red rimmed, and that made him look unwell, especially against his ruddy coloured skin, which was usually pasty hued. 'I was wondering if you'd like to go to dinner this evening,' he said, then both eyes squeezed in a hard blink.

Toni's blanched. 'No. No, thank you.'

'Why not? I made a mistake and got angry, but you know me. And I am your solicitor, we should be able to go to dinner and talk.'

'Justin, you are not my solicitor. And I don't want to go to dinner.' No point telling him she'd have to be back at the station, that had nothing to do with it. Better a definite "no".

He hung his head momentarily. 'Of course, I thought that after all these years, you and I might …'

She shook her head. 'No, Justin.'

'I always liked to think you'd change your mind. Especially when I was so close to your dad, and so close to giving you the very thing you really wanted.'

Her eyes went squinty. 'What do you mean?'

His face darkened. 'Another night for dinner, perhaps, when things calm down a bit more.'

She tried to work out why she was getting a creepy vibe. 'Justin, what do you mean? When what things calm down a bit more?'

'Doesn't the station mean anything to you now?' He looked as if both eyes had an annoying twitch.

She wished her brothers were here with her. 'What a question, of course it does. But it's no longer mine.'

'Or is it just that lover-boy's taken over already? Do you know he intends to destroy everything out there and I'm the only one who could've stopped it?' He nodded at her vigorously. 'Did you know I have a way around the current situation?' His face was blotchy with colour fading and surging. He waved the envelope in his hand. 'I have a claim.'

'A claim. Really?' A bubble of anger welled inside, stemming the curl of fear in her chest. She squeezed the pen in her hand, then let it drop to the desk.

'This in here,' he waved the envelope again, 'means the station's been sold without due and proper diligence, and that the whole lot of you can be held accountable for the fall-out—'

'I don't have any idea what you're talking about.'

'Oh, I believe that you don't, but they do' He pointed somewhere over her shoulder. 'And I'll see to it that there'll be trouble over it.'

The moment he advanced, she shot up out of her chair. 'Then you'd better get out of here because I don't want to know anything about it.'

He stopped. 'What?'

'Don't you come barging in here blathering about ludicrous things,' she hurled at him. 'My father thought you were a decent man. That's why he chose you to execute his will, to look after his affairs. It doesn't quite look like that, now, does it?'

Shit, Toni—stop. Don't say anything about an investigation, or criminal activity.

'What?' His eyes darted about.

She calmed herself, lowered her tone. Was standing face to face with him. 'What am I to make of what you're saying?'

His demeanour softened. 'I can look after you too, Toni, if you'd let me.'

'You can't, Justin. Go and repair whatever damage you've done—'

'I'll ruin it for your Callum Parker.' His cheeks looked fit to explode. His jaw jutted forward and his bottom teeth were exposed.

'He's not my Callum Parker.' She stepped away quickly, to relative safety further behind her desk. 'Time you left, Justin.'

'If he thinks he can just walk in here—and with bloody Two Bob—undermining all those years of hard work, all the years of unpaid hard work and waltz away with the station and you, he's got another think coming. You'll be running to me before long,' he snarled, and shook a finger at her. 'I have all the information I need right here to ruin it for the lot of you. I own a portion of the place, now.' The envelope flapped overhead as he waved it at her again.

'You haven't even opened that bloody thing,' she said, glaring back at him.

'Right.' He ripped open the seal, pulled out the letter, gazed down at the text then back at her. 'I'll show the damn lot of you.' Smug anticipation moved over his features as he nodded at her, mouth set, then chin doubling as he looked down at the letter.

Whatever was in it, brought a deepening consternation. A dark furrow appeared between his eyebrows, before a shock drained his face of colour.

He glared up from the letter at her, vacantly, his bloodshot eyes unblinking. Then he turned on his heels and marched out the door, slamming it behind him.

Her hands shaking, she locked the door. Toni rang Paul's mobile first, then Evan's but both went straight to message-bank. She checked everywhere looking for them, left messages until she learned they were with a stock agent and couldn't be contacted immediately. Paul eventually got back to her and finally they turned up. It had been an anxious hour.

Paul sat her down in her shop with a coffee and then they all started at once, all with some tale to tell about Justin West.

She held up her hands. 'Justin feels that I owe him some sort of—affection.'

'Bloody hell. Yeww.' Evan curled his lip.

'And something he said about a claim on the place, ruining it for Callum Parker. About wanting to look after me, and all the years of unpaid work. Are you aware of any money owing to him? That he owns a portion of the place—could he have a claim on the place?' Toni looked at her brothers. 'Any part of the sale that might be illegal?'

Evan blanched. He glanced at Paul. 'No way.'

Paul shoved hands in his pockets. 'Maybe he feels he's done more than required in the line of duty.'

'That doesn't make me feel any better,' Toni said. 'I think he's up to something stupid. What if he goes back out to the Run?'

Evan spoke up again. 'If he's a threat to the place, the police have to know, and now. Because there's a helluva lot of people out there, all sorts of engineers and other blokes. Architects.' He flopped in a chair opposite Toni's desk. 'The bloke supplying the extra dongas for accommodation is on his way, too, so there could be a whole mob of people out there. If he wants to cause trouble—'

'You really reckon he'll try something out there?' Paul asked.

'He looked crazy enough to do anything.' Toni tried to smooth out the frown lines, two fingers rubbing between her eyebrows.

'Did he say where he was going?'

She shook her head.

Paul's brows twisted. He looked distracted, as if he was searching for something. 'I don't believe he'd be involved in anything illegal. I know Cal's company.' He glanced at Toni, who shrugged, palms up. 'They want huge development on the place,' he mused. 'Will make it a tourist attraction. It's only in the planning stages but I'm sure Justin's got nothing to prevent any of that going ahead.'

Cal's company. Callum and her brother were openly discussing about the new plans and the impending development, even though settlement on the place hadn't happened yet. Why had Callum not confided in her? She shrugged. Maybe he hadn't the time to speak to her privately. Annoyed at the direction her thoughts were heading, she tried to push it aside. He didn't have to confide, did he? Surely, he'd explain at some point. Or perhaps he'd dodge her altogether. The thought slugged her. She couldn't bear to think he'd just leave her behind, keep her in the dark about something to do with the station. She couldn't believe he'd do that.

Even if he was pissed off. Even if he was distancing himself, he would still be professional with this side of things.

Toni dragged herself back to the conversation. Something was on the tip of her tongue, something from the reading of the last codicil—a thought that had struck her then, but she hadn't followed it through, her mind dimmed with grief and outrage.

She held her hand up as her memory released its secret. 'I know what it was,' she said, suddenly, and stood up.

Paul's head came up. 'What?'

'Justin. He had access to all of Dad's files.'

''Course he did. He was dad's solicitor.' Paul waved the idea off.

'I hope he hasn't done anything illegal,' Toni said, staring into space. 'Oh, my God.'

'I'm not with you,' Evan stated, looking from one sibling to the other.

She looked at both of them. 'What if Justin was a contender for the station—that would make sense of what he was saying.'

'He'd be off his trolley,' Paul said. 'Where would he get the money for a start? Sounds more like he simply hates Callum's guts.' He scratched his head. 'We've handed all the dodgy-looking paperwork to the lawyers.'

'They'll contact the accountants, won't they?' Evan asked, digging hands into his pockets.

Toni nodded but kept talking as thoughts tumbled. 'Wasn't Justin Dad's signatory? Didn't Dad have him as his co-signee on the bank accounts after Mum died because none of us were of age?'

The boys stood in silence.

'And nothing changed when you turned eighteen, did it, Paul?'

After a moment, he shook his head. 'And that was sixteen years ago.'

Her mind raced. Perhaps that's why Justin mentioned all his unpaid work. Perhaps he meant to reap the benefits of the estate after the event of her dad's death, and none would be the wiser. But how? And why would he want the station? Everyone knew it had impossible debts. Where did he think he'd get the money, or the backing?

'Oh—bugger. Maybe it was because of Justin that the station failed,' Toni said, echoing her thoughts aloud. The three MacDonnells stared at each other.

'You're talking embezzlement, or fraud, for sure,' Paul said.

'But the sort of money he'd need would be massive. It'd stand out like dog's balls,' Evan added.

'It would, so why haven't we found it? I better call the cops, even if it's just to flag suspicions. Can't hurt.' Paul looked at his siblings. 'It's got to be somewhere in the paperwork—'

The side door banged open, and Ben burst into the office,

hanging in the doorway. 'Come quick—it's the Run. I've rung the cops.'

'What?' Three MacDonnells rounded on him.

'Lorraine's just rung me.' Ben looked at all of them, puffing, out of breath. 'She couldn't get you guys, said Justin turned up there half hour ago, ranting and raving about making sure no-one would get in his way.' He sucked in a deep breath. 'Apparently, he started to clobber Two Bob, but Lorraine chased him off with a big stick. She said he was going berserk out there, smashing up the machinery, other stuff. Then the phone went dead.' Ben stopped to dust himself down. 'The cops are on their way and so's the firies and the Flying Doctor.'

Paul dug in his pocket and pulled out his car keys. 'Let's go. I'm not letting West destroy everything—'

'Wait,' Evan warned. 'It's not our place anymore. The cops—'

'Bugger that,' Toni said. 'I'm going out to Lorraine.' She grabbed up her tote bag, her jeans and boots.

Ben waved a hand. 'I'll follow you… Just gimme a minute to catch my breath. I'll lock up here for you.'

Toni rushed for the door. 'Leave a note for Mary-Anne,' she called over her shoulder.

Evan and Paul leapt ahead of Toni into the big vehicle parked at the back entrance. Toni tumbled in the back seat then they were away. Seatbelts on, they sped out of town back over the same road Toni had travelled so many times in the last few weeks.

*

In the hotel's coffee shop, a long black cooling, Callum checked his laptop for emails before he rang his sister.

'Marnie, hi. Good. How're things progressing with the finance at Central? Great news—told you they'd bypass her. They ought to toughen up their lending officers ... I know, I know, big-headed. But she had no control over the final decision ... Here? That's why I'm ringing. Nothing I can't work out. I'll scan and email the plans and get you and Bill to start the ball rolling. Toni? Her brothers did most of the work for me there. And they're pretty happy with the package we put together … Yes, they'll continue with us ... Just playing it wisely, hoping to forestall any problems.' He waited a beat. 'How are you going?' He knew his voice had softened. 'That's good. No, no. Just checking to see you're okay. Um, how're the twins? Good. Good … Dan's a laugh... 'Course, he is, takes after his uncle. And that niece of mine?' He nodded, smiled. 'Georgie's a good girl. One in a million.' He stopped, listened. 'All right, all right, I'm not getting soppy. I'll talk to you later.' He finished the call to his sister and rang off.

One in a million. Toni MacDonnell. He'd need more time to tackle what she'd told him, to make sure he could settle any fears she had, fears he might have had. He'd got through a whole life unscathed, so far, by nothing more unwelcome than a failed marriage. Bad enough, but in the bigger scheme of things, he'd had no lifetime infections after his sexual liaisons, no sordid affairs, no bad money times, no impossible hurdles. The only deaths were of those gone before him, not those of children.

All he had was a determination to get what he wanted, and he had the drive to do it. If he lost out, he picked himself up and got going again.

But this with Toni? She couldn't have kids. He'd thought long and hard about his own life after they'd learned his sister, Marnie, couldn't have any more. That had been devastating for her. For himself, he hadn't been overly concerned, having kids had been a long way off in his big plan at that time, and even though he was told he might not have the gene his sister carried, he hadn't opted to be tested. No point.

He scoffed aloud. At that time, he'd never really thought it would bother him one way or the other. And since Sylvie, no one had interested him enough to consider it. It was luck, or otherwise, on both his and Sylvie's part that they hadn't had kids. Sure, he and Sylvie had been spontaneous some of the time. Sure, they'd used protection when they thought of it. They hadn't been too worried. Overall theirs had been a healthy and happy—married—sex life. While it lasted. They'd never really talked about kids. It just wasn't in their vision at the time. If kids had come along, oh well …

But how would they have felt if they'd wanted kids and couldn't have them? Pissed off? Devastated? Would he have blamed Sylvie if her fertility was compromised and he'd opted out? Would she have blamed him if his had been? Did he know how he even felt about that?

He looked at it. He'd said—in a throwaway line to a woman who was about to work for him—that his job in the family was to have more kids, to keep up the tradition of a long line of twins. *It was just a throwaway, for chrissake.* He'd had no idea of the impact.

He flattened his mouth. Toni was his kinda girl, and she'd been honest. It had taken a lot to tell him. He knew that. Thank Christ he hadn't done his usual and jumped in feet first, both sideways, and played the rescue card—that's what Marnie called his style of approach. He needn't do any of the work for Toni. She had to come trust him herself, however long it took. He didn't want any misunderstanding between Toni and him. Not now. Not ever

But she'd closed the door on them. So, why insist they have blood tests if she had no intention of—? Maybe she thought she'd get a rejection. Or maybe she thought enough of him to tell him straight up.

He sucked in a breath, rubbed a fleeting ache in his chest. She'd slipped neatly under his skin from the time he'd first set eyes on her. *Bah.* Just a crazy infatuation—maybe it wouldn't last long.

He laughed at himself. *Who are you kidding, Parker? You got it bad this time.*

Ducking his chin, he thought more about the investigating other fertility options— What the hell was *he* expecting to do? He wouldn't come out of that scot-free. Toni would tell him to mind his own frigging business. Or worse. Besides, too early to talk about having kids.

But that's what she meant, wasn't it? If at some point he might want kids, and, if in a relationship with her, she would be at risk of his rejection. It made her vulnerable. He understood that, too.

If Toni gave one inch, he would go there—but no charging in like a desperate, no leaping into the sack and just going for it. A steady strategy to win her trust. And hope the hell it worked. And if they got that far, they'd investigate to have kids, how to make it happen, if that's what they both wanted. Would that even be what Toni wanted? They'd both feel like crap if it went badly.

Now he was messing with his own head. *That's enough of that. Stop.*

Callum leaned back in his seat, rubbed his face with both hands.

There were other things pressing on him, other things he could deal with, and wanted out of his way. *Get on with it. Move your arse.*

The phone jangled. 'Parker,' he answered.

'Hi, Callum. Ben Whyte here. Won't beat about the bush. Something bloody rotten's happened at the Run. Justin West has gone ballistic with a bull-dozer out there and the old house has gone—'

'What?'

'And he's burnt the rest of it to the ground. But that's not—'

Callum bolted upright, spilling coffee and paperwork. 'Where's Toni?'

26

'Oh God, what's he done?' Toni cried, hanging out the car window straining to get a better look. Dust and stones and twigs whipped up and stung her face.

Inside the vehicle, Evan had hold of her skirt. 'Get the hell back in here and put your belt back on,' he shouted over the din of the wheels roaring over the track. 'You'll break your bloody neck.'

Still fifteen minutes out of the station driveway, the thick palls of black smoke coming from the home paddock area drove Toni's fear deep.

Paul stood hard on the accelerator. The 4WD took another surge forward, but it was the longest drive ever before it skidded into the home run.

Then from the house gate, they could see one half of the place was a tumble of rubble, the bulldozer still jammed in it. Smoke poured out of Toni's bedroom and out of the front room that her mother had so lovingly furnished.

Police officers, maybe three or four, were checking the sheds. Firies aimed a blast of water at the house, but it didn't look as if anything would be saved. Smoke billowed, and hot ash floated around her.

Oh my god—the dogs.

Toni scrambled out of the car screaming, 'Chipper! Sudsy!' then tried to whistle them up but her voice was broken. 'Chipper, Sudsy,' she sobbed, the last of her strength laid flat by the thought that her dogs might be hurt, or worse.

A rusty flash, a frothy charge and both dogs leapt out from behind the sheds, did excited, worried round and rounds around her, barking and yipping and being crazy. She sank in the dirt with them and tearlessly sobbed her relief. They were all right, unharmed. Their excitement, fear, frenzy all rolled into one as they jumped on her, licking and whining and barking.

She ordered them into Paul's vehicle, kissed both their heads, secured them in the back and let the windows down. 'Stay,' she instructed.

The police had cordoned off the immediate area surrounding the house. Toni flew from the car straight into Constable Hemmings, his khaki uniform smudged with smoke and soot. 'Toni, get some boots on, the ground's burning over there. Paul,' he yelled across to her brother, 'get your vehicle well back behind those lines the boys have roped off.'

Toni dived into the car to grab her boots. 'Where's Lorraine and Two Bob?' she asked him. Snatching at her boots before Paul took off with the car, she hopped foot to foot, ripping off her sandals to pull on the Blundstones.

'Haven't found them yet.' He shouted across to his superior. 'I'm going to go look around the far shed.'

The sergeant waved his response and sent some men back around the other side of the house.

'That house is theirs,' Toni shouted and pointed to the crumbling debris that was once her second home. Clearly the bull-dozer had done its work on Lorraine's rustic little old cottage. 'Where's Justin West?'

'Bugger's gone bush but can't have gone too far. He'll be easy to spot.' Hemmings pointed at a helicopter buzzing overhead. 'We got Geoff Cooper taking a look for us.' He turned back to the squad vehicle.

Toni ran around the side of the main house hitching her skirt as she went. She heard the old timbers inside, dry and brittle with the heat, crackle ferociously as the greedy lick of flames raced through the house. She despaired for the photos left inside, for her mother's last few bits of china and linen, and silently kissed them goodbye. Wasn't worth her life trying to save anything now.

Then the noise, the hissing from the flaming timbers, the popping of glass and metal and plastics all went quiet except for the rush of water from the fire hose. The flames had done their job and finished everything to ash.

Don't think, don't feel.

She headed straight for Lorraine's demolished house. 'Lorraine,' she yelled, running around the crumbled pile of mud brick. She coughed as smoke and dust sucked the air around her. 'Lorraine,' she cried again. She dropped on her hands and knees frantically looking for the trap door to the old cellar near Lorraine's house. Scratching at the dust and rubble of the old wall, she tossed bits off, desperate to find the cellar door—

Despite her frantic scrambling, she could hear low ululating. 'Oh no,' she breathed. She tried to catch the fleeting wisps of keening. 'Lorraine,' she screamed and spun around in the dirt. If Lorraine was singing like that, Two Bob must be dead. She scurried around on hand and foot listening for the noise—

There. The handle of the old door. Finally.

She tugged at it with all she had, heard Lorraine's keening float up to her from below as the door creaked open on dust-crusty hinges.

'Lorraine,' she shouted into the darkness. The keening didn't stop, its horrible sadness striking her heart.

Oh no, not Two Bob. No. no, no.

Heaved at the door with all her might. She gained centimetres, wedged her foot to keep it open and heaved some more. With leverage, the old door gave way and she fell hard on her backside.

Scrambling back in the dust and rubble to peer inside, skin scraped off her knees. Daylight sent bright shafts into the cellar, and she saw Lorraine kneeling by Two Bob's body, his head on her lap. Toni let out a cry. She could see blood dripping onto her old friend's hands from a wound in his head. 'Lorraine—Lorraine, I'm coming down.'

The woman's eyes were blank as she looked up.

Toni shuddered. She'd only heard of this expression of grief, never seen it. She slid down the ancient ladder, heard her skirt tear and felt splinters jag her thigh—oh, for her jeans. Gave her friend a quick hug. Forced herself to look at Two Bob.

The awful keening continued. Toni grabbed Two Bob's wrist to locate a pulse. His hand was warm. She wasn't sure she felt the rhythmic beat of his heart there, so she placed two fingers on his neck and there it was—a strong, steady beat.

'He's alive, Lorraine.' She shook the other woman's shoulders. 'He's alive, Lorraine. Alive.' She kept yelling until Lorraine looked at her with some recognition. 'Look.' She pressed two of Lorraine's fingers to his throat. 'He'll be fine, just knocked out.'

Lorraine nodded her understanding and looked down at Two Bob's head in her lap. She stopped singing, and just kept nodding.

How to get them out? That was the next thing. She clambered up the rickety stairs, poked her head outside the trapdoor, but couldn't see anyone close enough to help.

An engine screamed. Careening around the rubble, hurtling straight for her, Justin West was at the wheel of a 4WD.

She yelped in fright, twisted her grip on the top rung ripping it from its precarious hold. She slid into the cellar with a crash, jarring herself hard enough that the breath whooshed out of her in a grunt. Some of the ladder pieces rained down on top of them.

Lorraine gripped her arm for a moment. 'You all right, Toni?'

'Yeah,' she said, but after a moment became aware of ferocious pain in her wrist. She hissed in a breath. 'You all right, Lorraine?'

'Yeah.'

Toni could hear the vehicle screaming around the yard. Justin was in a mad frenzy. She started up what was left of the ladder, stilled as she heard firecracker blasts in short succession. She dropped like a stone to the bottom of the cellar again. 'Oh, my

God. Guns.'

Did Justin have a gun? Who was shooting? Where were her brothers?

Justin didn't know about the cellar, but he'd seen her in her hidey-hole. With the trapdoor flung open it wouldn't take him long to find it now.

Get it closed. Maybe wait until she the police caught him. *Bugger that.* She began to shinny up the rickety stairs, but this time Lorraine stopped her.

'Stay down, Toni. Bullets could hit anything. He's a mad bugger, that one.'

'I have to close that trapdoor, Lorraine, else he'll come straight here.'

Lorraine shook her head. 'The police will get him. Just wait.'

Toni looked at Two Bob again. His face was shiny with sweat, but at least he was breathing normally. Maybe just got a bump on the head.

Another gunshot, then an explosion—

An almighty crash sounded above them, the engine of a vehicle screaming, the grinding of metal against metal screeching interminably over and over as they sat cowering in the cellar underneath it.

A white flash flew above the opening of the cellar. Toni shrieked as a hub cap belted down the stairs. Then an enormous pounding thud as the vehicle slammed into the mound of rubble that had been Lorraine's house.

27

Silence followed, eerie after the cacophony of moments before.

Toni poked her head out of the cellar, after tiptoeing on scraps of ladder rungs still clinging to the earthen wall. She couldn't see past the broken-up vehicle but could see booted feet running and yelled, 'Evan, Paul. We're in the old cellar.'

Evan got to them first. He slid down to her on his backside, leaping the last step off the old ladder.

He helped Lorraine out of the musty cellar, had to leg her up with Paul tugging her from the top. She staggered upright and waited for them to get Two Bob up.

They legged him up the same way, up what was left of the rickety old wooden steps. Carrying him between them, the older man's legs barely touched the ground. They ran from the mangled and smoking vehicle and back behind the cordoned off area to the Flying Doctor gurney.

Toni, waving off a hand, clambered out and ran behind them. Charged past the officers who were trying to wrench open the door of Justin's vehicle to get him out.

He'd driven the four-wheel drive directly at her. When she leapt into the cellar to escape, he'd swerved to miss the hole and plunged the car into what was left of Lorraine's little cottage. He was trapped inside the cabin of the vehicle.

Poor bastard. Poor bastard, nothing. She slowed, turned back towards the wrecked car. If he wasn't dead, she was gonna kill him.

Smoke plumed out from underneath it.

Oh God. Was he still inside? She made a start back towards it when she was swooped off her feet—

'Oh no, you don't, Toni MacDonnell.' A steely arm swung around her and propelled her back in the right direction. Callum ran with her the twenty metres to safety. He slid them to the ground and pinned her bodily alongside him.

She struggled to sit up under his weight. 'But Justin is still—'

'They have him.' Callum pointed out two officers who accompanied the Flying Doctor crew. They ran, stretchering Justin's prone body to the closest cover, the police vehicle. They disappeared behind it. 'Keep down,' he said to her, 'because any minute now—'

The car exploded. A fire ball spewed metal and smoke high into the air above.

Callum drew her close against him, the noise deafening, the air buffeting with waves of energy. Falling debris crash landed nearby, scattered, and then silence fell. Bursts of smoke puffed up as dry earth smothered sparks. As abruptly as it started, the roar of the inferno died.

Callum lifted himself away from Toni, just in time for Paul to skid body-length alongside them, give her a quick hug, and peck her smudged and dirty face.

'Lorraine and Two Bob?' She held onto her brother as they stood up.

'They have to stitch up Two Bob, but they're all right. You?'

'Fine,' she said, holding her throbbing wrist. 'But look at our house,' she cried desperately. 'And that car.' She pointed at Justin's vehicle, blackened, scorched, derelict. She clutched Paul's arm. 'Where's our car—and the dogs?'

'They're fine, it's safe. You all right, Cal?'

'All in one piece.'

Paul gazed at the burning wreckage. 'Remind me to buy a

bloody diesel next time.'

Evan found them in a couple of leaps and hugged everyone, planted a kiss on all foreheads, including Callum's, then gripped his hand hard, as did Paul in turn.

'Thanks. My sister would be bits and pieces by now if you hadn't grabbed her.' Paul echoed Evan's gratitude, and squeezed his sister's shoulder while he scowled at her.

'I would not.' Toni turned and whispered a 'thank you' at Callum, pressed his hand only a moment then tried to let go. Her gaze roamed over his face.

Callum didn't want to let her go. 'Nice look with the boots,' he said, trying to catch her eye.

Toni looked down at her best linen skirt, torn, red-dirty, soot-smudged and then at her scraped shins and knees, and the blundy-boots on her feet. Her fingers slid out of his grip. 'If I start to laugh, I'm never going to stop crying.'

The Flying Doctor's nurse strapped Toni's wrist, told her he was sure it was a bad sprain, nothing broken. Then the plane took Lorraine and Two Bob into Alice Springs and would deliver them to the hospital.

Evan and Paul, and the dogs, followed the police back to town to file their statements. Constable Hemmings took a quick statement from Toni on the spot and made her promise to drop into the station as soon as she returned to Alice.

'I'll drive you back,' Callum offered as her eyes met his. 'Get your arm seen to. We can't stay out here. I don't fancy camping in the sheds now.'

She nodded. Weary to her bones, she stepped into his car and waited as he wound up with the police. Seemed like ages. Ages and ages that he spoke with them.

Adrenalin had gone, the shakes had passed, and the weary had set in. The ache in her throat and in her face had lessened. her wrist felt stronger, though it throbbed dully.

She rested her head, for only a moment she was sure, and closed her eyes. At some point, she was vaguely aware of someone snapping her seatbelt closed.

In Alice Springs, Callum took her first to the police station for her final statement, then to the hospital for an x-ray. No bones broken, so a new bandage was applied. From there they drove to the house on Cromwell.

He pulled up. 'Let's talk, now. Today. Even after all this.'

Her heart sank and she looked out the window. To her, the tone of his voice said it all. He'd distanced himself, she knew that, she could tell, but couldn't that wait? She didn't want to talk. She didn't want to think. Or hurt. 'Not right now,' she said. 'I don't think I could string two words together. Can we leave it for a while? Too much has happened, all too quickly. I need some time out.'

His eyes darkened, and there was a deep furrow between his brows. 'All right, for now.' He rested an arm on the open window. 'There'll be lots to do from here, in town, anyway, if you're up to it. Next few days could be tricky. Maybe we can use your shop office for—?'

'Sure, that'll be no problem. Plenty of room.'

'I'll call you, then,' he said. 'Take a couple of days off. Sleep.'

She thanked him for the ride home, thanked him for helping her at the station and then she left his vehicle without a backward glance.

Paul and Evan had left the dogs inside at Toni's house and they went crazy again when they heard her coming up the driveway. She kept them inside with her, didn't want to lose sight of them. Needed them.

Collapsing in her bed after a long, hot shower, she was too exhausted to think of Callum Parker, too tired to weep over her old home, too tired to think, or to feel the pain in her heart. Just far too tired.

28

The next morning her head ached like a bitch. She tried to pull her hair back into a plait but gave up as pain starburst up the back of her skull. A pounding throb banged behind her jaw. Her eyes hurt. Her neck felt like it was caught in a vice. Her whole arm ached from the wrist where it was bandaged. Knees were scraped but not bloody, fingers and nails were ragged.

Sleeping through the onset of a tension headache meant that nipping it now was the only way to stop a full-blown migraine. Otherwise she could write-off at least the next couple of days. Not surprising after the last few horrible weeks.

Staggering from bed to the bathroom cabinet, she groped for the bottle of ibuprofen and downed two tabs. If the bloody thing hadn't loosened up in twenty minutes she'd down two more.

At the kitchen table in her old night shirt and boxers, she sipped water cooled in the fridge, glanced at the clock. Eight forty-five a.m. A body should go back to bed, wait for the anti-inflammatories to work some magic. Or go stand under a hot shower again. That was a better idea. Get loosened up a bit. Do some neck exercises.

She let the dogs outside, threw handfuls of chow into their bowls, filled their water buckets and gingerly crept back inside.

In the bathroom, she unpeeled the bandage at her wrist, releasing another round of throbs. Untangling herself one-handed from her night-clothes, she flicked on the shower taps. Under the steaming water, her neck eased. Soap stung the scrapes on her legs—sliding into the cellar was not the best thing to do in a skirt. There was antiseptic somewhere. She'd have to douse herself with it.

Without the bandage, her forearm looked swollen. She'd wrap it again when she found the strength. The bruises would be days coming out, and so would the fresh grief over the loss of the old house, and her mother's things.

Crying, tears blending in the hot water pelting down on her uplifted face, she felt her neck ease some more. Maybe it was tears she needed. Maybe she'd been holding onto too much for way too long.

Dried off, but hair still damp, Toni flopped on her bed, loving minute by minute that the awful pain in her head was receding, slowly but surely.

Her mobile rang. Nicky Cooper. Still flat on her back, she answered, and heard the whoosh of airspace and the staccato shake of a vehicle.

'I'm on the way into town,' Nicky shouted. 'Had to check you're all right. You up for a visit?'

'Sure, come on around. I'm not much company, though.'

'Figured as much. I'll swing by the shops and bring us some treats. I'll be thirty minutes.'

'See you then.'

Nicky would be a welcome sight. Not to mention that she'd cluck around like a mother hen and make sure Toni was fed, watered, comfortable and happy. At least three out of the four, anyway. Sitting up carefully on the end of the bed, noting that the banging and clanging inside her head had almost totally subsided, she thought about getting dressed.

She'd no sooner stepped into a pair of cargo pants and shrugged on a loose t-shirt when the doorbell rang. Couldn't be Nicky unless she'd decided to come to the house before going to the shops.

Chips and Sudsy out the back barked loudly enough to make her wince. She made her way to the front door on bare feet.

Through the frosted glass, she could see a huge bouquet of flowers.

And as she pulled the door open, a shaky smile on her face, her worst nightmare appeared from behind the cheerful, fabulous, joyful mass of roses, tulips, and gerberas.

29

Toni stared, wide-eyed. One mighty drum was pounding once again inside her head. A queasy rush slid into her stomach.

Sonny Murphy thumbed over his shoulder at the van driving away. 'I told the delivery guy I'd handle it from here.' He held the huge bunch out to her. 'Hang on a minute. The card says—' He smirked, juggled the flowers as he squinted at the card in his other hand. '"Hope these help make you feel better, love CP."' He lowered the bunch. 'Aw, Tones. You have a boyfriend.' He pushed the flowers at her again.

She snatched the bunch. 'What do you want?'

He came up the step. 'I want to come in.'

'Not going to happen.' Toni stood her ground. 'What do you want, Sonny?'

Thank God the flowers were between them. Toni would've shoved him with all her might otherwise. Then again, the last time they'd confronted each other, he had lifted a fist at her, and she wouldn't do anything to risk that happening again. This time he might follow through.

Reining in the rage, hating the thudding pulse at the base of her neck, she prayed Nicky would show up soon.

He came straight to the point. 'I need more money.'

'More than you already stole?'

'Whoa.' He held up large hands, then flicked the floppy mop of dark brown fringe out of his eyes. He wagged a finger at her. 'You mean, "borrowed" against our investment. I saw that you'd made some adjustments to the bank account, so I had to come face-to-face to retrieve more funds.'

'You were at some airport leaving the country,' she sputtered.

'Leaving Sydney for Darwin. Heard there that your dad had passed away, that you sold the station. Feel sad you didn't tell me that at the time.'

My arse, you feel sad. And Dad would've booted yours to hell and back.

'So, I made a little detour south.' He smiled at her. As friendly as a malignant tumour. 'I figured after the sale, you'd have some loose change by now.'

Calling him an arsehole to his face came to mind. But she wouldn't antagonise him. She had no idea what he'd do. There were no witnesses if he decided to clock her one. The police would not act without there being witnesses, and so-help-her, she didn't want to be clocked with or without witnesses.

'No more money,' she croaked. 'You have no intention of paying it back. You stole it, deliberately.' Toni swallowed. 'You're a thief and a liar.' Heat of the day bore down on her and the throbbing in her temples had only got worse. But the fire in her belly had her shaking with a cold, clear fury.

Why had she never noticed his huge flaring nostrils before now?

He shook his head. 'Now, Tones. Ten grand is what I need. You can bank transfer that for me and I'll be on my way back to Darwin.' He came a little closer, peering at her. 'Looks like you've been roughed up a bit.' His eyebrows rose only a little, as if curious.

Would he have heard about the fire? Who knows? She stepped back, thoughts pinging, and bells ringing alarms inside her head. The flowers rustled in front of her. 'You want ten grand,' she stalled. That paper from the real estate office was ready for him to sign. Thoughts danced some more around the pain in her head.

Where the hell had she stashed it?

He looked hopeful but calculating. 'Yeah, ten grand.'

'So, sign an agreement to sell the house.' The bunch of flowers found an edge of her hip and she perched them there.

He cocked his head to one side. 'Then my pocket money will dry up, Tones.'

'Sign the papers, Sonny. Move on. Leave me alone.' Something in the bunch of flowers was irritating. 'Sign and I'll send the money.' Her eyes watered up. Her nose twitched. Damn.

'I hate it when you cry.'

Sanctimonious prick. Her blood boiled, but she held her tongue.

Over his shoulder, she saw Nicky's F100 slow down, then thunder past to park down the street. She was waving her mobile phone at Toni.

A look passed over Sonny Murphy's face. 'So, get the paper. I'll sign. Anything for money.'

Fleetingly, hope leapt. But to get the papers, she either had to leave him at the door, or have him follow her inside.

No way inside, no way.

Shoving the flowers back at him, she whirled back into the house, slammed the door shut and twisted the lock. Head pounding, heart thudding, she scurried into the office, grabbed the agreement. Ran out—scrambled back for a pen—and charged to the front door.

When she wrenched it open, Sonny had thrown the flowers to the ground. Standing with fists bunched by his side, his mouth had twisted nasty. 'Not your hospitable self, Toni.'

The paper shook as she held it out to him. 'Here. You said you'd sign. Sign. Right here.' She shoved the pen at him. She pointed with her other hand, her wrist and fingers thick with bruising. 'All filled out, waiting for you.'

He made no move. He cocked his head to the side. 'Better get a good price. I won't be agreeing to just any offer.'

Of course, he would say that. Of course. That was a battle for another day. He might sign the agreement to sell, he just didn't have to agree to any offer that came their way. But things might change a whole lot by that time.

'It's worth it, so why wouldn't it get a good price?' She shook the papers again. Felt a shift in him across the space between them, though it fairly crackled with her rage.

Sonny snatched the paperwork, leaned on the porch rail and skimmed over it. He looked at her once, then curled his lip. Grabbed the pen and scratched out a signature. Dated it where indicated. He offered the papers back.

Toni plucked them, checked that it was, in fact, his signature, and not that of Batman, and whipped the papers behind her back.

Nicky Cooper marched up the path, her phone to her ear. 'Yes, Paul,' she said loudly. 'I'm here now and he's still hassling her.'

Sonny barked a laugh, held his hands in the air. He retreated, made to bump into Nicky but she neatly side-stepped him, still talking into her phone.

'You're on your way? Good.' She snapped her old phone closed. 'Get lost, loser. Her brother wasn't the only one I rang. Police are on the way.' All five foot two of her stood in front of Toni, arms folded, mouth downturned.

Sonny made a face. 'Ooh. I'm scared. I'm going.' But his smarmy smile this time was a little wonky. He pointed at Toni. 'Ten grand.' He turned and sauntered off. Only quickened a little as Paul's 4WD careened around the corner and skidded to the curb.

Paul leapt out, slammed his car door and sprinted after Sonny.

Toni sank to the concrete step pushing the bunch of flowers out of her way, paperwork clutched in her hand. 'Didn't need that surprise.'

'The bastard brought you flowers?'

'No. That would be too weird, even for him.'

Nicky sat down with her. 'You okay?'

Toni nodded. 'Got his signature agreeing to sell the house in Adelaide.' Her hand shook as she held it up. 'That's the main thing.'

Nicky clutched her friend's hand, stopped the shaking. 'Good. Get it on the market today. He didn't touch you?'

'You would've beaten him to a pulp. He knows that.' Toni covered her friend's hand with her other fat and sore one. 'Thanks.'

Nicky flexed her biceps. 'Shifty bastard met his match today.'

Toni blurted a shaky laugh.

The police car cruised by. Nicky pointed them on down the road just as they heard rubber squealing. Sonny Murphy's hire car sped by. The cruiser made a swift U-turn and followed.

'Hah,' Nicky said. 'They'll nab him for dangerous driving or something. Maybe nab him just because he's a dickhead. I told them, I said, you might call him "a person" but I call him a loser shithead. That's what I told the police. I think one of them thought that was funny. Reckon they got the message all right.'

Toni blurted another laugh. Her head hurt. 'I need one of your strong coffees.'

Nicky checked her watch. 'Ten-thirty. You should have had a few strong coffees before now. I'll make it. And maybe even drop a slug of Jameson's into it.'

'Sis, are you all right?' Paul jogged up the path, stared at the discarded flowers, his eyes agog. '*Jesus*—did the bastard bring you flowers?'

'Great minds,' Nicky said.

Toni brushed herself off. 'Not him. I'll tell you about it inside.'

'What did he want?' Paul squinted at her. 'You still don't look too good. I hope he didn't—?'

'Nah.'

Nicky looked up. 'Did you clobber him, Paul? I didn't but I could have.' She put up her dukes again.

'Those muscles are scary.' He shook his head. 'Didn't lay a finger on him. Wish I'd got the chance. He took off too quick. Bloody big brave bastard he is.' Paul pushed the front door and beckoned the two women ahead of him.

They traipsed inside, the bunch of flowers in Nicky's arms. He had to duck out of its way as she marched past him. 'That's a serious bunch of flowers, Toni. What's going on?'

The police returned to report that they had escorted Sonny Murphy to the airport just so he wouldn't get lost before boarding his flight for Darwin. They'd waited in the lounge terminal until he boarded.

Toni agreed to file a complaint. It'd be no use, and she knew it, but at least it would be on the record somewhere that Sonny might be trouble. More trouble.

Maybe, just maybe, police presence would finally shake him off. Certainly, the Sonny Murphy she first knew would have been embarrassed by it, but she wasn't so sure there was any of that man left in whoever Sonny Murphy was now.

The thought left her cold. And when she examined it, she realised that for the first time, she couldn't care less about him. That she didn't feel a thing. No thud in her chest when his name was mentioned, no anger, no tears welled, no ... nothing. Gone.

Nicky had unpacked her car of groceries and the takeaway lunch—a cooked chook, now cold, and a creamy coleslaw sat on the benchtop.

His elbows on the bench, and his chin resting on his clasped hands, Paul said, 'You won't be giving him the ten grand.'

'I said I would. But I won't.'

Paul shook his head, his dark eyes under a frown. 'Good. Just fob him off until there's an offer on the house. Promise?'

Toni nodded. 'Promise.'

Nicky gripped her friend's hand. 'He's a friggin' coward. He won't be back if he thinks the police are on to him.'

'That's what a normal person would think.' Toni squeezed Nicky's hand in return, then rubbed her temples. 'What a couple of days.'

A couple of sharp raps and a few manic ding-dongs of the bell, and the front door banged open.

'That will be the younger brother,' Paul said. 'No surprises there.'

Evan shot into the kitchen, his hat hair looking more odd than usual. 'What's happened? Why's everyone here? Everything okay?' He stared at his sister, glanced at Nicky, nodded, looked at his brother.

Paul picked up his coffee. 'You missed all the fun.'

Evan grabbed a mug and poured a coffee. Hunted in the fridge for the milk. Empty-handed, he turned back to the bench and saw Nicky waving the carton for him. She poured. 'Thanks. The way you shot out of that meeting, bro, I thought some other bad thing had happened.' He loaded two sugars and stirred. 'And I'm not the only one worried. Callum's on his way.'

Toni started, slipped off her stool and went in search of something big enough to take the enormous bunch of flowers.

The boys were heading back to the station. They told Toni and Nicky that the meeting they'd attended had been to set up a roster for the repair crews, and to get initial orders for new timber, iron and steel underway.

The insurance bloke was flying in by special request and someone would meet him out there. It wasn't Callum Parker's problem, not technically, but he'd pulled some strings to get things moving for the MacDonnells.

Two Bob and Lorraine were setting up temporary house over by the machinery sheds, close to the old generator. At least the workers would be fed and have water for ablutions. Not to mention—and most importantly—cold beer in the fridges.

Toni stood on the doorstep as the boys were leaving, intending to wave them off, to show that she was fine. She wasn't fine, she felt sick. As Callum pulled into the curb by the house, she retreated, head thudding, wrist pounding, heart skipping. She and Nicky watched from the front room window.

All three men stood, leaning on respective vehicles, arms folded, nodding, talking, heads tipping in the direction of the house.

'God, they look good,' Nicky breathed.

'Shut up.'

The boys headed off. Nicky headed back to the kitchen, loaded Toni's dishwasher after the takeaway lunch, and didn't linger afterwards. 'Call me whenever,' she said, pressed her cheek to Toni's then headed out the door. With a smiling glance at Callum, who'd stalked into the house and had taken a possie in the doorway, she waved fingers at Toni. 'See you.'

Toni glanced across at the gleeful flowers, cheerful despite their ordeal and happily sitting in a bucket of water. 'Thanks for organizing things, Callum. And for these. They're beautiful.'

'Pleasure.' He'd been leaning in the door jamb while the boys and Nicky took their leave, so now he paced across to the breakfast bench and took up a seat. 'It all happens around here, doesn't it? How are you feeling?'

'Like a truck's run over me.'

'Understandable.' He reached over and touched her cheek. 'Paul tells me the police escorted some bloke away from here.'

Toni ducked her head a moment. 'Maybe escorted is a slight exaggeration. But yes, he's gone.' Her heart thudded. She was sure it had nothing to do with Sonny Murphy this time.

'For good?'

An open question, deserving of an open answer. She nodded. 'For good. He's the reason for the blood tests. He couldn't be trusted. I don't know if…' She stopped. Didn't want to go on.

Callum Parker sat there just looking at her. Something responded in her, deep down. Something she couldn't keep at bay. Something she knew she should put a cap on, walk away from, something that made her eyes well up again at that thought. She let go of a long breath.

'Then, we'll wait to find out.' He let a hand drop to one of hers.

'Anything else I can help with?'

His hand was warm. Dry. When she glanced down, it looked capable, strong. His hands were dependable. Dependable? Where did that come from?

He dropped his other on both of hers, covering them. They felt good. Man's hands. Fingers scarred a little, callused a little, scratchy on hers. One ring finger bent at a funny angle, not straightening up. Nails broad, one blackened where something must have hammered it, or fallen on it. Maybe he scraped and tore a couple when rolling around on the fire blackened dirt of your homestead in the last day or so. You know, helping you out. You know, when he hoisted you away from an exploding car and dropped you to the ground under him, shielding you from being blown up. You know, that time.

She curled her fingers carefully through his, tugged a little, released. Somehow, sometime, she would go there, with him. Somehow, she'd try and forget the things she couldn't have, and—

'Toni, can I do anything else to help?' he reiterated.

The concern on his face was touching. Her mind worked, garnered all its processes.

Then it came to her like a bolt out of the blue. She straightened; her thoughts clear for the first time in days. She licked her lips, tasted cold roast chook flavours, picked up a paper towel and wiped them. 'I bet you happen to know a really good real estate agent in Adelaide.'

A smile lit his face. 'I happen to know a great many people in the business.' He rubbed her good hand in his. 'Tell me what you need.'

*

Callum glanced across. She'd fallen asleep on the couch, a forearm over her face.

After putting him in the picture regarding the house in Adelaide, about how this Murphy guy had taken funds meant for the mortgage, and how she'd used half her new salary to keep it out of foreclosure, she'd lost her puff.

She'd already tried insisting that she go back out to the station, following her brothers. Cal told her all available temporary huts were for the demolition workers, and then the repairmen. A hut for her hadn't been ordered.

And no, she wouldn't be going out to the station and swag it. When she felt better, there was work to do from her office in the travel shop. She'd protested, but he held up a hand stating that that's what they'd agreed. Grumbling, she had acquiesced, and sank to the settee, knocked down tired.

He fired up his laptop at her kitchen table. When he looked over his shoulder she was flaked out, asleep.

Callum turned his attention to the sale of her house in Magill. He'd scanned the agreement her ex had signed into his laptop, and the email was ready to send to the real estate agent. He'd chosen someone who'd be the best fit for the area.

After Toni had explained her predicament, he'd gone quiet for long moments. Then a plan emerged. When put into place, the house would be sold—almost immediately—to one of Callum's companies. The offer to the ex would be one he wouldn't refuse.

Toni protested, until he asked her to hold on. The plan ensured the weasel ex wouldn't be hanging around waiting for the market to bite. Or to bite Toni for more money. Then, Callum's company would sell the house on, to recoup its outlay.

Her ex wouldn't refuse the offer. Because Callum knew a lot of people, and one of them was a helluva good QC.

*

Toni woke up, groggy. Only a few aches and pains. Her forearm was sore, but not badly, and it looked as if some of its puffiness had subsided. She'd re-bandage it soon.

The house was quiet. Carefully sitting up on the settee, she looked about, listened for Callum. Nothing.

She stood up slowly, stretched only a little, took a couple of deep breaths. Noticed his laptop open on the kitchen table, and a note propped up against the screen.

5.15 - Gone to pick up pizza for us, be back soon.

She checked the clock. Over fifteen minutes ago. Food. That would be good. So, a shower would be even better. A quick one at that, if he was returning. A splash down would freshen her up, sluice off the crazy antics of the morning.

In and out of the bathroom quickly, her hair bundled atop her head in a scrunchie, she changed into a fresh tee, and dragged on a clean pair of shorts.

Her head clear, and her future looking not quite so tangled as it had earlier. A warm hearted, good looking man was bringing pizza home. To her.

Heading for the office, she booted up her computer and studied at least one website looking for some answers. There had to be answers. There had to be new developments that could give her some sort of hope.

Maybe a follow up trip to the GP for news on the fertility clinic.

Twenty minutes later, Callum texted to say he was on his way back.

Toni watched him wipe the paper towel over his mouth.

'Gourmet vegetarian with salami. What better pizza to have?' he asked and sat back. 'They do a good job, there.'

'Goes exceptionally well with the red.' She gave a little salute with her glass.

They sat side by side on the settee. The open, empty box of pizza on the coffee table looked out of place with the fine bottle of shiraz he'd brought back as well.

His shoulder nudged hers. 'Feeling okay?'

'I feel odd that you've come to the rescue with the Magill house.' Toni stared at the colour of the wine. Deep, rich, earthy red. Darker, of course, than her beloved red hills of home, nevertheless bold, and full of life. And her life was changing, quickly.

'I meant after Justin West's little pyro-demolition act,' he said. 'And you being tossed into the cellar.'

Toni met his gaze for a moment. 'You came to the rescue then, too.'

He smiled, rueful. 'Didn't rescue the damsel from total distress.'

She let out a sigh. 'It hasn't sunk in yet. This,' she raised her re-bandaged forearm, 'Reminds me that I got away with my life. That Lorraine and Two Bob are okay. That my dogs—' she looked over at Chipper and Suds lounging on their mats, 'are fine, my brothers are fine.' She stopped then. Ducked her chin and looked up again. 'That you're fine.'

After a beat, he nudged a little closer. 'I'm fine. And as for the Magill house thing, treat it like it's business. You get a fair and reasonable price for the house to get rid of it, and at the same time, you'll get rid of the other problem. Then my company will sell the house on. Might even make a profit. So, you see? A business decision.' He flicked her a look. 'Not a rescue.'

'Right.' Toni knew that without Callum the way ahead would have been so much tougher. As it was, she could only hope that Sonny Murphy would soon absolutely be past tense. The fact that Callum would be making a profit on the house in the long run, sat a whole lot easier with her.

As if he'd read her mind, he said, 'I have my reasons doing it. All legit. You're someone I care about, and you're my employee. I have a responsibility to look after you in that regard. You've spent half a year's salary already, and I still need you on the payroll. The other reason is because Phillip looked after my dad.' He reached for the bottle to refill both glasses, and then his eyes met hers. 'All of this buying the station, deeding land back to Two Bob, offering you and your brothers your jobs back, it's all part of the same.' He touched his chest near his heart. 'I know how much your dad's friendship meant to mine. So, when we saw the station up for sale, and I met with your dad… It's part of the original deal, which I

might add is working for all of us.' Callum bumped her shoulder
with his again, slumped a little further in the seat. 'And my
companies have the funds to buy and sell. That's all I'm doing
with your house, too. Buying it to sell. Because I can.' He took an
appreciative sip.

Her scepticism faded a smidge.

When he glanced at her again, he saw it. 'You still have to pay
the conveyancer, the real estate agent's commission, any mortgage
discharge fees. I'm just making sure it's all dealt with quickly.'
When still she hesitated, he said, 'You can thank me later.'

She laughed. 'I thank you now, believe me. I just don't want to
be—'

'You're not under any obligation whatsoever.' His voice had
hardened a little.

She was grateful. She accepted the help, no obligation. He'd
certainly charged into action, and he needn't have. Then again,
he'd been charging into action around her for a while now.
Warmth curled in her belly. Something lower down pinged,
sending a ripple waving through her, and she squeezed her eyes
shut a moment against the fierce blush creeping up her chest and
across her cheeks.

He pressed her hand. 'Okay, I know you're tired. Knocked out.'
He sat forward and closed over the empty pizza box. 'My car's all
packed. I'll head out to the station maybe four tomorrow morning.
I thought, if it's all right with you, I'll doss down on the floor here,
tonight.'

Startled, she sat up. 'Of course, it is, but I'll be okay here.
Sonny's gone. Besides, I should come out to the station, too.'

He shook his head, stood up, took the pizza box to the kitchen
bench. 'I need you at the travel shop office, remember? Besides,
once I've checked the station is as good as it can be from my
company's point of view, I'll go straight through to the airport
from the station. I'll take the red-eye to Adelaide. Have to spend a
week or so tidying up a few things.' He reefed car keys from his

pocket. 'Back in a tick.' He headed down the hallway to the front door.

She heard his car door open and moments later, slam shut.

Her heartbeat raced for a few seconds, and her breath was short. Head throbbed as she sat up too quickly.

True, there was too much to do and they did need an office. There was an enormous amount of work to trawl through, now. The insurance issue on the station, for one. At least from the travel shop, she could handle both jobs with relative ease. Though she wasn't sure 'ease' was the right term.

There were statements for the police, for insurance, for the prosecutors … God only knows what. Not to mention whatever Mackies and their forensic accountants came up with after the boys had put their suspicions forward. There was a mountain of paperwork to finish before settlement, the hand-over to Mary-Anne, the—

Callum returned, swag gripped in his hand, and leaned it against the wall just inside the lounge. He dropped an overnight bag beside it. 'You look done in, Toni.'

'It's not even eight p.m. Too early.'

'Nothing like an early night. I'll clean up here.' He waved a hand at the half empty wine bottle, their glasses. 'Don't worry about anything. Just get a good night's sleep.'

She took a breath, her stomach flip-flopping. 'I'll be fine on my own here, you know. You don't have to stay.'

He grabbed the wine, screwed on the lid, picked up the two glasses. 'No trouble. I'll be quiet as I can, won't disturb you in the morning.' He turned back towards the sink.

Toni wrung her hands. Nothing to lose, nothing to lose. Everything to lose. What if he rejects—

She took a breath. 'But I'm glad you are staying.' *Coward, Toni.*

He glanced over his shoulder and said, 'It's fine.'

A deep breath. 'In that case, just so you know—you don't have to be in here on your swag,' and held onto what was left of her breath.

He took his sweet bloody time turning back from the sink to look at her. Her hand wringing stopped. He didn't look happy. He didn't look unhappy. He didn't look anything. Just stared at her, as if he was concentrating on her nose, or something.

Oh God. I have so said the wrong thing.

30

Toni put down her pen and glanced into the mall. At least she had Mary-Anne at the shop for company this last week. Parker Inc would have office space while all this drama was sorted out.

Shoppers, tourists, locals all ploughed along the paved thoroughfare intent on their business. The bright blue sky of midmorning bore the promise of another scorching few days before the official start of summer.

M-A didn't need any help with the travel side of things. More like Toni needed something to occupy her rabid mind. Straighten things out. After that, she'd have to move back to the station and to the extra temporary huts Callum had secured for their separate quarters and the office.

Heart heavy, it was a dull ache that didn't seem likely to shift. Not only the station house gone, and with it the sixty-odd years of history, but gone also, the man who'd come here to take up the reins, who'd made it clear he wanted to spend time with her. He'd run for the hills a week ago when she made her offer to him.

She picked up her pen and chewed the tip. Scoffed. *Not exactly what had happened, Toni.* Hah! What did she expect? So why was she so floored by what he said? It was exactly what she suspected would happen. It showed why she could never—would never—ever go there again.

Staring down at the haphazard stack of papers messing up her desk, she blinked hard at the repeated thoughts. *Just gotta stop going there. Let it go.*

Another breath sucked in and puffed out—puffing like an old steam train, Mary-Anne had commented earlier—she mentally turned away from the internals and concentrated on the tangibles.

After the fever of Justin's assault on her family home had passed, Parker Inc's work had begun to roll in. Her desk was now covered in paperwork relating to a number of project activities, none the least of which were the plans and council approval submissions for the work at the station that would commence day after settlement.

Not long to go now.

Then there were the builders undertaking the repair work who had their own stack of paperwork for her to sift through.

'And what's happened with your hair?'

Toni swung towards the door and looked at Ben Whyte. He stood inside her office, a mock scowl on his face.

'I've been busy,' she said. 'I feel lousy, and there's a lot more to do yet. The settlement is day after tomorrow and I haven't finalised things with the insurance people about Justin's little incident. That was on our watch, you know, being the vendors. It's a mess. There's even more things going on, so don't hassle me about my hair, of all things.' She'd grabbed it this morning and tied it back in a loose ponytail, which meant it had all but escaped the scrunchie.

'Hey, whoa. I've got things going on, too, you know.'

'Sure.' She bent her head over the paperwork again but not before catching Ben glance at Mary-Anne who shrugged as if to say that she couldn't help, either. 'What?'

'And you've lost weight,' Ben carried on.

'Really.'

'No phone calls, then.'

'From whom?' Toni knew very well "from whom". It'd been a week since Callum had left, and every day he'd called her. She'd returned his calls only after they went to message-bank. That way, she could gather herself and answer the enquiries politely, diligently, and do the work he requested. 'I'm not expecting any calls.'

'Er, duh.'

'Don't.'

Ben walked to her desk, leant over and squeezed her hand. 'I'm sorry it turned out this way, Toni. Awful about the station. I just can't imagine it how it feels. All those memories.'

The concern on his face suddenly beat down her temper. She relented. 'Thanks,' she said, softening her tone.

'You feeling all right now? I mean, are all bruised bits healing?'

She nodded. 'I just have to head-down-and-bum-up and push on through to get it all done. I'm sorry, Ben, I really am under the pump,' she said. 'The boys are out mustering what's left of our cattle to go to auction and I have to do all this station paperwork myself.'

Ben leaned a bum cheek on her desk, folded his arms. 'You don't have to do it all before the settlement.'

'I do. I want it all out of the way. The insurance issue is a nightmare. I'm going to try and stall working for Parker Inc until all this is sorted.'

He looked at her, wide-eyed. 'Get out of the employment contract?'

She shrugged. 'Maybe. Find a way to pay him back what I owe.'

'There's only one way, fool. And that's work for it. Not a good idea to hold them off.'

'I'm going to try.' Shrugging again, she waved her hands at the paperwork in front of her. 'What did you just drop in for?'

Ben pushed his backside onto her desk, swung his legs. 'To tell you of my good news. Mo Reddell called me up. Wants me to take my old job back.'

Toni stared at him. 'Really? I thought you had a big falling out—'

He shook his head. 'Not so much Mo and me, as the dud things going on there he wasn't seeing and didn't believe I was telling him. And,' he tapped his nose, 'He's asked me to go along tonight for farewell drinks for Eric Roycroft. Maybe that's why I've got my job back. Eric's finally retiring.'

'You never liked him.'

'Cunning bastard reminds me of a rat.' Ben tapped his chest with a thumb. 'It'll be a smack in the face for him to see me at his farewell.'

'But why even go if you don't like the guy? Catch up with Mo another time.'

He inclined his head side to side, as if tossing up the idea. 'Had the same thought myself but Mo was ahead of me. Insisted tonight would be a good night to show up. Anyhow,' he stood up. 'I'll get going. I was just checking in with you. I'll report back later.' He winked at her. 'See you, Mary-Anne,' he called as he left.

Toni watched him go, vaguely heard a phone ring and Mary-Anne answer it. Curious how Eric was leaving. He was another of the contacts her dad had over the years. With Justin in the hospital awaiting assessment, there was no—

'Call for you,' Mary-Anne said, handing her the cordless and walking away.

And Toni knew straight away who it would be. 'Toni MacDonnell,' she answered, plainly.

'Ah, got to speak to you in person at last.'

'Hi, Callum.' Cheery, breezy, professional. Talking to the boss. No strings. No dumb come-hithers.

'Would you pick me up at the airport this afternoon? I'm on the four pm.' He was to the point, his voice light, friendly.

She had a moment's twinge of embarrassment but shooed that away. Wondering why he wasn't catching a taxi in from the terminal, or the shuttle, she said, 'Can do, but why don't you—'

'Great. There's a bunch of surveyors due out at the Run tomorrow. They're driving down the Barkly Highway, so I said we'd be out there to meet them. That okay with you? Will be an early start tomorrow. We can drive up together.'

Toni stared at the stacks of paper on her desk.

'You there?' His voice floated down the line.

'Settlement's the next day.' She eyed off the papers, the stack of which now looked enormous. *Oh, please, anything for the dusty paddocks and getting into the dirt again.*

'Technicality. It's just a phone call from the conveyancer advising it's all gone ahead okay.'

The conveyancer would have been Justin and would now be an agency guy from Adelaide. She tried to stall. 'Look, I might have to put off starting work out at the station. I have the insurance to wrangle—'

His voice floated down the line again. 'Sure, but that won't stop settlement now that we've squared it away. You're on our books, and that's that.'

She had nothing. No room to wriggle out of the employment contract.

Callum continued, 'Besides, probably better to do hand-over out there. We'll be face-to-face with all the plant and equipment.'

None of that had been damaged in Justin's rampage. He'd really shown her it was personal, an attack on her possessions, on her parents' legacy.

Resigned to it. Just another load to carry, she said, 'Sure. See you at the airport.'

They disconnected. She glanced at the time. Five hours to go. A person could knock over a lot of paperwork in five hours.

She absently reached for the jellybean jar.

31

Eric Roycroft checked over the last of the files he'd left on the office computer. Nothing likely to look suspicious to anyone. He shut it down. He pulled out empty desk drawers to check one more time. Then peering into his 'take-home' box he figured he had everything with him that he should have.

Glancing into the main office area, he saw the delivery fella bringing in boxes of pizza. The aroma of wood-fired pepperoni and onion wafting across prompted a stomach growl. The air was heavy with roasted garlic. Trays of bread-somethings were on every cleared space, and the boys were loading an esky with ice and beers.

It was the only type of send-off he wanted; nothing at his place or at a fancy hotel. Just at the office with a few invited clients as well as his colleagues, and that was it. And that was enough. He'd be out of town so fast after packing up they wouldn't see him for dust. He couldn't wait to get out.

No one had come knocking on his door when the police had picked up that nutter, West. He'd held his breath for a day or two, kept his head down. He'd murmured his surprise when the gossip reached the office about what had happened at MacDonnell's Run. And … nothing.

Wasn't taking any chances, though. He'd drained the AgAnswers bank account of all but a few thousand, closed Biosoil+ and converted the funds to cash.

Sure, anyone looking would be able to see clear as day now, but his passport was good to go, the money already offshore by way of good old Australia Post, mostly in American dollars.

First stop would be—

Shit. That looks like the MacDonnell boys. His gut tightened. Ah well, nice of them to come along. 'Cept I didn't know they'd be coming along. Christ, and that nong, Ben Whyte, is with them.

Sniffing, pulling at his open collar with one hand, he gave a wave with the other to show he'd be five minutes. He wasn't gonna rush out to schmooze. Besides, he felt sweaty, didn't want to look as if he was nervous or anything.

Steve Russell poked his head in the door, two stubbies of beer held by their necks in one hand. 'Here you go, Eric. Wet your whistle.'

'Thanks, mate.'

Steve landed a beer on Eric's desk, swigged from the other then headed back to the main room.

Eric spun around on his chair. Can't ferret around much longer in here, nothing else to pack up, I'm gonna have to—

Aware of a sudden silence in the outer room, he lifted his head. Saw everyone out there staring in at him. And his world stood still.

'You Eric Roycroft?' A tall, middle-aged bloke wearing a white shirt and suit-trousers stood in the doorway, his face bland. Another younger bloke, dressed the same with his suit jacket over one shoulder, stood just behind.

Eric nodded and stood up, one hand on the desk for support.

'Detective Senior Sergeant Mulholland.' He opened an ID wallet and held it steady. With a lift of his chin he indicted the younger man. 'Detective Sergeant Casey.' He pocketed the ID while Casey flashed his. 'You're under arrest for the embezzlement of funds from the estate of Phillip MacDonnell, for fraud charges relating to the embezzlement and for money laundering.'

Eric stood rooted to the spot. He looked at the lone beer on his desk, condensation dripping onto the blotter pad. Not even time for one last drink, and that felt like the most important thing right then. Saliva dried in his mouth and all he wanted to do was take a piss.

The older cop's mouth was moving again. Probably reading him his rights. All he heard was a whooshing sound, that of his hoarded stash, the product of his lies and deceit, whisked away by the wind.

The only other thing he heard was the clink of handcuffs around his wrists.

32

The arrivals board flashed that Callum's flight from Adelaide had just landed. It would be maybe fifteen minutes before emerging from the terminal.

Toni sat near the big sliding doors at the entrance, able to get out quickly soon after he'd grabbed his luggage. She was happy for the benefit of the air-conditioning inside.

On the drive out to the airport, she'd revisited—over and over—the last of their conversation at her place a week ago. That conversation was the one when she'd let him know she was going to jump his bones. The one where he took his time before he finally spoke. The one where she thought she would dissolve in a puddle of mortified embarrassment and go gurgling down the plughole, one murky slurp at a time.

Afterwards, when he left, she'd called her older brother, Paul. 'What does it mean when a guy says, "let's take some more time about this"?'

Paul barked down the line. 'What?'

Toni could hear steers bawling in the background. 'Does it mean, "no way, not going there", or "let's take some more time"?' she shouted.

There was a moment's silence and more cattle bawling. 'It means, he wants to take some more time,' her brother shouted back.

'Yeah, but what for? So, he can change his mind, or get out of it or—'

'For crissakes, it just means he wants to take some more time. Maybe wants you both to be on the same page.' Paul hesitated, then yelled, 'Cal Parker, isn't it?'

Toni winced but sailed on. 'And what does it mean when you ask a question and he just answers "okay"?'

Another hesitation, more cattle complaining. 'It means "okay",' he shouted.

'Yeah, but okay to what?'

'Whatever the hell you asked him, Toni,' Paul bellowed. 'For crissakes, what did you ask?'

'Nothing. Nothing. Don't worry about it.'

'Well, get off the phone, then. I got jobs to do.'

Paul. No help. And Evan certainly wouldn't be any help, so she didn't call him.

She recalled how Callum had leaned his backside on the bench near her sink, and stared at her, thumbs now hooked in his belt loops. Those steely blue-grey eyes met her gaze, and the zazz spiralled all the way to her feet before bouncing back to her nethers. She went weak at the knees—because of what, she wasn't sure. Hormone-frenzy? Or complete and utter shame.

'…You don't have to be in here on your swag.' That's what she'd said.

A little smile had played at his mouth, and the dimple had twitched. 'I don't?'

She'd swallowed. 'No. You don't have to swag it when I have a perfectly big, comfortable bed.' Hands crept up to smooth and tuck locks of annoying hair back into the scrunchie.

Tilting his head, the smile still in place, the dimple a definite promise, he'd asked, 'And where will you be sleeping?'

A red-hot blush had swept across her cheeks, needling her face in its rush. 'In my bed.'

'So, two of us in your big, comfortable bed?'

Oh God—he doesn't want to. He's thought about all the things, all the stuff, and changed his mind. She'd blinked hard.

He'd glanced down at the floor for a few seconds. 'This isn't anything to do with the rescue thing, or the old lover-rebound-thing is it? Maybe a thank-you thing.'

'What? No!' Horrified, she'd stepped back. 'This isn't a—thank-you thing, or anything else. God no. I'm not—sacrificing for the greater good. I'm thinking it might be maybe fun, even.' Another rush of heat hit her cheeks.

He nodded and the dimple had taken a life of its own. 'It certainly would be fun.' The smile still in place.

Tentatively, she'd smiled back. 'Good—'

'But not now. Not tonight.'

Stock still, she'd kept her tone light. 'Right. Then, sure, roll out your swag.'

He advanced a couple of steps, bear-hugged her before she could retreat. 'I must be completely out of my mind, but not tonight,' he said into her hair. 'I want you to be absolutely sure—'

'I'm sure.'

'—that you won't feel lousy if we go there.'

She froze in his arms. 'Look, I take full responsibility for how I feel—'

'Good.'

He'd been pulling back. Kissing the tip of her nose, he released her. All so matter-of-fact. All so clinical. All so perfunctory. Like a job.

She'd felt a whole lot unsure of herself, then. 'You're right. More thinking required. Okay.'

'Okay.' He stepped back to the sink and leaned on the bench again, took a slow breath in. 'So maybe now you better go off to that big comfy bed of yours.'

She'd nodded. 'Right.' *Just refuse to be embarrassed, Toni, you big galah. Refuse. Hold your head up.* Her chin came up. 'You know where everything is. So, um, I'll see you when you get back.'

'Sure. Goodnight.' He still stood there, almost wary.

What's that look on his face? Jeez, I'm no good at this stuff. Then it struck her. 'We're still good, aren't we?' Nervous at his slight hesitation, she blurted, 'We're okay, right?'

A hesitation again. 'We're okay.'

And then she'd marched herself off to her bedroom, undressed, crawled her aching body and sore head into bed. Pulled the sheet over her head and gave herself a good talking to.

Now, a whole seven days later, she watched the throngs of people emerging from the airport arrival lounge and make bee-lines for the baggage carousel. Her heartbeat thumped loudly in her ears. Any minute now he'd— There he was. Striding. Carrying a cabin bag. Wearing jeans, and a finely striped blue and white shirt, sleeves rolled. Boots. Making directly for her, a big grin on his face. Dark hair tucked behind his ears. More metro meets country.

She jumped to her feet. 'Hi.'

'Hi.' Bent to kiss her cheek lightly. 'Thanks for coming out.'

'It's fine.' Lost her words, it seemed, because she didn't say anything more.

'Yep, I had a good flight. Yep, let's get going. I only took this bag with me, so no luggage to pick up.' He guided her through the sliding door and the dry heat outside enveloped them.

They walked briskly across the driveway to the car. Once inside her 4WD, buckled up, the air-con switched on full-blast, and his bag slung into the back, he twisted in the passenger seat to look at her. 'Is your bag packed ready for the station?'

Toni reversed out of the park. 'Sure is. Early start tomorrow, you said.'

She detected a scent, maybe aftershave. Citrusy, woody undertones. Faint, but tantalizing, even though his chin and jawline sported what might have been a neat three-day growth. He looked good. Real good.

'I'm thinking we should go to your house, grab your bag and go straight out there tonight.'

She changed the gear into first. Stared resolutely ahead. 'Sure. Fine by me.'

'Right.' He settled back in his seat. 'Seems all the temp huts are at the station now. Paul's worked a minor miracle.'

'Great.'

'Great.' He grabbed hold of his seat belt, anchored his hand on it.

He seemed edgy. Might be a long drive.

She left the 4WD running in her driveway, ushered both dogs into the back bay of the car, and hauled her bag into the back seat. It monstered Callum's and looked slightly ridiculous.

Callum lugged out both their swags from the house, tossed them atop the car and strapped them down.

They were headed out of town by five thirty, the ninety-minute drive ahead of them. He kept the conversation light, chatty, as if there was nothing like an elephant in the room, so to speak. He talked about the people he met, especially his mate the QC, who said he'd take care of things.

Toni glanced across at him. 'Still can't believe a QC is on the case. I can't pay—'

'It's one letter. If he charges, and I don't think he will, I'll pay it. Believe me, it'll kill your problem stone dead,' he replied tonelessly, and kept on talking.

The agent he'd decided would sell her property already had buyers lined up. He was sure it'd be under contract—all being well—within a week or two.

'Very glad about that,' she said, and breathed a sigh of relief. Could it be that easy? She'd have to wait to see if Sonny Murphy would sign the contract, then she remembered again about the QC letter. He would sign. The QC had given him many reasons why it would be in his best interest to sign and reminded him that his 'borrowings' would come off the top of his share of the net profit.

Callum held a very good one-sided conversation. Toni didn't

have much input except to let him know that Eric Roycroft was in remand in Darwin, and most likely a flight-risk so no bail would be imposed. Justin West was still under sedation, awaiting competency assessment. Yes, there were large tracts of money fraudulently acquired by Roycroft, it seemed, but whether it could be recovered was another matter. The few thousands they'd uncovered was only the tip of the iceberg. It looked more like hundreds of thousands of dollars. Maybe more than a million.

Callum said he had more details to share with her, and that he'd fill her in on it later. 'Either way, it sounds like the threat to everything from both West and Roycroft is over.'

Toni blinked away the smarting behind her eyes as she thought of her sick dad, and how easily he'd been betrayed when he first learned of his illness.

She didn't stop the vehicle at her favourite spot along the way. Heading into dusk, wildlife would be roaming, and steers were likely to be on the move. She decided to keep going.

Halfway up the drive to the old homestead, lights twinkled in a different area to where she'd been used to seeing them all her life. Campfires were dotted near the old yards. The sooty hulk of her old homestead sat on their left as she pulled in by the rickety house yards. This was the time the tears would not be forced down or stopped from trickling over her cheeks and on to her shirt. Her lungs expanded painfully and a lump jumped in her throat.

Callum was already stepping out of the vehicle and shouting greetings to the team. He opened the back door for the dogs and Chipper and Suds shot out, leaping in a frenzy for the makeshift camp and the workmen.

Untying the swags, he dropped his to the ground. Was about to drop hers, too.

Toni rubbed her cheeks, sniffed and clambered out. 'Leave mine. I'll go out a little way, camp overnight. Be back early.' Maybe cry a little bit, heal a little bit, the bit she could heal.

Before Callum could answer, Paul jogged over, Evan behind

him. Back slapping and shoulder bumping all round, offers of beers and steaks for Callum, bear hugs for Toni. A wink from her older brother. If he noticed any tears, he didn't say, just hugged her harder. Didn't help.

She resisted the invite to join them. Despite her brothers' protests, she headed towards the old house. Stood solemnly by the shell of her family home, the deepening dusk slowly giving way to the night sky.

The boys had been able to save a few of the remaining things out here that she'd treasured. Some books. Some old photos in frames that were on the far wall away from the fire. Her mother's ancient trousseau box, which was a family heirloom, and an old clock. All a little bit sooty and smoky, but intact. Luckily, most of the real prized possessions were already stored in Alice at the house on Cromwell Drive.

Everything salvageable was tucked into a shed that had previously housed a couple of ancient tractors, now removed. It was smoke damaged, but at least they had something.

Scanning the destruction, she thought of Justin. His overworked mind must have suddenly snapped under the strain of her father's death, the embezzlement, watching his livelihood sneak away from him. Her rejection. Then the DNA results, which he hadn't even looked at, and which had mocked him even more when he did look.

No use making excuses for him. She shuddered when she thought of what he'd done to Two Bob, who thankfully would recover easily. Justin would go to jail or an institution for a very long time. He and his accomplice, that Eric Roycroft man, sitting in Reddell's cooking the books. It didn't bear thinking about what they'd nearly got away with. Hundreds of thousands of dollars.

She walked back to the camp, a nonchalant glance at Callum, who caught her glance, lifted his beer towards her. She nodded, smiled, just a stretch of her mouth, really. Found Paul.

Despite more protests from her brother, he helped pack a camp box for her—a light and gas bottle, a chair, a little table, a mozzie tent. Heaved it into her car.

She packed a small esky with a cold bottle of white, grabbed a handy stack of plastic cups, a box of crackers and a plate of cheeses Lorraine must have cut for the men.

Shoving it onto the back seat, she climbed behind the wheel and drove west, following the sun, a huge blood orange ball low in the sky.

A few kilometres along, the rough track petering out, she pulled over at a small clearing. Stepping up to untie her swag, she threw it down, unpacked her little camp utilities, and settled in with a book she'd brought with her from Alice. Not the time right now to face the issues of a burned down old home, and of Callum Parker. She'd do that in the morning, when back at the homestead, amid the hustle and bustle of workmen. His damn name thudded like a boulder dropping in her stomach.

The boys would be up and at it early tomorrow with Chipper and Sudsy and their own dogs. They'd be somewhere shifting the last of their cattle off land no longer theirs, and into trucks to go to market. When that was done, they'd be back in the mix, helping with the repair work. She would start work for real out here.

Under New Management.

First thing, she'd catch up with Lorraine and check on Two Bob. Her priorities in that direction would never change. For now, she just wanted to sit. A bit later, she'd quietly drop off to sleep under the great night sky over the central desert. At least for now, she could still steal some time to herself. The sun was fast making its way down to set, but there was still an hour or so of light left.

She hauled out the esky and set up a couple of solar lights to cut what would become dense night darkness. Her gas lamp would attract too many bugs and crawlies, and she hadn't brought a fly-proof tent, so she didn't light it.

Having eaten ravenously at lunch, she'd snacked on some fruit before picking Callum up from the airport. Tonight, a nibble of cheese and crackers was all she wanted.

Retrieving the bottle of wine, she realised she'd grabbed one of the older ones –one with a cork in it. Not fancying tonight without a drink, she rummaged in the glovebox, full of hope, and with an 'aha', found a corkscrew.

Just like the boy scouts said, be prepared.

A rumble of a vehicle in the distance.

Ignored.

She'd toast her new life—whatever that was going to be—with a glass or two or four from this icy dry white. Ironically, she'd brought enough plastic cups to hold a party, but had no one to party with. Not on one bottle, anyway.

Look forward to rebuilding your life. You don't own the Run any more, but still, there might be a good future working it.

Bury herself in work at the station, keep the travel agency going with Mary-Anne at the helm, get up and running full tilt again. All she had to do was ride out the year with Callum Parker and Co. How hard would it be?

At least there would finally be some money for each of Philip MacDonnell's kids to come out of the fiasco of a sale, from the trust, and from the last of the stock. Not enough to give each of them a lifetime of luxury, just a degree of comfort, enough to help her pull the threads of her existence back together again and get on with it.

God only knows what money would come back to them after the court cases. Maybe nothing after legal expenses. No one could tell her whether any stolen funds were retrievable.

Hard to say what would be secured for her out of the sale of the Adelaide house, either. But perhaps a little something to look forward to, or even just enough to give Sonny Murphy a two-finger salute. The QC would work that out, make sure she'd get her fair share after Sonny's attempt at swindling.

The corkscrew fit neatly into the centre of the cork. Which took a great deal of concentration because she heard the roar of a big four-wheel drive speeding along the track.

She knew who it would be. Couldn't ignore it any longer.

Holding the bottle by the corkscrew stuck in its neck, she watched as the vehicle skewed to a halt and Callum Parker stepped out of it. 'Nice place you got here.'

Her voice jagged. 'Huh. Surely not a surprise.' She gave him a small smile, dying to step into his space.

Callum grabbed a swag from the back seat of his car, Paul's vehicle, and threw it to the ground near her little table. 'I want to talk to you.' Curt.

'You talked all the while in the car coming out from town.'

He unpacked the rest of his gear—another esky, a chair, a table and a wicker basket. 'About something else. Time wasn't right before. Needed to catch your brothers. I want to clear up some big misunderstandings.' Brusque.

Bridling, she sat in her chair. 'Not on my part, though. I'm clear, now.'

He looked over. 'If you grip that bottle any harder, you'll snap it,' he said. 'May I sit down?'

'Of course, you can.' This was being friendly. This was nice and easy, civilised, with a smile, and a nod.

Callum set up a chair and eased into it. 'I'll have a glass, if you're offering?' he said, eyes averted from hers. He opened his little fold-away table and set it on its legs. Then leaned over, took the bottle from her, removed the cork and poured himself a glass. He handed back the bottle, watched her. Seemed a little fidgety.

She filled her glass.

'I have an apology to make,' he stated.

'What for?' Toni's thudding heart made her voice sound unsteady. She knew what was coming, for sure. She knew he was going to say that he was sorry for leading her on. Sorry that she'd had "misunderstandings", that she had misinterpreted after all. Right? Her heart thudded so hard she was glad to be sitting, otherwise she might have keeled over and fallen flat on her face, sure as anything. 'Nothing to apologise—'

'Hear me out.' He rubbed his face with both hands. 'Much as it looks like it, I don't have the patience of a saint.'

His quiet words brought quick prickles of heat to her hands. 'Nothing to get upset about. I just wanted some peace and quiet, here,' she said. 'Just a night out here in the dirt, on my own.'

'It's my place, now, too.'

The three-day old stubble darkened his cheeks and chin, a contrast to the red ember glint the setting sun sparked in his hair. His now crumpled blue-and-white shirt was open, striped along one shoulder with red dust from the seatbelt of Paul's car. His trademark white T-shirt underneath was smudged with desert dirt as well. He looked at home, work-weary and tired.

It's my place, now, too. Her heart—the damned thing—lurched around her chest.

'Someone rang me the day I left for Adelaide to say that you were backing out of the employment contract.'

She just knew who that would have been. Her Loyal Friend, no doubt. 'Not true. A discussion point at best.'

He kept on. 'Then I had to do boss-PA-travel-shop-manager games for the week I was in Adelaide. Pretty frustrating.'

She started to roll her eyes, then stopped. *That would not be nice and friendly.* 'I didn't want—'

'So, I get on the first available flight after all my jobs were done to come and see for myself what state things were in.' He took a long drink of cool wine. 'And I figured out—all by myself, you'll be pleased to learn—that someone had told some porky pies.'

Toni shook her head. 'Not lies exactly, but Ben shouldn't have passed anything on about our conversation. He's never learned boundaries, never figured out when I'm just blowing off steam.' Her gaze rested on his usually serious face, softened now by fatigue. 'Is that what all this is about?'

'Ben wasn't the only culprit.'

'He wasn't? He usually is.' Toni took a tentative sip of her wine, and then another. 'Who then?'

'Marnie, my own flesh and blood. My sister. She only told me she'd heard a rumour from a well-respected source. She only suggested strongly that I fly back here sooner rather than later to get it sorted quickly. No actual fibs involved.' He looked at her. 'Perhaps Loyal Friend had got to my sister, too.'

She flicked a glance at him. 'You didn't come all the way back up here just because of that.'

'That, and a number of other things. For one, I wasn't about to let you out of the employment contract. I'm glad, at least, that rumour was wrong.' The clear grey eyes studied her. 'You wouldn't take my calls.'

'I answered when I had the information you needed.' A lump rose in her throat as his scowl deepened. She didn't want to do this. 'Callum, I wanted some privacy here for a little while, tonight, even if all this,' she waved her arm around, 'isn't mine anymore.'

'You said. But we have something to talk about,' he insisted. Looked at her out of the corner of his eye. 'When was the last time you ate properly?'

She sparked. Ben and his bloody judgements— 'If you're going to remark about my weight—'

'I don't care about your weight. I care about your wobbles.'

'Oh. I ate properly at lunch time, thanks.' She looked away from his six foot plus solid frame draped nonchalantly on the small camp chair. God, she didn't need a lecture on her wobbles either, as well as everything else. 'This will be fine for now.' She pointed at the crackers and unopened cheese.

He nodded. 'Fine.' He took a deep breath. 'I'm a partner with my sister and brother-in-law.'

'I know that.' She took a long drink of wine.

'I have to start an explanation somewhere. I'm a full partner. We developed a limited company specifically to buy the station, and we divvied it up. Now Marnie and Bill have a third share, Two Bob has a third share, and so do I.'

'I understand that.' She stared at her glass, downed half the contents and topped it up, ignoring his.

He stood and refilled his own, taking the bottle with him. 'You weren't the push-over I was referring to when you overheard me on the phone. It was the lending clerk in the financial institution.'

Toni nodded. 'That was all cleared up, too.'

'She did eventually finalise our dealings with the bank. Didn't need too much prompting after I put it to them straight up—any more problems like that ever again and we'd take our business elsewhere.'

'Right.'

'You were never a push-over, I never considered you that.'

'Okay. I get it. It's okay. I did misinterpret at the time, but now I'm good.'

He stared at the liquid gold in his glass. 'I didn't want—I don't want that sort of thing to come between us. I knew, even before I met you, that I wanted to be as close as all this would allow.'

She studied him a moment, a little wary. 'What do you mean by that?'

Scraping a hand through his hair, he said, 'Shit. I don't mean to sound like a bloody stalker. I visited your father for the last time just before he died. We'd been in direct negotiations with him, as you know, before he took that last decline. What you didn't know, perhaps, is that after Marnie's first contact, way back at the beginning of all this, he came after us.'

'I didn't know that,' Toni said. 'We were never brought into the negotiations, even after Dad got sick. He believed he had it all under control.'

Callum lifted a shoulder, glanced at her then away again. 'He decided he wanted Two Bob to get some land back. He propped on that point, among other lesser ones, and when we looked at the Two Bob plan, it seemed good, solid. More paperwork, more government stuff as well, but it would work for all of us, a win-win. All business.' He sat forward on his seat. 'We agreed. That's still going through proper process. So, then your dad came up with the other devices, like the one to keep you in a job.'

Jeez, Dad.

'Once things got further down the track, and you finally made it into the contract period—you'll admit to a certain reluctance—I wanted to make you secure on the property.'

Toni let her half empty glass dangle in her hand. A few quips popped into mind, but she let them go. 'Secure me on the property,' she repeated, instead.

'I had in mind to run a proposition by you.'

She glanced across. 'What proposition?'

He shifted again. 'I knew that for you to feel secure, there finally seemed to be a way. The same kind of way as for Two Bob and Lorraine.' He looked at her. 'I went back to Adelaide after the fire to square it with my legal people. And yes,' he stated flatly at her questioning glance, 'with legalities, and financial wrangling and so on, it took a week to get back here. And it's not over yet. And I did ring every day. You know that.'

She sniffed and eyed her glass. She should've answered the calls, despite being so mortified by her own proposition. She should have …

Was she getting tipsy? She didn't understand what he was saying. Toni put the glass down on the table in front of her and picked at her dry biscuits, took up the cheese and cracked the packaging.

'Did you hear me?' he asked. She nodded. 'Do you have any idea what I'm talking about?'

She glanced across, his big frame sprawled only a metre or two away. Toni shook her head. 'No, not a word.'

'It's important. I didn't come out here just to pass the time of day, Toni.'

She lifted her shoulders, dropped the unopened cheese to the table. 'I can't read your mind, for God's sake.' She waved a hand. 'My home is gone, and I'm embarrassed to say my brothers and I let it go without a fight. My dad himself wanted to sell out, so what would we have been able to do, anyway? My dad's solicitor is a loony and probably a thief and totally a pyro, not to mention a basher of old men. Eric Roycroft, my dad's rural advisor, is going to jail for embezzlement and fraud and God only knows what else. Ben rats on me, makes up stupid stories and you think I might get the wobbles. That's enough for me.' She took her glass again and slurped. 'I don't suppose you do want to pass the time of day. Neither do I.' But the fire in her blood had run its course.

He lifted his chair and plonked it down beside hers, removed the glass from her hand and set it on the table.

Tears wanted to come. *Well, they bloody wouldn't.* 'Where's my damned water bottle?'

He pulled a flask of water from his esky. He threw her wine out, refilled her glass with water, held it out.

She took it. 'I don't need you to look after me.'

'I know that. There's still something else I've been meaning to tell you.' He sat back. 'About how we first met your dad. I mean, about how I first met your dad.'

He held up his hand as she started to speak. 'Hang on a second. We don't have any fires to put out, or meetings to rush off to, or… Just let me go through it all.'

She let her breath out in a quiet whoosh. 'Go ahead.'

'I told you that night I'd come back from the paddocks with Two Bob that my dad had met with a bull that sat on him. It broke his back as well as lots of other bones.'

Her gaze was on his sombre face.

'Dad lost it big time—' he tapped his temple, '—once they got him out of what rehab they had in those days. It was your dad, a mate from a few stations over, who spent a lot of time with him, who talked to him. Talked him out of doing the worst possible thing Dad might do.' He took a long swig of wine, refilled his glass. 'I was about fifteen, I suppose. A long time ago, now. Your dad didn't really know me, I was a kid, but I knew enough of what was going on. Anyhow, Dad got himself well enough in his head, and once Mum and Dad decided to move us to South Australia, the families lost touch.'

He shifted in the seat, noticing that her gaze was still on his face. 'One thing after another, Dad passed away, the result of the injuries. Mum passed away not long back.' He topped up his wine, emptied the bottle. 'Marnie had got married to Bill a while before. They'd done really well financially. I'd done okay with my business. We decided to partner up to look for a good property in the Centre, a small enough one we could manage. And one day, Marnie sees your station up for sale. She contacted your dad.'

'Sounds like a shorthand sort of version.' Her voice was soft.

'Yep. Then I came up to close the deal, to talk to Mo Reddell. He told me your father was in hospital. He was really sick by that stage, and I wanted to do something for him. For what he'd done for my dad. I'm sure Phillip saved Dad from suicide.' He reached into his shirt pocket and handed a photograph to her. 'Anyhow, that's why the clause about your employment was a good one. It put his mind at ease. He gave me this.'

Toni took the photo, looked at her own smiling face beaming out. 'I haven't seen that pic for years.'

Callum took it back from her. 'Looks like he treasured it.' He put it back in his pocket. 'He told me you were headstrong and stubborn, and that you can get all hot and bothered at times. That you hate being called Antoinette.'

Toni shot him a look. 'And don't you dare. That's my mother's name.'

'That you are as beautiful as your mother was, he said.' He tapped his pocket. 'I was head over heels the moment I looked at your pic.'

Her heart wasn't thumping any longer. It was clanging and banging a gong inside her.

Callum studied his wine. 'But that's not the best way to be feeling when you're employing that someone. Can lead to … being inappropriate at the very least.'

She allowed herself a smile. Sort of.

He inhaled loudly. 'You have your heart and soul here, in this land, on the Run, and when I knew you felt that there was something genuine between us as well, I thought I could make it work. I took a punt, I admit.' He rubbed the side of his face. 'For all of us, really, your brothers as well. They have their jobs here. They knew that long before the fire. And I'd been in discussions with Two Bob for a while about the deed-back. Then Justin West's little antics came to light. And I would never have known about Eric Roycroft if not for your Loyal Friend. It all seemed to happen at once, especially when the boys told me you all had your own suspicions.' He stood up. 'I have something else.'

He went to his vehicle and withdrew a large postal tube. Returning to his little table, he moved things aside and pulled out a roll of papers, unfurled them, flattened them and pinned them down with the wine bottle and the cheese plate.

Toni peered at the top sheet of paper. Couldn't believe what she was looking at. Felt as if she was watching an opening episode of something magical.

'Freelands. The Wildlife Park.' She pressed a hand to her chest, her breath hitched. There were plans for its construction. There were architect's drawings, final impressions…

'Incorporated in the plans for the whole concept. They're on display as of Monday in the council chambers in Alice. A bit hurried, not totally comprehensive, we'll submit better drawings later, but it's there nonetheless.'

Her beloved wildlife park. She stared from the drawings to him and back again, turning each page to study what her dream might finally look like. 'How?' She knew her eyes were wide, and her voice had a squeak in it.

'It's taken a while, but finally all the pieces slotted into place.' He downed his wine, refilled his glass with water and downed that, too. 'Starting back a bit, we know that Eric Roycroft had been ripping the homestead off once he knew your dad was sick. Then Justin West got in on that, tried claiming indigenous rights to the property based on shared—but non-existent in any way as it turned out—DNA with Two Bob.'

Toni shook her head. 'How Eric and Justin got together on it, I'll never know.'

'We do, now. Eric saw Justin as a 'mark', an easy way in for his scheme, so he encouraged West to follow up on making a claim. Justin has told police that they'd met often, that Roycroft had promised Justin part of the money he'd been ripping off.'

Toni sat and slumped in her chair.

'Ben had become suspicious of Eric Roycroft over the MacDonnell file at Reddell's, couldn't work out why 'consulting agencies' were needed out there at the station. He always thought Roycroft was shonky, shifty, but couldn't put his finger on it. He blew the whistle but without any real proof, but Mo Reddell had thought Ben was being a stirrer, had almost accused him of being malicious. Ben couldn't prove anything, so didn't take it to the police, didn't want to upset you. He resigned, instead.'

'And I was away... I know he tried to tell me something, but my mind was on other things.' Toni thought back to the day Ben had met her in her office after the last letter from her dad had been read. 'Can hardly believe this was happening right under our noses,' she said, and looked up. 'Do you have another bottle stashed in your car?'

'I do.' Callum retrieved another bottle of white, unscrewed the lid and poured a glass each for them. He shifted his chair closer, sat the bottle in the chiller between them.

She sipped. 'I mean, Justin had seemed a bit creepy to me for a while, but I never thought he'd rip Dad off. Or us.'

Callum reached across and gave her arm a squeeze. 'While all that was going on, Marnie and Bill and I went ahead and purchased the leasehold on the station. Ben had met me in Reddell's before he finished up, told me he didn't like Justin West, either, suspected something odd. I'd already met your dad again, didn't like to think an employee was doing the dirty on him. Parker Inc had engaged Justin's services for conveyancing, up until that point—all interests declared for transparency—but I didn't like it anymore. That's when you heard me in his office.' He glanced across.

Toni shrugged. 'The pressure on him would have been big. He would have panicked, maybe wondered if he'd been found out.'

Callum nodded. 'Apparently so, and he fronted Eric with the DNA thing. Roycroft told him he was an idiot. But part of me thinks he knew he was barking up the wrong tree. He'd just dug a big hole for himself.'

Toni shuddered, made a face. 'He must have come to my office after that. He hadn't even opened the letter about the DNA.'

'That's what tipped him over the edge,' Callum said, flexing his shoulders as if to loosen up. 'He had definite proof that his last resort was closed to him. He had no relationship to Two Bob's father, had no claim at all on the station. No matter how long he'd been working with your father, he had no right to try and claim any part of MacDonnell's Run. That's when he took off for the station. And the bulldozer.'

Toni knew the rest about Justin. He was arrested, given a bedside hearing, had a mental health assessment and was carted off to God knew where. He'd be in the system a while yet, a prosecution perhaps a long way off, if ever.

Eric Roycroft on the other hand, would be convicted of his crimes. Thankfully, some of the funds had already been intercepted and his remaining bank accounts frozen, pending investigation.

'I'm truly sorry you've been hurt in this, Toni. No one wanted that for you.'

Again, Toni looked from the plans, to him and back to the plans, her heart lurching and the throb of a good cry aching in her throat. Out of all of it, the only thing that meant anything, was Freelands. It was going to go to public consultation. She'd never have been able to take it to that point. And Callum had done it for her.

What had Nicky said? *Look at what he does.*

Daylight was quickly slipping away and she couldn't study the plans as much then as she wanted to. She stood and rolled them up, held on to them.

Callum set his drink down, rolled his hands together. 'I never expected things to go between us the way they have. I came out here to...' He pointed at the roll of plans.

Most unlike him to seem to be lost for words.

He threw up his hands. 'A partnership.'

Her eyes lit up but only for an instant. Reality kicked in. She laughed shortly. 'Oh, I see.'

'I don't think you do.'

Still clutching the papers to her chest, she said, 'It's wonderful. All of this. But you know I could never pay for the privilege. You know all about the Sonny Murphy thing. Even when the house in Adelaide sells, I won't have the kind of money to buy back in.' She rubbed her forehead. 'Let's forget it for now. I'm just going to roll out my swag and go to bed.'

Placing the plans gently on the table, she smoothed her hand over them before they curled into a tight roll again. It felt like things had been so close...

A thought flitted through about being 'friendly', and the work schedule ahead, what the next twelve months might look like. She wanted to tell him she was grateful. 'This was great of you, thank you. To do all of this.' Her hand rested on the roll of plans. 'It is really wonderful. Before now, it's always been an impossible dream.' She patted the plans and turned away. 'Now, you have a truly great idea in place for the station.'

Callum's voice rose. 'It's not for free, Toni. It's part of a deal. I had a mate cast a glance over it, put a price on its worth. If you're willing to sign over the plans for Freelands, in exchange I'll sign you over an equal share in my third in the property.' He stopped only for a beat. 'I've squared it off with Marnie and Bill. Just have to make the transfer, if you agree. I've got no other way to pay you for it.'

Her voice caught in her throat and she turned back to stare.

Callum kept talking. 'I mean it. That's the deal on the table.' He stared back at her. 'Freelands. The concept is worth it for the place. It'll belong to all of us. Even your brothers as well, if you want. Right on MacDonnell's Run. Right where it belongs.'

Toni tried to hide her scrunched up face as she struggled with a rolling wave of emotion. She spun back to the vehicle and, keeping her hands busy, retrieved her swag. She dropped it to the ground, tugged at the ropes that bound it tight but couldn't budge the knots.

He came over. 'Here,' he offered, and knelt on the rolled swag, undid the ties, flattened it out for her. Then got to his feet. 'I know you care a great deal about the land, and you know I care for you.'

Still trying to take it in, she licked her lips. 'It's a helluva lot to think about. It's just come from thin air.'

'Not from thin air, it's a solid concept. Worth probably more than half my share. But that's all I've got to work with right now.' He ran a hand down her arm. 'And I want you in my life, Toni.'

Pride, and fear, started to peel away. She stared into his blue-grey eyes. 'I've told you that I don't know if—'

'If you can't, we can't. I don't have to personally increase the Parker family head count.' He waited, hands dropped by his side. 'We won't know until we find out. So, we'll take it from there. What do you think? Give it a try?'

Her face was still screwed up. 'I never believed another relationship would work for me. But at the same time, I never really thought of myself as a getting to be a lonely old woman.'

'God forbid.'

The smile in his voice made her smile. She took another breath. 'What if I wanted to explore those new technologies, sooner rather than later?'

His chest expanded. 'I'll explore right along with you.'

'But what if there's still nothing—'

'We'll look after us, Toni,' he said, and reached across to touch a lock of her hair. He held out his hand. 'We'll do everything and anything, if that's what we want. We'll be careful with us.'

She took his hand, squeezed her eyes shut. 'We'll still need to be careful—'

His arm tightened around her. 'We'll explore lots of interesting ways to make the earth move, don't worry about that.'

Toni's fingers curled into his other hand as he drew her into to his chest. His heart pulsed against her ear and she rested her head there, desperate for the peace she felt in that moment.

Rocking against his chest, she felt his kiss on top of her head. He wrapped both arms around her. 'You've no idea how long I've wanted to do this, waited to do this.'

She mumbled into his T-shirt. 'Twelve weeks, maybe?'

'A lifetime.'

'Big call.' She dared not believe it.

'Yep.'

'What do we do now?' she asked, holding her hand up to his chest.

'Let nature take its course.' He took her wrist in his fingers, kissed her fingertips. His other hand wound itself in her hair, tangled in the scrunchie, and she didn't want to do anything but keep her body pressed to his.

He broke away and hugged her to him. He smattered kisses on her forehead and nose, brushed his stubbly chin on the curve of her neck. He pulled her down on to her swag, kicked his into reaching distance and undid its ties. Side by side the swags lay and he tugged her over to him.

Propped on one elbow, he draped his free arm over her hip. 'Tell me you care.'

'I care.'

He rasped his chin lightly down the smooth lines of her throat, scraped his three-day old beard over her neck, its soft bristles tickling.

Oh yeah.

Warm lips nipped her shoulder as he pushed aside the collar of her shirt. A hand cupped her breast, stroked a nipple and a sweet ache bloomed deep inside her. 'Callum.'

'Yeah, okay.'

He pushed a hard thigh between her legs, fingers popped the buttons of her shirt. His mouth, over the full breasts beneath, closed over a nipple thrusting from under a cotton bra. She clutched at his shoulders, the insistent tug on her breast irresistible. A whirl spiralled in her belly.

Hot and heady anticipation swept through her. He snapped open her bra and caressed a breast, its heavy warmth in his palm.

He pulled off her open shirt and bra, tore at the belt buckle and the button of her jeans, ripped the zipper down and shucked her pants. Tugged off her undies.

Naked.

She squirmed under his gaze.

'Wow.' Callum stripped, reefed a hand into his jeans pocket, tossed his clothes aside, and slid along her body once again.

She gazed down at a beautiful part of Callum Parker, then lifted her gaze to his.

'Roll this on me,' he said, hoarsely, and held up the foil packet.

'I'll be a bit fumbly, I haven't—'

'It'll come naturally,' he breathed.

She laughed.

'Pardon the pun,' he ground out.

Trust him trust him trust him ...

33

With his free arm, Callum felt around and held up a pair of undies. 'Here.'

In the dim light, she gazed at what he was holding. 'They're yours.'

'Bugger. Hang on.' He fumbled alongside again. 'Here, these are yours,' he said, holding up her lady undies.

Legs akimbo, they lay side by side, kisses smattered between them. Gathering her to his chest, he kissed her forehead, tilted her face up to kiss her nose, her mouth. Then he settled beside her and breathed rhythmically into that deep afterwards slumber.

Toni drifted off, snug against him. Exhausted, and on a tiny hopeful high, she whispered to a man she thought was asleep, that she loved every bit of it, that she loved him. She was certainly glad he couldn't possibly have heard the involuntary slip because what she said was just silly.

Just plain silly.

Side by side, awake, the stars bright as the new moon rose. Toni had no idea of the time.

He'd earlier joined the swags and had thrown his open sleeping bag over as a bottom sheet. He threw her sleeping sheet over their near-naked bodies, and she snuggled into him, loving the closeness of him, despite the heat of the night.

'We must think about consolidating our partnership,' he

murmured into her ear. At her hesitation, he added, 'Our personal one.'

Hugging him tightly, she was content to lie there until she thought it was time to do more than just be content with lying there. She found the new condom herself.

In the light of morning just before dawn, they made love again. Then ate what was left in their eskies, cheese, crackers and some apples.

They washed with water out of the jerry cans, always filled and always ready in the vehicles, laughing because they had to hurry, to scrub up and rinse off. The water wouldn't last too long between them.

Dressed, Callum stood behind with his arms around her. 'I knew it would come to this,' he said in her ear. 'I'm happy.'

She pressed against him. 'I sort of hoped so, though I didn't believe it, not for a second. I'm happy, too.'

Mindful that they had to head back to work, they packed up. Kissed before each stepped into their vehicles to turn for home.

The makeshift camp back at the old homestead was just rousing for the day. Men leapt out of swags to go find a place to take a wee break. Dogs bounced around them as Toni's and Callum's vehicles pulled up.

Parking her car over by the old homestead, she got out to stand by what had been the front veranda. Callum followed.

Shouts from her brothers, 'About time,' and 'Slackers, get on with it,' met them from across the yards. Toni waved them off, only to be answered by loud whistles, and a fair bit of sledging. Dogs bounded around her, and red dust puffed around her feet.

'We'll rebuild it.' Callum slung an arm across her shoulders. 'Just as it was. Better, even. We'll put in a bigger place for Lorraine and Two Bob as well.' He went on, ducking his head to her neck, a smile in his voice. 'I believe you're not a cook, so we need to keep her on.'

Toni gave a snort. 'You do that, Callum Parker.'

'And the personal stuff for us. I know it's early days. I know it's all new, but you said you love me.' He took a breath when she stiffened in his arms. 'Yeah, I heard,' he said. 'I have loved you, Toni, ever since your dad showed me that photo. We'll get through, no matter what comes our way. We'll keep working on it. We'll do it for us. Together.'

She turned away from the old shell of a building, leaned against him, her head pressed on his chest. 'We'll get through,' she repeated and believed it. *No matter what comes our way.*

He kissed her neck. 'So, it's a deal? All of it? No arguments?'

She listened to her head for some moments, to her heart for half a beat. Gripping his forearms, she hugged them tighter around her. 'It's a deal.' Then she stared up over her shoulder at him, made a deep frown. 'I just can't guarantee no arguments.'

He laughed, a delighted, happy sound. 'I can live with that.'

ABOUT THE AUTHOR

Will of the Heart
is an older work first published in 2014
at half its current size

Darry Fraser's first breakout novel with HarperCollins, *Daughter of the Murray* (2016) is set on her beloved River Murray where she spent part of her childhood. *Where the Murray River Runs* (2017) is her second novel set in the same era, 1890s. The Christmas story, *The Drover Comes Home for Christmas* is another Australian historical was released in an anthology, *Our Country Christmas*, also in 2018. *The Widow of Ballarat* set in 1854 released in November 2018. The Good Woman of Renmark is due out November 2019. The novel for 2020 is part way finished.

The Australian landscape is home and hearth - the rural, the coastal, the arid lands and the desert. The history, the hidden stories, the catalysts create the powerful connection between her characters and are the drivers in her stories. Apprenticed on a number of contemporary novels and novellas, she returned to writing Australian historical fiction, which is her favourite genre.

She lives and works on the beautiful Kangaroo Island off the coast of South Australia, and you can follow her journey at www.darryfraser.com or on Facebook https://www.facebook.com/darryfraser0210